# THE WISHING OF TREES

JOE TALON

Vinci Books

vinci-books.com

Published by Vinci Books Ltd in 2026

1



A CIP catalogue record for this book is available from the British Library.

Paperback ISBN: 9781036716431

The EU GPSR authorised representative is Logos Europe, 9 rue Nicolas Poussion, 17000 La Rochelle, France contact@logoseurope.eu

## By Joe Talon

Griffin Woodbury Supernatural Detective

*Music of the Damned*

*The Wishing of Trees*

*A Cathedral of Demons*

A Valentine Investigation

*For Whom the Willow Weeps*

*Seven Tears of Heaven*

*An Agony of Lies*

Lorne Turner Supernatural Thrillers

*Counting Crows*

*Money for Old Bones*

*Dead of the Winter Sun*

*Salt for the Devil's Eye*

*Bad Waters Run Deep*

*The Alchemist's Corpse*

*The Spirit Glass*

*The Dead Also Have Secrets*

# Prologue

Jennifer stared up at the stars. She imagined they rode the blackness like tiny fairies performing a ballet created by the musical whims of the universe that harmonised with the camp's earthbound musicians. The stars danced through the dark as her eyes swam with tears. Their presence always filled her with such a sense of freedom and joy, she couldn't help but allow it to overwhelm her.

For so many years, her life had been nothing but mundane middle-class chores. She'd married young, surrendered a promising job as a secretary in a large firm of lawyers to raise her daughter and look after her successful husband. Then her daughter escaped to university and suddenly, Jennifer—never Jenny—found herself caring for the wicked witch. Or the mother-in-law. Years of washing, cleaning, cooking, gardening, polishing, and bloody sex with a man who, it turned out, had a thing going on with his own secretary.

Bastard.

She'd left with all the money she could muster and started her new life. Right here, right now.

Still smiling at the dancing stars, she let the tears fall, her heart aching with love. The world had more grace in it than she'd ever thought possible. So much light and love.

Even after her divorce settlement came through, and she bought her tiny Cornish house, she'd kept her van. It made her feel free. She'd come down here to Madron to help preserve a tiny, but significant, woodland from becoming a hotel and golf course. With all these beautiful souls around her who believed in the cause. Jennifer wanted to save this place for her grandchildren, for everyone's grandchildren. Its importance to the world, to history, to the souls of so many generations of people, couldn't and shouldn't be wiped away by bulldozers. The rich could go and knock their balls around somewhere else.

The thought made her chuckle.

"You alright, Jennifer?" asked a heavy, almost lumpen voice.

"Hello, Aggie. Isn't it a beautiful night?" Jennifer took a deep breath, almost smelling the sea on the clean, cold air. The end of April still had a nip in it. Though, tomorrow was Beltane and May would begin. Her favourite month.

"Aye, it's canny, Jennifer," said Aggie, her Northumberland accent thick as treacle. Some would say, as thick as the treacle in her head, but Jennifer knew Aggie to be the kindest of souls.

A rowdy rendition of a Levellers' song began among the older residents of the camp. The younger members might not remember the violence of the Bean Field, but some of these people had lived it, some of them knew it from others who'd been there, or their parents. Travellers, protesters, eco-warriors, they all came together here in Madron, for the sake of the cloutie tree and the ancient woods.

Jennifer pushed herself off the damp grass. "I'm going down to the wood. I want to go and hug some of the trees."

"I can come," Aggie suggested.

Jennifer patted her hand. "No, dear, you stay here with the others. When I get back, I'll make us some hot chocolate. Just don't tell anyone." By the light of the nearby fire, Jennifer saw the wide smile on Aggie's plain face.

"That'd be awesome, like," Aggie said, pushing her glasses up her nose. The lenses were so thick, her eyes looked like they belonged to a fish in a bowl.

She straightened her thick skirts out of long habit and walked around the fireside party. Her clothes and long silver hair now smelt of smoke, rather than tinned air freshener from her husband's house. The others gathered here most evenings, unless the rain threatened to wash away the camp, and your sanity with it, but tonight was special somehow. She felt drawn to the wood more strongly than at any other time. It called.

No, that wasn't quite right. It whispered. The trees in there, so old and gnarled they might've come from a fairy-tale, murmured only to her. She'd heard them, felt them, growing inside her for over a week now, and tonight, tonight she'd listen to their song and maybe sing back to them if they wanted to listen.

She knew if she walked into that wood, she'd have some kind of epiphany. A blessing from the universe. She'd enter some liminal space, and she'd glimpse the other realms they needed to save. Tonight, Beltane's eve, was magical.

She walked through the field, her night vision fully adjusted, her torch on low and held close to her leg. Then she took the lane to the footpath that wound its way through the trees, alongside the hesitant stream, and deep into the magical heart near the cloutie tree.

Her boots found sure footing, not slipping in the mud and avoiding the rocks. Jennifer had discovered the more she shed of her old self, the greater her woodland skills grew.

As she reached the cloutie tree, the rags making the branches look as if they'd been draped with Spanish moss in the darkness, her senses detected a change in the atmosphere surrounding her. Instincts, long dormant, woke up in the back of her brain and began squeaking, rising over the alluring, soft whispers of the trees. Neither gave her words to formulate something as mundane as logic, but they rivalled each other and wrestled for attention in her mind.

She looked around. Listened with her ears, not her heart. Nothing. Only the rustle of something in the undergrowth. A badger, or hedgehog. Maybe a fox. There would be plenty of things hunting on a night like this.

Shaking off the odd, and unfamiliar, sense of fear, she continued towards the trunk of the cloutie tree.

Leaves, among the spring growth of ground elder, rustled again. Jennifer frowned. There was barely any wind. Certainly, nothing to pull at low-lying plants. She swallowed hard, her mouth suddenly dry as if it, and her now jellied knees, knew something the rest of her didn't.

"Hello?" she called out. *Dammit, where did that wobble come from?*

Nothing came back. Not even the startled movement of a deer.

"You're a daft old woman. Go hug your tree and get back to the others," she muttered, even as her stomach twisted and anxiety made her chest ache.

The beautiful whispering trees in her heart were almost

forgotten. The coming epiphany vanished like mist on a summer's day. Ancient, human instincts, now had control.

Jennifer, primed for any movement in the creamy black of the woodland, took another step towards the cloutie tree. Movement in the dense shadows to her left made her lift her torch. It tried to penetrate the space between the moss laden trunks, but it failed to offer peace of mind. The narrow beam no rival for the honest joy of sunlight, and it trembled.

"It's night. We're primed to fear the dark," she told herself aloud.

She knew the truth. The science of fear and where it came from was well known to all. Logic must be the prevailing motivation here. Though, logic didn't prevent her heartbeat from rising further. It didn't stop her palms from sweating. For the first time, she wished she'd never come to Madron.

The shivering leaves became an audible whisper. No longer did she hear the siren call of the wood in her heart. She heard it outside her head, and it didn't promise some great connection to Mother Earth. It really didn't.

Jennifer swallowed hard. "I'm not alone," she called out. "I have friends nearby."

*There's no such thing as monsters. No wolves, no bears. This is England.* Her thoughts panicked and rambled as shadows began to move.

Tall, broad shapes came out of the dense black. Jennifer's torch wobbled, catching flashes of naked chests, thick legs, heavily muscled arms and faces that were not human. Not human at all.

"Who are you?" she croaked. "I… I don't mean any harm. I… I…"

Words failed. She turned her back on the cloutie tree

and began to run. Two paces, four, six, her thick skirts were tangling in legs, but she might just make it back to the easier bit of the path and from there the lane, with its tarmac and sanity.

Her foot hit a rock on step number nine. The pain of the impact shuddered up her leg and threw her forwards. The torch hit the ground and rolled off into the water, surrendering to the smothering black forever.

Jennifer cried out. She'd jarred her entire body. Her hands burned where she lost skin on her palms. Her knees hurt, and she'd probably twisted her ankle. Grateful she hadn't smashed her face on the ground, she'd started to scramble upright, when a strange clicking, whistling murmur began behind her.

Jennifer whipped her head around, over balanced in her haste, and landed on her backside in the mud. Cold water hit her buttocks, and her skirts became heavier.

The shapes stalked their prey.

"This isn't real. This isn't real. This isn't real," she whimpered. Images of her daughter, living in Australia with her husband and two beautiful children, filled Jennifer's mind. "I love you," she whispered. "I love you, Chloe. I am so proud of you."

The shapes of the beings became more solid as they approached. Jennifer scrambled backwards, trying to stand, trying to run, failing at both. Fear had its maw around her mind and was chewing on logic, spitting out the pieces in total contempt.

Jennifer tried to babble about how she loved the trees. Loved the land. Loved Mother Earth and wanted to preserve this place forever. That's what she tried to say, but nothing like real words filled the space between her and the advancing... what? Aliens? Is that what they were? Had she been lured here by aliens?

Hands reached for her. In vain, she tried to batter them away. Nothing worked. They were so immensely strong. Stronger than her husband had ever been. They pinched her skin and bone. Pulled her long hair. Dug into her soul and filled it with terror.

The unforgiving black of the woodland cracked open as they carried her—how many hands now—towards a strange oily-looking rainbow.

At last, Jennifer screamed.

# Chapter One

Groaning, I stood and stretched my back out. It cracked.

"Please tell me that's the last one?" I begged.

Sid smirked, his dark brown eyes twinkling. "I only needed the five, the rest were just for my amusement."

I scowled at my companion. We'd been working closely together for a few months now, and Sid loved nothing more than to watch me scramble about setting up his equipment, as he gave the orders and tested the various connections. Today, we were back at the Brane long barrow. The site where, six weeks before, we'd almost died thanks to an incubus. I'd spent the morning checking the vibrational sensors, recording devices, and cameras inside and outside the long barrow's entrance. I'd had to crawl into the small, square hole and out again several times while Sid calibrated the distances for the audio and seismic sensors. We'd occupied ourselves for weeks touring the sites of different Cornish ancient monuments and setting up all kinds of equipment. He spent the time behind his laptop screen, leaving me to do the fetching and carrying. From Land's End to the Lizard, we had it covered in gizmos.

These, in the Brane cairn, were the most important. The alchemists and a priest had come down from the main London branch of the Department of Paranormal Investigations, or DoPI for short. Their job had been to clear the space.

Our job? We just wanted to make sure they'd done their bit properly. We were both suffering from the effects of being inside a liminal space in our world, where the dead could scream at you and beg for release. Some of the souls the incubus had trapped in that stone burial chamber could've been there for centuries. Some of them were young, victims of the rave parties they'd attended. Those were the ones that gave us nightmares. I knew their names, had their files on my desk, and their photos.

Still, it could be worse, Sid and I had come close to joining them. Far too close. This was the one place Sid hoped not to capture the memories trapped in the stones.

He didn't know it, but I'd visited the location at least once a week since the incubus incident. That horrible night, while I'd been crawling out of the netherworld we'd stumbled into, with Sid draped over my back, my mother had stepped into the void and held back the dead long enough for us to escape. The barrow drew me like catnip. It was the closest I'd come to her because, despite all logical reasoning, I knew she'd been there. Not in a dream, like so many times before, but actually been there with us. It had been almost three decades since I lost her, and even though her grave was in a Redruth cemetery, this was the place that pulled me in and gave me some kind of solace, even if it didn't give me answers.

Shaking off the feeling of loss that never really left, I

returned to Sid, where he sat on a folding stool in the field, his laptop balanced on his knobbly knees. The sun had started bleaching the tufty Afro that haloed his head, hiding much of the grey among the deep brown. He looked happy in his world of ones and zeros. The countryside might make him shudder with revulsion sometimes, but he was gradually adjusting to life outside the M25 ring road around London.

As for me, nothing much had changed. I'd hardly seen Megan, and we kept a distance between us at the few family events I'd attended at Aunt Iris's insistence. I knew Megan had started dating someone called Adrian because Iris wanted to know why he hadn't been invited to the big Easter lunch. Megan mumbled something about family only and left the room, avoiding my gaze. It sliced through me, but I'd known it was coming, and it was very much for the best. We'd come too close to crossing a line that first cousins really should never cross. The invisible Maginot Line between us must remain.

After Brane, and the deaths I'd caused both there and in Carrine Manor, I'd endured days of debriefs and interviews. Sanchez, our boss, had reprimanded me for excessive force. I considered the death of potential rapists a bonus, but that was hard to explain to the powers-that-be. I'd also failed to capture the *para* involved in the murders of so many young people, and the collapsed mental health of many more. Dozens of people would never be the same after those raves. I'd answered the questions, accepted the bollocking, and tried not to remember the sight of body parts sprayed over walls. Pulling the trigger on this mission had been all too easy. I was having problems coming to terms with the monster inside me, the one the Royal Marine Commandos had trained, the one I spent my life denying existence, until the moment came when it was them, or me and mine. Under the circumstances, regret was impossible, but I'd spent many hours staring at my bedroom ceiling, or gazing into the bottom of my whiskey glass, wondering what kind of man I really was under all the self-proclaimed reluctance to be that Marine. When I needed to find the violence inside, it came with the dizzying speed of a tornado, and I squeezed that trigger without a moment's hesitation.

Just because I told the world I was on the side of the white hats, I had no idea if it was true.

I spent my life denying the rights of the *para-world* to come into ours. Did that really make me a good guy? In the case of the incubus, yes, it did. No one wanted another Ajax and Mephistopheles in the world. They encouraged the worst kind of misogyny and violence, but what would I do if I faced a *para* I believed in? Could I really give one over to Sanchez and DoPI's scientists? Could I really help her build the *para* version of an atomic bomb, whatever that looked like?

These questions haunted me whenever I stopped long enough to allow my mind to wander off into the long grass. Rather than think about that, or Megan, I'd taken to working hard and training. My fitness had slipped, and I needed to gather it back up, so I ran miles, worked out in the gym and spent time swimming, battling the tides off the Cornish coast despite the cold. In a wetsuit. I wasn't a complete psycho. I also continued to allow my hair to grow out, the military style long gone.

The last of our small group of survivors, Dr Lucinda Carmichael, had left on a lecture and book tour, attending universities around the country. She and Sid were dating, but neither of them seemed anxious to hurry things along. I had the sense they'd both been stung before and wanted to take things very slowly.

Despite all the mental flagellation and disappointments, I thought of myself as content. Being in Cornwall gave me the room to breathe that I'd denied myself for years, and I felt my soul starting to expand. I'd even popped up to Exmoor to visit Lorne and Heather. They were expecting their second child, a boy this time, and seeing them so happy made me envious.

"Griffin," Sid called out. "We can go home. I've got everything I need. Get me out of this field before things start to bite me." He really didn't like the countryside and all its crawly things.

I watched a butterfly tumble about in the rising breeze. "Office or home?" My phone buzzed in my pocket. "Hang on a sec." I fished it out and felt that familiar squeeze on my heart. I kept convincing myself that I'd tidied away my feeling for Megan, then a text would turn up and that ache would start all over again.

*Hey cuz, meet me at the office? There's something going on tonight if you fancy coming along with Sid and Luce.*

So, not a date invite then. It must be work. For the last six weeks, two of which she'd been on a walking holiday in Scotland, Megan had maintained her normal routine as the uniformed police officer, Sergeant Ackley. Arresting drunks, dealing with domestics and keeping the peace in Cornwall. Also, filling out reams of paperwork.

"Megan says to meet her at the office," I said, walking over to Sid.

"Office it is then. It'll be good to see her, right?" he asked as he stood. Whip-thin but even taller than my six-two, he peered down, checking on me.

"Yeah. It's always good to see Meg." I managed a smile, picked up his large equipment bag and stool and started to stride over the stony field at a pace which meant he'd find it hard to pepper me with questions.

We'd parked in the farmyard, DoPI currently managing the estate, the original farmer having been found dead in the outbuildings. The post-mortem didn't find anything specific that killed the poor man, so we figured he'd been another of the incubus's victims. Drained of life, his soul would've been trapped with all the rest. For the other residents of the small hamlet of Brane, DoPI had concocted a story about a terrorist cell being busted. So far, the narrative had held, but then, DoPI had been telling lies about the *para* world since the seventeenth century; they'd had a lot of practice.

I loaded our equipment into Sid's vintage red Mini, and shrugged into my bike gear, then I tapped out a reply to Megan, agreeing to the meeting and giving her an ETA. I'd reach Redruth faster than Sid, and I didn't know if that was a good thing or a bad one. Throwing my leg over Quacker, the name bestowed on the Kawasaki 800 Café by Heather, I told Sid I'd meet him there. The engine burped to life, and I decided to enjoy the ride back.

After endless rain in March, April had come with blue skies, mild winds, and birdsong. The British peninsula of Cornwall, a land choked with myth and legend, moved at its own pace, and these few weeks were just bliss. Soon the place would be packed with tourists, but right now, we had a hiatus of peace, and I made the most of it. The bike ambled through the narrow lanes, and I smiled at the wash of white from hawthorn and cow parsley. The blaze of yellow from dandelions and rapeseed. Fields of happy, fat lambs drew my eye, and budding trees promised to make an appearance any day now. It was good to be alive. When I hit the main trunk road running through the spine of Cornwall, I ripped up the speed and played with the traffic until I reached Redruth.

The industrial estate that contained our disguised office hummed with activity. The local businesses came and went constantly, with Redruth still trying to be the industrial heart of Cornwall. The small sign outside our office door read, *The Department of Rural Security*. Currently, a short, blonde, police sergeant leaned against it, scrolling through her phone with a smile on her face. Messages from the lovely Adrian, no doubt. The thought soured my mood at seeing her standing there in her uniform. She'd lost weight.

Megan looked up at the sound of my bike, and the smile widened. Waggling her phone at me, she called out, "This is the funniest dog video I've ever seen. You should get a dog. It would make you happy."

My mood flipped back so fast I almost felt sick. Dog videos I could get onboard with and enjoy. "A dog won't fit on the bike," I said, pulling off my bike's helmet.

"Get a sidecar. I reckon it would be cool." Her blue eyes mirrored the depth of the sky.

"Why the sudden interest in me having a dog?" I asked, climbing off the bike.

"I worry you get lonely," she said. "I want to see you happy."

*You mean you want me off your conscience.*

The thought was uncharitable, and probably undeserved.

I needed to change the subject, and by the look on Megan's face, she realised she'd gone too far as well.

"What brought you up here?" I started the laborious process of gaining access to our office. Seriously, our security system put the vaults at the Bank of England to shame.

"There's an event you and Sid might enjoy. It'll

certainly be up Luce's street. A pagan ritual at the oldest of Cornwall's cloutie trees and a holy well." Megan followed me up the short, concrete corridor with its health and safety posters, before the next lot of security made me pause.

"What the hell is a cloutie tree, Meg?" Even as I asked the question, a tingle ripped up my spine and crawled through my hair. It made my breath stop. Many would dismiss the feeling as a stray cold wind, but for me it felt like… What? A premonition?

That made no sense. A premonition to what? We weren't working on anything specific right now, this was just natural DoPI inspired weirdness and paranoia. Besides, even with my issues, I'd never had a premonition about anything.

We walked in and headed straight for the kitchen area of the large office space. Over the last six weeks, Sid and I had begun to make the area more comfortable. The obligatory X-Files poster adorned one wall, asking if we believed, which we did—well, in fairies and demons; aliens were another matter right now—and a second-hand sofa we'd found in the street one morning. Sid had photos on his desk of his sister's kids, who were back in London. I had no one on mine.

"A cloutie tree is a place people go to make wishes. They take a piece of fabric, sometimes torn cloth, sometimes a ribbon, and they tie it to a branch, then make a wish. As the fabric rots, the wish comes true. A fairly new coven has started doing rituals there over the last few years, and I've always wanted to see one. I thought it would be right up your alley."

"Adrian coming?" I couldn't help myself, dammit.

Megan's cheeks coloured. "No. He's away. It'll just be

us." With Sid and Luce in tow, of course. A situation I could handle.

I nodded. "Sounds interesting. What time? Do you want to come on the bike?" I met her gaze, daring her to turn me down, she loved being on a motorbike.

Her grin made it worth the question. "If we meet up at five, your place? And yes, the bike is a good idea. There'll be very little parking. I knock off in a bit, so I'll grab something to eat at my place. You'll let the others know?"

"Sure."

She reached into her black trouser pocket and drew out a small blue velvet bag. "I keep forgetting to give this to you, but I wanted you to have it. Seems appropriate somehow."

I took the small bag from her hand. "What is it?" The last time someone had given me a spontaneous gift was… Well, I couldn't remember. I pulled apart the drawstrings and tipped it up into my palm.

A small stone tumbled out, dark with jagged lines of white running through it, and a perfectly smooth hole ran through the top half. Megan had placed a rough string of leather through it.

"It's a *milpreve* in Cornish, or witch's stone in English," she said. "You can look through the hole and see if the person you're viewing is a witch or a fairy. With your job, it might save your life one day. I found it in a stream in Scotland we walked through, and I thought of you." The last came out in a rush, and I glanced up from the stone to see her turn away, hiding something in her expression.

"You becoming a believer?" I asked. Her denial of the supernatural world she'd stumbled into, with my help, had caused her problems before her holiday. As I'd only seen her around the family, we'd been unable to talk about it. Or, she was ignoring both me and the issue.

"Jury's still out. To be honest, Griffin, I remember very little of what happened in that mine. Of what we did, said… I just liked the stone and the legend that goes with it." She still didn't meet my eyes. It made me sad. Very sad.

"Thank you, Megan. I love it," I said quietly.

"Good, well, I'd better be off. Forms to fill out from this morning's arrest of a drunk driver totalling his car. At least no one else was involved."

I watched her leave, my thumb playing over the smooth black surface of the stone, before slipping it over my head and tucking the gift under my shirt.

# Chapter Two

Sid arrived soon after Megan left, and he agreed that an evening watching a pagan ritual would be fun. Even if it meant he had to spend time in the dreaded countryside. He rang Luce, who'd returned home from Cardiff a few days before, and they planned the evening. Megan texted me the location, a place called the Holy Well of St Madron, and I found it on a map. After a thirty-minute ride, first down to Penzance, then to Madron village, we'd be using progressively narrower roads. It would be beautiful in the evening light, very romantic. For Sid and Luce, of course, not for me. We'd have a bite to eat at home, then I thought a pub somewhere for a bigger meal. Maybe on the coast. It would be interesting. A good opportunity for the team to do something nice, rather than just dealing with chaos and dead bodies.

Back at Turpin Cottage, Sid and I changed clothes. I dressed in a clean pair of black cargos and new shirt I'd just bought. Soon enough, the rumble of Luce's Land Rover made Sid second guess his choice of a Hawaiian-style shirt for the warm evening. I watched, amused, as he hurriedly swapped it for a plain black t-shirt.

Then he said, "No, she has to accept me the way I am, and I want the shirt." Off came the t-shirt; on went the eye-melting shirt. It was covered in skulls and mushrooms in vibrant purples. I'd grown used to the random packages turning up at the cottage with 'interesting things' in them. Sid was a hoarder in comparison to my spartan way of living, but I hadn't really had a home since Mum died. The small lockup I had in London, which contained things like my dress uniform, a few bits of furniture and albums, had made it to another in Cornwall. Moving it into the house felt like a commitment I wasn't ready for yet.

When Sid opened our front door, I saw Megan parking on the road and climbing out of her ex-police Ford Vectra. She wore her bike gear and police-issue boots and her blonde hair was in a braid down her back, ready for the bike helmet.

Unable to focus on Luce's bemusement at the shirt, I approached Megan. "You look great." She did. She really did, despite the weight loss. The sunshine had brought out the freckles I remembered from our childhood, and the biker-style jacket suited her perfectly.

"You look fitter than ever," she said, trying hard not to focus on my chest.

I'd had a lot more practice at meeting a woman's eyes rather than her attributes, so it made me grin. "Yeah, well, I have to do something with my evenings. Lifting heavy things is a good option." The deep green shirt I'd chosen didn't hurt; the fit was snug.

Megan declined to comment. Rather, she said hello to Luce and Sid. The women had an odd relationship, and one I didn't understand, but Megan seemed more relaxed this time around.

We sorted out the vehicles, taking Sid's Mini as well as the bike, and left Redruth. The road down to Penzance was easy enough, but when we reached Madron, the very narrow lanes began, and so did the traffic. It slowed us considerably.

With Megan on the pillion, sitting tight against me, the ride had been as electric as I'd hoped and feared. At least for me. For all I knew, she dreamed of her next date with Adrian. The late afternoon was certainly romantic enough. Light turned the world hazy, its questing fingers drawing a veil of damask-like fabric over everything, blurring the edges and turning Cornwall into a dreamscape. The beech and sycamore trees lining the low hedgerows were mellow green, and the fields rolled off towards patches of higher moorland. Bluebells hid among the high grass of the verges. I followed the Mini and sat upright, one hand on my thigh.

As we drove down the narrow lane, we began to see large signs on one side advertising a new development. A familiar company name, Whist Industries, branded the hoardings that described a new hotel and golf course development. We couldn't be more than half-a-mile from the location of the sacred well and chapel's entrance. Over the hedge, I saw heavy industrial machinery and long fencing with warnings in yellow all over the place. It looked ugly and disorienting in the gentle evening light coming from the west.

On the other side of the lane, I saw a camp. Despite going slowly, I couldn't count the number of vans, trucks, tents, caravans and other mobile living arrangements filling the field. People milled about here, whereas the hotel site was quiet now that the working day was over. There were homemade hoardings on this side of the lane declaring everything from independent Cornwall to the disillusionment of the monarchy. To be fair, the Duchy of Cornwall was the major landowner, but my loyalty, as a Royal Marine, would always be to the Crown.

"I love it down here," I said, visor up. "Despite all this." I waved a hand at the two sides of the lane.

Megan flipped up her lid as well. "You've always loved the wilder places. It's your nature. Not tempted to go back to London?"

"God, no. Nothing for me there. It was never home, just a place I lived. Have you ever wanted to leave Cornwall?"

A longer pause than I expected made me twist slightly to glance at her. "Megan?"

"I've been offered a post in Bristol. A possible move to CID. I applied months ago, didn't hear anything, then came back from my holiday to find the letter. Adrian says he'll put in for a transfer if that's what we want." She sounded tense.

I now had both hands on the bike, attention fixed forwards, ears humming with tinnitus like they did after a firefight, heart racing. Is this why I'd had that weird feeling as we'd walked into the office earlier? Was this the premonition I'd been expecting? Megan was going to leave me.

The right thing to say eluded me. I panicked. "Well, it sounds… like a good opportunity for your career. Working with DoPI might be a dead end. It is for most of us, really, so if that's what you want, then city policing is where you should go." I was babbling.

The cars lining the verges started to build up, and Sid indicated that he'd be parking in a Mini-shaped hole. I rode further down the lane, almost blind to what was happening, until Megan tapped me on the shoulder and said, "That's the footpath we need to take."

I glanced at the entrance and rolled to a stop. People were milling about, some in stout walking boots, others in wellingtons. A few, obviously tourists, were wearing less suitable footwear. April might've been dry, but not that dry. I had no doubt the track we'd be taking had its muddy patches. I found a good place to leave the bike, and Megan climbed off, removing her helmet.

The surrounding feeling was one of a festival. A joyous adventure shared by many people, none of whom really knew what would be happening. I felt dislocated from the celebratory feel of the event.

"I'm sorry for shocking you, Griff," she said.

I shook my head, making busy-work with my security locks. "No, don't be daft. You must always do what's best for you. I'm sure you'll make the right decision and your bloke," I couldn't bring myself to mention his name, "will be fully supportive."

She stepped towards me, hand out for some kind of reconciliation, but I heard Sid call. I slipped sideways before Megan made contact.

"Hey, guys. Looks busy," I said, the brightness of my voice sounding like shards of glass in my ears. Was this heartbreak? I'd had disappointments, and I'd been badly hurt a time or two, but this felt different. It felt like I was allowing something truly special to escape.

Luce smiled at me, but Sid frowned, his eyes darting to Megan before his jaw tightened.

"You alright?" he asked.

"Fine," I lied.

We joined the crowd going down the footpath that ribboned its way between fields and copses. The trees slowly closed in around us and I shivered, my body reacting to…

What? The cold? This was Beltane, and I was a toughened Marine, I didn't feel a chill. Shaking it off, I tried to pay attention to my companions.

Sid said to me, "Do you even know what a cloutie tree is?"

"Wishing tree, right?"

"It is a wishing tree, but this site is so much more," Luce said. "The cloutie tree is an interesting Cornish phenomenon. This is possibly one of the most popular in the area. The site itself is an ancient one. Boswarthan Chapel and Well date back to the early Christian missionaries from Wales. It's believed the site might've been dedicated to a Celtic goddess known as Mordon, but we obviously have no written evidence."

Megan, who walked next to me, murmured, "Obviously." Which made me chuckle.

Someone from behind me said, "The Christians banned goddess worship."

Luce frowned, opened her mouth about to argue the point, when Sid placed a hand on her arm and shook his head. "Some fights are just not worth it."

"Ignorance is no defence," Luce announced.

The voice became a person. A woman, younger than the rest of us, strode up beside Luce and glared at her. In the dim light of this bit of the track all I could make out were large dark eyes, straggles of black hair and lots of silver jewellery. "I'm not the ignorant one. These trees," she continued, "are tied with strips of cloth or ribbon that allow the petitioner to ask for healing. As the cloth rots, the ailment heals. It's sympathetic magic. Women's magic."

I looked around; we were beginning to come to the area where people started to tie things to the trees. "I'm not sure tying nylon or polyester to a tree is a good idea." It was meant to lighten the coming storm. It didn't work.

"No, of course not," the young woman snapped. "It should be a natural, undyed fabric, or it doesn't rot. Besides, we have to consider the environmental impact of using unsustainable fabric—"

Sid said, "I think we get the idea. Plastic bad, hemp good." The tone in his voice reminded me of London and Sanchez. Sid was about to lose his temper with the young woman.

I hid a smile but tried to keep Luce on track. "What do we know about the supernatural things in the area?"

"We have the holy well, and the chapel," she said. "They are meant to be healing. The tree is for wishes." She glared at the young woman. "The spring water rises here, as you can see."

We walked alongside a very shallow stream, and the ground was marshy. Many of the trees growing in the thin soil and granite rocks were obviously old, but they had spooky twisted trunks clothed in moss and lichen. The weather kept them shorn and pointing away from the most common south-westerly wind, though I knew from experience that during the spring, Cornwall and Devon could be battered by a strong north-easterly. They had been bitterly cold when we'd been training on Dartmoor.

The young woman said, "They were placed here to dominate—"

"Excuse me," Luce said. "Do you have a PhD?"

The young woman glared. "I can read."

"Yes, dear, but can you study?" Luce asked.

Sid muttered, "Ouch, burn."

"If you think bits of paper qualify you—"

"Well, yes, I rather think it does," Luce said. "I appreciate your passion and if you want to learn more, then I can suggest some very good courses in Falmouth. I even guest lecture on occasion."

We watched the young woman storm away through the water, her boots sloshing. Luce smiled and returned her attention to those of us listening.

"There are creatures called spriggans," Luce said. "A type of woodland spirit in Celtic lore. They tend to be wicked, often cruel and more prone to do harm than good. People can't appease them by leaving gifts. Much like our young friend over there."

Several people around us laughed.

Even Luce grinned. "Cornish piskies are another, different spelling to pixies, and these can be helpful to humans if treated well. If not, then look out; bad things can happen."

Someone asked, "What about dryads?"

"Strictly speaking, they are from Greek mythology. We don't know whether the druids had a similar concept. They are female tree spirits. Some are able to live in a woodland, away from their tree, but others, like the hamadryads, are tied to their tree, and if it dies, they die."

"What about male versions?" a man said from behind us.

Luce considered this for a moment before she said, "Well, we have satyrs, of course. They are bacchanalian in nature, with goats' legs and human torsos. We have little written evidence of something called a dru, which is meant to be the male equivalent of the dryad, but it's rarely mentioned in surviving documents." She managed to stop herself giving a full lecture.

I listened with interest but had to admit with only half an ear as she continued on answering people's questions.

The deeper into the wood I walked, the stronger the

prickle became across my back, up my neck and into my hair. It made me want to shiver and shrink away. I peered into the thickening trees lining the path. The air smelt of humans, and damp disturbed soil. Nothing seemed out of place.

Megan put a hand on my arm. “You okay?”

I dragged my attention back. “Yes, of course, I’m fine. I just…” Once more, my focus went into the woodland. It was thick beyond the path. The early evening light seemed to need an invitation to scramble between the ancient trunks and jutting, broken tooth-like boulders strewn between them.

“Griffin, are you sure?” Megan asked.

I forced myself to look at her and smile. “Yes, it’s all good.” Though, it wasn’t. Something here had my instincts standing to attention. Was it the mass of people? This was the most I’d been around since those horrible party nights we’d attended to flush out the incubus. Or a quirk of my PTSD? Though a Cornish woodland had little to do with the desert landscapes of the Sahel, the cities, and the pirates. Wishing it was PTSD seemed like a betrayal of all those people who had it far worse than me. I shoved the thought to one side.

No, if I were honest, something in this wood made my skin want to crawl off and look for a safe place to hide, dragging the rest of me with it.

Not wanting to spoil the evening for the others, especially Megan, as she’d invited us, I forced the feelings away. I’d come back, when it was quiet, with one of Sid’s gadgets and try to figure out why this strange squirrelly feeling of dread marched in heavy boots up and down my spine. It was burrowing long, gnarly fingers into my guts, and tugged at the curling hair around my collar. It almost felt like it was trying to rub its ugly face against the stubble on my jaw, a wicked cat, enjoying the beginning threads of terror it wanted to induce in its prey.

I forced a shiver to run through my body, trying to rid myself of the feeling. This was a wood. Not a haunted house. There were no ghosts in this place, and I was being a paranoid fool.

# Chapter Three

Stepping carefully through boggy and rock-strewn woodland, we reached a grove with a huge tree covered in wishing rags. Its roots dug into the marshy land and shallow stream that wove between the rocks. There were so many pieces of cloth tied to the branches that, due to this only being May, I couldn't tell what kind of tree we were looking at, but the width of the trunk made it old. Enough people were gathered that we stopped, thinking this must be the site of the ritual we were here to witness.

"The spring's beginning is further into the woodland," Luce said. "It's a bit of a hike."

"You've been up there?" I asked. I badly needed some breathing space. After pushing away my paranoid, DoPI inspired fears, I wanted to ground myself in the real world. Between the nagging sensations of the woodland, and Megan's news about moving to Bristol with her boyfriend, I was beginning to struggle to see the point in the evening festivities.

Luce nodded, distracting me. "I've been here a few

times over the years. The chapel is really only four walls, most of it rebuilt, and it's tiny, really tiny. There's a font that's supplied by the spring water and an altar that has space for a saint's image, or if it was originally pagan, a deity of some description."

"Do you really think this was a pagan site?" Megan asked.

"There's no reason to think it wasn't. The woodland here is ancient. The trees too misshapen to be of use for building houses or ships. Many of the woodlands of Britain and Ireland were stripped of trees for various wars over the centuries. Here, if you were a gnarled old oak, then you'd be safe." She lifted her boots out of the mire, gradually sucking us down.

I wasn't surprised by anything she'd said. The moment the ancient wood closed its branches over our heads, I began to feel it as a liminal space, one between worlds. It's an odd sensation many feel. If a person just picks the right spot, the space between two trees, or maybe the back of a wardrobe, they'd slip out of reality and experience something else. Maybe these spots were soft places in the flow of time, or thin places between dimensions? I certainly expected to see that strange oily twist in the air that meant I'd glimpsed the veil. This place was steeped in *para-energy*.

"Griffin, are you sure you're okay?" Megan asked again.

Startled, I realised she'd snuck up beside me. Commando training had clearly been lost on this Marine. "Yeah, I'm fine. All good. Great. No problems."

Her eyebrows rose.

I managed to stop myself before more words tumbled out of my mouth. Like my fears about the wood. Instead, I asked, "When do you leave for Bristol?" That's what she wanted to talk about.

"I don't know. I haven't accepted the post yet. I'll have to serve out three months' notice down here, anyway. So, there's time." She bumped herself against me. "You'll come up to visit, right? Now we've found each other again?"

I made the mistake of looking down. Her eyes, too bright, too blue, gazed up with hope. Fortunately, I was saved by the bell. It tolled nearby, and the procession began. Luce tugged on Sid and led us further back from the crowd, higher up the small stream. It gave us a great view.

When the procession appeared, I was surprised. They wore robes of deep green, like monks, or those freaks I'd 'met' on Bodmin Moor. Rather than a cross being carried by a priest, like it would be in a church, these guys carried a staff which morphed into a knotwork circle. Inside the circle was an equilateral cross marking the four compass points or maybe representing the elements. It had also been carved using the knotwork motif.

Behind this priest, I saw four others carrying a bier, as they do in Catholic countries. Only rather than the Madonna or Christ, this bier was entirely natural and not overly large. It had four small metal bowls on the corners of the central platform, all of them with flames glowing in the lowering light of the evening. In the centre of the dais rose a beautifully carved statue of a couple, male and female, obviously representing the unity and balance of humanity and the gods.

The priests themselves wore masks, which after tangling with the incubus, didn't make me comfortable, but these were of deep blue and green, some representing the sea, or blossom, some the trees in full leaf or crops. Whoever designed this event really knew their stuff. It was beautiful. Those not carrying the bier held simple drums, tambourines, and acoustic guitars. Scattered among the musicians were singers.

The crowd fell silent, and I watched with a growing sense of the veil being close to us, thin and permeable, as the procession came closer.

I had to say something. Warn someone. I whispered in Sid's ear, "We might have a problem down here if we aren't careful."

He glanced at me with a frown and nodded. "I hear you, brother. It feels different." So, I wasn't alone. He felt it as well. His dark eyes were full of concern. We both forced ourselves to focus on the ceremony.

The singing, lovely as it was, made the hairs on my neck stand up. The words weren't in English, maybe Cornish, and they rose and fell in the harmonies you'd expect from a professional choir. When the procession arrived in the glade, the people spread out, many of them standing in the water, soaking their robes, as they continued to sing. Some in the crowd began to mimic their sounds, and an enterprising lad brought out a tin whistle, probably one of the protesters, catching the melody and spreading it through the group. The man carrying the staff lowered its point into the soft soil, and I belatedly realised there were four low pillars of wood in the correct places for the bier to rest. I watched it being placed carefully down. The manoeuvrer almost made me hold my breath, half wishing for the comedic possibilities of it falling in the water.

The priest removed his mask, thank goodness, and raised his voice to quiet the crowd.

"Brothers and sisters, we are gathered here today to celebrate this…"

I tuned him out because at our feet, weaving among the stones, I saw something I didn't expect. Or perhaps I did, and that instinct is what made me see it even in the dim light of the evening. A faint trace of dark liquid in the crystal clear water coming from behind us. It looked like blood.

I nudged Megan and pointed down. The light in the grove was dimming quickly now, making it harder to see the difference in colour between the water, surging over peaty soil, and the brighter trail of red. Megan shook her head, not understanding.

I leaned close and whispered, "There's blood in the water." This wasn't my imagination. No crawling, sneaking dread, making me wish grown men could hide under the duvet. This was fact. Logic. Good sense. My job.

She glanced at me, disbelief warring with horror. "Seriously?" she whispered in return. The priest's speech about thanking the local goddess for her benign help during the coming summer season had gone quiet as he led the prayers.

"I saw it, Meg." Twitching my head upstream, I moved through the few people standing behind us. Megan followed, and Sid made to do the same, but I held up my hand and shook my head.

Following the stream, which turned into more of an ooze the further from the cloutie tree we walked, Megan and I picked our way with care. The trees and underbrush continued to thicken, and it became harder to see the footpath, more mud than walkable track. The still air held the scent of water, fresh and clean, now that we were away from the people, but after maybe a hundred metres, the smell changed. I sniffed like a bloodhound, and the metallic scent, along with other strong odours from the human body, built up like a wall pushed outwards by the thin breeze.

"Oh, shit," Megan muttered, joining me in the sniffing.

We switched on our phone's torches and continued our careful walk.

"There," she said, pointing to a flash of colour she'd seen. "Be mindful of evidence, Griffin."

Combining her torch beam with mine, we approached the scene. Stepping on stones rather than the mud, we managed to reach the body. She lay trapped by her left leg in the tangled roots of an oak tree. Her back was turned towards us; her skirt and woollen jumper of bright colours, soaked. Long strands of white hair trailed in the slow-moving water.

Working hard to keep to the stony surfaces, I moved around her body and leaned against the tree in which she was trapped.

A woman in her mid to late sixties, a nose ring glinting under the soft light from my torch. She had something wrapped around her throat.

It took a lot of effort on my part, but I lifted my gaze to meet hers. The eyes were blank, open, with a death-grey film over the surface. She'd been here at least two hours, probably longer considering the number of insects trying to make a home in her corpse.

"She's dead," I told Megan.

"Bloody hell. I'll call it in." She glanced over her shoulder, the sound of more singing coming to us through the trees. "This is going to be a shitshow with that lot here."

"Let's keep it quiet. There's no reason for them to come this way. Do you have your police ID on you?" I remained crouched near the body.

"Yes, fortunately. Give me a minute while I explain to my inspector what's happened." With great care, she stepped back onto firmer ground and made the call.

I tuned her out. The minutiae of police procedure

meant very little to me. Knowing I shouldn't be touching anything, I removed the Leatherman I kept on my belt and opened the pliers. With great care, using my phone's torch as a guide, I lifted the victim's cardigan's collar from her throat. Laced around it, like a choker, or Bronze Age torc, was an intricately woven necklace of ivy, but that hadn't killed her or caused the blood in the water. Despite the heart not beating, the amount of blood on her clothing had made a stain in the sluggishly moving water that eventually reached us. That blood had been caused by a hunk of wood, probably more than thirty centimetres long and as thick as my wrist. It stuck out of her smashed rib cage, directly over the heart.

I began to take photos.

"Hey, you can't do that," Megan said, returning to me and the body.

"It might be *para*," I stated, continuing to snap. The flash might alert others to our presence.

"You don't know that."

"I know she's here with a wreath of ivy around her throat and a wooden stake in her heart," I said. "That's not the way a normal person would kill."

Megan came closer, still using stones and firmer ground. "Normal people don't kill."

I glanced up at her. "You know that's not true." Movement near the body caught my attention. Among the roots of the tree, I saw the oily, rainbow-looking mist that made me think of the veil. "Trust me, Meg, this is a *para* death." I turned away from the mist, making sure I didn't touch it. The thought of it sliding over me made my stomach clench.

"Griffin, this has to go through CID first. You know that. I'm your police liaison for a reason."

Ignoring her for the moment, I pivoted on the balls of

my feet and angled the torch to the surrounding ground. With great care, I started taking more photos, often moving the camera at different angles, so the flash would highlight the mud, water and roots in different ways. Gently, I moved further upstream from the crime scene, examining the ground. Every few steps, when the soil was rich and thick, I stopped and looked with more care.

"Meg, can you come over here and lend me your torch as well?" I didn't move from my location. She approached, grumbling about the bollocking she'd get for not controlling me, and crouched beside me.

"This," I whispered, "is a footprint. There are a few more marks down there, but near the body they are muddled." I pointed.

Megan leaned over, the smell of her hair in my nose, I almost groaned at the ache it caused. "That's not a footprint. It can't be."

"It's not an animal. I'm no tracker, but I know the basics. No animal makes a mark like that one." The print was no more than the length of a woman's foot, maybe a bit more than twenty centimetres, but it was the wrong shape for a human, with a very narrow heel and most of the shape was made up of long toes and a high arch.

"It looks almost chimp-like, only way narrower," Megan said, just as quietly.

We had no reason to whisper, but with the body behind us and the ancient trees tangled together overhead, it didn't feel right to break the sad sanctity of the place. Besides, it suddenly felt like we weren't the apex predators in the area. I shivered again and tried to force out the feelings of being watched.

"Let's go back to the body," Megan said. "I don't like it here."

"Glad I'm not the only one." With both of us sensing the wrongness of the place, I became even more certain this was a *para-event*, even if Megan wasn't.

I reeled off a series of shots, taking in the surrounding area, the footprint and the treetops. Why I did the last series of images, I had no idea, but I was paid to trust my instincts.

We made our way back to the body. Megan stood and gazed at the woman for a moment, before shaking herself and saying, "I'm going to have to make sure no one comes in this direction."

"I'll stay with her," I nodded to the corpse, already wishing it wasn't necessary. All thoughts of a pub supper were long gone.

"You don't have to."

"I know, but it's wrong to leave her alone. It's not a problem. Whatever was here, it's gone. If you see the others, tell them about this, but make sure they go home."

Megan hesitated for a moment. "I can't believe I'm saying this, but do you think it means something that she died on Beltane?"

"Sadly, yes. It has to, but what it means…" I let the sentence trail off into the darkness.

Megan shook her head. "It has to be a human. God, please let it be a human." Her muttering continued until she was out of my view.

I sat on the roots of the oak tree, the moss making my shirt damp up my spine, and looked at the woman in more detail.

Her hair had long since gone grey, but it was a thousand different shades and would once have been deep brown or even black. Her eyebrows were certainly very dark. The hair looked naturally tangled, maybe with some matted dreadlocks among the more free-flowing sections. The nose ring wasn't her only jewellery. There were a mix of pendants, from crystals to pentagrams, and the fabric of her layered clothing had to be natural. She wore silver rings but had a simple gold wedding band on her left hand. It made me sad that somewhere out there was a family waiting for their matriarch to come home. On her feet were heavy, well-worn, but expensive boots. Good quality. This woman had money. She carried a little too much weight, but it filled out her cheeks, and she probably looked younger than her years when she'd been smiling, laughing, singing and dancing. I had no doubt she hailed from an alternative community. A great many of them existed in Cornwall, and I suspected we'd find connections to the protest group just up the road.

It made me feel lost, the familiar sense of sad loneliness rising. "I'm sorry this happened to you," I murmured to the woman. "I very much doubt you deserved it, and I promise we'll find out who, or what, did it."

# Chapter Four

From a distance, I heard Megan arguing with someone. It concerned me enough to apologise to the dead woman and leave her alone among the roots of the tree.

Once more, being careful of my steps, I approached the rapidly heating debate.

"I'm sorry, sir, but you cannot go further into the woodland," Megan stated. "I have the authority to stop you, and if necessary, arrest you."

"We have religious rights to this site. You're behaving as if this is a fascist country."

"If you give me your name, sir, I can—"

"Withers, Geoffrey Withers. I am the priest of our community, constable?"

"Sergeant Ackley, Mr Withers," Megan bit off. "With respect, sir," her voice dripping with contempt, "you have no idea what a fascist country might be like to live in, so I'd wind your neck in. Please." I swear I heard her teeth gnash.

"Sergeant Ackley?" I called out from behind her. "Is

there a problem?" Walking out of the wood, I kept my military bearing obvious.

"No, sir," Megan said, picking up on the game and playing along.

She'd been arguing with the man who'd carried the pagan cross and who'd led the prayers and other rituals. He looked to be in his fifties, and in the better light of the glade, I saw an expensive watch on his wrist. The robes weren't too modest, either. Up close, I noticed they were of a fine woollen weave and looked to be new. He'd pushed his hood back, as had the others behind them, and I noticed many faces with good quality haircuts, fine jewellery, and the confidence of the middle classes. Very few of those who'd watched the ceremony had followed the pagan group into the wood. Perhaps, I wasn't the only one picking up on the weird vibes among the darkening trees, and that was before we'd found the corpse. Sid and Luce were nearby watching, but they were the only outsiders.

"Good, then I suggest we disburse this group and wait for the rest of our colleagues to arrive," I said in my best impression of a Royal Marine sergeant.

"I was attempting to explain to Mr Withers that very fact, sir."

I stared hard at Mr Withers. "I'm afraid you can't go deeper into this part of the woodland, sir. It just isn't possible at the moment."

"And as I was trying to explain to your," he looked Megan up and down in a way that made me want to punch him in the face, "Pitbull here, that we have a ritual to complete."

"I'm sure the deities of the wood can wait another year for you. It's been several centuries, if not millennia, since the last one, and the world hasn't come to an end."

His eyes widened, and a woman—small, slim, with a complex series of braids holding back the highlighted hair, making her look like an extra in a fantasy film—stepped forwards. "Your contempt for this ceremony is bordering on harassment of a minority religious community."

Megan stepped up. "And you are?"

"Mrs Beechwood, defence barrister." She smiled with the kind of smug power that reminded me of the cat from our previous lodgings in Redruth.

"In that case, Mrs Beechwood, may I have a private word?" I asked, opening my arm to indicate I wanted to separate her from the herd.

She didn't glance at the man, who obviously thought he was in charge, and stepped towards me. I led her nearer Sid and Luce, giving them a quick nod.

Keeping Megan and the small crowd in sight, I turned Mrs Beechwood so she couldn't see her audience. It deprived her of their power. A neat trick if it worked.

With my voice pitched low, I said, "We need your co-operation, Mrs Beechwood. It's important, or we wouldn't have interfered." I glanced behind me. "We've found a body, and it's not a natural death. Sergeant Ackley doesn't want to start a panic. We don't need a stampede. People will get hurt among the rocks and trees. If I could ask for your help in sending people home, that would be useful. We really don't mean any disrespect. Like you, we were here to enjoy the evening and haven't attended in any official capacity. We're just trying to do our jobs."

One of the things my unit in the Marines had always relied on was my ability to calm the locals and talk us out of problems. I'm a good diplomat. Also, with a childhood laced with emotional explosives both at home and school,

I'd eat humble pie like it was made of lamb and potato if I thought it would help.

Even in the dimming light of dusk, Mrs Beechwood's face paled. "I see." She gazed past my shoulder, then met my eyes. "Are you sure?"

"Very. If you assist Sergeant Ackley in moving people away from the site, and take the details of those you can, we'd appreciate your professional help."

The small woman's shoulders squared, and she gave me a brief nod. I approached Sid and Luce. "We need as many number plates as possible. Can you get back to the cars ASAP and photograph the vehicles before they leave? Just in case."

"There's really a—" Sid looked sick at the thought of saying the words.

"Yes, and we need to move fast. Megan thinks this is a mundane crime. I'm not so sure. Either way, we need to do our bit and collect as much information as possible."

"Okay," Sid said, obviously keen to escape.

"And, Sid?"

He turned back to me.

"Be careful. Don't get lost in the wood. Something here is…"

"Off?" he suggested.

"Yeah, that'll do for the moment."

We shared a nod before he took Luce's hand and vanished back into the crowd.

Enlisting Mrs Beechwood proved to be one of my better decisions. First, she organised her people, asking them to lead others safely through the dark woodland, using the torches they'd brought with them. It turned out these pagans weren't daft. They'd thought to bring, not only their carved statues but also boxes with towels for their feet, walking boots, hi-vis vests, and electricity. In short order, she had her people guiding the few stragglers back down the tricky path without too many arguments.

Megan, now with a police issue cap on her head that all but hid her features, walked back with the crowd to wait for her colleagues. Once again, I was alone in the wood. The long twilight of an English spring evening waned into full night as I stood there among the twisted trees, thick undergrowth and ribbons full of wishes. The fitful breeze died completely, and the stream, now undisturbed, barely made a sound. I tried to control my imagination, but to be fair, I knew what might be out there. Perhaps not specifically, but as one of DoPI's door-kickers, or the point of their spear, I'd seen more than my share of the darkness in the supernatural world. It always seemed to be at odds with humanity, as if we couldn't exist in the same place. My boss, Pilar Sanchez, really wanted to make sure we didn't. No sharing. Not in her reality.

Now that humanity had left the glade, life eked back. Small rustlings in the low brush, a flutter of wings as silent owls approached their feeding grounds. I tried to remember which kind of owl hunted in woodlands. Tawny, that's right, tawny owls hunted in places like this. There would be stoats, weasels, voles, mice, rats, and more night creatures. Some like badgers, hedgehogs and foxes might appear. It would be fine. I wasn't alone.

*You're scared of the dark? Really?*

Yeah, well, a murdered woman lay among the roots of an old tree just a few metres away. A man could be forgiven some trepidation, surely. What could've done that to her? What made me feel that cold, gnarled hand of dread the moment we walked into this beautiful place? The shadows might not be lunging at me, but they weren't friendly either.

Years of experiencing *para-events* made me highly sensitive to shifting atmospheres. I hadn't liked this place when we walked in surrounded by other people. Now, I wanted whatever was out there, to stay the fuck away for the moment.

I just had to hold the line, not solve the problem. Time to think about something else. My brain instantly went to its favourite torment.

When we'd arrived for the evening's festivities, I'd been looking forward to spending a few hours with my favourite person in the world, and now she was leaving Cornwall to live with her bloke in Bristol. I knew I couldn't stop it. I had no right to stop it but damn it hurt bad.

Trying to force that away as well, I pondered the implications of this being a *para-event.* Megan might not recognise it as such, but I'd seen the oily twist of the veil around the dead woman. The way the wood oozed discontent. That strange footprint and the ritual aspects to the victim's death. It had been just a few short weeks since the last one, and it worried me for the future. What did this mean for the safety of the area? Maybe Sanchez had it right; we needed to close down the *para* leaks, and we needed to prepare for the worst in the future.

Something flashed in the darkness, and with unmanly relief, I realised the police had arrived. Megan came with the first responding officers. I heard her talking to them as they picked their way through the mud.

"Hey," I called out.

"Griffin, thank goodness, I'd forgotten how long the path was," she said, appearing out of the gloom.

For the next couple of hours, I explained repeatedly that I worked for Rural Security, and where I fitted into Sergeant Ackley's official life. Also, the SOCO team arrived, the pathologist followed soon after, and CID made a nuisance of themselves. I spoke to a gruff detective inspector from Penzance who made it perfectly clear this had nothing to do with my department, so thank you, but piss off.

I wondered how he'd feel when Sanchez called the Home Office, and they leaned on the man's boss to turn the crime over to me. Probably not very happy. I didn't give the bloke a hard time, it wouldn't help Megan, and he was just doing his job. Quickly enough, I faded into the background.

While I waited for Megan to find me, I forwarded Sid the images I'd taken and asked him to start work on the identification of the victim and the footprint.

I soon received a message back that said, *What, now? It's late, man.*

*Yes, Sid, now. I'll meet you at the office.*

He didn't reply. I guessed I'd be less popular than a case of herpes by the time I reached Redruth.

"Hey," Megan said, sloshing her way to me through the stream.

"Hey, do you want a lift home?"

She glanced behind her at the gentle chaos that accompanies a sudden death. "Well, I'm not needed here. CID will want boots on the ground tomorrow to interview people, but I guess that depends on what you'll need from me?"

"This'll become a DoPI case, I'm sure of it, so I'll need you with me if that's okay?"

She nodded but didn't look convinced. Slowly, it now being full dark, we began walking back to the bike. "It hasn't really done my career any harm working for Rural Security, you know." She grinned and put the name in air quotes. "Though my team in Redruth don't like it very much. I'm an experienced beat sergeant, and we don't have very many of those."

"I'm glad it's helped. Though, for most of us, it's a career dead end. We burn out. Our regiments wanted shot of us in the first place and don't want us back. Is that one of the reasons Bristol wants you?" I asked more out of politeness than really wanting to know.

"I think so. Collaboration with outside agencies is a good thing in the modern service. It'll be a wrench leaving Cornwall."

"Yeah. I'm sure it will."

We slumped into silence, and it didn't feel comfortable. Rather, it spiralled around us like a weak tornado full of unspoken words and the knowledge that something special would die when she left me.

We rode back to Redruth, and I didn't hang about. Megan lay tight against my back, her arms around my waist and her head resting on my shoulder blade. Her thighs were tucked under mine. I focused on the road, the night sky full of cold, distant stars, my heart empty of hope.

It was a relief to reach the office and see Sid's Mini parked outside. "I can take you home," I said to Megan over my shoulder.

"No, I should be with you during the initial stages. I'm still not convinced this is a *para* crime, but I can't do my job if I don't know all the facts on your side of the fence. I also need to know how to handle the fallout when CID throw their toys about."

"Roger that," I murmured.

Once in the building, I saw Luce sitting with Sid and the pair of them interrogating the web. The office smelt of pizza and energy drinks. One of those I could definitely go for, and it wasn't the chemically induced high of the drink. Fats and carbs were more appealing.

"Your pizza's in the kitchen," Luce said as we walked in.

"Thank you." My stomach growled audibly, making her chuckle.

I noticed Megan biting her lip as if the thought of pizza was worrying. Odd, she loved food, though her weight loss was noticeable.

Sid had printed out the most relevant images and stuck them onto a large board. I guessed Luce had done the writing because Sid's was unintelligible at the best of times, and he couldn't spell. Apparently, you didn't need to spell when you wrote code.

With pizza in hand, Megan and I pulled up the more comfortable chairs we'd ordered for just this kind of situation.

"What do you think at the moment?" I asked.

Luce rose and pointed to the stake and the ivy around the woman's throat. "These are ritual plants and trees in folklore and magic. Ivy you'd think, would have a negative connotation because of its association with graveyards and dead things in general; it has a suffocating nature, after all. However, that's not the case. Ivy is generally thought of as a benign plant. From binding friendship to protection, fertility and good luck. The fact that it's around the woman's neck is very odd. You'd think that would be negative, and perhaps it is, but I've been thinking that maybe this is about all those things I've just mentioned. Protection of a home, fertility of the land during the Beltane fire festival, and a binding."

Megan asked, "Like that Mephisto thingy did? Binding souls?"

Luce shrugged. "Maybe, but I don't think it's that kind of binding. This is different. It's a more sympathetic magic."

"It's a practitioner?" I asked with some hope. Catching a human foe would be a great deal easier than something purely *para*.

Sid replied, "It could be. We think the stake is likely to be ash wood."

Megan huffed. "How would you know that? No one at the scene knew."

"It's one of the most significant trees in many Western mythologies." He said this as if Megan should just know it as a fact, which annoyed me. We weren't all experts in the crazy of the world.

"If it is ash, what does it mean?" I asked.

"In British mythology, it's about protection and healing. You kill vampires with it, obviously. It's the World Tree in Norse and used for druidic wands."

Megan laughed. "Wands, that's just so silly. I'll never be able to take this shit seriously."

"That poor woman obviously did, and she died horribly because of it," Luce said.

Here we go…

Personally, I was with Megan. A bit of gallows humour is something the armed forces and the emergency services share. It's about survival, and Megan was right; wands are a very odd concept to those not interested in casting spells.

The tension between the two women escalated quickly. I tried to smooth things out. "I think what Megan was trying—"

She rounded on me. "Don't tell me what I was trying to say. I know what I was saying. I've spent the entire evening with the corpse. Sadly, I had to watch as they rolled her onto a gurney so she could be carried out of the wood. She was small, alone, scared and defeated when someone ran that fucking stake through her heart. I'm trying to find a little light in what's become a very dark world. So back off and just accept the fact that sometimes, those of us on the front line of this, have to remember to find a little silliness in the world."

Silence. I watched Luce's expression, and it hardly shifted. Sid opened his mouth, but I shook my head. They needed to sort this out.

Luce's eyes unfocused for a bit, then she seemed to come back online. "I understand. I'm sorry. You're right. What I said was unkind. However, I'd like you to remember that it's often difficult for those not on the front line to understand, and people in the emergency services often have little patience with us."

Megan nodded. "You're right. I'll do better."

"So will I."

Sid and I remained wrapped in awed silence. I think we'd half expected it to become a punch-up.

Eventually, I asked Luce, "Okay, so, erm, ash trees?"

"It's the protection theme being repeated. The stake through the heart makes us think of vampires, but it could be about releasing the heart blood for fertility of the land. There are many common themes between the two plants."

Megan said, "Someone might be using this as a way to throw us off the scent."

I frowned. "What do you mean?"

"Well, let's be honest, the three of you are always looking for the supernatural narrative. What if it's someone from the property developers down there? Maybe a fight with the protesters got out of control? Or perhaps it's as simple as someone wanting to break up the protest group? Making this look like an occult murder is a good way of forcing the police to react to the eco-warriors."

"Are they a problem for the police?" I asked.

Megan leaned back in her chair and put her feet on the edge of my desk. "They've been calm so far. We were called out initially, but the farmer invited them onto his land, so the developers can't do anything, and neither can we. Despite what everyone thinks, people still have a right to protest. What they can't do is negatively impact businesses and property. Though I will admit I don't like enacting the new legislation. We try to take a gentler approach down here than they do in the cities."

I wanted to say it wouldn't be like that in Bristol but managed to hold back. Starting that conversation in front of Sid and Luce would make me too vulnerable. "Okay, so it could be the developers—meaning those working for them—who went too far in trying to break up the protest site. What else could it be?" I had my ideas, but I didn't want to dominate the conversation.

"A blue-on-blue attack," Sid said.

"A what?" Luce asked.

"You know, like when you shoot someone on your own side because you mistook them for the enemy, or you didn't like the person and used the cover of a firefight to get a bit of revenge." He looked at me. "It happens, right?"

"Sadly, yes. Though it's usually the former, an accident through cross-communication. Or just the chaos of a battlefield fight. It's one of the reasons we train to move in sync with each other, so we know where everyone is, even in a high-stress situation. Though I'm not sure what you mean this time, Sid."

"Well, maybe she just pissed off the wrong people in her group? It could be another eco-warrior dressing it up as an occult ritual, or something spooky. They'd certainly have the imagination to do it."

I rose from my chair, suddenly tired and in need of being alone. "Tomorrow, we need an ID, and once we have that, we can run a background check. Right now, we need to sleep. Megan, I'll take you back to the cottage, and you can go home from there. Sid, Luce, you're finished here for the moment?"

The pair of them looked at each other and nodded.

Luce said, "There is one more possibility that it could be."

"What?" Megan asked.

"A supernatural assassin interested in feeding the land the energy of the dying woman's heart blood. If you want a *para* explanation, then that's a place to start, I should imagine. You don't just go out with a rope of ivy and an ash stake. That's a planned event." She pointed to the pictures. "Be this human or otherwise, this was carefully thought through. When we discover who the victim is, we might begin to understand the objectives."

I gave a quick nod. "Then we're on the track. Let's reconvene here in the morning, 09:00 hours. I want to make sure we're ready when CID hands over the case."

Megan rose but looked sceptical. "I'm not sure that'll happen, Griffin, but I guess we'll see."

# Chapter Five

*The call came again, and I knew I had to answer. Nights had slipped past without the summons, and I had been still. Fighting the call never worked; it was impossible. Resistance was useless; only acceptance brought peace.*

*I threw back the bedcovers, rose and dressed. Over many years, I had become accustomed to the movements needed in this state of* otherness. *Sometimes the call came from nearby, sometimes from a long way off. Then there were times I couldn't understand the call's demands and became lost.*

*Tonight, I didn't need the motorcycle. I would walk. The call itself was not an audible sound. It drew me with a vibration that centred on the core of my being. I had no choice but to obey. The imperative was so strong nothing could impede my progress. The ground under my feet was cold, the town quiet, the night in its middle age. It wouldn't take long. At a good pace, I would reach my goal in time. Plenty of time.*

*When the moon's light broke through the gathering clouds, I turned my face to the light. It helped. It made the journey less lonely to have the silver brightness of her company. My long legs soon arrived at their destination. No gates barred my way, not that it would have mattered. I walked through the long grass, the moon kissing the flowers and turning them from bright gold, to silvered shadows. Bats spun overhead, owls sang for their mates, and a fox loped between the rows of headstones.*

*The call tonight was the clearest I'd received for a long time. The last took me to the place of the dead far from here, an ancient site, which left me confused and lost, but tonight was different. The pull felt stronger than ever, and I knew why. The veil moved inside me with more vigour. I'd walked among the cries of the dead, and I had heard them, listened to their pleading and begging. Then, I'd ensured their release. The dead were now my silent companions. I saw them lying still under the thick soil, their peace like blankets of silk made by dew and spiders' webs.*

*I approached the one grave I had not seen during my waking life. Dropping to my knees, I dug my fingers into the grass and began to pull.*

The moment consciousness began to come back, I knew I wasn't in my bed. For starters, despite it being May, I was cold and wet. My feet were sore, and my fingers hurt. Opening my eyes, I rolled onto my back and groaned. Muscles in my chest and arms ached appallingly. Tears pricked my eyes as I gazed at the branches of the cherry tree in my garden, the leaves a light green against the pale blue just making itself known overhead.

"I can't do this," I whispered, tears pricking my eyes. "I just can't keep doing this." Fear wriggled through me and nestled like a viper in my heart, waiting to strike. I heard the back door creak open.

"Griffin?" Sid's voice sounded panicked. "Oh God, Griffin, I should've set some kind of alarm." He hurried over the grass and threw a blanket over me. "Come on. Let's get you inside and cleaned up. You look like you've done ten rounds with a mud monster."

Too exhausted, cold and miserable, I didn't reply.

Instead, I allowed Sid to wrap me up and hold me to his body as I hobbled down the garden path. At some point in the night, I'd dressed in a t-shirt and a pair of black fatigues, but that was all. No boots, no coat against the rain that must've come.

"Bath first?" he asked. The last time this had happened, him finding me in the garden, his kindness and practical care had shocked me, until he'd confessed that, as a child, he'd supported his mother during her addiction.

"Shower will be fine, easier to clean off the mud," I croaked, my throat parched.

Sid rubbed my back and said, "Hey, come on. It's alright. We'll figure this out. I'll have a record of where you've been."

I glanced at him. "How? I thought you were going to use a drone?"

"What, and stay up all night trying to track you? Nope, I went for the nanotech option instead. I've put a small tracking device into all your belts."

We were halfway up the stairs, but I stopped and looked at him. "Why didn't you tell me?"

"Why would I? We don't know what's happening, and for all I knew you'd remember in your sleeping state and remove your belt. You're welcome, by the way."

"But that means you've been tracking me for weeks," I said, horrified at the thought.

"Yeah, because your life is so interesting. Besides, after what happened with Mephistopheles, it's a good precaution. With just the two of us down here, and the London teams at best an hour-and-a-half away, I need to be able to pull your arse out of whatever fire is currently burning it, like this one."

"This isn't a fire," I muttered. "It's marsh gas that builds up and explodes."

Sid chuckled. By the time he'd stopped, he'd manoeuvred my tired body into my shower room. "Get clean. Don't think too much. I'm going to make breakfast and log into the tracker software."

I managed to pull off my clothing and shuffle into the shower. The hot water burned for long seconds, and my feet howled in protest as the water stung the many small wounds, but I started to use soap and flannel to work the grime off my arms, face and those poor feet. I felt better. Wrapped in a towel, I threw the clothes in the laundry and redressed in a soft shirt, another pair of the same trousers and my softest woollen rainbow socks after slathering them in disinfectant cream. Comfort clothing.

The smell of food soon lured me downstairs, despite my embarrassment. I'd done my best to keep my brain in neutral, knowing a panic attack wouldn't help, but the meaning behind the trance, or absence, or whatever the fuck was going on with me, veered dangerously towards the panic red zone.

Sid had his laptop next to the cooker and appeared to be emptying our fridge into the largest frying pan we owned. He moved deftly between the two.

"Right, soldier boy, I know where you've been. We just have to figure out why. And how many sausages do you want?"

"I'm not hungry, Sid."

"Bollocks, you aren't. Two should do, with the fried egg, toast, tomatoes, beans and some bacon." Sid had started shopping at the local butchers rather than the supermarket, as I'd started digging the veggie patch over in our garden. Neither of us knew much about growing things, with me forced into a dysfunctional boarding school and him surviving a sink estate in London, but we'd learn.

I sat, knowing I'd never manage even half of what he cooked, but I didn't have the heart to argue. A cuppa tea waited for me at the table. "Thanks, Sid."

"You're welcome. Now, what we have here is an interesting conundrum. You went for a walk, at quite a pace I might add, to the nearest cemetery and to a specific place. There you remained for several hours until you walked back about an hour before sunrise."

I felt sick. No, I was going to be sick. Pushing back from the table, I rose and ran to the downstairs bathroom. Bile exploded out of me, and I began to shake. I heard Sid yelling something from the kitchen, but I couldn't answer. My stomach twisted again, but this time, nothing came up. I broke out in a sweat.

"Hey, what the hell?" He brought the smell of the kitchen into the small room, and I groaned as it made my head swim. A glass of water appeared. "I've put the food in the oven to keep warm. Take your time."

When I managed to lean back on my heels, I murmured, "My mother is in that graveyard."

Silence for a beat. Then, "What the St Day Road one?"

I nodded. "I don't go there, but that's what she wanted. To be close to her family, her sister and the farm." She'd left a note. I never saw it; my brother said our father had destroyed her final words to us. To me.

Sid leaned against the door frame and studied me, his expression serious. "We'd better go down there and check. Can I ask why you haven't visited it?"

I glared at the cistern, rather than at Sid. "What's the point? She's been dead for decades."

"But you've been down to the Brane dolmen at least once a week—" So he did know.

I surged from the floor. "I know…" Then tailed off because a dizzy spell hit me. "Bugger it."

Silently, Sid handed me the water again.

"Sorry," I whispered, not sure which bit of my behaviour I wanted to apologise for. "The tracker?"

"The tracker. It downloaded all the data. I wasn't spying, Griffin."

"Yeah, alright, sorry. I'm just…"

"A little raw? Come on, mate. Let's get some food inside you, and I promise it won't look so bad."

It turned out, you stick a fried breakfast in front of a Marine, he's going to eat it regardless of what his brain says, and it did make me feel better. At least physically. Psychologically, I was a mess and aware of time slipping away. Luce and Megan would soon be at the office, and I needed to speak to Sanchez.

Which brought with it an entire maelstrom of thoughts. How could I do my job like this? These events were more than just weird wanderings; they had a purpose. I'd woken once at the Carwynnen Quoit and seen the burial ritual of someone in some kind of dawn-inspired vision, and now this? At school, I'd been found more than once at the site of the death of a student from years before. Had all my other wanderings been trying to take me to some kind of burial place? What the hell did it mean?

I knew one thing for certain; it meant I shouldn't be trusted by my colleagues. If we didn't know what this was, I might do something to place them, or myself, in a dangerous situation. If I were hurt, that was one thing. But someone else being hurt due to my actions? No, I wouldn't tolerate that. I'd been considering resigning from the Royal

Marines anyway, but this brought it home. I couldn't be trusted, and if I wasn't a Marine, then continuing to be a part of DoPI seemed like a remote possibility. They wanted their investigators in the Armed Forces, which meant we were disciplined and highly trained to deal with stressful combat situations with calm, detached minds. Or that was the theory. After my experiences on Bodmin, and then with the damned incubus, I knew things with me were changing for the worse. Whatever *para* threat we faced with this new death, well, maybe I should back off. Megan was leaving Cornwall anyway, so returning to London for a full assessment before being retired from the field might be the sensible, safe option.

Megan. Cornwall. My mother's grave. All these thoughts and more tumbled about like marbles in a bag being shaken by an imp. They clanked and crashed, fell out and rolled away.

A sharp rap on the table's surface brought me back to the present. Sid peered at me. "Whatever's going on in there, I'd pack it away."

"I'm fine. I need to report to head office, after doing the washing up."

Sid went upstairs to change, making no comment, but obviously worried. Who could blame him? If I were him, I'd be asking for a new investigator to partner with, rather than trying to keep a failing one on the team.

Of course, my phone rang the moment I had my hands in the washing up water. I dried and pulled it from my pocket. At catching sight of the name on the screen, I had a brief moment of wondering if she'd had my brain bugged and could listen in.

"Ma'am," I said, knowing there was no point in asking

after her well-being. I wasn't entirely sure she had a well-being that needed looking after.

"Corporal, why didn't you inform me of last night's events?"

Shit. "It was late by the time we left—"

"You should have phoned me from the location if that was a concern."

I saw her sitting in DoPI's office. The mind-melting artwork on the wall behind her desk, which I'd stared at more than once while waiting for her to acknowledge my presence.

"I'm sorry, ma'am." There was no point in trying to explain or find excuses.

"Well, having received a report from Mr Dalton, I have been speaking with the Serious Crimes team, and they've agreed to hand over the case to Rural Security. Your police liaison will update you on the investigation's details as they stand at the moment."

Sid had notified Sanchez last night? Why on earth did he do that? They loathed each other. I didn't have the time to think it through in detail.

"Very good, ma'am, at least the team is working well together." I stared at a blackbird in the grass. He looked at peace with his lot, and I felt a pang of envy. "There is something I need to discuss with you, ma'am. It might be wise for me to come up to London."

A pause. "This is an active investigation, Corporal."

"I'm aware, ma'am, but I think this is a priority." Was I really about to do this? My heart pounded in my chest, and the hand holding the phone trembled. "It's an HR issue."

"What's he done?" she sounded resigned.

"No, erm, it's not Sid, it's me. I'm the problem."

A longer pause. She did this. My boss weaponised

silence like no other person on the planet. I waited, long used to her habits. "And what do you believe is the problem, Corporal Woodbury?"

I licked my lips. "Ma'am, I no longer think I'm fit for duty. Not as a Royal Marine, or as an investigator for DoPI."

For the first time in four years, I heard Pilar Sanchez chuckle. "And why on earth, Griffin, would you think that?" It was the first time she'd ever used my given name.

"I think my personal issues are getting in the way of the job."

"You mean your PTSD, which none of us are sure really is PTSD caused by your service?"

I opened and closed my mouth a few times, not sure what to say. I was pretty sure frowning at the blackbird wouldn't help, but it was all I could manage.

A long sigh came all the way from London. "Griffin, you're one of my more talented spear points. That's why you're down there on your own. You have a knack for seeing the *para* influences in places most wouldn't. Take this murder, for instance. I don't need to list the reasons it looks like a normal murder, if there is such a thing, and some weird bastard decided to dress it up as something pagan. You see it clearly as a potential *para* event. That's important."

"Thank you for your faith in me, ma'am, but my mental health—"

"Is something you can deal with down there. In the fresh air. Griffin, we both know you aren't going back to the Royal Marines. I'm not stupid. Despite what you think, you were damned good in the service, and they'd have you back if you passed the psych eval."

That was news to me. I was about to break in, but she was quick to continue.

"Working for DoPI causes problems for those on the front line. We know that; it has done for centuries. You operatives are often untrained sensitives, psychics, or mediums, which can be a problem, but also a benefit. I'm assuming Sid knows of these issues?"

"Yes." I was confused by this conversation.

"Then he'll report if you collapse in a heap, gibbering like a madman and drooling into your porridge, right?"

"I suppose so, yes."

"Then whatever nightmares, terrors, sleepwalking, and trances you endure, so long as no one is in danger—"

"But that's just it, ma'am, I don't know if they are."

The blackbird spied next door's cat. He took flight, screaming in irritation at the big fat thing. The cat didn't seem to notice.

"No, you don't know, but that doesn't mean you should stop work. You're no more dangerous than someone who suffers from depression getting behind the wheel of a car in a state of utter misery. You aren't going to kill someone in your sleep. From all we've assessed of your previous records and the reports you've given to our welfare team here; you are still able to perform your job."

"The episodes are getting worse."

"Good, then maybe you can figure out what it all means. Now, get on with it, Corporal. I don't have the time to babysit your conscience." The connection was cut between us.

I stared at the phone. Never in all the years I'd worked with the woman had she called me Griffin or spoken to me like she cared.

"You talked to the wicked witch?" Sid asked from the doorway.

"Have you been reporting to her?"

His skin darkened further. "She asked me to keep an eye on you. Spear points need to be well maintained to keep functional. Her words."

Paranoia leaked over the confusion of the call like a sticky blanket. "Why didn't you tell me?"

"Because I didn't want you to look at me like you are now, and I wanted us to build a friendship first. It's not a big deal, Griffin." Sid approached, his hands out, body language open. "Look, I'm not easy, I get that, but you're one of the few people I rub along with, and that's mostly because you're really relaxed. You don't make demands, and you put up with all my crap in the house. I wrote to Sanchez about your trances, especially after the last major *para* event, because I wanted to know if the alchemists and healers in London might be able to help. You took a huge dose of MDMA, and if you think that isn't going to affect you in the long-term, you're mistaken. With your sensitivities to the *para,* it'll do something to you. Who knows what? Right now, I'm thinking it's made you more aware than ever, and this event, this new mystery we have, it's sparked something that caused you to trance out last night. Or maybe just bumping up against the veil during the Beltane festival was enough? Who knows? Just stop giving yourself a hard time, and for once, listen to the boss lady."

"Well, that's new, coming from you."

"Yeah, well, don't expect me to make a habit of it. The woman's a plague." He grabbed his coat from the back of the chair. "I'm heading for the office. Meet you there?"

I wasn't exactly happy with his reasoning, but right now, I didn't know how to deal with his help. It seemed rude to reject the consideration he'd given. "Sure. See you in a bit. I'll finish the washing up."

Sid nodded and left the house. A moment later, I heard the unmistakable rumble of his ancient Mini's engine.

My phone buzzed. A message from Sid. *We need to see what you were doing at the grave you went to last night. We'll go later. Maybe with Megan?*

I felt a strange, unfamiliar pang in my gut. Support. I had a support network with this, even if half of it wanted to go to Bristol. Right now, I had friends. It felt good. Then I wriggled my feet and felt how sore they were. I might have friends, but could they help with the issues plaguing me?

## Chapter Six

By the time I reached the office, the Land Rover and Megan's Vectra were parked outside. I pushed the bike close to the wall and locked her in place. The double security system annoyed me, as usual, but when I finally entered the office, the smell of coffee welcomed me.

"Here he is," Megan said. "Can we get on with the briefing now?" She held a folder in one hand and her mug in the other. "And you look like shit. What happened?"

Luce handed me a coffee. "She's eager to get started."

I ignored Megan's question and said, "What have you got so far?"

"I was sent these first thing this morning. I did printouts, and I've emailed the details to both of you. The initial findings aren't all that different from what we knew yesterday, except for one thing. The cause of death is not the massive blunt force trauma to the chest."

"That's a relief," I said. "I hate to think she suffered."

"Well, that depends on how you feel about having your

throat cut. From initial interviews, she'd also been missing for twenty-four hours."

I frowned. "Did anyone report her missing?"

"No, not to us. They're aware of how missing people are treated by the police, especially those in their alternative community. Though, they looked for her. No sign found."

I pondered this as I said, "I didn't see enough blood on her neck and chest. Any neck wound usually produces arterial spray."

Megan nodded. "It's a small incision directly into the area between her neck and clavicle cavity." She held up the image related to the wound. "They did a preliminary autopsy very early this morning to help with a press release. Overnight, there was a lot of unhelpful speculation online. With so many people at the Beltane festival, the press got hold of this very fast. Then one of our uniformed officers posted something stupid, and it's all gone a bit crazy."

DoPI's press office would be having a heart attack about now, trying to control the flow of news. I wondered how they'd spin this death.

Sid chuckled over the rim of his mug. "It's the perfect story for a wild conspiracy."

"Sadly," Megan agreed. "Anyway. If you look here," she pointed to a small wound on the woman's neck, it lay just over the area where the neck and shoulder met. A thin slice in the pale skin was clear. "If a sharp blade is pushed in here, apparently, the artery can be opened, but the blood pours into the chest cavity, rather than spurting all over the place. It's a ritual location."

"Why so much blood with the stake?" I asked.

"That was probably put in seconds after the heart stopped. It caused the massive amount of blood in the cavity to exit through the wound. It became a spill, not a squirting fountain."

Luce shook her head. "This is not good."

"You don't have to be here for this," I pointed out.

"Maybe not, but it helps. Besides, ritual death is one of my areas of interest. It's very important in all manner of myths and legends."

"Okay, well, it's good to have you here." I pointed to the images Megan was adding to our board. "This is a very difficult and specific form of death. It would take a lot of practice to do it correctly. As we thought last night, this is a well-planned act of violence."

"Which means it might not be the last," Megan pointed out. She tapped the woman's face. "Meet Jennifer Mancore, age sixty-seven, just retired and recently divorced, despite the wedding ring she's wearing. She moved to Cornwall six months ago, according to her daughter, and has been at the protest site for three weeks, living in a small camper van. She has a cottage in Crantock, near Newquay. Jennifer's become increasingly interested in the alternative lifestyle and is an activist in the Just Stop Oil campaign, even getting arrested several times in London. Though she hasn't committed any acts of violence against artwork or at a sports event. It's more about passive resistance. She isn't a leader, just a supporter. We can speak to her daughter, but it'll have to be via video link, as I don't think anyone has the budget to fly to Australia for a one-to-one interview."

"She must be devastated," Sid murmured.

"Yeah," Megan said. "She is, by all accounts. Jennifer's husband isn't a particularly nice man, apparently, and this was seen as her fresh start. He's also been notified."

"Possible suspect?" I asked.

Megan shook her head. "Very solid alibi. He's a mason and had a lodge meeting with countless others in Newcastle. There is no way he could've made it to Cornwall and back again to commit this crime."

"She wasn't local then?" Luce asked.

"No."

I glanced at Luce. "Could that be important?"

She frowned. "Maybe. Spilling an invader's blood can be important in certain myths. I'll have to do a quick refresh to pull out specifics."

"Only do that if necessary. I'm not sure that's likely to be relevant," I said. I returned my attention to Megan. "What else?"

"That's more or less all the team managed to gather before your boss pulled it from Serious Crimes."

"How annoyed are they?"

"Apoplectic probably covers it," Megan admitted.

Sid asked, "Can you confirm it's an ash stake?"

She nodded. "Yeah, sorry, that's important. It's green ash, unseasoned, cut recently and most likely hewn with an axe rather than a saw. Interestingly, someone thought to mention it might not be a metal blade on the axe. It could be stone."

"How the hell would they know that?" asked Sid.

"Shape of the cuts and the depth," I said. "Stone axes are distinctive in the way they cut wood."

Luce asked, "How the hell do you know that?" echoing Sid perfectly.

"He has a degree in digging up old stuff," Megan answered for me. She smiled at me fondly. "Wished you'd stayed doing it."

"So do I most of the time," I replied. We held our gaze

just a little too long. I broke contact first. She was going to Bristol. "Is there anything else we know for certain?"

Blank faces all around. I slapped my thighs. "First step, I want to talk to someone at the proposed hotel and golf course. Sid, find me the name of a foreman down there. Megan, I want you with me. Luce, if you could avoid vampire stories, find out more about ash stakes and their history, would you?"

She nodded. "Happy to help."

"Sid, full background on Jennifer and her husband, just in case it turns out to be domestic."

"Yes, boss."

"Bike or car?" asked Megan.

I didn't look at her. "Car." I couldn't do another trip with Megan behind me, holding tight.

"It's almost tourist season, are you sure? It'll be faster on the bike."

"Car is fine. I'm knackered." The look of disappointment on Megan's face almost made me change my mind, but it turns out I'm not that much of an emotional masochist. The briefing broke up.

I sat in surly silence, gazing out of the window, not seeing the world as it ripped past and realised, I was being a complete… well, the list of descriptives was a long one. Megan certainly didn't deserve my behaviour and was probably confused. She needed support from me if she was moving to Bristol, not someone who made her feel guilty about trying to expand her horizons and career.

Forcing my shoulders to relax, I tried to engage. "You'll have to introduce me to this bloke of yours before you move away."

Megan glanced at me, then back at the busy road. "Yeah, sure." Her hands twisted on the steering wheel.

Was she nervous? "You want to move in with him, right?"

Again, she glanced at me. "Can we talk about something else? I don't want to think about Bristol right now."

"I thought you'd be excited."

"So did I. How do you want to approach the building site people?"

Her change of subject surprised me, but I'd go along with it if it made her happy. "We'll find the foreman—"

"Foreperson might be better?" Her mouth quirked up in amusement.

I rolled my eyes. "Okay, whatever, foreperson, though if it is a woman I'll eat my boots."

"And I'll supply the steak knife you'll need."

"Silly conversation aside, we'll hunt down whoever is in charge of the site. Right now, I don't want to disturb the owners of the site. Do you know anything about them?"

Megan shook her head. "No. Though they've spoken to the chief constable because she's been giving my inspector and our CID team a bit of a hard time. We're supposed to be finding evidence of wrongdoing among the protesters, giving us an excuse to clear them out. To be honest, we haven't been pushing because no one really sees the point. The last thing any of us locals want is more luxury accommodation. Most of us struggle to pay our rents, never mind mortgages. The protesters are being very careful about staying within the new legislation. It's peaceful, they don't damage property, but they are gaining many supporters through social media."

"I'll get Sid onto that. He can track the different groups, cross-reference with people labelled domestic terrorists from the Security Service."

She glanced at me again. "It's weird when you say things like that."

I frowned. "Why?"

"Makes you sound like a real grown-up with a scary job."

My bark of laughter filled the car. "Do you always think of me as eleven?"

"No, mostly fifteen."

I didn't know what to say to that and steering us onto more solid ground seemed wise. "With this initial interview, I want to hear the general reaction to the news about the murdered woman. Feel our way through the politics of the site, the thoughts of the workers about the eco-warriors."

"You want to see if any of them hate the protesters enough to kill?"

"Basically. And I want to know how they feel about the owners of the site. It could be they're offered bonuses to finish quickly, and if the protesters are in the way, slowing construction, then hostilities could escalate fast."

"Nothing motivates the anger of strangers like money."

Driving through the lanes we'd used the day before on the bike felt odd. For a brief while, I'd been so caught up in the romance of the ride and the soft elegance of our surroundings, I'd forgotten to guard Megan from my childish emotions. Projecting my need for connection onto another person in this world was foolish. That wasn't her fault. The blame lay with me.

When the site's entrance appeared, it stripped all romance from the surrounding countryside, or what was left of it. I murmured, "I thought a golf course would be less destructive."

"I guess this is for the new buildings going up," Megan replied.

We'd reached a security gate set into a long fence. The track we were on consisted of large metal grids, which I guessed kept the heavy vehicles from bogging down in the thick Cornish farmland. I saw ancient stone walls being dismantled, hedges ripped up and the edges of the woodland that contained the cloutie tree and holy well, torn into and pulled down. There were a few trees left standing, but the golf course wanted something that nature couldn't give, so humanity was making it happen. In the distance, we saw the concrete foundations of buildings being worked on, and the old farmhouse that once stood in splendid isolation now found itself knocked about to accommodate the needs of the new owners. I guessed it would become the clubhouse, and behind it the hotel would rise.

"Progress," I mumbled as a security guard came over to the driver's side.

Megan opened her window and showed her identification. "Sergeant Ackley and Griffin Woodbury, we'd like to speak to the site fore," she paused for a moment, then said, "foreman."

I hid my chuckle.

"There a problem, Sergeant?" asked the guard. He was about my age, burly, with a shaved head and a hard eye. "The protesters have been restless, but—"

"Maybe you could help us find the foreman, and we can speak to you both? I should imagine your team will need to know."

He looked a bit startled at this suggestion but nodded. "I'll just go make some calls. Give us a minute. You're welcome to wait in the cabin if you want?" He indicated a small portacabin on the other side of the gate.

"No, it's okay. We'll wait here until you're ready."

We sat watching the site. Diggers ambled about, lorries

trundled, and people hurried. The mostly dry month meant dust clouds twisted and billowed in the sullen air, obscuring the piles of building material.

"I think I sympathise with the protesters," I admitted.

Megan didn't comment, but I saw the sadness in her eyes. She came from a farm not that different from what must've once been here. I knew her family struggled to keep operating, and she must be wondering if this was its fate.

The security guard returned with a friendly wave. Once he dropped the fearsome stare he adopted for unknown visitors to the site, he appeared younger, softer and his hazel eyes were kinder. I wondered if the same thing happened to me when I switched into the man who could shoot without my conscience getting in the way.

"I can't leave my post," the man said, leaning on the roof of the car and looking in, "but you can drive down to the main site. Go into the old farmhouse and you'll find Steve Denzel down there. He's the man you wanna talk to, and he'll let our security team know of any problems. We're a bit short-staffed right now." His southwest accent sounded more Somerset than Cornish.

"You live down here?" I asked.

"No, most of us are from upcountry, but we can't employ foreign workers easily, and it's making it hard to recruit. Same with the builders."

"Okay, thanks," I said as he tapped the top of the car before opening the security barrier.

"Think that's relevant?" Megan asked.

I shrugged. "Who knows at this point? It means they won't have people here who understand the land and have ties to it. That can matter in a DoPI case."

"It can matter in a normal crime as well. It means these guys are less emotionally invested in what happens around here. They are more likely to react to negative engagements with locals or the protesters. No ties mean they can move on easily. We need to ask if everyone showed up for their shift this morning."

I grunted in acknowledgement.

The track we followed bumped and dipped, working the Vectra's old suspension hard. Megan took it slowly. When we arrived at the torn-up farmhouse, the front looked dusty and forlorn. I saw a man, who must be in charge, walking towards us. He wore a plain blue t-shirt under a fluorescent vest and had a small paunch hanging over the top of his blue jeans. I'd place his age at around fifty, and under the white hard hat the man was bald. We climbed out of the car, and he approached with a wary smile.

"Sergeant Ackley?" he asked Megan, holding out his hand. It surprised me; most people assume I'm the sergeant when we're out together.

"Mr Denzel?" she asked.

"Steve is fine."

"Megan." They shook hands, then all attention turned to me.

"Griffin Woodbury, Rural Security. We liaise with the police on certain problems they face." The man's handshake came in hard, but not aggressive. His palm was rough and dry. He obviously still did his share of using building materials. He had a solid but plain face, with small grey eyes, set deep. Despite being wary, he came across as friendly and open.

"How can we help? I didn't think it worth bothering you guys with the break-in we had last night, but as you're here…" His eyes darted between us, unsure of who might be in charge.

I gave Megan the floor.

She said, "Break-in? Yes, we'll want to know about that, but we're here for a far more serious crime. Can we come in?"

"Of course, of course, and if it's alright, we'll have a coffee, or I can do tea? You'll need to wear hard hats."

We followed the man into the shadows of the farmhouse. A pile of yellow hats occupied a rough table in what once would've been the main room. He handed one to each of us, and I grinned. To be fair, I was more use to a battle helmet or my bike's one, but something about wearing a yellow hard hat turned me into the five-year-old boy who'd played with diggers and trucks in our small garden.

A few men milled about with planks, Acrow Props and wheelbarrows. It was clear the old building would retain only the walls. They were probably on some heritage list.

"My office is actually out back in a cabin. I can't work in here, need somewhere quiet." We followed him over some boards where new pipework lay next to rusting old ones and cabling looped overhead. The air smelt of dust and damp stone, with a hint of old mud. A dented metal sink stood filthy and stranded in what must've been the kitchen, with stained taps leaking water into the basin. Out through the hole where the back door used to stand, the property opened onto a farmhouse garden, and we saw a larger portacabin on the remains of a lawn.

Steve let us in, removed his hat, and set about making instant coffee. He had a fridge, so the possibilities for the milk wouldn't be too grim. "Sugar?" he asked.

"No," we both said.

He looked between us with a puzzled smile.

"We've known each other a long time," I stated, taking hold of a spare plastic chair and placing it in front of the man's untidy desk. Fine dust covered everything. Not being familiar with building sites, I wondered if they were all like this. It reminded me of the bomb-ravaged villages I'd known.

I watched the man settle down behind his desk. No signs of discomfort or stress from having us here.

He asked, "What can I do for you?"

Megan glanced at me, and I nodded consent. She took the lead. "We're here to ask a few simple questions. You'll know about it soon, because it'll be all over the news a bit later. Last night a woman was found in the woodland, near the cloutie tree, and she'd been murdered."

Steve's eyes widened. His ruddy cheeks paled. "Who? How? Oh God, this is… it's… that's horrible. Are you sure?"

Megan, far more used to delivering bad news to people than I am, nodded. "We're sure. She appears to have come from the protest group over the road. How much do you know about them?"

Steve's eyes were unfocused, his gaze turned inwards. "I… I think I need a minute." He rose and hurried out of the office.

"That's new," Megan murmured.

"I might know why." I nodded towards the corner of the office. On a filing cabinet stood a pile of books, one of which was a Bible, another of which said, *How to Live a Good Christian Life in the Modern World.*

"Ah." We waited and drank our tea.

Steve returned full of apologies, still using paper towels to wipe his face. "It's a shock. They aren't bad people. Total opposite in our experience. Friendly and really quite lovely once you move past their weird lifestyle."

"And faith?" I asked.

He laughed and glanced behind at the filing cabinet.

"Well, yes, we are at different ends of the same pole. Or so they think. To be honest, officers, I have a lot of sympathy with their arguments, but I'm paid to do a job. We can't all afford to live completely on our whims and fancies. I have a family to provide for, and a mortgage to pay."

"Are relations between the workers here, the security staff and the protesters cordial?" Megan asked.

Steve nodded. "On the whole, yes. When it first began, we had issues, that's true enough, but these days it's quiet. They yell at the lorries, yell at the security guys, sometimes yell at the workers leaving the site, but it's just yelling. I've had a few complaints from my people, grumbling about how unpleasant it all is, but really, we can't do anything. They have their rights; we have our jobs."

Megan made notes. "Does everyone feel like you do? As reasonable?"

Steve laughed. "No. Of course not. But I won't have any bullying on my site. We've a lot of big men, some of them not the most…" He searched for a tactful word. "Educated of people, emotionally, I mean. It's erm… Well, it's a building site. Many of the protesters are young women, or skinny guys with too much hair. The two worlds do collide occasionally. We've got a good team on the gate, though, and they keep things civil."

"I'd like a list of people who work here, if possible. Any absences today you weren't expecting?"

The man frowned, his eyes sharp. "I'm not sure if I'm allowed to provide a list of names. I'll have to speak to head office. If I do that, I'll email it." He made a note on a pad. "Do you want our security team as well?"

I could just ask Sid to find out, but this was more appropriate.

Megan nodded. "Thank you, yes. The absences?" she pushed.

He shook his head. "No, everyone turned up for work this morning. I've no one missing, though, I will double-check the rota and if anything is amiss, I'll let you know."

"Were you here yesterday?"

He nodded. "We were warned by the Cornish Sun people that they'd be holding a ceremony and the roads would be busy. I told the men to knock off early. Nothing creates bad blood like men not being able to get home on time because of traffic, and these lanes can be a nightmare."

I'd never had a normal job, but if I did, I hoped my boss was like this man. Steve seemed like a good bloke to have in your corner.

His thick, work-worn fingers twisted on his desk. He looked at Megan. "Can I ask how the lady died?"

"We can't discuss those details."

"No, sorry. Of course." His cheeks pinked.

She continued, "You mentioned a break-in last night?"

"What? Oh, yes though it feels… well, irrelevant now."

"Nevertheless, if you could give me the details?" Megan pressed. "At this point, everything is important."

"Yes, I suppose… Of course. Um, well," he rose from his chair and came around the desk, picking up a paper carrier bag on the way. "I kept it, just in case. I can't find anything missing, but this was left on the floor. I took photos before picking it up."

"Left where?" I asked, taking hold of the bag.

"In the farmhouse itself. I suppose, strictly speaking, it wasn't a break in, as there aren't any doors on the place right now, so maybe trespass is better. Still, it was odd.

Pagan, obviously. Probably kids from the protest group. Nothing was taken. We lock all the tools away."

I opened the bag. A wreath of ivy and at the bottom a collection of red berries. They were wrinkly and old-looking. "Do you have CCTV on site?"

"On the gate, but total security is impossible right now. That'll be different in a few weeks once the initial buildings are under construction."

"It's going to be a big change for the area," Megan said.

Steve rubbed his bald head. "Yeah, it is. Not sure it'll work. I mean, would you travel to the end of Cornwall for golf?"

"People do it in Scotland."

He didn't look convinced. "It just seems a shame to be taking down the old hedges, the old stone walls and biting holes in the woodland. I came down here before breaking ground to help plan our clearing stages, and it was so wild and beautiful. That was in the autumn. The trees over there," he nodded to the woodland that contained the cloutie tree, "they're old. I tried to talk to the management team putting this project together, even emailed the boss, Sir Pierce Alanson, but they wouldn't listen. The council had given the go-ahead, so…" He shrugged. "I just try to keep the damage to a minimum." His eyes strayed to the books on his shelf. "Though, it still doesn't feel like the right thing to be doing."

I recognised the sentiment. How many times had I stood on the foredeck of a ship, aiming my rifle as the Royal Navy tried to stop the pirates? The guys in those tiny vessels were hardened criminals, but they were also desperate for their slice of a pie heavily weighted in our favour.

"Can you forward the photos you took of this display?" I asked, showing Megan what was in the bag. Too much of the professional, she didn't openly show her dismay, but I could see the tension ramping up in her body.

Steve looked at me, confused by the request. "Sure, I'll do that."

I gave the man my card, with my Rural Security details on it. "Just email me. This is going to be an odd question but bear with me. Have you or your men sensed or reported anything odd about working here? Other than the obvious with the protesters?"

The man's eyes darted between me and Megan, doubtless wondering what the hell I was sniffing to make me ask the question. "Seriously? What kinda thing… I mean… Well, I guess…"

"What my colleague is trying to ask in his rather ham-fisted way," Megan glared at me, "is important. I know it seems odd. The police are only really here to deal with facts, but Rural Security is a bit different. Moods and odd things happening can affect people in different ways, and we're anxious to gather as much information about the location as possible."

Steve's thick fingers splayed over his desk's surface and wiped at the dust. He wanted to say something but struggled to find the words. "The men, back when the evenings darkened earlier, and the mornings were dark, they didn't like being here. They aren't wrong to be worried. It's a weird place. I kept finding myself checking over my shoulder."

I leaned forward in my chair. "I'm sorry to ask this, Steve, but is it in the house, or on the land that you feel disturbed?"

He glanced at his Bible again. "Look, I'm not comfortable—"

"I know, but it might help us establish what happened to

the victim of a serious crime. We need to keep the details quiet, but the items you've just given us, they…" I allowed the sentence to fade, letting his imagination fill in the blanks. Then, I sat back and waited in silence. It stretched. Megan and I watched as he wrestled with an internal argument.

"You're going to think I'm crazy," he eventually said, meeting my eye for a moment before flickering away.

I smiled. "Trust me, I won't."

"I'm a religious man and not easily spooked. I don't believe in the hocus-pocus those traveller types over there," he nodded in the direction of the eco-camp, "believe in. Still, even the Lord said there are strange places in the world, and anyone who is troubled by the occult, or practices it, should return to the fold. He doesn't condemn it Himself, but He's obviously not a fan. That being said, there's something bloody weird in that wood and on this land. Some of the men, they've seen shadows move oddly. Wood that's left out can be moved about in the morning. Never the bricks, or concrete, only the wood. And…" Again, his gaze darted between us. "There's been footprints. They're muddy, or wet. We see them on the dusty floors in the farmhouse and on larger pieces of wood."

"Can you describe them?" I asked.

"I can send you photos."

Oh, all my Christmases had come at once. "That would be great, thanks."

"We've tried to be sensible about it," the man said, "but it's not easy. At one point, around Easter, I thought I'd have a revolt on my hands." He grinned sheepishly. "There was talk of curses and getting my church in to do some kind of exorcism. I put a stop to that."

"Why?" asked Megan, and I could tell, by the tone of

her question, that she was curious rather than seeking an answer to go into a report.

"Well, exorcisms are a serious business and not the kind of thing you mess about with. Besides, whatever is here hasn't done any harm, and it's not satanic. It's just a bit disturbing."

"Until a dead body turns up nearby," I said.

His expression became rueful. "Aye, until that happens. Look, this is a wild place, full of ancient sites of worship. It's going to be a bit odd. Do I think the place is haunted? Who knows? I believe in things many think impossible, or at best highly improbable, so I'm not going to be the most impartial person in the world."

"I have to thank you, Steve; you've been patient and helpful. If you can email all the relevant images to my office, that'll be great. For now, we don't have any more questions." I rose, and Megan matched my movements.

Back at the car, we both worshipped the heat and light for a moment before climbing inside. "What do you think?" asked Megan.

"I was halfway convinced we had some clever prankster setting up someone at the building site to take the rap for the murder in the woods."

"Yeah, me too. It all seemed a bit too convenient to find that wreath the same night the woman's body was found with ivy wrapped around her throat. It's a very human game that's being played." She leaned on the bonnet of her car and looked at me over the top. "Do you still think that's possible?"

"It's the footprints, Meg, and the obvious problems the workers have faced for a long time. The spooky vibe they sense…"

"Could be imagination."

I nodded. "One of the many downsides of my job, trying to unpick reality from a brain fart."

Megan laughed. "Brain fart, love it. Lunch somewhere? Then back to the office, or just back to the office?"

Lunch with Megan sounded like a great plan, but also a really bad one. However, I needed to talk to her about something other than work. "Lunch, I need to talk to you about something."

# Chapter Seven

Discussing my little nighttime adventure would be tough, but Sid had been right that morning, I needed help. Of all the people in my life, Megan had known me longest and through some of the toughest parts. I trusted her above all others, even though she was about to leave me.

*Emotive much?* bitched my internal monologue. He had a point.

Megan, sensing my deepening mood, only talked about the case as she wound us through the lanes. "What did you think of Steve?"

"Nice bloke. I'm pretty sure he knows nothing about Jennifer and her murder. Unless you think differently?"

She shook her head. "No. You're right. He's innocent of the murder."

"Makes it sound like he's guilty of something else."

Megan chuckled. "Old habits. Everyone is guilty of something, we just haven't caught them at it—yet."

"Oh, ye of little faith, my friendly cynic on human nature."

She huffed at me. "At least I didn't ask him about ghosts."

I grinned. "Yeah, the job is a bit mental sometimes."

"I noticed." Her hands tightened on the steering wheel. "His reaction to the questions was interesting. There seems to be something at the site disturbing people."

"I'll make a believer of you yet."

"For all you know, it's marsh gas causing their brains to pick up on something, or there's a problem in the local water. Let's keep it sensible for now."

I smirked.

She scowled at me. "You can get that look off your face. Just tell me what you think about his disturbances."

"I think we have a problem down here. Though I'm not sure what it is. For footprints to be left, we know it's corporeal, which rules out any number of nasties that are in pure spirit form."

"You're joking?"

"No. For instance, we know it's not going to poltergeists. What we do need to do is figure out if it's something that's been given a manifest life through some misguided conjuring, or some human individual trying to set it up to look like a monster. We need to talk to the coven who did the ceremony last night." Was it only yesterday? It felt like a week ago.

"I've got their details; it won't be hard to find them."

"That's where we're going this afternoon. Right now, I need to refuel."

She glanced at me. "You really don't look too clever. What happened last night?"

"I'll tell you once we're eating. What about this place?" I pointed to the pub, King William IV. The door stood open, and the car park looked busy, which was always a good sign. The place wasn't large, but they said they served food, and that was enough for me. The exterior of the building was stone with large windows filled with old glass. I'd lay money on this being a miners' pub during Cornwall's industrial past.

Megan pulled into the car park and, almost before she stopped the car, I was out and heading for the bar. I needed a pint. Or two.

In the pub, the owners had gone for a light, bright, cosy feel, and they'd pulled it off. Lots of places to sit quietly, books lining one wall, and mirrors cleverly reflecting lamplight. It felt like walking into someone's living room and was very welcoming. In the places they didn't have books, they had modern seascape prints, some nineteenth century, and one of the king they'd named the pub after. He glared down at us.

*No good staring at me like that, my regiment existed before you took the throne.* We were proud of our heritage in the Royal Marines.

A woman stood behind the bar, about my age. "What can I get you?" she asked the moment I approached. My mouth watered. Not because of her, but because I could smell pies. The bartender slipped off her stool and put her book down. An actual book.

"Two pints of..." I examined the draft ales. "Doom Bar, and are you serving food?"

Megan appeared beside me. "I'm on duty."

"Then I'll drink both," I told her.

She tutted and told the bartender to make one of the pints sparkling water.

"The menu for lunchtime is on the board. Vegan options are available, you just have to ask."

I ran my eye over the menu and said, "Steak pie and chips."

Megan shook her head. "I'm guessing you're still being paid by London ratings?"

I grinned. "Have whatever you want, on me."

"Same as him." She didn't hesitate. "But no chips. Salad."

I frowned. "You like chips."

"They don't like my hips, and Adrian isn't going to want to go to Bristol if I put on too much weight."

"Adrian needs re-educating about how women should look," I mumbled over my pint.

"I heard that."

I couldn't help myself. "Doesn't stop it from being true."

Megan manhandled me away from the bar and towards a neat table in the corner. We'd both have our backs against a wall.

"What's going on with you?" she asked.

I eyed her. "You're going to think I'm going mad."

"That ship sailed long ago, cuz. Just tell me. I can't help if I don't know." Her blue eyes were soft and inviting. I'd get no judgement here.

I pulled on the pint, and a third of it vanished. "My nighttime wanderings are getting worse. A few weeks back, during the previous nonsense, I ended up at a quoit. I'd ridden my bike. I don't remember anything. Sunlight woke me. I was under the stone lid of the quoit, surrounded by lambs." The words had to be delivered quickly, as if I were giving a report to my senior officer in a combat situation. I'd never get through it otherwise.

"Jesus, that's horrible."

"Yes. I had a weird vision of the dead as well, but that's not really the point. There's more. I keep going walkabout in Redruth." I drew circles in the condensation rolling down my glass. "The time before last, Sid found me freezing to death. I didn't know it, but after that event he put trackers in all my belts. I'm now dressing before leaving, but I seem to forget my boots—except for the jaunt down to the quoit." I realised I was avoiding eye contact, but I didn't want to see her pity, or possible scorn.

Her hand reached out and held my wrist. It felt warm and grounding. "What happened last night?"

"He tracked me to the cemetery on St Day's Road." That's when my eyes flicked up, and I watched her mouth drop open.

"Your mum…?"

"Yeah. I'd been digging. My hands were filthy. Actually, everything was covered in mud. I don't remember anything, Meg. I tried telling Sanchez how bad it was, that I should be pulled out and resign from the Marines, but she's not having any of it. Says I need to figure it out, and no one who does my job comes out of it unscathed."

Megan's eyes widened. "That's reassuring for your long-term mental health."

I didn't disagree with her. "Can you come with me later? Go check out the grave? I—"

"Of course I can, Griff. Of course, I can."

My throat tightened. "Thanks," I managed to croak.

"What do you think is going on?"

"I don't know. It's weird." I stared into the distance. "When we were in the mine, having taken that MDMA, I had this vision. Usually, people would just say it was a trip and get over it, but it felt like more than that. In this job, you learn about the human psyche and the power it has, the secrets it keeps. I was being shown something." I went on to describe the vision. The vast tapestry of my life, and how

I'd flown over it on the wings of a raven. The different colours of thread and the long, thick silver line that ran through everything. How I'd chased that line backwards, seen it pull me into my mother's tapestry, and how I couldn't read her colours the same way I did mine. She seemed to be missing chunks, or rather, people, including her sister, Megan's mother.

My cousin sat back and considered. "What do you think it means?"

Our food arrived, and we tucked in. Food always came first. After demolishing half of my excellent pie, I mumbled through a mouthful, "I don't know what it means."

Megan started in on her salad. I took pity on her and lifted my plate to deposit half my chips. There weren't many people in the world I'd share my scran with, but Megan was definitely one of them.

"Before you say anything, it's free food, therefore, no calories."

She laughed. "I don't think it works that way."

"Well, it should. Besides, you look great. Always have."

Her cheeks coloured. "Thanks, Griff."

I thought I ought to move the conversation on before I dug myself a hole. "I can hazard some guesses about the meaning of my mother's tapestry." I sighed when Megan peeled off the lid of her pie and dumped it on my plate. Rather than say anything, I just started cutting it up. Whatever was going on with her, it would require a careful hand.

"Go on then?" Megan put brown sauce in a neat puddle well away from the remains of her salad and groaned at the taste of the chips.

I laughed. "The tapestry I saw might not be complete because I'm not meant to see it. That's the simplest explanation."

"It sounds like there's more to your thinking."

I waggled my hand around. "Maybe… It's all wild speculation."

"Out with it, Woodbury."

"What if pieces were missing because the vision was trying to tell me something?"

"Like?"

I stared glumly at my remaining pie. "Dunno."

"Try a different angle. What's the silver thread mean?"

"That could be the connection to her child."

"But you didn't see it fork off towards a tapestry that could be your brother."

"No, that's true, I didn't." I gazed off into the distance. I'd been thinking about this for weeks, but as Megan was the first person I'd shared my thoughts with, I didn't have them buttoned down.

"Bearing in mind," she said, "I have a limited ability to take this seriously, I'm going to suspend my natural scepticism and offer a few options. Maybe the silver you're seeing is what enables you to work for DoPI? That it leads you towards the dead. If your nighttime wanderings have shown us anything, then it could be that."

"Doesn't explain why I went walkabout on the farm as a kid."

"You're joking, right? Griffin, farms are full of places where animals have died. Remember when the dog died? That summer, you were really active trying to leave the house. We'd buried him in the garden."

I'd forgotten. "That's the link between me and Mum? The dead?"

She shrugged. "Why not? It seems logical to me. Have a think about your past missions and see if they match up with your night wanders. Make a list."

"Sounds cheerful. Making a list of the dead." If the pie weren't so good, that thought might just put me off my food.

She shrugged. "We do what we have to do." Her phone buzzed, and she removed it from its belt holder. I saw Adrian's name, and she swiped the red button with a grunt.

"What about the holes in the tapestry?" I asked.

"They bother you?"

"I can see them clearly, and that bothers me. It's like they're as important as the thread." I dipped chips in my pie's gravy. It was good.

"We can ask my mum? She might know something."

Aunt Iris, would she be able to shed some light on this mystery? "I'd have thought she'd have said something if she had secrets about Mum."

Megan huffed. "Don't you believe it. She's like a steel trap with secrets. I've known her to keep mine forever."

"Like what?"

"If I told you, they wouldn't be secrets." Her colour rose again, making her freckles stand out.

"Then we'll go talk to her, without the rest of the family cluttering about. Maybe see those photos you promised me weeks ago?"

She grinned. "That would be lovely."

We finished the food, I drank my pint, and we both felt better. Megan already had the details of the pagan group we'd watched at the cloutie tree, so we headed off to meet with Mr Withers and Mrs Beechwood, who just happened to have the same address.

We were heading to Marazon, which had once been a small fishing village on the other side of the bay to Penzance. It had been transformed into yet another tourist destination, and house prices had risen accordingly. When I checked my phone, I discovered Godolphin Drive had long views over the harbour, and the particular house we were visiting had the best of those views. Not surprisingly, neither of the people who'd headed up the pagan group seemed short of a shilling.

I dozed off in the car, the pint and food doing a good job of sedating me. Only Megan's hand on my thigh made me come back to the world. She smiled and told me to get my lazy arse up and my head in the game.

After parking on the road, we headed to the front door. This house, like many with good panoramic views, had been built upside down. By which I meant, the living area was upstairs, the bedrooms down. It had a large balcony and garden. Megan knocked.

"We didn't check if they were at work," I murmured.

"I did when I asked for their details, they work from home."

I grunted, then twigged that the steep drive had two cars on it, a large Mercedes E-class and a smaller electric car, make and model unknown to me. The door opened.

Megan flipped out her police identification. "Mrs Beechwood, remember us?"

The woman, now out of formal robes, looked expensive but frighteningly normal. She could've just stepped out of a catalogue for 'upper-middle-class women who dress well'. Though I doubted women of that sort would use a catalogue when they shopped.

"Of course I remember you, hard not to, considering how we met. Is this about the body? They're now reporting it on the news."

I had no doubt DoPI had a heavy hand in that 'verified' press release.

"Yes, if you wouldn't mind, we'd like to talk to you and Mr Withers?"

"Geoff's not here at the moment, but he'll be back fairly soon. We have two rather demanding dogs. Do come in. We're all devastated about what happened to the poor woman. The entire coven is praying for her and the woodland, obviously."

*I'm sure the woodland appreciates it.*

Megan's mouth twitched, trying to hide a smile. "May we come in, Mrs Beechwood?"

"Bridget, please call me Bridget."

We followed her inside. The interior surprised me. Though neat and well maintained, these people were obsessive about their dogs. Blankets covered the furniture, piles of toys took up corners, and dog beds smothered the hardwood floors.

"They're a pair of working German Shepherds. We're hoping to have puppies soon. Both parents have straight backs. The Kennel Club wants to remove the sloping hips if possible."

"Sensible," I murmured, following her up the stairs. The entire house had been covered in expensive wooden flooring, not just the downstairs. I guessed it helped to keep the mess down, but despite everyone's best efforts, balls of dog fluff rolled about as we moved.

Bridget tutted and began picking up the random dust bunnies. "Spring and summer, I just can't keep the hair under control. In the winter, at least I stand a chance, but then you have the endless muddy paws. Sometimes, I wonder why I bother."

I smiled. "Because you can't resist their big brown eyes?"

"Something like that. I'm sorry, I never did catch your name and rank."

Dammit. I didn't think she'd remember. "Griffin Woodbury, Rural Security." I showed her my ID.

"Yes, I've heard of your lot," she frowned. "You had something to do with that odd business in Brane. I've a client in the village who says they have post-traumatic stress after a rather noisy arrest."

"It wasn't that bad," I said. "The locals weren't really involved."

"You were there?"

I glanced at Megan. "We tracked the terrorists to the location. They opened fire. We were unarmed." Officially. I'd taken one of the M16s and had my sidearm, but I wasn't going to confess that to a defence solicitor.

"That's what I thought," she said. "Still, I'll have to pursue the case." She sighed, then asked, "Tea or coffee?"

"Tea," Megan said, and I agreed.

We sat on the balcony, and I had to spend a moment just enjoying the view. The sea had her tranquil aspect on her, and the colours were a deep blue right across the wide bay. Sea and sky met on the horizon, kissing each other in perfect harmony and balance. No arguments between them today. Penzance rose up from the harbour, but behind it lay the hills that rolled into the centre of the Cornish peninsular. The breeze smelt rich from a nearby lilac bush and the salty air.

"This is beautiful," I murmured.

"We're very blessed. It's been tough, but this is a good home. We're both second time around on the marriage stakes, though Geoff and I haven't set a date yet. I still use my married name because of work. It can be difficult to untangle yourself from your previous life."

I liked Bridget Beechwood. A part of me felt like I shouldn't, she was a bit of a cliché, but she came over as honest and kind.

After taking a mouthful of tea, Megan kicked off the questioning. "How long has your coven, if that term is okay to use, been doing ceremonies at the site?"

"Two years, Sergeant, and coven is fine. We aren't practicing Wicca, more the druidic path, but I'm sure you don't need to know that."

"At the moment, we're collecting data, so everything is useful," Megan said with a smile. "What made you start celebrating Beltane at that site? There must be others easier to use."

"You mean the stone circles and such in the area? Well yes, they would be easier, but we use Madron because it's a living monument to the old ways. Its traditions have survived for a long time. We're in the process of identifying what might be thought of as a living tree henge in the ancient woodland. It might help save the rest from that blasted developer."

"You support the eco-warriors?" Megan asked.

"I support the protest group. They, we, aren't terrorists. We aren't warriors. We are protesters, Sergeant. That shouldn't be forgotten. I'm not at war with anyone. Words matter."

Megan gave a single nod of her head, accepting the point. "They do. Alright, you support the protest. What can you tell me about that?"

Bridget gazed out over the view. "They are a kind people on the whole. Well-meaning and progressive thinkers who want to save our countryside for the future. If we have to cut down trees to build new houses, let's make them affordable, both to the people of Cornwall who need them and the environment."

"You should run for the council," I said.

"I probably will, but if the press finds out I'm a practicing druid, there could be problems."

"Not if you're upfront about it. It'll put some off, but if you state that your faith supports your credentials, I bet it won't matter so much."

She laughed. "You looking for a new job as a press officer for a politician, Griffin?"

"No, I just think it's a waste to lose that passion for your people." I gave her one of my winning smiles, and she laughed, her cheeks flushing a lovely pink.

"You're good for the ego," she murmured, eyeing me over her mug.

Megan coughed. "Have you noticed conflict between the developers and the workers on the site?"

"Nothing untoward," she stated. "It can get a bit noisy, and a bit of roughhousing has come to my attention, but on the whole, it's been cordial. There is one group among the protesters you might want to talk to, and that's Anwen's Children. They are more fundamentalist than our band. We worship at these sites, trying to keep them alive and in the public's mind. We also try to tread lightly on the land. Geoff is working towards gaining government grants for property we own so we can convert it into an outdoor worship area for all. A place people can gather to be together with each other and nature."

*Yeah, but he's not willing to give up his Merc.* My thoughts were uncharitable. These people wanted to do the right thing, and that's always a place to start.

Bridget added, "Anwen's Children are more radical. They have a…" She licked her lips, and a small frown marred her brow. "Um, they're different from us. They have a way about them."

I made a note that they needed checking out.

"What about the people in your coven? Do you know them well?" Megan asked.

Bridget nodded. "I've known some of them for years. Others are more recent members, people who've moved down to Cornwall to get away from the rat race and want to live a more sustainable lifestyle. They don't think of themselves as religious, but they want to connect to the environment in a way that holds a certain amount of ceremony. You see, Sergeant, it's about focusing the mind. Asking people to meditate is all well and good, but many of us struggle with that kind of mindfulness. A faith like ours can give back to nature because we learn to appreciate her more. We understand her cycles and her bounty. We recognise her dangers and her cruelty, but also her beauty. Our ceremonies, songs, prayers, they offer guidance to a mind beset with the clamour of the modern world."

She certainly sounded plausible.

"Do you have a membership list?" asked Megan.

Bridget smiled. "We have names and phone numbers, but there is no membership as such. And I'd need a warrant. I'm sorry, Sergeant, I'm happy to chat, but giving over—"

"I understand. You don't have to explain. We'll set the wheels in motion. One more question from me, Bridget, is anyone in your group a radical? A disruptor?"

"You mean, are they capable of murder?"

Megan remained silent and blank-faced, not revealing her thoughts.

Bridget paused before answering the question she'd

posed. I was impressed with her calm acceptance of Megan's questions.

When she did speak, the words were measured, weighted carefully, and came from a mind trained in criminal law. "It's an impossible question to answer honestly, Sergeant. I'm sure you're aware, we are all able to commit extreme acts of violence under the right, or wrong, circumstances. If this were a spontaneous act, then I'd have to say I don't believe any of our members could commit murder. We are, by definition, a peaceful tribe of people. You were there throughout the ceremony; no one left our group long enough to kill and return. If the murder was done before we arrived, then I'm sorry, we had no members vanishing for an extended period."

"You can vouch for that?" Megan probed.

"I can. We arrived in a hired minibus with a transit behind us, carrying our totem. At no point did I lose sight of anyone."

I butted in. "That's a lot of people to keep track of."

"Yes, I'm aware of that. However, we all had our jobs to do. It was busy, and we were nervous, pleased that such a crowd was gathering to watch our ceremony. I cannot categorically state that no one snuck off to commit murder, but it's highly unlikely."

"Maybe we could confirm that with Geoff?" Megan asked.

"Of course."

I piped up again, "What would you think if the murder was planned and happened some time before your arrival?"

"All I can say is that every member of our group was with us before the ceremony and afterwards. We came down to Madron together. We changed into our robes together. And we walked to the site together. The people who you saw at the event, they were with us all the way through. No one acted oddly, either in speech or manner. We were excited, but no manic behaviour. I've spoken to murderers, those who plan and those who commit it during the heat of the moment. I saw nothing that would raise a red flag in my mind."

*Members of the jury, it's your time to decide.*

I had to give her credit; she was good. I believed her. At that moment, the front door opened, and chaos erupted as two large dogs wanted to know why their home had invaders in it and what their humans were doing about the problem. At least, I assumed that's what all the noise was about until Bridget took control. They were beautiful dogs and friendly once they'd decided we weren't going to do anything horrible.

We went through the same questions with Geoff, who gave the same answers as his partner, if in a slightly more surly manner.

As Bridget showed us out, she said, "If you would like a puppy, then let me know via email. We have a waiting list, but we're checking each potential owner."

"Bit too much dog for me," I said. "Besides, I only have a motorbike, and we work long hours."

Back in the car, I relaxed. "If I do ever get a dog, then I want to rescue an older one."

"Very wise," Megan agreed. "Let's get back to Redruth. We have an appointment with a grave."

In all the excitement, I'd forgotten.

# Chapter Eight

I called Sid. "We're on our way back, coming in via the cemetery."

"You told Megan?"

"Yep."

"Good. Want me there?"

I thought about it for a second. "Might be best. Bring some equipment. The EMF and EPV recorder." I needed to be analytical about this, not emotional.

"An hour?"

"Bit less."

"See you then."

"A what?" asked Megan when I killed the call.

"One measures fluctuations in electromagnetic fields, the other picks up sounds beyond human hearing. Though, Sid has his own version. I doubt these tests will do anything. We're not expecting to feel ghosts, but if there is a trace of the veil energy, they might find it."

"Interesting," Megan said. Her scepticism remained

verbally bottled, despite being written in big black letters all over her face.

"Just go with it."

"Afterwards we could go to the farm, talk to Mum?" she suggested, eyeing me as if I'd suddenly become glass.

"I've reports to write for London. It's important we keep this event low-key after the problems in Brane. Besides, don't you want to spend time with Adrian?" I think I managed to keep the attitude out of my voice.

Her raised eyebrow made it clear I'd failed. "He's away, remember?"

"Ah, yes, so I'm the easy option after him," I muttered, feeling edgy at the thought of Mum's grave.

"You're never the easy option, Griff."

I wanted to ask her what she meant, but her phone rang in its holder, and I saw her inspector was calling. Megan took the call and reported her status and location. The rest of the journey remained quiet, except for my fingers beating a relentless tattoo on my thighs.

We arrived after the school run, meaning the roads were fairly quiet. I saw Sid's red original Mark III Mini parked up outside, and he leaned against the bonnet fiddling with one of his gadgets. The familiar kit bag I used to lug his equipment around sat on the ground next to him as Megan pulled to a stop. The St Day Cemetery was beautiful. Spring encased it in colour and scent, despite the busy road bordering one side, and houses on the others. This was an oasis of quiet for the restful memories of those who'd left this world. I looked through the open entrance and realised they kept the grass long and full of wildflowers. Trees and hedges protected the boundaries, and in the centre stood a small Victorian mock-medieval chapel, long since left to time's ravages. The tiny arched windows were blocked up, the double wooden doors left to rot at the bottom. Even at this distance, its grey face looked glum. Squinting against the sun, I realised there were missing tiles off the roof as well. We were not great at caring for the dead in Britain.

"You alright?" Sid asked as we approached.

"Fine, we have some good intel on the new case. I'll catch you up as we walk." I lifted the familiar heavy pack and slung it over my shoulder. Setting a pace that made Megan scramble to catch up, I walked into the cemetery.

Sid and Megan followed in my wake. I knew I marched as if on a parade ground, but my limbs were unable to do anything else. Just like those moments when the switch in my head flips, and I can kill a man, I knew I'd become the commando, not the son of a woman who'd killed herself.

Despite never having visited the grave, even when I'd moved back to Cornwall, I knew where it was because I remembered that day.

*I stood in new black shoes that I'd been made to polish to a shine, and a new suit that had made my skin prickle in the heat. Shouldn't it be raining on such a sad day? The sun beat down on my head, making the odd-smelling goo Dad made me use to control the nest of curls, dry and crack. He said I'd be having a haircut the moment we went back to base. I knew what that meant. I'd look like him and my brother.*

*They stood behind me. The weight of them ever-present in my life. I stared over the deep hole in the ground and saw my Aunt Iris and my cousins. My uncle had to stay with the farm, something about the vet. Though I think he just couldn't be around my dad. I didn't blame him. Megan, with her blonde hair in a neat ponytail and her legs sticking out from under a dress, looked just as uncomfortable as I did in the suit. She cried quietly. Her eyes looked at me with such love…*

I cut the memory dead. It made my chest hurt, remembering the pain I'd seen in her eyes and how it had filled me with dread for my future. How another layer of understanding wrapped its cold fingers around my little heart and pulled the pieces further apart. I was shattering slowly that day and all the days afterwards.

Nine rows in, ten columns back from the main entrance, the grid firmly fixed in my mind. I marched onwards but now began to slow. A man stood next to the headstone I'd never seen erected, with a spade in one hand and his sun hat in the other. He must've been well into his seventies and had once been broad and strong. Now, his back had a stoop, and his naked scalp held more liver spots than Megan's nose had freckles.

"Oo'r'u?" he asked, his accent so thick, it took my tired and barricaded brain a moment to figure out he'd meant, "Who are you?"

Megan arrived beside me and flipped out her police identification. "Hello, there. I'm Sergeant Ackley. We're here because this gentleman came to visit his mother's grave and realised it had been disturbed. We're happy to take over, mister…?"

The man frowned, his eyebrows meeting like two off-white foxes about to have a scrap. "Ma'be not a good—"

Megan stepped in front of me. "Really, it's fine. If you could give us a few minutes. Leave your shovel, we'll finish up."

The man, obviously the caretaker of the dead, huffed and puffed a few more times before he said, "Not the first time she's been disturbed these last months. Don't know why."

I remained still and quiet, unable to process anything with a stranger among us.

"That's why we're here," Megan said. "Maybe if you have a record, you could bring it up to the police station in town? My card, just ask for me and they'll…" She held out one of her police-issue business cards, but the man backed away, propping his spade against another headstone and stomping off in his heavy boots.

"That was weird," Sid mumbled. "What's he hiding?"

Megan hummed, but her focus became the same as mine.

The hole the man had begun to fill in.

We all stood on chunks of grass and dead wildflowers that I must've pulled from the ground before starting to dig into the thick, rich soil. I stood there and stared. All day I'd been wrapped up in the death of a different woman, and I'd never given myself a moment to consider how this would feel. What would be waiting for me.

Sid walked around the site of my mother's grave and opted to be the one to break the gathering storm of my silence. "I'll take some photos, Griffin. Then, do the basic tests. We can fill in the hole, mate. You don't have to be here."

I didn't move. My throat was locked closed. My heart beat in my ears, and my chest rose and fell hard. With my hands in such tight fists that they ached, I tried to process the scene.

The vegetation lay in small, dying, scattered mounds. Some older than others, indicating I'd been here more than once in the last few weeks. Dry soil also lay scattered about in the living grass, like a huge hound had pawed deep into the soil and chucked the dirt about with wild enthusiasm. What I'd done in my 'other' state had caused a hole of perhaps half a metre deep but the length of a coffin to be scored from the earth. No way did I do this in one night. I'd obviously returned and removed the loose soil the old man used to refill the grave, then dug virgin ground.

Finally, my eyes went to the headstone. It read:

*Hazel Woodbury*
*Born 13th November 1960*
*Died 30th June 2000*
*Loving mother and sister*
*Forever missed*

My throat tightened brutally, making it feel like I swallowed boulders, and the world blurred. Unable to remain still, and fully aware of what the inscription meant, I turned my back and stomped away from my companions.

The sun pounded on my shoulders and head. My hands ached from the unspent tension in my fists. I knew who to blame for this, but for decades, I'd pushed it down. Held it in place with brutal physical demands on my body and the endless pursuit of the country's enemies.

"Griffin?" Megan broke into my thick bubble of rage and loss.

"Not now." A snarl of sound. With the world flickering into a dark place, I wasn't the man she knew, or even the one she glimpsed when I killed people. For this moment, I wore another disguise. I was the untamed monster that hunted other monsters and brought them death or banishment. Not all of those monsters lived beyond the veil; some of them lived here, in our world, and I could find them. One of them looked a helluva lot like my father.

Megan's footsteps were slow and careful. She didn't touch me, but she came to stand before the monster. "Griffin, it's okay to be upset."

"Iris put the headstone in, didn't she?" I couldn't meet her gaze. My eyes remained on the spring grass and one particular dandelion.

"Yes. Your dad—"

"Fuck him."

"Well, yes, that's pretty much what Mum said when she decided to add a proper headstone rather than the wooden marker."

"My brother?"

Megan nudged a piece of masonry with her booted foot that came from a nearby grave far older than my mother's. "He… um…"

"Didn't want to know either?"

I felt, rather than witnessed her shrug. She said, "Troy is a product of your dad, you shouldn't blame him—"

I held up my hand, finally able to release the fist, but unable to surrender the tension. "Don't make excuses for him."

She fell silent. "I'm so sorry, Griff. This shouldn't have happened to you."

"It shouldn't have happened the way it did. Not that any of us really knows the truth—" My words were snapped off by the wail of technology from behind me.

"Erm, guys, I think you need to see this," Sid called.

I turned, and he stood near the headstone, waving the high-spec gizmo over the disturbed grave.

Megan approached and the machine in his hands squealed in terror. "What the hell is that?" she asked.

Sid held the device in two hands. It was about the size of a controller for a large drone, but with more buttons, switches and lights than the USS Enterprise's helm. "It's my pride and joy." He beamed, showing all his crooked teeth.

"That doesn't help explain—" Megan began.

A long finger pointed to a projection from the right front of the controller. "This bit is an EMF meter. This one…"

Megan waved her hand to forestall him. "It's a very clever machine, designed by you, built by you, that surpasses anything anyone can buy online. Right?"

He nodded like a nodding dog being driven over several cattle grids at high speed.

"Good," Megan drew out. "What's it telling you?" She asked this slowly, obviously worried about the answer.

His expression wavered between a frown and excitement. I had the eerie feeling that if it weren't my mother's grave, he'd be bouncing with glee right now, saying something like, "We have a live one." Just to take the piss out of the situation.

For the moment he kept his glee closed down, and I admired his restraint, well aware of how much it cost him. Megan and I joined the boy-wonder scientist, and I felt some of the tension slip away into the long grass as my investigator's mind took control of my emotions. It came as a relief.

He glanced at me, the machine still screeching as he waved it over the grave. "These readings are really strong, Griffin."

"What does that mean?" asked Megan.

I fielded that one. "It means the tech is picking up on spirit activity in this location. Or it could be our mobile phones setting it off." I removed mine and put it on airplane mode. We were a long way from the houses, so I guessed it wouldn't be the technology from the housing estates, like laptops, routers or tablets. Besides, Sid calibrated for that stuff, making his equipment highly directional. Megan watched and switched her phone off as well. The noise calmed down, but not by much.

"What? Like a ghost?" she asked, interested despite herself.

I said, "Maybe, or it could be something else pressing against the veil. We might have a thin spot here, which just happens to be my mother's grave. It doesn't mean we have zombies, vampires, or any other undead variations living under the soil."

"Bit of a bloody coincidence if it's a thin spot that just happens to be located here," Sid mumbled, wisely not lifting his eyes to mine.

I glared at the top of his head. "Just take the measurements of nearby graves. We need to see how far this problem has spread."

"Yes, boss," he said in his best Creole accent, bobbing his head.

"Fuck off, Sid."

Which just made him laugh. I closed my eyes and tried to rationalise my feelings. Over several weeks, I'd come here to my mother's grave and tried to dig a hole with my bare hands. I'd also taken a motorcycle trip to a quoit and seen a vision of the dead from millennia ago. Then I'd had other visits to locations associated with the dead. Why? How were these things linked? Were they linked at all?

My mind hummed with possibilities. Connections formed, dissolved, reformed in new patterns as I discarded and rebuilt theories faster than any computer. I gained no answers, but I had a list of questions that might lead somewhere. Removing my phone, I started to make notes.

Sid co-opted Megan rather than me into helping him with another electromagnetic field detector. This one designed to DoPI's high spec demands, but much smaller and easier to operate. The kind of thing they could trust with a grunt like me. They were slowly stepping between the graves, waving the devices over the ground. No squeals accompanied them until they came within one pace of Hazel Woodbury's grave.

# Chapter Nine

Rather than standing still and pondering the unknowable, I opted to put my bulk to some use. Stepping around the grave, I picked up the shovel and began undoing much of the damage I'd inflicted on the site. It felt very odd replacing the dirt over my mother's body. I remembered everything from that day. From the limp sandwiches at the tiny wake my father allowed in the nearby pub, long since defunct and turned into a bed-and-breakfast, to the 'hot, sweaty little hand pushed into mine, as Megan tried to give me silent comfort. She'd just turned eight. Her little face was carved into lines of solemnity no child should have to encounter.

Moving soil is always hot and heavy work. I allowed the memories to bubble up as I dug the shovel into the dirt, then I held them as I moved to the grave and let the images flicker out as the soil poured back over the still hidden casket. It became a moving meditation and gave me some time to shed another layer of my grief. Maybe if I'd had a supportive parent, I'd never have carried this pain into adulthood like it was a virus in my blood. Aunt Iris did all she could, I knew that, but months in that lonely arsed school in Scotland handed me a darkness I fought every damned day. I'd become adept at hiding. Had something come to dig me out of that hiding spot and expose me to the light? God, I hoped not.

"Griffin, I think we need to set up cameras and sound recording equipment here." Sid and Megan were back.

I dug the shovel into the hard ground beside the grave and realised I'd completed my maudlin task without being conscious of the physical effort. "I agree. We need answers." It helped to keep it DoPI related, not personal. "How did the detection of other sites in the area go?"

Sid shook his head. "I get why you'd like it not to be localised to this site, but I'm afraid it is. The only signals we're receiving are from your…" He glanced at me, and opted for, "*…this* grave."

I heaved in a lungful of afternoon air and realised it held a level of humidity that made me look up. Large black clouds now hovered, like demented airships, over the centre of Cornwall. Blue sky edged them, probably well out to sea, but the gathering heat of the day now beckoned a thunderstorm.

"Let's get this done before the heavens open," I said.

The three of us, with Megan guided by Sid, began sticking highly sensitive motion detectors around the site. These were usually used by seismologists at volcano or earthquake sites. Then we added wildlife cameras with night vision, sound recording equipment, infrared detectors and remote EMF recorders designed by DoPI's geeks. They'd record any activity in the electromagnetic field and note the time and variation.

When we'd finished, my mother's grave looked like it had sprouted electronic aliens.

Megan reviewed our work with her arms folded across her chest. "You know, someone will come and nick this lot and sell it on eBay."

Sid shrugged, tweaking something close to the ground. "DoPI can afford it. I'll just replace whatever's missing. Besides, who's going to come and steal off a grave?"

"The dodgy bloke whose spade we're using, for a start."

"It's a shovel," I said. "And he won't be disturbing anything. I'm going to give this back." I hefted the item in question and strode off towards a small hut I'd noticed in the back corner of the cemetery.

"Griffin," Megan called. "You can scare him, just don't break anything." I could imagine her muttering. "The last thing you need is me arresting you for grievous bodily harm."

I should've been disturbed by her knowing me that well, but my focus remained on my objective. As I neared the wooden shed, I smelt cheap whiskey and cigarettes. Approaching the old man's salubrious daytime accommodation, I flicked that switch and felt my body shift. It's an odd sensation. One moment you move like a normal human being, the next you're loping almost wolf-like, with rounded shoulders, head on a swivel, and your senses alert. Everything about you becomes primed, and the normal world takes a backseat.

The smoke came from inside the shed. Its flimsy construction made it obvious it'd come from some DIY store, rather than being constructed by real builders out of thick wood. I didn't bother knocking, I just pushed the door open and strode into the six-foot by eight-foot room.

"What the fuck! You can't just—" The old man half

rose, realised it was me, glanced at his shovel, and sat back in his deckchair.

"Thanks for the loan." I put the shovel down. Having empty hands would help make sure I didn't do anything too stupid. An old iPad sat on the guy's desk, and I saw some adult entertainment playing. Nice. At work. Real nice. Not only that, but this location would often have children and grieving family members walking among their relatives. Beside the iPad sat a packet of tobacco that didn't look legit. No tax tag on the outside.

"No problem. Thanks for bringing it back," he muttered, his accent still thick enough to glue fish together.

I leaned over him, which made his mean little eyes widen in surprise, then shock, then fear as they stared into my face.

"We've left scientific equipment at the site of my mother's grave. Any interference with that equipment will be seen in a very dim light. My police colleague will pursue any theft through legal means. I don't have to play by her rules. I don't have to play by anyone's rules."

The man swallowed hard, and a fine tremor ran through his body. "I get it."

"By the looks of your tattoos," I glanced down at his fists, "you've been in prison. Keep the porn away from here. Do not give me a reason to find out you're watching something other than consensual sex between adults. My other friend out there can, and will, hack all your devices. He'll know. I'll know. Understood?"

A slow nod.

"Don't go near my mother's grave. Ever. I'll be back." Yeah, okay, cheesy last line, but I couldn't help myself. It relieved some of the pressure inside me to have vented on the old git, but I also had a measure of shame. Bullying old men shouldn't become an attribute I fostered, no matter how gross they were.

Even from the other side of the cemetery, I saw Megan and Sid making their slow way back to the car, carrying the large DoPI kit bag slung between them. Now jogging, I soon caught up.

"All good?" Megan asked as I lifted the thing onto my shoulder.

"Yeah, though you may want to do a PNC check on him. Sid, he probably needs your services. Find out if he's doing more than buying illegal fags, drinking on the job, and watching porn."

"Really? After doing one of those, I always want to wash my eyes in bleach."

His moaning did not improve my mood.

"That's why I don't work in cybercrime. Give me a nice, clean street brawl and some innocent heroin addicts any day," Megan muttered.

"Back to the house?" Sid asked.

"Can't," Megan replied. "Paperwork at the office." Did that mean she had to go and have a chat with her boyfriend?

*If she does, then that's her right, you nutbag.*

I huffed at myself, feeling itchy in places I couldn't reach. Like inside my chest cavity. "I'll walk back to Turpin Cottage. Sid can take the gear in the Mini. We'll need to talk about how we want to handle the next phase in the investigation."

Megan nodded. "Visiting the people in the camp. It won't be easy. They don't like my badge. You might be better off going alone, or with Sid. Besides, some of them might recognise us from the Beltane ceremony."

Sid pulled a face. "I'm not stomping about a field

talking to smelly hippies, thank you very much. I've a pervert to hack." He nodded towards the cemetery.

"We'll go in undercover," I said. "I don't want to be seen as officials. It's unlikely they'll recognise us. We dealt with the Cornish Sun people. You wore your police cap while moving people around. It was dim under those trees and until Jennifer was found, we just looked like all the other normies. Without a trusted introduction, we'll never get anywhere if we take this through the official routes. We'll take the bike down. Wear something you'd use on the farm. Come up to the cottage at whatever time suits you tomorrow morning and we'll head out. Bring a change of clothes in an old rucksack and some food and water. We might end up staying the night."

"You have a plan?"

I shrugged. "Maybe. If anything changes, I'll message you."

She nodded, walked towards her car, then turned and hurried back. Before I knew what she'd done, she hugged me. "It'll be okay," she whispered. "We'll figure it out. I promise." Her hot body was gone before my arms had a chance to wrap around her and hold her even closer.

I knew she didn't mean the DoPI case we were working on. She meant Mum. I watched her drive off. Sid, making a meal out of packing the stuff back into the Mini, eyed me when she pulled out onto the main road.

"You know she loves you, right?" he said.

"Fuck off, Sid."

"You've said that to me a lot today. If I were more sensitive, I'd take it personally."

I just stared at him, and his hands went up in surrender. Without another word, the tall man folded himself into the little car and rumbled off. I began walking home, a path I'd only taken in my altered state. I couldn't call it sleepwalking. Sleeping people don't dig holes in cemeteries and fall unconscious on the lawn when they arrived home. It was an altered state of being. As I strode through the humid afternoon, the spring having turned mysteriously into summer for a few hours, I realised that maybe it wasn't an altered state as such. Maybe I was being possessed, like Lorne Turner had been with his jinn?

The thought sent chills through me even as the first fat raindrops fell. The tarmac became a canvas for the splat of water, and the scent of petrichor filled the air. People began to hurry along the pavements, their dogs double-timing it beside them. The more rain fell, the more the cars swished as they passed me. I turned my face upwards and welcomed the soaking. Within minutes, I was drenched, my t-shirt clinging to my chest and back, a cold second skin. Walking up the hill, with evening collaborating in the sudden cloudburst, the day became gloomy right up to the moment lightning scored the sky and thunder unleashed its burden of sound as the broken air snapped together again. Suddenly, I felt alive. My spine tingled, energy rushed out of the top of my head. It reached into the blackening, roiling clouds, pulling my face up to meet the pounding, brutal rain. As I stared into the dark underbelly of the sky, each raindrop became visible as it raced down towards its individual doom, only to become part of a new embodiment of itself.

Another flash, the inversion of the world's colours dramatic, vivid and a reminder that we poor mortals might live longer than the individual violence of the earth's power, but in reality we are too fragile to survive forever. We are the lightning within an epoch that will stretch far beyond our petty existence. The boom of thunder made my teeth rattle, and the cars began to crawl, unable to cope with the deluge.

Crops would be ruined already, blossoms smashed, frail newborns battered in their fields. I began to run, unable to hold on to the rawness inside me any longer. My boots splashed through the flooding water, drains unable to cope with the drama of the moment and vomiting their contents into the streets.

That's what this weather exposed. The rawness inside me, ripping me apart. The hill grew steeper, and I ran harder, head down now, focused on the agony inside. What if I wasn't digging at my mother's grave while under the influence of some malign force? What if I were doing it from trauma? Simple, unremitting childhood trauma? The pain and loss of years, the confusion and loneliness. The sadness. As my boots hit the pavement and I crested the hill onto Highway Lane, I started to slow, and the raindrops slowed with me. Gradually, my heavy breathing eased, and my heart rate dropped. The cold seeped through the agony and made me shiver at last.

Maybe my work with DoPI offered the easy option: the supernatural. Perhaps I just need a good therapist?

*Don't we all? Besides, you know that's bollocks. The EMF meter practically screamed supernatural at you. Something* para *is happening, and you need to shake off this self-pity and flagellation.*

I pondered this bit of feisty self-analysis. It was a true statement. Yes, I had no doubt my mother's death had left me with unresolved trauma, but that didn't change what I'd experienced in the Brane long barrow, or during that odd vision on Bodmin Moor. It didn't explain how the night wanderings so often led me to the places of the dead. As if I had an affinity for them.

When I reached Turpin Cottage, I felt thoroughly cold, and I tramped around the back, my boots squishing. The garden looked bedraggled after the deluge, and the birds were silent. Reaching the back door, I stripped off my t-shirt, fatigues and boots, leaving them in a pile. Even my underclothes were wet, but I'd lost my dignity too many times in front of Sid to want to walk through the house naked.

After a hot shower and dressing in jogging shorts and another grey t-shirt, I realised the smell of Sid's Cajun chicken wafted through the house. With my stomach complaining my throat must've been cut for it to be deprived of such sustenance, I returned to the kitchen.

"Some storm," Sid said, standing at the cooker. "I've put your stuff in the machine and filled your boots with paper to help dry them out."

"That's very domesticated of you, Sid. Thanks. Luce coming for dinner by any chance?"

Sid glanced at me over his shoulder. "What made you say that?"

"You're not likely to cook me Cajun chicken, mate. Don't worry, I'll keep out of the way."

"As it happens, I am cooking for you. Luce cancelled. She's busy with an article her publishers want by the end of the week."

I peered over his shoulder at the pan. "Can I help?" I wondered if I could distract him enough to steal something to eat.

He shoved against my chest with his bony shoulder. "No. Bugger off."

I laughed and sat at the table while we talked about mundane house stuff, gossiped about DoPI and watched as the black clouds broke up to reveal a Cornish sunset any filmmaker would envy.

# Chapter Ten

The following morning, I dressed in my oldest pair of fatigues, a t-shirt with a faded print of a Norwegian band I loved, and my still damp boots. I packed my daysack, suitably battered, with a jumper, a dog-eared novel, and the usual accoutrements of a DoPI field operative. Holy water, salt, a small iron dagger and snacks. The last was for me. I heard the front door open and Sid welcoming Megan into the house. I grabbed a two-way radio system in case our mobiles didn't work, and a couple of notepads. Sometimes, analogue was best. I also rummaged around to find my small tent and the sleeping bags I'd lifted from the quartermaster's stock.

I jogged down the stairs, feeling better than I had done in weeks. A good night's sleep will do that for a person, and I'd slept very well. No wandering, no dreams, just nine hours of unconsciousness. What had I done to be so blessed?

"Morning!" I called out. Then stopped as I caught sight of Megan. "You alright?"

She gave me a wan smile. "Yeah, just tired. Long night."

I frowned. "Something I did?"

Her eyes rolled at me. "Yeah, sure, my life is entirely about your drama, Griff. I do have other things going on."

*Adrian.* I repressed the urge to snarl. "You don't have to come if you don't want to, or if you have other plans. I can handle this alone." Though it wouldn't be anywhere near as much fun.

She shook her head. "No, I want to. It's my job, and my inspector is pleased to lend me to DoPI for the entire investigation. He seems quite taken with our work. Though, it does save his budget when we take on a major crime."

I chuckled. "I wish I could say that about Sanchez."

Sid appeared, wiping his hands on a cloth. "Breakfast. I'm not letting you two out there without a belly full."

"Feeding me again?" I grinned.

He pointed a long finger at me. "You're doing the washing up, and the bathrooms need cleaning. I don't mind doing the cooking, but I'm not doing it all."

"Roger that." My promise made, I headed towards the smell of toast and bacon.

"I'm fine," Megan said. "I had some fruit."

I backtracked, walked up behind her, and pushed her into the kitchen. "Sit, eat all you want. We can't do this properly if you're hungry."

"I'm on a diet," she complained.

"And you look like a washed-out dishcloth. Eat, Meg." I pushed her down into a chair, grabbed what I guessed to be my plate of heart attack food, and shoved it under her nose.

She looked up at me with tears in her eyes. "Thank you." Her voice, so small and frail, worried me as much as the dark circles under her eyes and her thinning cheeks. She hadn't been with this bloke long, but I could see how her battered jeans hung on her hips differently, and her old shirt fitted her oddly. I didn't like the changes. They were too sudden.

I didn't say anything, aware I'd only end up causing her more grief. Today, I'd make her happier, one way or another, and I'd see that bright smile I cared about.

Sid, without verbal comment, served me another plate, but he said plenty with his expression. I gave a short shrug and sat with Megan.

"What are your plans?" I asked him.

He sat and began tackling his own food. "I think a deep dive into the company that owns the new golf course. If you feed me back the names of key players in the protesters' camp, I'll do the same with them. I want to ask Luce about the location and, as you'll be out, I'll have her help with the intel we'll have gathered overnight down at the cemetery."

"Sounds good." Being bachelors on London wages, Sid and I had far too much cash to spend on luxuries. The bacon was organic and local, as were the eggs, the bread, and the fried tomatoes. I'd be raiding the cupboard for more treats before we left, like the sourdough loaf I'd bought at the bakery earlier in the week and the veggie bacon in the fridge. We needed to take food to share. Somehow, I doubted we'd be welcome with a ton of meat in my rucksack.

In short order, Megan and I had the kitchen cleared. I grabbed my bike jacket, despite it being newish, because for me, safety came first, and Megan shrugged into her older version of the same thing. We went outside, and I tied the small tent and bags to the bike. I slung the daysack over my chest, making sure Megan had room on the back of the bike, and she climbed on after me. Her arms snaked around my belly, and she leaned against me, even her head resting on my shoulder. I reached down and rubbed her thigh in solidarity, making her hug me tighter in response for a moment, before I gunned Quacker into life.

After the rainstorm of the previous afternoon, the world smelt cleaner than ever, and the landscape opened out with colours to rival the bejewelled surface of a monarch's crown. I rode fast enough to give myself the thrill of the chase until I hit the narrower roads. Then good sense took over, which was just as well, as tourists who didn't understand the lanes made it more dangerous for us than it had been on the main road doing seventy, maybe a little more. Still, we made it back to the camp near the Madron Well site without incident. The hoardings from the golf course on our right were now covered in graffiti, a new addition from the previous day and a step up in action.

Megan, finally sitting upright with her visor lifted, said, "That's unhelpful."

I gave up trying to read the curly letters. I'd always struggled with odd fonts, or words written in a stylised form. "It won't help keep the peace. You know these guys are going to be jumpy after last night. They lost one of their own."

Megan leaned over my shoulder to talk. "Many of them were questioned last night. They all said the same thing, in a variety of ways. Jennifer Mancore went for a walk to the wood, no one saw or heard anything else. You're right, though, they'll be spooked."

When we reached the camp's entrance, I parked the bike on the verge, not willing to risk her after the storm of the day before. Spending an hour or two hauling my bike out of the mud didn't inspire me. Quacker was no trail bike. Megan slipped off, and I slung my daysack over my back. We locked our lids to the bike and just strode into the field containing tents, vans, caravans, trucks, and even a few small yurts and teepees.

The fields here weren't steep, they rolled over the land like the Cornish accent rolled gently off the tongue. I guessed that's why it worked for the golf course, but they'd need to do something about access, the lane was narrow even by Cornish standards.

Together we strode into the field. Megan said, "We didn't discuss a plan. Mainly an exit if they recognise us."

"Just blend in, keep your ears open. They won't remember us."

"You don't blend in anywhere, Griff." She stared up at me. "Try to walk like we aren't on a parade ground or storming a gun emplacement."

I laughed. "Not much chance of that. You'll just have to introduce me as a convert to the cause, recently released from the Armed Forces."

"That I can manage."

Three people headed towards us, an older woman and two men, both about my age. They'd obviously been in the lifestyle a long time. The tribal symbols of the alternative scene were the dreadlocks for one of the men and the woman, the other bloke had a shaved head. Baggy clothing, heavy boots, and piercings with the odd flash of a tattoo on a forearm or neck.

Megan stepped in front of me and said, "Hello. Is it okay for us to join you? We're here for the protest. My name is Megan. The big guy is Griffin."

I watched to see if anyone recognised us. A lot of people were watching, but no one commented. No pitchforks, no screams of traitor, or 'It's the pigs', so I forced myself to relax.

"I'm Leaze, this is Denny and Mitch, we're on duty for

meeting newcomers today. It's good to have you here." The older woman held out her hand, and Megan shook. I followed suit, making sure I remained friendly and not reacting to the stink eye Mitch gave me. The woman, Leaze, had red eyes and a strain that her face didn't naturally recognise. Denny too looked sad under the general droopiness.

"We're planning on closing the lane tomorrow with a sitting, silent protest. It'll mean a few arrests, I'm sure, but that's all part of the cause. It'll be good to have new spirits among us," Leaze said with a sad smile. "We lost a beautiful soul last night."

Her eyes were hazel, her shoulders rounded, but her hair held a shade of red I doubted even henna could pull off. It was hard to tell her age, as she'd long since turned naturally brown from the outdoors lifestyle. Despite being taller than Megan, she didn't take up enough space, her body too thin. Her voice held a hard edge to it, somewhere southeast of London, and it was pitched to slice through my head. I wouldn't want to spend too much time listening to Leaze, it might make me a bit stabby.

"I'm sorry to hear that," Megan said. "What happened?"

Leaze's eyes filled with tears. "One of our people was…"

Mitch took over. "Murdered." The brutality of the word hit Leaze like a punch in the kidneys.

She gasped. "Sorry. I'm so sorry. We're supposed to be a welcoming committee, and here we are spilling our sadness all over you." Tears leaked out of her eyes.

"That's terrible," Megan said, reaching out and rubbing Leaze's arm. "Do you know what happened?"

Denny shook his head. "No, man, but it was bad." His

gaze drifted to the wood, a silent stand behind me. "Something is rising in there and it ain't happy." His eyes roved around the camp as if seeking some gremlin in his machine of peace and love.

"This is so sad. We've taken some time off work, so we're happy to pitch in to the community, if it'll help ease the burden," Megan said.

"Where'd you come from? What work?" Mitch asked. I glimpsed the man's teeth as he spoke and saw the damage that came from drug abuse. He had a scar through his right eyebrow, and pockmarked skin.

"Mitch, we talked about this," Leaze warned, as she patted her eyes dry.

"They could be scabs," he said. "One of us was murdered, we gotta be careful now. They're after us, and they'll do all they can to scare us away from the bastards over there."

I took that to mean the Whist Industry site. I finally located his accent. Nottingham way, I guessed. Scabs being the word for those who crossed the picket line and continued to work during the miners' strike. Not even a memory for me, but I'd seen the documentaries and films.

Mitch would never trust us, so I answered truthfully. "I'm sorry for your loss. As for what I've been doing, well, I've just been kicked out of the Royal Marines. I want to do something useful with my life."

Sort of honest, anyway. Megan then surprised me by sliding her free arm through mine. "We've been together a while. I've been in Scotland counting birds on the islands."

To say I was shocked at her decision to make us a couple was an understatement, and counting birds? Where the hell had that idea come from? I'd expected a bit of adlibbing, but Megan was going off like this was a poem by Homer.

"Environmentalists rather than protesters?" asked Denny. His words were a slow drawl, and his gaze far less intense than Mitch's. The distinctive scent of weed floated in a soft miasma around his body.

"Yeah, well, me more than him." Megan nudged me with her shoulder. "But I'm converting him. Love not war, right?" She delivered one of her best smiles to Leaze.

"Amen, sister." Her grief was under control for the moment, but I saw it bubbling under the surface. It needed testing to see how real it was. She said, "Come, I'll show you around. I can see you have a tent, but we have community lodgings if you need them."

I let Megan go and watched as she blended effortlessly with Leaze and Denny. Mitch stomped off, muttering something about keeping an eye on me, but I wasn't worried. A strong puff of an asthma inhaler would knock him over. Following the women and Denny, we wove between small encampments. They kinda reminded me of refugee camps I'd walked through in Somalia, only with a lot less despair and more welly boots. There were a good number of tents mushrooming between the trucks, vans and caravans parked around the edges. These would be the hardcore protesters, I guessed. Many of the people nodded a welcome at least, some an actual hello. There were preschool children running about, and a selection of dogs. The multi-generational, and diverse backgrounds of the protest group blended together to form a positive and oddly cohesive whole. It felt safe, even if a general air of being subdued because of Jennifer's death meandered about.

Then I noticed at the top of the field a group set apart. There were five vans, all decorated in a similar livery of a muted kaleidoscope of colours and images. They weren't bright, psychedelic images, but more natural. In the centre of the semicircle that the vans formed, stood a teepee.

"Who are they?" I asked, lengthening my stride to catch up with Megan.

Leaze and Denny looked at me vaguely, so I pointed.

"Oh, them," Denny said. "They're our heart group." He tapped his chest with his fist.

I lifted an eyebrow, so Leaze interpreted. "They're a hardcore group of warriors and profoundly spiritual people. They're really connected to the Mother. You'll see them later. Anwen's Children is their name, and we're blessed to have them here."

Megan flicked her eyes at me, and I gave the briefest of nods. Anwen's Children needed a closer look.

By this time, our amble through the camp had brought us to a yurt. I'd never seen one in real life, and I had to admit to being impressed. The cloth sides of the building were pinned back, revealing its carcass. The design reminded me of a toadstool with just the rounded cap sprouting from the ground, and no stalk. The heavy cream canvas covered a felt insulating layer, and under that, the lattice of wood formed its skeleton. I'd learned to build temporary shelters, but this was magnificent, and I instantly understood why they were used by nomads in Mongolia and similar places. They'd stand up well to the strong winds and deep snows of the tundra. Very different from the more upright teepee design.

"This is our shared space," Leaze said, not hiding her pride. "We come here to eat together, share our stories and sing. Visitors can stay, provided they respect the space and our intent. We are social anarchists. You know what that means?"

"That means no rules, except mutual respect for each other and our shared property," Megan replied without a moment's hesitation, once more surprising me.

Leaze smiled, pleased with her reply. "Cool, yeah, you've got it. So, you're welcome to stay, though you'll be sharing the space with several other people. I live over there in the blue van. Denny's in the one next door. We've travelled together a long time."

Megan lifted the small tent I'd brought out of my hands. "It's okay, we have this, but we'll be happy to share our food while we're here. Maybe we can pitch up close to this beauty," she patted the yurt, "and get to know a few people?" Again, she brought out her smile. It always worked on me, so I didn't see why it wouldn't melt the hearts of these poor bastards.

Of course, she got her own way, and I was soon building the tent right next to the big yurt. Megan pottered about, meeting and greeting the locals. I knew I had a way with people; it's one of the things that made me a good investigator, but watching her work was a study in careful manipulation. She mirrored the people she spoke with, matching their postures, enjoying the conversation and actively engaging in opinions that I knew she didn't share. On several occasions she thickened her accent, which in this community, made her seem more legitimate. I kept my mouth shut, smiled and nodded in the right places, while I watched and listened.

Much of the talk was of Jennifer's death. Rumours mostly. The favourite conspiracy seemed to be that the Security Service had killed her as an example to the rest of them. That they'd have to fight 'The Man' with real force. If the government wanted them dead, then they had to fight back. It wasn't the kind of talk I wanted to hear.

However, most of the people around us were passionate about the environment, community-minded and friendly. In fact, Mitch appeared to be the only one I'd classify as 'dodgy'. At least so far. During the morning, we met people with a range of backgrounds, from a retired barrister to a young mother who wanted her children to have a future in Cornwall. There were a few older teenagers, and one lass who looked like she'd just stepped out of a TikTok video for eco-tourism. Personally, I'd want to know why she wasn't in school. She didn't seem to fit somehow with her bright blonde good looks and white teeth. We also unearthed more information about Anwen's Children, and it became clear we needed to speak with them.

By lunchtime, we had quite a group around the community kitchen. It was an outside space with an open fire in a well-built pit that provided better food than I'd managed in the field on training exercises. The group dynamics meant Megan and I could finally talk alone.

"What do you think?" I murmured over my lentil stew.

"Same as you, we need to speak with that group up the hill. I've heard nothing that makes me think they know anything about Jennifer's death. Though it's hit them hard. She just walked to the wood and vanished. They spent most of yesterday looking for her, in case she fell. No one found her body."

"That's bloody odd." I considered this for a moment. "Where was it hidden until we found it?"

"Who knows. We just have to keep listening and find a way into Anwen's Children."

"What do you reckon, it's a cult?"

She shrugged and bit into the soda bread we'd brought and shared. Around her chewing, she added, "How are we going to make that happen? They don't mix much with the others."

"Walk?"

A soft nod. She allowed herself to be distracted by a young man holding forth on the terrors of warfare and how peace should be the only option. It took a lot for me to hold my tongue. The peaceful option didn't really work when someone else had tanks rolling over your population. I was sorely tempted to ask what conflict zones the boy had seen in his vast experience of life, but Megan held my thigh in a vice-like grip. I was a bit concerned she'd remove my entire group of quadriceps.

After cleaning up, we disengaged from the group and walked first towards the woodland that contained the cloutie tree. Even from this distance, a sense of wrongness leaked over me. However, it was good to escape the intensity of the camp itself. I hadn't been around that many people since the raves I'd been forced to attend while tracking down Mephistopheles. The crowds of London had a tendency to freak me out, and these people were few in comparison, but they were so earnest it became overwhelming.

"Phew," I breathed out once we were well clear of twitching ears.

"Yeah, a bit much, even for me, and I've a lot of sympathy for them," Megan agreed.

"Can I ask you a question?" My stomach swirled, unused to the heavy lentil stew. I'd enjoyed it, but it seemed my belly didn't quite know what to do with the healthy option.

"Let me guess, why make us a couple the moment we arrived?"

I didn't say anything, just kept my eyes on the treeline at

the edge of the vast field we occupied. A stoic expression seemed best.

"I know it's a bit weird," she confessed, "but as a couple we're both saved from having potential problems. You're a good-looking bloke, Griff, and I could do without being hassled myself. We don't have that kind of time."

A number of things came to mind. She was in a relationship and could've explained that we were cousins, and that she had a boyfriend. We could've been brother and sister, though I didn't look anything like her real brothers, but our seamless shared history meant it would be easy to blag. Her option basically closed down any chance I had of finding a flirtation. Also, I very much doubted anyone would hassle my cousin for long, with or without me being around. The woman was a police sergeant, for heaven's sake.

"Megan, I don't mind. It's not that. It's just…" I saw the metaphorical shithole I was about to fall into and managed to step to one side. "It's just that you're with Adrian now."

Megan remained quiet.

"Meg?" I stopped walking and gently took hold of her arm, tugging her around to look at me. "What's wrong? You've not been right for days."

Rather than speak, she stepped into my space and wrapped her arms around my waist, her head burying itself in my chest. I held her, uncertain what kind of hug she wanted. Platonic was the word emblazoned on the front of my brain.

*Don't do anything fucking stupid, Marine.*

She said, "I don't know what to do. He… He's very popular at the nick."

"Okay, but you must be as well," I said to the top of her

head. *Tread really lightly here, mate, she'll never forgive you if you get this wrong.* The thought made me nervous.

"Not like he is. It's different for men, you know that."

"No women have made it through the commando training and stayed, Meg. I work primarily with men, and in DoPI I work mostly with blokes as well. The world of women is a bit of a mystery, which is why I'm single." More or less accurate.

She pulled out of our embrace. "I guess the Police Service and the Royal Marines aren't all that similar. It's not like you usually work in the community."

"True, but that's not the point. What are you trying to tell me, Meg?" Genuine concern began to fill the cracks inside me that her romance with this Adrian had caused.

"I don't really know, Griff. Sometimes, I think it's all in my head, but the last few weeks… Since the offer came through from Bristol, he's been different."

"Like what?"

She started walking again, but her posture was hunched, her footsteps slow and heavy. "I dunno. It's weird. Like this morning, he said it was good I was learning more about how to be undercover, but I should remember that women are always used for vice stings rather than real operations. He made it sound like I was only going to be of any use to Rural Security if you started investigating some prostitution ring in the villages rather than cities."

"Unless another sex demon turns up, I can't see that happening."

She smacked me in the chest hard enough to hurt. "That's not the point."

*Well done, dickhead. There's the shithole you just managed to fall into.*

"No, sorry, you're right."

"Forget it. I shouldn't be talking about it with you anyway." She increased her walking pace, striding over the field and leaving me to scramble to catch up.

"Hey, wait, don't take it like that. I didn't mean—"

"Who's that over there?" she asked, pointing and changing the subject completely.

I'd failed. Maybe I'd be permitted to find another way in later. We had the rest of the day and the night. "Let's go find out." I gave her an exit from our conversation. Though the more I thought about the implications of her odd statements, the more I worried.

As we strode over the field, we no longer felt like the single unit we'd become while working together in the camp. Megan's walls were in full operation, and if I wanted back inside the compound, I'd have to work bloody hard to get there. I was annoyed with myself.

Focusing on our objective, I reined back the mental flagellation. It was time to assess our situation rather than worry about my companion. On the edge of the field, a small group of people stood around a tree that had made it beyond the woodland and into the hedgerow that bordered the farm's usable land. There were nine individuals, and even from this distance, we could see they were different from the others we'd met in the camp.

"Anwen's Children?" Megan murmured.

"Reckon."

"Tread light?"

"Best way."

"Understood." Megan's smile came out of the cupboard as we approached, and she lifted a hand in welcome.

No one acknowledged it. Considering how friendly the

rest of the people we'd met that morning had been, it surprised me. It also disturbed me. The waves of hostility coming from the group clustered around the tree felt disproportionate.

"This is a private affair," said one of the men in the group. "If you're part of the camp, then just go back. If you're tourists, it would be better to leave the area."

"We're part of the camp," Megan said. "We were just wondering if you needed any help?"

"Nope, we're fine, you can go."

There were five men and four women in the group. All were dressed in various shades of green and brown. The fabric looked natural rather than manmade. They wore their hair long. Even with them clothed, I realised they shared the same tattoos over their hands and up their throats. It meant leaving this group wouldn't be easy, forgetting them, impossible. One of the women had a baby in the sling across her ample chest. The chap who'd told us to bugger off looked like he'd stepped out of a fantasy novel and wanted to continue to play the part of the grouchy wizard. Among the group stood a figure set apart from the others, but in a way I didn't understand. Other than being far younger than the rest, a boy really, he was dressed the same, and yet, something in his eyes…

I recognised him, or an element within him. It left me with a discomforting feeling that I didn't immediately recognise, and I sensed it would take me a while to figure it out. He watched me with large grey eyes, his blond hair past his shoulders and perfectly straight. There'd be many a catwalk model that would envy his ethereal beauty. I doubted he'd be much more than fifteen and had that long-limbed thinness to his frame.

"Hello," I said, with a smile.

"Dydh da," he murmured in return.

I glanced at Megan, and she looked shocked. Very slowly, she said, "Prn kewsel kernewek?" Then she looked at me. "I just asked if he spoke Cornish. At least I think I did, it's been a while."

The boy nodded, and his pale cheeks coloured, eyes dropping to the floor. With small movements, he shuffled behind the largest of the women.

"You still need to leave," said the same man again, stepping towards me.

I focused on him and felt the desire to flip that switch that always lay just below the civilised surface. Megan's hand brushed mine to remind me we were here to ingratiate ourselves, not to start a war.

She stepped towards mister bad attitude. Thickening her accent, she said, "We just want to understand and become part of the protest. These people," she waved a hand in the direction of the building site, "they don't get it. The sacredness of this place. You can feel it, even here." She held her hands out to the woodland, as if warming them against a fire. Personally, I felt a chill coming from the trees, but it could've been my imagination. The previous night's events were all too vivid in my mind.

Knowing how little Megan liked any of this 'religious bollocks'—Megan's term, not mine—I was impressed with her ability to become such a chameleon.

"You know nothing of the suffering in this place. Please leave, this is a sacred rite," said the matron of the group. Her hands were on her rounded hips.

I caught sight of the boy again and noticed his eyes were filled with tears. It disturbed me greatly. Though I couldn't place why or how he'd made me feel so alien inside my skin. Reaching out, I took hold of Megan's arm. "Let's go."

She looked around me, a frown about to turn into an argument on her lips, when she registered something in my face. Stepping back, she said, "Namaste." As if she'd been using the word her entire life.

# Chapter Eleven

We walked away, feeling the eyes of the group on our backs, heading towards the top of the field once more. It made my back itch and my left hand twitch for my sidearm, but I'd been eyeballed by scarier people than Anwen's Children. Besides, the feeling of dread from the woodland, far surpassed anything a few humans could offer in the way of fear. Why weren't more people worried about the wood? Everyone seemed focused on Jennifer's death, not the anger I'd sensed among the trees. Was I the only one paranoid enough to feel it, or was I being too paranoid, and the trees were just trees?

I pushed the thoughts to one side, wanting to escape them for a few minutes. A fresh perspective was necessary.

Beyond the field, lay a small patch of heathland. The gorse and heather battled it out with rough grass and a few stumpy trees.

I'd decided it would be good to have a full understanding of our current location in the geography of the area if we were spending the night. However, right now, I had more pressing matters to interrogate. "Really?" I asked once we were out of earshot. "Namaste?"

She grinned. "Yeah, I know, but loads of these people will use it and get the meaning wrong. I just thought it'd help make me look harmless and a bit of a fool." We'd reached the stone wall and the pair of us climbed over, heading up through the last year's red-brown bracken.

"Well, you certainly achieved that," I replied with a grin.

"What about that boy?" she asked. "He should be in school. And speaking Cornish? That's not normal for most kids his age."

"He was a strange lad. It might be worth trying to get a photo of him for Sid to run some checks. I don't like minors being involved with tight groups like this. It didn't seem like any of them were his parents."

Megan breathed out heavily. "Dangerous path, Griff, but I agree. It felt off."

We turned at the same moment. Now, on the crest of the hill looking back, we saw the camp laid out like a haphazard post-apocalyptic village of survivalists. Also, in the shadows of the trees, we saw the small group of Anwen's Children. They were standing with their arms raised, the boy in the centre of a semicircle with his hands pressed against the large sycamore tree rising, king-like, in the hedgerow. On the breeze, we caught the murmur of chanting voices but couldn't make out the words.

"Yeah, definitely need a photo of the boy for Sid," Megan agreed, a frown deepening the blue of her eyes. "I don't like the look of that at all."

The afternoon passed as the morning had, with domestic chores to help the protesters. I saw Mitch watching me and muttering to a couple of blokes and a woman who had more in common with starving wolves than the rest of the fluffy bunnies surrounding us. Despite the knowledge that we were here to infiltrate the group to discover their possible involvement with the dead woman, I had to admit to having fun.

In the Royal Marines, I'd done a lot of roughing it while on training exercises, or when deployed. Our all-male units would set up camp with typical military efficiency and preparedness for anything that could come at us during our rest periods. In this camp, I found myself helping several younger women carry water in buckets from a tank that sat near the field's gate. Then I lent a hand to the children, who were busy painting new banners and struggling against the rising wind. I found them stones heavy enough to pin down the cardboard and helped with the spelling. A woman called River worked with me, someone obviously experienced with the scene. When I tried to engage her in a conversation about Jennifer Mancore, she shut me down. I had the feeling it pained River, but she was a private person, and you'd have to go a long way to be awarded any trust.

Megan and I peeled vegetables, and I offered to lend a hand with the compost toilet. Not a job I wanted, but I'd done my share of digging holes and using them. Besides, I'd be using flushing loos soon enough, and these poor bastards were here for the long haul. The entire afternoon passed in a flurry of shouts, giggles, noise and laughter, despite Jennifer's passing. There were tears. Leaze spend a long time with a young woman called Aggie, someone who'd been close to Jennifer. We'd need to talk to her soon as well.

Megan fitted in with the other women, helping with the smallest children, reading stories, changing nappies and doing other domestic chores I'd never imagined her being able to perform.

I had to ask about the nappy thing. "How'd you do that?" I pointed to the small human, whose fat legs and arms pumped the air as Megan held him out to his exhausted mother. The baby grinned at me. I backed up. Despite being a godfather to Rowan Turner, I hadn't dealt with the intricacies of her care.

"I've nieces and nephews, you fool," Megan said.

I grunted, once more reminded of my abandonment of Megan's family for so many years. It left me with a pang of loss I didn't expect. How much had I missed? Why had I missed it? For a long moment, I gazed at Megan, who continued to coo over the baby. I'd always told myself that my feelings for her kept me away, but it wasn't just that; I'd been scared as an adult by the responsibility that came as part of a loving family. I didn't really understand it, and I didn't know how to relate to it, how to merge with the whole. If I were honest, it intimidated me, almost to the point of fear.

As I helped out around the camp, I thought about this and realised how unfair I'd been to myself for years. I'd lost so much by rejecting my family, Megan's family, and if I'd just plunged in with both feet and submerged myself in their willing embrace, I might be a happier person. Could that be why I kept trying to dig up my mother's grave? Was it really that simple? A kind of plea from my subconscious to make me join in family life?

The children were fed early, and many were packed off to various vans. As the late spring twilight stretched its arms overhead, dropping veils of colour towards the horizon, we adults ate together, and soon enough music began around the safely contained bonfire. I had to admit; these guys were organised.

More people joined the growing party around the fire

pit, and a jamming session began. My fingers now ached for my guitar, sat alone and unloved for far too long. One of the men playing said he wanted to rest, and Megan did something I could've strangled her for doing. She said, "Griffin can play. He'll take over if you're okay with that. He's a lefty like you."

Within seconds, I had a guitar's familiar body pushed into my belly and my arms embraced the instrument as if they'd known her all her life.

"Thanks, Meg," I muttered.

"What you gonna play?" asked one of the younger adults.

I felt the panic rise. Performing in public like this was not in my repertoire of skills. Megan's hand reached for my knee and squeezed. She smiled and said, "Remember how good you were at *Eleanor Rigby*? It seems kinda fitting if what I hear about poor Jennifer is right."

"What's that song?" asked an ignorant idiot, as murmurs of agreement came from several people. Leaze sat with her arm around Aggie, who sniffed regularly.

It was enough to prod me into action. My fingers raced up and down the frets. I tweaked the tuning just a little, dancing over the strings. I'd lost the guitar calluses; this would be uncomfortable.

Closing my eyes to block out the audience watching me from all around the fire, I picked out the chords and began to play. I'm not Lennon or McCartney, but I play well enough and I have a reasonable baritone. It didn't take long before other people joined in, and soon enough, I'd started on *Nowhere Man*. Happy songs were never really my thing as a distraught teenager, and in the years since, I'd stuck with the sad, sad songs. That's the one I picked next, *Every Rose Has Its Thorns* and wondered how the hell I'd manage the guitar break. By this point a few more people joined us, and I realised some of them were from Anwen's Children, one of whom picked up my fumbling efforts and carried us through the complex licks DeVille made look so easy.

With night now in full control of the sky, the stars a vivid display overhead and a low moon waning on the quarter, it felt magical. Megan sang beside me, her voice a soft contralto, and laughed when I spoofed knowing the words. We were both happy and at peace.

Until a tall woman strode into the fire's circle and everyone fell silent.

If ever a goddess decided to be made manifest in this world, then surely, she'd arrive in the skin of this woman. Her face held no deep lines, though her straight, waist-length hair was silver. The firelight made its strands flash red. She had to be almost my height and held her slim body upright, strong chin proud. The tattoos we'd seen on the others in the group wrapped around her bare arms, under the long pale tunic dress she wore, and swept up her neck to nestle against her ears. Pale blue eyes took us in as our silence stretched.

I heard someone whisper, "This is Eloise. Our teacher."

Megan acknowledged her thanks for the explanation, and I handed back the guitar.

Eloise looked at me. Or rather, into me. Over the years, I've been stared at by some scary-arsed dudes, but this woman made all my instincts ping with warning. She didn't radiate anything but dominant, controlling peace, and yet… Something felt off. I tried to pinpoint it as I listened to her speak. Everyone else in the group looked mesmerised.

"Daughters and sons of the Mother," she began, making sure she walked the circle around the fire to gather everyone's attention. "Blessings be on you all." Several of the people at the front of the gathered group rose and moved back, giving Eloise space at the nadir of the community. Most of them murmured their blessings to her in return. I kept my mouth shut. This would be the opportunity we needed to really see the dynamics of these people.

She continued in her strong, modulated voice, accented slightly for the West Country, but obviously educated. "We are gathered together tonight in a state of union to celebrate our connection to each other and our Mother." She paused for a moment. "Especially after last night's tragic events." Everyone bowed their heads in remembrance of Jennifer. Eloise continued, "Many of you know our teachings among Anwen's Children, but some of you do not." Her gaze settled on me and Megan. "We are a peaceful people who wish no harm to come to our Mother, her sacred spaces, or each other."

I had my doubts about the last one. The miserable wizard from earlier stood in the crowd, scowling at everyone. I had a sneaking suspicion, or maybe a wish, that Anwen's Children had something to do with this mess. If they did, I was going to rip the happy little cult into tiny little pieces and feed them to Sanchez.

Eloise said, "We came to this place when our tribe heard of the coming desecration of this ancient site. Mother's heartbeat is strong here, and yesterday we were gifted with Father Sky's as well."

*Okay, she's as mad as a March hare marching towards that cliff lemmings like to use, while carrying a box of pissed off frogs.*

I tried to tamp down my inner sceptic, though I felt Megan straining at the seams to keep herself quiet.

"Our Mother speaks to us through the Seismic Pulse. Every twenty-eight seconds she lets the world know she is still there, still alive and in need of our support and love. All mothers need the love of their children, right?"

Murmurs from the crowd acknowledged this as fact. My love for my mother hadn't been enough to keep her alive, so I didn't comment.

"This heartbeat is now straining. There are changes in her core that we need to hear in order to survive and thrive during this difficult time. We are on the brink." She raised her hands, fists clenched and shook them. "The time to be passive, as our Mother is raped and abused all over the planet, has gone. If we don't protect her, and the sacred spaces in this world that she uses to communicate with us, then we are doomed to repeat our mistakes forever. Father Sky's pulse is different. His words to us come through the lightning that penetrates the Mother. He lights the atmosphere that gives us and Mother life. Oh, the heretics dismiss this signal, this heartbeat. The Schumann Resonance, they like to call it, as if it is owned by them. But the truth we know is that it exists all over the world and has done long before the science of man. We were gifted with his deep voice yesterday, and Mother received his bounteous tears."

I almost laughed. As part of DoPI's investigations into various small cults over the years, we'd come across these two, perfectly scientific phenomena being twisted into something spiritual, but I'd never heard it personally. Sid would love to listen to this as *mister science.*

Up until this point, Eloise had spoken with passion, in a resonating voice. The kind you'd hear on a Royal Shakespeare Company stage. Now, it dropped to a near whisper, but still it carried over the fire's crackle and hiss.

"Places like this, with the holy spring, the beautiful cloutie tree, the ancient sacred circle of trees our young mystic is learning about, give us hope that we can reach out to Mother Earth and Father Sky. That we can commune with them, let them know we are listening to their hearts as they hear ours, and through that connection find healing. Our healing, as we beg their forgiveness and give thanks for their bounty." Her voice became stronger. "If we allow this atrocity to happen," here her finger stabbed the night, "we will be cutting off one of the few places in this country where we can hear our Mother's wisdom. We need to listen, daughters and sons; we need to listen and to find the courage to act. No longer can we be passive as our Mother is silenced by the greed of the few for their pleasure and profit. No longer can we be passive as our Mother is denigrated and humiliated. We must rise up and speak and act and defy those who would take from us our lungs, our bellies, our hearts as they destroy our world. Our sister Jennifer knew this and her sacrifice will never be forgotten!"

The crowd around the fire roared in approval. I noticed the TikTok girl in her expensive woollen coat recording Eloise on her phone. Her attention was rapt, avid, devoted. Yep, the woman would appeal to the photogenic youngster.

I had no end of nuggets for Sid to interrogate when we went home. However, I also heard in Eloise's words some elements that disturbed me a great deal. The 'young mystic' was obviously the boy we'd seen. Naming him a mystic, as with Joan of Arc and countless like them worldwide, wouldn't end well for the lad. Also, the rising up bit sounded like too much of a war cry to me, and war wasn't something I'd allow, either as a Marine or an operative for DoPI. The general premise I understood, though I could do without the flowery magical rhetoric, and I supported their efforts to save the woodland and the cloutie tree. But hearing the earth's heartbeat through communion with such places? Yeah, well, I wasn't going down that rabbit hole.

Science couldn't yet explain either 'heartbeat' completely, but they did happen. I knew from the lectures we often attended, presented by DoPI's academics, that the seismic one centred around the Gulf of New Guinea had something to do with waves, the sea floor, and the earth's internal structure. The lightning had something to do with electromagnetic frequencies, and that just about ended my understanding.

Also, the way she'd tacked on Jennifer's death at the end of her speech, framing it for her agenda, didn't endear the woman to me. If this were a human using *para* inspired knowledge to kill, then this Eloise had floated to the surface and flashed a warning beacon in my head.

The crowd settled. Eloise thanked everyone for listening and appealed for them to stay strong, that Mother would hear their prayers, especially for Jennifer. She shook hands with some, laid hands on others, and spoke to a few. An air of mystery surrounded her, and I was certain I saw a cult leader in the making. Give her a few years and Anwen's Children would be drinking the Kool-Aid in protest of climate change.

Megan leaned into me, smelling of bonfires and honey, though that last one could've been my imagination. "I don't like her," she whispered.

"Bit of a worry," I muttered in return. "Time for bed?"

"Yeah."

Megan and I rose, backing out of the circle and into the dark, rather than cross the firelight. We walked around the large crowd and headed for our shared tent.

I let her go first, having been raised a gentleman by my

mother and then my aunt. It took a while for us to settle, with compost loos, outdoor tooth brushing and struggling with clothing in the small tent. I opted to sleep on top of my sleeping bag, fully dressed except for my boots. Partly I was worried about another nighttime episode, but mostly, I had the feeling I needed to be ready for action. I liked these people, and most of them were harmless. However, as with all groups of this nature, there were elements more interested in the fighting part rather than the protesting part.

As I settled down on my sleeping bag, I tried very hard to focus on our problems in the camp, rather than on Megan. She lay inside her bedding, wearing a t-shirt and shorts. I hadn't noticed her braless state, or her rounded thighs. Really, I hadn't.

"Today's been kinda fun," she murmured from beside me.

"Yeah, I've had a good time. I've never done this with women and children around. It's been educational."

Megan chuckled. "You're hopeless. You know most of the women in this camp are desperate to catch your attention?"

I didn't say anything.

She tried another ploy to get me talking. "Remember camping when we were kids?"

I did. "The river on the farm? Of course, I remember. We loved it down there. I think Iris was worried we'd moved out of the farmhouse altogether by the time August came around."

Megan laughed. "She started insisting we turn up at the house for breakfast and our other main meals. God, we were feral that summer."

I smiled, remembering the pool we built out of stones in

the river on their land so we could have somewhere to swim. With Megan's dad helping out initially, we learned to use a camping stove, though he banned us from having a campfire. I couldn't blame him. I had just turned eleven, and Megan wasn't yet nine. Her older brothers had made a nuisance a few times, but they were easily bored with our company, being teenagers already. I doubted we spent the whole summer in the tent, but that's how it felt at the time and in my memory. The boy who'd lost his mother found a little piece of his childhood returned to him in the company of his determined cousin.

We reminisced for a while as we listened to the camp settling down for sleep. It didn't take long, everyone familiar with their routines after a long day outside in the sun.

Megan rolled over towards me and whispered, "Interesting dynamics among the people here."

"I think that Eloise is a problem."

"She won't do anything herself. She's the sort to wind them up, give them an idea and convince them it's their own."

"That's what worries me."

"And the boy."

"Yes, and the boy. He's obviously special to them, but—"

"There's something more to him?" she asked.

I grunted in acknowledgement. "Did you find anything out about the dead woman?"

"Loads," Megan whispered. "I don't want to be overheard, though, so we'll save it for tomorrow."

"Good plan."

"Night, Griff."

"Night, Meg."

She rolled over to her other side, and I heard her take a deep breath. I lay awake, listening to the world outside our tent, and wondering when I'd detect a problem.

It didn't take long.

## Chapter Twelve

I dozed rather than slept, so when the furtive sounds of movement began, I woke. It was the whispers and the occasional curse I caught as several people tried to move around the crowded campsite without tripping over ropes and gear.

Glancing at Megan, I knew it hadn't disturbed her, but I'd need her help. Leaning over, I slowly covered her mouth, then nudged her shoulder. She woke with a start, but the dark prevented me from seeing her eyes.

I hissed into her ear. "I hear something. No speaking. Get dressed. Follow me."

She nodded into my palm, and I let her go.

Slowly, so I wouldn't make much sound, I unzipped the tent and wriggled out. Pulling on my boots, I also shrugged on my bike jacket. In my daysack, I had a torch, but I didn't switch it on. The night was dark, but cloudless, and we had just enough light to see the ground if we didn't look at it directly. One more thing came out of the bag, two asps and a can of pepper spray. I heard Megan dressing in silence, and when she appeared just seconds later, I handed her an asp and the spray. She nodded her thanks and stuffed them in different pockets.

Together, we followed the sound of the people moving. They headed towards the field's gate. Special Forces trained, they were not.

I didn't want Megan and me to present a clear bulk of black against the horizon, so I went right. She went left after I gave her a signal. Quietly, because we were trained, we followed the group of five individuals down to the gate. They exited, turning right. This meant they were heading in the direction of the golf course's new entrance.

Megan jogged to my side, and we crouched in the shadows of the old wall and hedge, watching the group go up the road. They weren't interested in maintaining discipline and silence.

A soft voice breathed in my ear, making me shudder. "What are we doing? Following? Do you think they're the killers?"

"Just wait," I whispered. This didn't feel like an abduction and murder. I had my money on something very different.

The group rounded the bend, and we ran up behind them, then moved slowly as we came around the corner. Once more in the thicker shadows, we stayed close to the ground and continued to watch and listen.

The group now stood in front of the security gates protecting the site. These are open during the day, with just the barrier there for the guards to check as deliveries and visitors arrived.

I recognised Mitch, and one of the others who'd been watching me during the day. Another figure looked to be a woman, she was much smaller than the others. The two strangers to me were a mismatched pair. One bulky bastard with a shaved head, the other a skinny lad with long lanky hair.

The security gates were no joke for the site. They were corrugated sheet metal, with electronic locks securing the two halves. I wondered if they had dogs patrolling the site, but I guessed these guys had done at least some nighttime surveillance. The group crowded around the lock, and much to my dismay, I heard the beep, beep, beep of a code going in. It wasn't familiar to the user because it took time for them to key it in and a constant reference to a text or something on a phone, but it was correct. The gate released.

"We need to get in there," I whispered. "Get ready to run, then hide."

Megan stared at me in shock. "The last time we tried this, we almost died."

"Yeah, but we didn't die, did we?" I watched the group slip through the gate as it continued to roll back on its electronic mission. The moment the area cleared of hostiles, I raced forwards with Megan on my heels. At the edge of the entrance, I did a quick peek and saw the group running towards the old farmhouse we'd seen a few days before. They weren't protecting their backs.

As the gate started to rumble closed, I grabbed Megan's wrist and, at the last moment, slipped inside. We both remained still and in the shadows.

On the site, there were security lights going all night, so the trespassers were easy to spot.

We heard their conversation, despite their attempts at being muted.

Voice One said, "The message this'll send is a worthy one."

Voice Two said, "It's the only message they understand. It worked for the IRA, so it'll work for us."

Megan cursed. It made my stomach plunge. Invoking the name of the Irish Republican Army filled every British serviceman and woman with dread.

The woman in the group said, "The timer is set to go off in an hour. We need to be clear of the area. I've designed the explosion to rip through the metal of the gas canisters on the site. That should set up secondary explosions that'll wipe out several of the earthmovers and destroy the farmhouse. It'll take the fire brigade too long to get here, so the prefab buildings will go up as well."

Voice Three said, "They'll know it's the protesters."

Voice Four now joined in. "I think we use the guns on the first responders. Get the job done properly." He had a thick Scottish accent.

"Fuck," Megan whispered. "I need to call this in."

"It'll take forever for them to get armed response down here and the bomb squad," I hissed back. "Go, get out of earshot of this bag of dicks, and I'll follow them. If I can stop them, I will."

"Griffin, there's a bomb, and no one here to help if you get hurt. Just let them do what they want. We'll warn the others coming in." To say she'd reached the end of her tolerance for my stupidity was an understatement. She looked like she wanted to grab me by the ear and drag me out of the area.

"And if that bomb goes off when your mates are swarming over the place looking for it? Or worse, there's a remote detonator on the damned thing? At the very least, I need to see where it's going."

Megan's expression was one of helplessness. She knew I was right. I had to follow, stop them if possible. Her reluctant nod of agreement gave me the green light to move.

The familiar hum of action rippled through me, and the switch flipped. I ran into the night.

Taking a different route to the group of would-be saboteurs, I raced along behind the reaching security lights and their puddles. The ground was hard underfoot, devoid of grass, and covered in the worn, smashed ripples caused by the diggers. It proved easy going, and I soon arrived at the farmhouse long before the others. Taking a knee behind the neatly parked earthmover, I watched the saboteurs arrive. The huge shovel on the front of the machine hid me well, and the jokers I hunted were completely unaware of my presence.

Voice Two said, "You sure you built it right?" He sounded nervous. I didn't blame him. More than one bomber had blown themselves up, and often along with everyone else in on the conspiracy.

"Fuck's sake, what'd you think?" snapped the woman. "I've been taught well enough, and it's a simple device."

Which gave me some hope of stopping this madness. I was more worried about the mention of guns. Voice Four must hold one of them. Were they all armed?

That voice, Number Four, came up with another plan. "We could set up a kill box at the gate. We have enough ammo."

*A computer trained wannabe? Or the real deal? What d'ya think?*

It was hard to tell at this point. He used some of the familiar lingo of the more extreme men I'd worked with, but as they used the same language in games and films, I'd have to see them in action to know if they were trained. Apparently, using this language made the games more realistic, but I'd rarely experienced a game that could replicate the real horror of a live fire event and people dying around you—because of you.

"And do you know how to set up a kill box?" asked Voice Three with clear contempt.

I watched him in particular. Quiet, more aware of his surroundings, with his head on a near constant pivot, and a set of shoulders that rivalled the machine I used for hiding.

Voice Four bounced on his feet. "Yeah, I've set up plenty—"

"World of Warcraft doesn't count."

Well, that answered that question. Four was a wanker.

"What's your big idea?" Four snapped back.

Three and Mitch shared a long look. "Keep it simple. We plant the explosive and leave. We can use the firearms if they attack the camp. It'll be our opportunity to escape."

*And a great way to kill women and children, you fucker.*

I needed to break up this happy little nest of vipers. It was the only way I'd take them down alone. First, I had to see where they put the damned explosive. They moved away from the circle of light and further towards the old farmhouse. I kept to the shadows and tracked them, silent behind the smelly vehicles. Old oil and diesel reminded me of the ships I'd served on, and the aircraft they'd used to move us around. It added to my readiness for action, and I had to take a moment to calm myself. I couldn't afford to be slap-happy in my approach. Only a rational attack would accomplish this task.

The woman strode towards the large tanks of various gases. They were all stored in safety cages, but that wouldn't help if someone stuck a bomb on the top or the sides. I guessed we'd have a volatile mix of oxygen for welding, methane and propane for other jobs like heating the porta-cabins. If they went up, the explosion would be far larger than they thought. She swung the bag she carried on her back around and dropped it to the ground. It looked heavy, and I winced, expecting my life to flash out in a second. I'd have treated an IED with far more respect. I'd had training with claymore mines, but I'd never had to use them in combat. Sadly, I'd seen more than one IED go boom.

The improvised explosive device was at least lifted out of the bag with care. The bomb maker and Mitch then strapped it to the tank cage with heavy duty zip-ties. In the darkness, I couldn't see it clearly, but it had the general look of a suicide vest's contents. A sudden flashback to that horrible walk along the stony beach outside Lynmouth on Exmoor ripped through my mind.

The memory made my palms sweat and my heart kicked up a notch. When a sound behind me alerted me to another's presence, I almost lashed out blindly.

Megan saw something in my face and backed up, holding her hands out in supplication.

I bowed my head and took a few deep breaths.

She approached. "You okay?" she whispered.

"Yeah, I just… I've never told you. I will. Let's just… We need to get this done. The explosive device is strapped to the gas tank cage."

"Nice. That'll make a mess."

The group of saboteurs were arguing among themselves again about the timer on the bomb and the possibility of remote detonation.

"Roger that. I need to separate them so I can hunt them down. Some of them at least have firearms, possibly all of them."

Megan nodded, understanding instantly what we needed to do. "We need to split them up."

I felt a surge of pride at her intuitive approach matching mine. "Go around the back of the farmhouse, make a noise. The moment I hear it, I'll do the same here. Then, I want you to run. Please, Megan, don't do anything else. Get back to the road, wait for your colleagues. I'll do what I can to disarm as many of these pricks as possible. Warn the first responders that I'm in here."

"Griffin," she only murmured my name, but it was enough to let me know she didn't approve of the plan.

"It's the only way. We have to keep them separate from the camp across the road."

She shook her head. "You're a magnet for trouble, Griffin Woodbury. Just stay alive, okay? Mum'll be really pissed off with me if you get killed." Before I could reply, she leaned close, gave me the briefest of kisses on my cheek, then raced off into the night. I watched her go before returning my attention to the collective group of idiots I'd be hunting.

Voices Three and Four were getting into a rumble about the kill box idea, and it was becoming feisty. With some luck, one of them might kill the other. I removed my asp from my pocket and pulled the batten to its full length, feeling it click to lock solid, rather than have it snap loudly in the darkness.

Some pushing and shoving began, with Voice Two and Mitch getting involved. The woman cursed them for fools and pointed out that it might be wise to leave the area of the explosion.

That's when a low rumble started from the back of the farmhouse.

"For fuck's sake, Megan," I cursed. Now was not the time for my police liaison to go all Special Forces on me. Although she was a farmer's daughter and what she didn't know about driving heavy vehicles around in fields could fit on the back of a stamp. She must've found a set of keys in something large and noisy back there. The machine's engine splintered the quiet of the night, and the group of saboteurs instantly stopped their arguments.

I started to bang on the side of my protective earth-mover with the asp, setting off a cacophony of sound. The group panicked. I heard a large piece of machinery begin to rumble towards us, but it wouldn't move fast enough to stop this lot running for the camp. Therefore, I sprinted into the light.

"Oi, fuckwits," I called out. "You've gotta problem." I gave them a saucy wave, turned and dashed back to the cover of night.

I heard raised voices over the sound of the machine as I headed towards the treeline and deeper shadows. Several shots rang out behind me, but they weren't even close, and it set off another argument. At least two of the men came after me. The large engine Megan drove changed tempo as she reached for maximum speed in the hulking vehicle. I should've gone with her, it would've been more fun.

A dozen tree trunks lay forlornly on their sides at the edge of the wood, waiting to be carted off, and a pile of their branches looked ready for a bonfire. It was a sad sight. Even as I dived behind them in the darkness, I could see the weird shapes of the lichen and moss on their ancient trunks. The things we do for progress.

*Focus, fool.*

I did. With one knee in the dirt, I readied myself for action. It wasn't one man that came after me, but three. Good times.

They rounded the corner of the tree trunks, and I pushed up from the ground towards the nearest body. With my asp smacking down on the arm holding a weapon, then flicking back into his face, Voice Four didn't stand a chance. I heard teeth shatter, and his forearm hung at a strange angle. Blood splattered my face. With a howl of pain, he collapsed. I'd smacked him hard enough to break bones.

The other two fools paused. Without taking my eyes off them, I bent and picked up the dropped weapon. Voice Four moaned and wept. I hoofed a boot into his hip. Killing him wouldn't help me at this point.

"Shut the fuck up." In my hand, I held an old Browning Hi-Power pistol. Until recently, the standard sidearm of the British military for decades. I had no doubt this would've come from the IRA, or some iteration of it.

The smallest and slimmest, also the quietest of the saboteurs, stood with eyes wide. He looked ready to bolt.

Voice Three sneered. "What the fuck do you think—" In the dark, I'd kept track of the voices, not the faces. That meant Megan was dealing with Mitch and the woman.

I shot at the ground between Voice Three's legs. "Put your weapons down. Back away, then get to your knees, hands laced behind your head." The barrel of the Browning didn't waver.

Shouting began to drift our way over the rumble of Megan's diesel engine. I needed to end this quickly.

"You think that scares me?" snarled Voice Three.

I sighed and shot him in the leg. Voice Two dropped to the ground with his face pressed to the dirt. His tears were almost as loud as the screaming from his mate. Keeping the firearm close to my chest, I approached Voice Two and nudged him with my foot.

"You armed?" I asked.

He whimpered.

"Get up, I need your help." I nudged again with a bit more force.

The man, if you could call him that, had the patchy

beard of a youth, his hair long, lank and thinning already at the front. Poor sod looked ready to have a breakdown.

"Please don't hurt me. I just wanna save the trees, man," he pleaded, actually putting his hands together.

"Pull yourself together. Do you have any weapons?" I sighted the Browning at his face, making it clear what I'd do if he buggered me about. Not that I had planned on shooting the kid in the face, but he didn't need to know that.

The kid emptied his pockets, hands shaking so much he barely managed it. Voice Three was making far too much noise. It annoyed me.

Trying to block out the demands for help, and the fact the man thought he was bleeding to death—he wasn't, I'd winged him at worst—I kept my focus on the youngest of the group.

"What other weapons do they have?" I asked. "Don't worry about what they think. They're going to prison. I want to save you from that, so help me to accomplish this act of kindness on my part."

The kid's eyes widened, and he nodded. "There's another gun and some knives."

"Search them," I ordered, with a slight wave of the barrel. Backing off, I returned to where I'd dropped my asp, and without taking my eyes off the Three Stooges, I retrieved it. Using the nearest log, I smacked it hard, unlocking the mechanism, and allowed it to reel in, before putting it back in my pocket. While I did this, the boy rummaged in his mates' pockets while they cursed him, nursed their wounds and swore at me.

"What's your name?" I asked him after Voice Two threatened to kill the lad's family.

"Todd, sir," he managed to whimper.

"Don't listen to them, Todd. I'll keep you and your family safe."

Voice Two found his bollocks and said through his broken nose, "You can't just shoot people. Even undercover. It's illegal."

I stamped on his ankle. "I'm not police. I'm far worse."

After he stopped screaming about my size twelve's making a mess of his ankle, he accused me of being a spy for MI5. I wasn't going to argue. It was close enough. From the distance, I heard Megan warning people to back down. It worried me.

"Todd, we need to move this along. I want you to start running away, far, far away. Go home and thank all that you hold dear that I let you go. Never, ever, let anyone talk you into doing something this fucking stupid again. Get a degree and get a job that'll let you make changes to the world from the inside." I waved the barrel of the Browning. "Go on, off you fuck."

The lad scrambled to his feet and, with effusive thanks through snot and tears, ran off into the night. Voice Two and Three stared at me. Oh, the temptation to just end this now. Among the debris the boy had pulled out of their pockets were more zip-ties, doubtless meant for the bomb. Happy days, it would save me the paperwork I had to fill in every time I killed someone for DoPI. I tied their wrists together and left them.

# Chapter Thirteen

I ran in the direction of Megan's voice.

It turned out I didn't need to worry too much. Sergeant Ackley had both would be saboteurs on the ground, her pepper spray in one hand, her asp in the other. She'd 'borrowed' a huge digger and parked it right in front of the metal gates, having smashed through the barrier we'd stopped at just a few days before. The bucket of the machine rested off the ground.

"All good?" I asked, jogging to her side. We both heard the distant sound of the emergency services.

"Yeah, I chased them down with the digger. Mitch fell over, which gave me the opportunity I needed."

"I've more zip-ties." I waggled them about. Both Mitch and the woman were crying and cursing from the pepper spray, which obviously meant they couldn't see clearly. Other than that, they were doing better between them than their colleagues. "Have you searched them?"

"Not yet." Her full attention remained on the prisoners.

I moved in and performed a full pat down. Both Mitch

and the woman carried firearms. They'd not been used against the huge digger Megan drove. I wasn't surprised. Amateurs. I searched the woman's bag and found written instructions for the homemade explosive. I also found a burner phone. After zip-tying their wrists and leaving them on the ground, I returned to Megan's side. She visibly relaxed.

"What's that?" she asked, nodding at the paperwork.

"They printed out the instructions for the bomb."

After the surge of adrenaline all this caused, we both laughed. With a bit of luck, if the police could find the computer attached to the printer that did this, they might be able to track back to the source of her intel.

Megan suddenly walked off, bent over and vomited onto the ground. I approached and rubbed her back as she continued to bring up bile.

"Sorry," she managed to gasp.

"Don't be. It was a scary situation. I've done pretty heavy damage to two of them. The last one was hardly more than a kid, unarmed."

Megan eyed me. "You let him go?"

"I let him run. Whether he manages to keep his freedom is another thing entirely. At least some of their antics have been caught on CCTV." I pointed to the track. One of the arc lights held a camera as well.

"Amateurs," Megan mumbled, wiping her mouth.

I handed her the bottle of blessed water I tended to carry around for emergencies of the DoPI kind. She nodded gratefully.

The sirens were closing in fast. "I'm going to have a look at the explosive. I have the phone, which might be the remote detonator."

"Leave it to the experts, Griff. We've done enough

tonight. I'm not watching you get blown up on home soil. It's been bad enough thinking of you out there in the deserts of the world."

"It's my job, Megan."

She snatched the rucksack out of my hands. "No, it isn't. You hunt supernatural nasties. You don't defuse bombs. Leave it the fuck alone, and that's an order. On UK soil, I outrank you." Her expression had become so serious, I didn't feel like I could argue with her. Even in the dim lighting from the digger's dusty headlamps, I saw her pain at my plan.

"Okay, no defusing homemade bombs," I agreed, admitting silently to myself that I was grateful for her intervention. Who wanted the often fatal decision: do I cut the red wire or the blue one? Just on the law of averages, you'd have to be wrong fifty percent of the time. "In that case, I'd better go and check on the other two. One of them has a broken arm. The other has a hole in his leg."

"Jesus, Griffin, did you have to shoot him?"

"I didn't kill them. Be grateful."

"What about DoPI? Are you—"

I shook my head. "No, I'm not bringing them in on this. It's not supernatural."

The sirens were very close now. Megan left me to move the digger, and I made Mitch tell me the code to the gate. I picked him up and moved him to the side of the track.

"You're a fucking scab. I bloody knew it." If the hatred in his voice could burn me, I'd be cremated by now.

I crouched down to look him in the eye. Or I tried to, they were so swollen from the spray, he kept them closed. My sadness at his actions made me say, "You've threatened the very existence of that group of good people through your actions."

He spat at me, but it proved ineffectual. "If we don't take direct action, the world will burn. This is the only thing anyone understands. Violence is the only language they know."

"Who? The poor bastards who work here? They might've died—"

"Collateral damage. Isn't that what your lot call it when innocent people suffer during war?"

I rose and left him blinking painfully. He had a point. Suddenly feeling very tired, I walked back to my prisoners.

The hours until dawn, well into the day, and then on into the evening went slowly. Endless rounds of explanations, checking of my authority—thank you, Sanchez, for bailing me out of trouble again—and waiting around for bomb disposal. They came from my old stomping ground in the end, Bickley Barracks. I kept out of the way, but I didn't recognise anyone, and that suited me just fine.

Some of the protesters turned up, and I managed to convince them to return to the site. The foreman, Steve Denzel, arrived early. The police rang him, and he almost burst into tears when he realised firearms and bombs were involved. He was a good bloke, and Megan helped him deal with the employees, who also arrived for work, unaware of the situation. I wondered if he'd resign, though I hoped not, the site needed him as a manager. He was instrumental in maintaining the peace with the protest group.

Inevitably, they were raided by the police. It wasn't pretty. There wasn't much we could do to stop it, and after the antics with the explosives and illegal weapons, having the authorities involved wasn't all bad. They weren't impressed with Megan and me, but again, we'd saved lives and further arrests. If that bomb had gone off, the consequences for their protest would've been devastating. Without involving the courts, the police couldn't force people off the site, so for now the camp was safe. Of course, all this meant we didn't move any further forward with the investigation.

My attempts to rationalise our infiltration of the protest camp just infuriated those we'd met initially. The woman, Leaze, looked like she wanted to spit roast me over a volcano. I'd never seen such an angry vegan in all my days. Still, I managed to leave a card, if not with her, then in her general area. I tried to tell her and the others to stay away from the wood, but they weren't going to listen to me in a hurry. I tried to find the woman I'd helped make banners with, River, but she'd vanished. When I made enquiries, it turned out no one had seen her since the bonfire and singsong. At some point during Eloise's pitch for humanity being bad for the planet, she'd gone. Her van remained at the site, though, which struck me as odd. People were worried, especially after Jennifer's death, but wouldn't talk to the police. I had hoped River would be more sensible than Leaze, and I'd convince her, as an experience traveller and protester, that people needed to stay away from the woodland. Especially at night. They'd all become convinced, during the long and harrowing day, that Jennifer's death was nothing more than the Security Service picking an easy target to dismantle their rightful protest. They saw it as an opportunity to once more change the legislation against freedom of speech.

River's disappearance worried me a great deal. This wasn't over. Not by a long way, and I wanted to know, before anyone else, the next time something bad happened.

Many of them had recorded the raid on their phones, and again, TikTok girl caught my attention. She seemed to be here alone but was so damned young. What was her story? I'd have to dig into it at some point, but not today.

By the time I extracted Quacker from the other vehicles cluttering up the narrow lane, and Megan climbed on the back with our tent and sleeping bags strapped on behind her, we were both exhausted. Twilight once more beckoned, and I had a sore throat from all the talking I'd done during the long day. Riding home took a while. Megan leaned into my back, and I swear she nodded off with her arms around me.

When we reached Redruth, I stroked her leg. "Hey," I said, slowing down so we could speak comfortably. "Your flat or my house?"

"I've no milk in," she muttered.

I chuckled. "Spare room it is, then." It felt right, taking her home. The last two days had brought us closer together than ever, and I wasn't ready to let go.

During the long hours we'd been waiting around for different sets of authorities to yell at us, I'd been calling Sid. When I pulled up on the bike, he opened the door. Megan climbed off the back and slumped into the house. I followed.

"Food?" I asked.

"There's a cold-roasted chicken and salad with cold potatoes, bro." He held my shoulder, keeping me still for a moment in the doorway. "You alright?"

I nodded. "Very, very long day. Lots to share, but I think we need to eat first."

Megan appeared in the hallway, gnawing at a slice of chicken. "Sid, can I marry you?"

Sid laughed. "No, but I'm happy enough to keep you fed."

She stared at me. "Marry him. I want him in the family so he can't escape." With that, she returned to the kitchen.

I smiled, watching her go. We were both filthy, tired,

hungry and mentally overwhelmed, but we still needed to put in our official reports and confer with the team about our findings and events. I heard Luce in the kitchen.

Sid took my daysack and tent off me, and I trudged in to find Megan stuffing her face.

"You couldn't have washed first?" I asked her.

"Leave me alone," she growled, ripping into another chicken thigh. Looking at it, she said, "You died in a good cause, don't feel bad."

I managed to wash my hands and face at the kitchen sink, then got stuck into the scran. Luce and Sid just watched us with some bemusement, before Sid grew bored. It didn't take long.

"Come on then, tell me what happened? What do we know about the site and the people? Did they kill Jennifer Mancore?"

Megan paused in her one-woman mission to demolish all the food. "I found her protest family." Her eyes widened for a moment. "Wow, that feels like last week." She blinked heavily and continued, "Here's what I know, and some of it we already discovered. Recently divorced. Daughter in Oz with grandchildren. Jennifer wanted to become the woman she thought she'd missed out on by marrying so young. Her career stalled when she had to look after her husband's mother at home, despite her daughter leaving forever as soon as she went to uni. So, Jennifer didn't have much of a life. By the time she reached retirement age, she'd had enough of cleaning up after hubby and just walked out. She took enough money from their savings to buy a large van already prepared as a home, gained her heavy goods vehicle licence, and she's been moving from one protest site to another ever since. Until she bought the cottage in Cornwall from the proceeds of her final divorce settlement."

"Any enemies in the camp?" I asked around a mouthful of spud.

Megan shook her head. "No, everyone seemed to like her. A few found her too posh, but others said she just sounded posh. She always mucked in with the grim jobs. Even helped a few people out with their finances and the paperwork when they'd been arrested. She believed in her cause. The planet was more important to her than anything except her grandchildren, which is why she became an activist in the first place. Apparently, her mother used to protest at Greenham Common, if you remember that, back in the eighties."

"There has to be something," I mumbled.

"If there is, I didn't find it. No smoking gun, Griffin. Her closest friend, Aggie, said Jennifer just went for a walk. She wanted to spend some time hugging trees during a beautiful night on Beltane's Eve. Probably in what the Anwen's Children people think is an ancient druidic circle of trees in the centre of the wood, near the spring."

I pointed a fork at her. "That could be something, right?" I looked at Luce.

She shrugged. "Maybe. Though, it's unlikely to be the remains of an original druidic circle. It would have to pre-date the Romans and survive Christianity. This area of Cornwall was trading with the Romans long before their invasion. There aren't any Roman towns this far down, but there are settlements at Chysauster Ancient Village. It's a well-preserved Romano-British settlement, and Carn Euny, which is nearby. Kinda. That would make the trees more than two-thousand years old. Which they aren't."

"What's this circle thing anyway?" Megan asked. "I wanted to know when they mentioned it, but didn't think it prudent to ask, as I was supposed to be an eco-warrior for the day."

Luce leaned back in her chair and stared at the ceiling, gathering her thoughts. "Well, not all ceremonial spaces for pre-Christian worship were stone henges or other megalithic sites. Some of them were woodhenges. In fact, they've discovered that Stonehenge and the Avebury circle also had layers of wood in their construction. There are many examples throughout the British Isles, but due to their very nature, we only have scant remains. What these Anwen's Children are talking about is something different. Druids worshipped in treelined groves. We know this from the written Roman records. I won't go into the propaganda the Romans used to turn the druids into savages, but it was bad. These groves contained a specific set of trees, like oak, ash, yew, and the rest. What we *might* have in this woodland is the offspring of these original trees."

"What kind of ceremonies?" Megan asked.

Luce shrugged. "Hard to say. We really don't have any written records. The druids were an oral faith, so nothing survived the Roman death squads that killed most of them on Anglesey. We believe it would've been similar to some of the ceremonies we know about from the Norse faith. Ancestor worship, appeasement to the deities that control fertility, war, that kind of thing. I'm not sure if this speculation will lead us anywhere."

I put my fork down long enough to say, "It's useful. What will modern worship look like?"

Luce picked at the rocket leaves left on her plate. "That depends on the type of druid. Some of them are full-on, with robes and a hierarchy. These types of groups go back to the 18th or even the 17th century and were more like the

Masons than a true religious order. Then Iolo Morganwg created a more music and worship based version in Wales. That's the more familiar aspect most of us know. These days there are countless small druidic groups, or covens, and many that practice alone. It's a faith, even more than Wicca, that strives to communicate with the planet. To understand but never dominate nature." She considered a bit more, then added, "It's a nature worship faith. I can't imagine a druid ever killing anyone."

"Not even in a wicker man?" muttered Sid, with a raised eyebrow.

Luce huffed but played along. "That's Roman propaganda, Sid."

I watched her begin to organise her remaining pieces of salad into a straight line across the centre of her plate. Then she carefully rearranged them into size and put them in a circle. Her brow furrowed, and she started again. Sid laid a hand on her wrist and brought it to stillness.

Luce glanced at him and then away. "Sorry," she murmured.

"It's okay. Tell us what's bothering you." He spoke low and evenly.

Finally, I realised something about Lucinda Carmichael. She wasn't cold or highly strung; her level of commitment and focus to her work hid wherever she was on the spectrum. I'd met men in the Marines like this, highly motivated individuals who followed orders like they were the word of God, and the grunts were Moses. But outside their area of expertise or in the field where things were often unpredictable, life often became complicated for them. Not all autism left you unable to cope with high-pressure jobs. You just had to find a way to function within your speciality.

Luce had found her place in academia, among myths and legends.

Megan and I shared a look. We'd obviously recognised the same thing. Shame on us for not realising sooner and taking more care.

"You can tell us, Luce. We're the last people in the world to judge," I said.

Her eyes flicked to mine, then returned to the circle on her plate. "There is something I'm not seeing. A connection that doesn't make sense." She shook her head. "The ivy and the ash stake are about protection, but someone killed a protector of the site." Her gaze met mine and held. "That doesn't make sense. Right?"

"No, Luce, it doesn't." A wave of exhaustion washed over me, the food kicking in and ordering my body to rest. I yawned, and Megan caught the bug.

"We need to clean up and sleep," she said. "I'm borrowing your sofa."

"No." Sid rose. "We tidied up the spare room. It's yours. You can use the downstairs bathroom or Griffin's shower room. Griffin wanted to make sure you had somewhere nice to crash the next time you needed to sleep over. It's all made up."

Megan looked at me. "You did that for me?"

The last time she'd stayed, the room had been Sid's dumping ground while he was still unpacking. During the last few weeks, I'd tidied it up, bought some good bedding, and made it comfortable. We didn't need a home office, as we both worked all over the house, so I opted for a proper spare bedroom. I wanted Megan to feel like she could be here any time she needed it.

In answer to her question, I just shrugged, like it wasn't a bother, but I felt the heat gathering in my cheeks. Megan just smiled, rose, squeezed my shoulder and murmured, "I'll steal your shower."

I watched her walk away. "I'll wash up." Meeting Sid's amused gaze wouldn't help my blushes.

Blushes? Seriously, I was a Royal Marine Commando, and I blushed. Hopeless. I was hopeless.

# Chapter Fourteen

The phone rang, slicing through the darkness of my deep sleep and dragging me out into the world. I fumbled about, my fingers feeling like sausages.

"Wha?" I asked.

"Is that Griffin?"

"Huh, hoo is dis?" I rolled onto my back and tried to blink away the soporific brain fog I'd been enjoying.

"Griffin, this is Leaze from the camp. Remember, you gave me your card yesterday when…"

My brain cleared instantly, and I sat up in bed. "What's wrong?"

Her voice sounded very small and quiet. "I think… I think something bad has happened, and I don't… I don't want to call the police. But… I think we need help. I'm really scared. It's River…"

"Are you at the camp? Are you safe?" I was already out of bed and moving towards the spare room.

"I'm safe. I'm in my van."

"Okay, stay there. We're on our way. We'll be thirty minutes. Do we come to your van?"

"I'll meet you in the lane."

"Only if it's safe, Leaze. Promise me. You'll only leave your van if it's safe. We can come to find you." I knocked on Megan's door.

Visions of River helping the children make the banners flashed through my mind. Fuck! I should've stayed and looked for her. Bloody Mitch and his cronies distracted me from the mission. I'm a DoPI operative, I don't get involved in mundane domestic terrorism. They had to be wrong, it couldn't be her. Please, don't let it be her.

"Okay, maybe the van is best." There were tears in her voice. "What's happening to us?"

"I don't know, but I'll figure it out. Talk soon." I ended the call and knocked again on the door. "Megan? I need you up."

Something resembling a few choice swear words floated out of the room. "What?" came more clearly.

I opened the door. Megan, sleep rumpled, sat up wearing one of my band t-shirts. It never looked that cute on me. "We've a problem at the protesters' camp. Leaze just rang me."

"What, the harpy that you tried to talk to yesterday, and she threw your business card back in your face?" Megan asked, blinking.

I chuckled. "Yeah, that one."

"Shit… it must be serious."

"She sounds scared. Five minutes?"

Megan nodded, already pulling on her filthy clothes from the previous day. I headed to Sid's room, then hesitated. Right now, there was nothing he could do to help. I'd leave a message for him. Opening the app, I started talking even as I pulled on more clothing. I heard Megan moving downstairs, and I followed. We both slugged back some water, grabbed some energy bars, and headed for the bike.

Dawn pressed hard against the night, shoving it back, demanding the right to dominate the sky with her pink dipped fingers. With the rising sun at our backs, we rode hard into the remaining darkness. The roads were quiet, very few people seeking out the new day. The birds, though, were mightily impressed with the clear skies. As we slowed to take the narrow lanes safely, their riotous noise overwhelmed the rumble of my engine. Driving past the entrance to the building site, I saw the white and blue police tape flapping about in the morning breeze. Approaching the camp, the sun's brutal assault on the night won, and it shoved the last of the darkness away into the west. In the distance, just outside the gate, I saw a small group of people huddled together. I slowed down.

"This isn't going to be good," Megan murmured from behind me.

"No. I don't think it is." A sickening feeling in my gut set up an ache in my chest. That familiar friend called dread rose into my throat.

We rolled to a stop and dismounted. Megan approached the huddle of people, who spread out in the lane. Leaze and Denny were there. Mitch had gone with the police the day before. I recognised all their faces and knew a few names. The Jennifer's friend, Aggie, stood next to Leaze and Denny.

"What's happened?" Megan asked in fully police sergeant mode.

Leaze and Aggie shared a look. The others shifted uncomfortably behind them.

Aggie shared their news. "We've found a dead woman."

Her hand went to her mouth as if she couldn't believe the words tumbling out.

Megan glanced at me.

The pair of us said, "Show me."

Everyone moved. Megan held up a hand. "No, wait, just Leaze and Aggie, please. The rest of you return to your homes. It's important we maintain calm and the integrity of the scene."

"We gonna get raided again?" asked one of the younger men in the group.

Megan sighed. I opted to field that one. "I very much doubt that'll be necessary. And we really are sorry about yesterday. None of us wanted that to happen. It was horrible and scary and not your fault. We really are here to help."

Leaze looked over the group. "Remember what Eloise said last night. We are non-violent. What Mitch and the others did was wrong, very wrong. We all paid the price for their actions, but it's just a setback. We have a moral responsibility to do the right thing. It's what…" her voice broke and she hiccupped her grief. "It's what Jennifer and River would've wanted."

Oh, God, no. The weight of failure settled on my shoulders. Rather than sacrifice my time and my bed to look for River, I'd gone home. Eaten like a king and slept like a drugged log.

As the group broke up, there were some grumbles from the younger people—TikTok girl included, though she was phoneless for the moment—but they returned to the field.

"Where is the body?" Megan asked. "Who found it? And when?" She pulled at the pocket of her jacket and removed a police issue notebook and pen.

"I heard something," Aggie said, her thick accent

marking her as being 'up-north', but where I didn't know yet. "After yesterday and what happened to Jennifer, I wasn't sure I could stay."

Aggie had neatly cut short, brown, fine hair. She wore thick lenses in her plastic glasses that made her hazel eyes larger than reality would allow. Her nose dominated the round cheeks, and her mouth had thin lips, but by the looks of the creases, she smiled more than she frowned. I guessed her to be about thirty.

Megan focused on her. "Okay, Aggie, tell me what happened next."

"I couldn't sleep, like. It's been rough since losing Jennifer, and I just wanted to feel the wood, the holy well, so I thought I'd walk down to the path and see if I could go near the cloutie tree. I wanted to offer a token for my friend. She was good to me." Aggie held out a strip of cloth. "This came from a shirt she gave me."

"That's a kind thought, Aggie," Megan said with a gentle smile.

I appreciated her reasons for taking this slowly, but I needed to get to the damned point. Shifting restlessly, Megan glanced at me and gave a small nod.

"Is that where you found the body? Down by the path?"

Aggie nodded, and tears pearled on her rounded cheeks. "I found her near the entrance. She's still hanging there." The last began on a wail, and Aggie burst into tears.

With that news, I left the women and strode down the remainder of the lane. At the entrance to the footpath, I saw it.

"Oh, fuck…" I murmured. Some desperate part of me wanted to be wrong. Wanted Aggie to be wrong. For the world not to be like this.

A woman's body hung from an oak tree just coming into

full bloom. The trunk rose thick and strong, the lower branches reached out to cover the path's entrance and the lane. The clothes marked her as someone from the camp, and as the breeze nudged her around, I saw her face.

With a hanging, it's often hard to see the features of someone you don't know well, but this woman I recognised. It was River. Images tumbled through my head. The squeals of laughter from the small children as she chased them, paint brushes in hand. The little ones putting their feet and hands in the paint and then on the cardboard, the words written by me, begging for their future. She'd spent most of the time laughing and chattering with the children, her tangle of long black hair pulled into a loose tail and her silver jewellery dancing in the sunlight. She'd told me she'd just returned from India, having worked at a school over there for almost two years.

"Oh, River, I'm so sorry."

Around her throat hung a necklace of ivy, more of which tied her to the tree. A large hunk of shaped wood stuck out of her chest, red staining her deep green dungarees. One of her boots was missing. The other hung, unlaced, at about my chest height. I wondered about cutting her down, but I couldn't do it with dignity, even with Megan's help, and we needed to preserve the scene.

It brought tears to my eyes seeing her there, and I turned away. Megan walked towards me, with the other two women remaining in earshot, but at a distance from the body. I saw Aggie weeping and Leaze trying to comfort her.

"Jesus, Griffin, this is awful," Megan whispered. "Is that—?"

"Yes. River. The woman I helped with making the banners. She went missing during Eloise's speech the other night."

"Why her? What the hell is going on?" Megan whispered.

"Call it in. Get SOCO down here."

Megan, giving the body one last long look, turned, and pulled out her phone. I ignored her and approached the footpath with great care. The tarmac of the lane petered out quickly, becoming road gravel, then good old Cornish mud. Even with the dry weather of the day before, the previous rainstorm had left this bit of the path thick and claggy. I searched the ground, keeping close to the greener verges. That's when I saw them. A cluster of those very strange footprints, the toes deeper in the wet soil than the heels. It looked like the toes were used to grip the ground. Was that so whatever did this could pull the woman up into the tree? These were larger than the last set I'd seen. Disturbingly larger. I glanced about. The trees lining the footpath at this point were only a single layer deep, only slightly more than a hedge, but that sense of human fear squirmed over me like I was in a bath full of dirty earth worms.

I took photos from several angles. Then from the same spot, I looked up at River. She didn't have the features of a woman who'd died from choking on a rope. No swollen tongue, bulging eyes, or blood infusion to the face making it distorted and bloated. I saw no obvious signs of her fingers having torn at her throat, trying to release the binding.

"Meg?" I called. "I think she died before the hanging. Same as Jennifer."

Megan approached but didn't look too closely at the dead woman. I had no doubt it affected her, to see someone she knew dead in such a gruesome way, but Megan battled to keep it professional. It took me a lot of effort to do the same thing. We'd both be haunted by this image for some time to come.

"Talk me through it," she said.

I pointed out the footprints, then River's features.

"You think she was killed like Jennifer?" Megan asked.

I nodded. "I expect so. It's the most likely explanation. There's a lot of blood on the ground, and other fluids from the body, but I can't see anything squirting. The hanging and the stake are ritual."

"Do you think they meant to hang Jennifer from the tree we found her under?"

"None of us looked up. Maybe she was hanging there, but the vines snapped?"

"Shit, we're going to have to go and look." She eyed the woodland's path. "I don't like it in there, Griff."

"Me neither," I said. "I'll call Sid. We need Luce to know about this." I took more photos, sharing them with the secure cloud server DoPI used. Then, Megan answered a call from her inspector, and I rang Sid.

"Hey, mate, you up?" I asked the moment the call went live.

"Yeah, what's up?"

I explained, feeling the pressure of this latest event building behind my chest wall. "You'll—"

"Yeah, of course, I'll get to it right away. Luce is here. I'll have her think about the consequences of this event."

I noticed he didn't call it a death.

"Cheers. I'll ring back a bit later. We need to start talking to people down here. Do some proper interviews. Call the foreman of the site." Poor Steve, he wouldn't want to know about this one.

The next few hours were terribly sad and harrowing for all involved. The fire department arrived, the only ones with the equipment necessary to cut River down safely. She was laid carefully on the ground as SOCOs moved in, wearing their white suits and masks. Megan and I gave statements to the police, Megan making sure they knew we had jurisdiction over the investigation. The grey areas of Rural Security made them wary of me and the procedures involved, but I told them everything would remain the same with regard to the evidence and witness statements, but I'd receive copies. The police would notify River's family. Their obvious respect for Megan's authority helped smooth the way.

One of the older police constables removed his cap at one point, his thinning grey hair shaved close to his scalp as he scratched the top of his head. "This is a right old mess, Meg, love."

"I know, Dink. I know."

"Well, I'm sure you'll figure it out. You always do." He smiled at her, the clotted-cream thickness of his accent marking him a real local.

"We'll try."

"You heard from Aid?"

He meant Adrian. I knew I should move away, but I couldn't make my legs shift.

"No, not today."

"Well, I'm sure you'll figure that out as well. You knows he just wants what's best. He's a good bloke."

My eyes zeroed in on Megan's face. Her usually warm skin tones paled, and the tension in her body ramped up several more notches. "Yeah, sure, Dink. Look, um, we need to go talk to people. Can I leave you here in charge of what's happening until CID turn up?"

Dink nodded. "No worries, my love. I'll keep 'em in line."

Megan didn't say a word to me; she just marched off back up the lane. I scrambled to catch up.

Rather than face the obvious problem head-on, I opted for a sideways approach. "Why's he called Dink?"

Megan glanced at me, obviously expecting an interrogation. Still, the question surprised her, as I'd intended.

"He's not the sharpest of our knives, but he's a good solid copper. Taught me the ropes when I joined up and returned to Redruth after training. He's called Dink because he has a nasty habit of putting dinks in the police vehicles. Even if he's just parking the damned things. Our inspector has banned him from driving. The budget can't stretch to his endless list of mishaps."

"That's cute."

"Don't say that to those who hold the purse strings. They aren't impressed. They want him to retire. He's an expensive police constable to employ. The younger ones are cheaper."

"That's a lot of experience they'll be losing."

"Tell me about it. Not the way to help community policing units like my old one."

"Um, Meg, about what he said when he mentioned Adrian—"

"Not now, Griffin. I need to focus on the issue at hand. My personal life is just that—personal."

Okay, that sounded like a 'fuck off, leave me alone'.

*We're not leaving it there, right, mucker?* No, we bloody well weren't.

"Nice, Megan, thanks for that. However, I'm not a colleague, not just a colleague, I'm your friend. Probably your oldest friend. And I'm your cousin, so please, listen." We were stomping up the lane at a furious rate. I caught hold of her forearm. "Slow down."

She yanked her arm away. "Not now, Griffin." The glare she shot at me had something else lying behind it. I saw confused desperation.

It made me pause. In an interrogation, I'd push until she cracked and gave me the answers I wanted, but if I tried that with Megan now, I'd ruin everything. Damn her, she knew it as well, and she was relying on my desire to keep the peace between us. I couldn't argue with that, I didn't want to hurt her.

"Alright, not now, but we are talking about this, Meg. You're in trouble. I can see it."

She didn't reply, just turned and continued her march to the group of protesters now gathered at the gate, watching events unfolding farther down their lane.

# Chapter Fifteen

To say the group were in a state of shock would be an understatement of the century, but there was no other word that would even come close to describing their angst. Two of the women they'd come to know had vanished for a day, then died horribly. Several more of their company had turned out to be more like terrorists than protesters. They'd been raided by the police and infiltrated by us. I'd expected hostility, but right now, they were just stunned.

Leaze and Aggie were at the central fire pit, and I saw several of Anwen's Children among them. TikTok girl was back, and she'd been crying. To be fair to her, she looked exhausted, shocked, sad, and very small in her woollen coat. A big pot of tea lay nestled in the glowing embers of the fire, and quiet voices shared what news they had gleaned.

As we walked up, they all fell silent. Megan glanced at me, so I opted to take the lead on this one.

Rather than sit on one of the straw bales they used, I knelt in the dusty grass. "I want to say how sorry I am for your loss. We're doing all we can to find out who did this to Jennifer and River."

*Except you didn't, did you?* The snide comment made me hate myself.

Aggie sat nearby, pale faced, clutching a mug between her hands. I noticed the chip on the rim as her thumbs stroked the bumpy sides of the hand thrown clay. Her thick glasses were spotted on the inside of the lenses from tears. She gazed at me with those overly enlarged eyes and whispered, "She was my friend as well." Her Northumberland accent stood out among the southerners.

"I know, Aggie. I'm so sorry."

"Why'd someone want to hurt River? She… Oh, God, I'm going to have to tell her son."

"The police can—"

"They won't find him. He's in France, working on building a medieval village using traditional tools. They don't have phones except in the main office."

Megan sat next to Aggie. "If you give me the number, I can make the call. It doesn't have to be a burden—"

"She was my friend!" Aggie exploded with fury, then burst into tears, dropped her mug in the soil, and ran off through the camp.

Leaze watched her go. "I think she was half in love with River. Aggie's a bit special. She sees the world in a way most of us don't, and River helped ease her through life in the camp. She's going to be lost."

"There seem to be fewer people here today," I said.

Leaze nodded. "No one likes being raided by the police, and our mission has turned…" She put her hands over her face. "God, I don't even know what our mission is right now."

Megan placed a gentle hand on the older woman's back. "To help us find the truth?"

A small nod. "Yes." Her spine straightened. "I suppose that's important. If we don't establish the truth, we'll never be free."

"What do you know about River?" I asked.

Leaze looked into the fire for a long moment. "She was amazing. Like Jennifer, but in a different way. She was physically strong. She'd go at a task for hours without seeming to get tired. Having lived on the road most of her life, she had a vast range of survival type skills. Without being bossy, I guess she was instrumental in organising us and making sure everyone did their share. Like with Mitch, when he first arrived, he just drank and did drugs. River told him that if he wanted to stay, he had to pull his weight."

"Would she have known about the attempted attack on the building site?" I asked.

A firm head shake. "No. She was nonviolent. Though she didn't lack courage. She's been to prison for the cause more than once over the years. Her son was born in the van over there." Leaze nodded her head towards a very heavily decorated horsebox that probably pre-dated Sid's Mini. "She made a good mechanic as well."

"She wasn't a true believer," said a thin, hairy man in the garb favoured by Anwen's Children.

"Sorry, sir, who are you?" asked Megan. She held her phone in her hand, and I wondered if she was recording the conversation.

"Mr None-of-your-damned-business," he snapped, glaring at Megan.

Her mouth quirked. "This is a murder inquiry, everything is my business. Name, please, sir."

Clearly not her first rodeo with a reluctant witness. He spat, "Jack McCracken."

"Well, Jack, what makes you say she wasn't a true believer?" I asked.

He glared at me. "It's all well and good, doing all this," he waved a vague hand at the sprawl of the protest camp, "but it doesn't make you a real believer." He sniffed and swept a work-roughened finger under his overly dramatic nose.

Leaze huffed. "Fucking zealots," she muttered. She'd changed her tune. I wondered what dynamics had played out after we'd left the area last evening. During the day, I'd been too caught up in the domestic terrorism to watch the impact of everything on the group.

"What was that?" Jack flared instantly.

Leaze glared at him. "You heard," she spat.

Megan put a hand out. "This isn't helping anyone. Leaze, I thought you supported Anwen's Children?"

"I do," she flung her arm out, "but it's like the rest of us aren't worthy to understand the deep mysteries of their bloody messiah. Eloise comes down here from her high perch," now she waved at the camp on the top of the field, "makes some bloody speech about how crap we humans are, then fucks off back to consult with their little godling." She meant the boy we'd seen, though her choice of words sent a chill down my spine.

Leaze's anger stemmed from the shock of the last few days. She looked older and terribly saddened by more than the deaths of her friends. "We just want to save the woodland from another bloody greedy capitalist. We don't want to harm anyone." The last came out on a wail. "And to be told we aren't worthy of the secrets of their fucking cult," she banged her chest, "hurts. It hurts a lot."

*Blimey, she's going to have me in tears in a minute.*

I coughed manfully. "Leaze, maybe we should speak to you alone?"

"No, I've nothing to hide."

Jack snorted, rose and vanished back into the growing crowd. It would be impossible to interview any of them like this. We needed a controlled environment.

"Look," said a voice from the crowd. I identified another woman with a small blonde girl on her hip. "River was loved here. She was like a spiritual mother to many of us, and a practical mother to our children. You aren't going to find enemies among us." A murmur of agreement went up from the assembled crowd. I scanned the faces, checking to see the truth of that statement. It was hardly scientific, but I really didn't see anyone with a flicker of doubt or fear in their eyes. Everyone liked River, just as they had Jennifer.

My phone rang. I checked the screen. Sid. "Excuse me." I rose and walked away, even as I accepted the call. "What's up?"

"Luce has a theory you aren't going to like."

"Do we need to come back?"

"No, we're coming to you." That's when I heard the familiar sound of the Mini's door closing and the glass rattling in its antique holding.

"Okay. See you soon."

Megan and I continued to try to dig a bit deeper, and with Leaze's and Aggie's permission, we went through River's van. The place was immaculate. The interior was laid out with separate living areas that blended together in a way my awful bedsit in London had never managed. The wooden surfaces flowed, and the fabrics used for comfort matched as they would in any ethnic designer home.

"What did she do for her income?" Megan asked.

"She wasn't on benefits if that's what's worrying you," Aggie snapped.

"It wasn't," I said, trying to soothe Aggie's temper. "I think we're just amazed at how beautiful all this is."

Aggie sniffed back another impending fall of tears. "She was an artist. Sold her work online." She opened a cupboard and somehow a laptop appeared with all modern conveniences. "Over the years, she's gone from painting to online designs. Albums and book covers. Albums mostly. She has quite a reputation among certain genres."

I nodded. "Find something you love, then find a way to make money at it."

Neither Megan nor I wanted to rip the tidy home to pieces, so we did a gentle fingertip search, and it showed nothing. I'd get Sid to interrogate the laptop and any external hard drives we found, but I doubted it would reveal some earth-shattering secret. River was picked to die, but not because of bad habits. Was it the wrong place, wrong time? Or something more sinister? And lest I forget, she'd also gone missing the night before she was found dead. Just like poor Jennifer.

It felt like someone from outside the camp took them off the board of life. But who? Or what? And why?

I heard raised voices outside the truck and jumped down, only to find Sid and Luce trying to explain to a group of distressed protesters that they needed to speak to us.

"Hey, it's okay, everyone. They're here to help us find out what happened to River and Jennifer. Ease up on them." I strode through the small throng and added my bulk to Sid's tall, thin frame. People muttered but backed off.

"Sorry," I said, "trust is in short supply."

"So, I see," Sid replied. "We've left the bag of tricks in the car." He nodded towards the lane.

"Okay, if we need anything, I'll go get it. I don't want to disturb the natives by setting up equipment unnecessarily; they are very restless."

Luce looked around her, quietly taking it all in and, I imagined, cataloguing it for future reference. She turned her large, dark eyes on me. "Do you have photos of the woman?"

I nodded. "I'm not sure you want to see them, Luce. It's not good to look at." As we talked, I led them out of the camp and towards the centre of the big field. It would keep us away from prying ears, if not eyes.

"I just want to check a few things," she said, her expression grave. "I have a worrying theory, but I don't want to share it until I've taken due care."

"Okay. But didn't you see the images I sent Sid?"

"No, Luce had gone home. I told her what had happened over the phone and just picked her up," Sid explained.

I found the right folder, selected an image I'd taken of the ivy wrapped around River's throat without her face being involved, and handed over my phone to Luce. She enlarged the image. "It's the same ivy as before, and the same stuff the foreman found at the building site." She glanced at me. "Were there berries at the scene?"

I shook my head. "Not that I saw."

"That's unique to the building site. Interesting."

Sid and I shared a somewhat exasperated look, and Megan arrived beside me.

"What are we talking about?" she asked me.

"I don't know, Luce has yet to explain."

Megan rolled her eyes, impatient with the academic.

Luce finally decided to share her thoughts. "Yew berries are highly poisonous. You can eat the flesh, but the seeds will kill in a high enough dose. The leaves, the wood, and even the sawdust are all toxic. However, it can also be a tree of protection and purification. Their place in mythology is complex and often contradictory."

Megan cocked her head to one side. "You think that's why the dried berries were at the building site, but not at the deaths? There's a significance we're missing?"

Luce nodded. "Yes. It's only a guess at this point, but I think the berries are a warning to the building site."

I frowned. "Why aren't they near the bodies?"

Luce's eyes gazed at the woodland behind me. "That's what worries me."

Megan muttered, "I need more sleep if we're going back into the land of riddle me this or that."

I realised I still hadn't given her the answer to the riddle I'd tricked Mephistopheles with.

"Let's sit, and I'll try to explain," Luce said, dropping into a neat crossed-leg sitting position with ease. Only years of yoga made that move possible.

The rest of us joined her, Sid groaning about his old bones. With the ground dry, the grass fresh green in this part of the field, it felt soft under my restless palms as I stroked it.

Luce fished about and retrieved some small stones. "Here we have the woodland." She placed a stone down. "The building site." Another. "And the camp." A third. "In the woodland we have the ivy, yew and ash growing in abundance. So, nothing was brought into the area to commit the crimes. This forms a crucible effect. The story plays out here."

"It's not a story, Luce," Megan said. "It's two murders and a break-in. That's pretty serious."

"I'm aware, but for this to work, we need to call it a story. Please just trust me for a minute, Sergeant."

Megan shrugged, and Luce continued, "The ivy and ash are predominantly for protection. The yew has two meanings but was found inside the ring of ivy, so it could be acting as protection, but I think it was meant more as a warning."

"You don't think the murders are warnings?" I asked.

Luce met my gaze. "No, Griffin, I don't. It's far worse than that. I think they are sacrifices to appease the ancient gods of the sacred grove in the woodland. We have the concept of the triple death. The piercing with a knife, probably one used for ritual, the hanging, and the stake in the heart. You're all familiar with that theory?" We all nodded. "I think these women were chosen because they represent the three phases of the goddess. The crone, the matron, and we might be on the way to another death."

"The maiden," Megan whispered.

Luce nodded, clearly worried about the prospect. "I suspect, though without the final death—which none of us want—I can't be definite, that the women's souls are sent to the afterlife with the blessing and protection of the killer, due to the power of the triple death they endure. Although we know they're dead before the hanging and stake. Whereas the building site was sent a warning that their time is nearly up, and they need to leave. The placement of the bodies is also significant. One was at the head-water for the spring, or near as makes no odds. The other is the entrance to the woodland. If we checked old maps, I should imagine that the path we walked the other evening is an ancient trackway through what once was a far larger woodland."

"Where would the maiden go?" Sid asked.

Luce shrugged. "Difficult to know without further examination of the wood. Maybe that druidic circle Griffin mentioned? I don't think we have time to amble about the woods making guesses. I think we need to move every young person out of this camp before someone else goes missing."

Megan twisted and glanced at the camp over her shoulder. "Not much chance of that, but I'll talk to Leaze and make sure the younger members of the group don't go anywhere alone after dark."

Sid coughed. "I realise this is a delicate thing for me to bring up, but does the maiden need to be a virgin, or just young?"

That floored Luce for a minute as she thought it through. "Well, erm… I guess she should be a virgin, but unless you want to ask—"

Sid threw his hands in the air, making swishing motions. "No, no, I really don't want to do that." His panic brought a smile to my face, despite the horrors of the occasion.

"Then I think we'll just assume it's any young woman. Just to be safe. From the age of twelve to twenty," Luce decided. It suited me. The more we had locked up, the less I had to worry about.

"What do the deaths achieve?" I asked Luce.

"That's the thing, I don't know. I've never read anything about this kind of death made by humans. There are lots of stories about stakes, lots of stories about ivy, but the small incision in the throat that means the chest cavity fills with blood that then pours out because of the stake? That's new. Or pre-written records, and we've never found the archaeological evidence for it. We understand the concept of triple deaths and their religious significance as a sacrifice to a god, but in this context, I'm blind to the potential meaning at this point."

Megan asked, "Why these women? They were positive people. Strong but quiet leaders in the community. Good, solid role models."

"I think you've stumbled over the point," Luce said. "A priest would sacrifice those that mean the most to appease the gods. Like the bog body that had evidence of the triple death. He may have been a fine warrior or leader who agreed to his death to save his community."

"That's dark," Megan muttered.

"It's horrible," Luce agreed.

This meant I still didn't have a scooby about which supernatural nasty might be committing these crimes. It didn't bode well for the future.

# Chapter Sixteen

"We need to talk to Anwen's Children," I decided. "They are the ones with more arcane knowledge than anyone else in the camp."

"I wouldn't mind a quiet word with their messiah," Megan added with a growl.

Sid said, "I think me and Luce should take some of the equipment into the woodland and see what's what at these death sites. Maybe try to find the druidic circle of trees. An EMF reader might pick up on something."

I stood up. "Agreed. We'll talk to the happy campers at the top of the field. You guys take the woodland."

"Is it safe?" Megan asked. "Maybe you should go with them? I can handle the dippy hippies."

I chuckled. "They'll be safe in the woods during the day. Right?" I asked Luce.

She nodded. "I think I'm way past my maidenhood days."

The meeting broke up, with Sid and Luce heading back

to the car. Two deaths were now linked to the wood and the victims coming from the camp, and I found myself scanning the people even more than before. With a possible theory we didn't want proving about a maiden going missing, I started to log all the female teenagers. Then I felt like a pervert, and stopped, but not before I saw TikTok girl again. Why was she here alone? How much of this horror was she sharing on social media? Did I have the right to have her locked up, and her phone surgically removed from her hand?

As Megan and I began to walk up the hill, I decided to tackle something only slightly less depressing than the threat of death to one of the young women in the camp. We'd deal with that problem later.

"When can we talk to Aunt Iris about Mum?"

Megan glanced at me, obviously surprised. "Any time, I guess. Though after this is probably best."

It felt more urgent than that, but she was right. I'd waited more than two decades. A bit longer wouldn't kill me. "I don't really know what I'm going to ask her," I confessed.

I had a lot of conflicting priorities in my head. The deaths, of course, were primary. However, Megan's problems with Adrian, and my problems with graves, shouldered their way to the front of the queue. Were they easier to think about? Definitely not, which is why my stupid brain wanted them solved, so it could move on with the more important stuff. Like my actual job.

Megan glanced at me. "I guess we need to ask her what she remembers of their shared childhood. If there was anything to suggest a link to what you're going through. Mum thought you'd grow out of the night wanders. When we tell her you haven't… well, she might come up with something. You never know, Aunt Hazel might've had the same problem, but Mum never wanted to share it with you."

I frowned. Aunt Iris was a farmer's wife. She didn't mince her words, and her practical view of the world could often feel like she'd slapped you with a wet kipper. It didn't stop her from being one of my favourite people. "She wouldn't do that to me, would she? Keep secrets like that, I mean."

"You know Mum. It would depend on what she thought was best. As your only female parent while you were growing up, she felt she had to protect you from as much of the past as possible. Let's not forget, Griffin, you haven't been around much as an adult man. She doesn't really know you. If she wanted to share something, you haven't really given her a chance."

That little shot of guilt shut me up. Moments later, we arrived at the camp Anwen's Children used. The smaller compact encampment had a less chaotic feel than the larger one down the hill. The vans were parked in a semicircle, all facing the same way and acting like wagons did in those old Western films I'd watched as a kid. They'd be a fine barrier to wind and rain. The large teepee had its back to the straight edge, and the stone wall behind it rose to about my chest height. Enough to keep errant lambs in the field and well away from the roaming dogs. Beyond that rose the heathland.

In the centre stood another fire pit, but this one held a complex set up of cooking equipment that wouldn't have looked out of place on the Third Crusade.

Seven pairs of eyes turned to stare at us as we breached their outer curtain of protection. Four women and three men. I didn't see that Jack bloke from earlier. They all had the strange tribal tattoos on their arms and throats. The largest of the women, the one who'd challenged us just a few days before, rose from her wooden stool.

"And what brings you up 'ere?" she asked, her south-west accent very clear.

Megan reached into her pocket and withdrew her police identification. "Official business, I'm afraid."

One of the men glared at her. "I'd have thought you did enough damage yesterday." His accent sounded as if he'd come from Harrow, not some rural community school. Younger than the others, blond, with a jaw chipped from marble. By the set of his shoulders as he looked at me, I began to wish I'd brought my Glock up the hill.

I pointed out, "Yesterday, lives were saved by the authorities. If we hadn't acted, you'd all have been arrested as terrorists."

The fool rose with the fluid grace of a fit man in his early twenties. I stepped back, as did Megan, both of us priming for violence.

He shouted, "And that's the fucking problem! We," he smacked his chest, "are the problem here. If people had died, maybe the trees wouldn't have to, and those of us who understand how to live sustainably can finally be at peace with the Mother." His glare left me ready to close him down if he took one step towards us.

"Will," came a commanding female voice from the left, "stop."

I took my eyes off Will and saw Eloise step down from her large truck. A glimpse at the interior, and I registered with some surprise it looked far more space-age than River's. I'd have thought these people would be even more heavily influenced by the ethnic lifestyle, but apparently not.

Will rounded on Eloise. "They have no right to be here. We haven't done anything wrong."

Eloise, her pale eyes fixed on her young acolyte, didn't say a word. A slight tilt of her head was all she needed, and Will sat. Air huffed out of him on the way down.

She said, "Will, we seek unity with Mother, but she will not listen to us unless we control our impulsive natures. After all, that's why she suffers so much. Humanity's impulsiveness strips her of her bounty. If we are to change the course of people's lives, to make them aware of their cruelty, then we have to rise above our base natures."

He mumbled gracelessly, while scowling, "I'm sorry, Eloise. I'll do better."

"You shall. Go and meditate. Find your centre and think upon your actions."

Will rose, gave a brief, stiff bow and said, "Forgive me all."

Everyone around the fire pit murmured, "You are forgiven. Go to find your grace."

Will said, "I shall return with grace. Thank you for your love." He stepped away and walked to the teepee, head down, shoulders slumped. A slinking dog who'd eaten his mistress's slippers.

*Oh no, this isn't a cult at all.*

Ritual words, ritual body art, clothes and shared doctrine… That defined a cult in DoPI's books. I should know; I'd read them. All I needed to do now was work out if they were murderers. If they weren't, and they proved mostly harmless, I'd let Sanchez know of their existence so we could keep them under observation, but I wouldn't interfere. Big Brother might well be watching, but they had no interest in stopping most of the foolishness people get up to in their own time.

Eloise turned her intense, pale gaze on us. Megan's spine straightened, trying to match the taller, slimmer woman for regal dominance. Sadly, for Megan, it didn't work. We were mere chaff to this woman's golden wheat.

"As impetuous as our young brother is, he's quite correct. Why are you here? Did we not suffer enough from your attentions yesterday?" She kept her voice light, almost playful, as if trying to distract us from the odd bollocking she'd given Will just moments before.

I decided to take over and placed a hand on Megan's shoulder before she could step in. "My colleague and I are investigating the death of another woman from the protest group. I'm sure you've heard about it. It's important that we speak to everyone." After a moment, I added, "Privately." This community living was all well and good, but I didn't want this lot hiding behind a shared narrative.

"We are a peaceful group of people… I'm sorry, I haven't seen your identification." She smiled with saccharine appeasement. Though I had some doubt that a chemical like saccharine ever came near this woman's lips.

"I apologise," I said, removing my Rural Security ID, and Megan showed her police credentials. Eloise took both and examined them with great care.

"Very well, Mr Woodbury, what can we do for you?" she asked.

"Perhaps we can speak alone?" I requested again, maintaining the polite but slightly hostile vibe we had going on.

"We have no secrets."

I doubted that. "Nevertheless, it's procedure."

"Very well." Rather than return to her van, which pissed me off because I really wanted to see inside, Eloise walked out of the wall of vehicles. It meant Megan, and I had no choice but to follow. She certainly knew how to keep control.

When we were a good ten metres from her coterie, she stopped, folded her arms and waited. The woman was clever; she had her back to the sun, forcing us to squint. I doubted it was an accident.

Megan moved around, so she had the woman's profile and little sun glare. I removed my military-style peaked cap from a pocket and reduced the light's effects. I needed to see the woman's eyes without dominating the interview. At the moment, I needed her to think she had control of the situation.

"We listened to your speech the other night in the camp. You're eloquent when it comes to sharing your thoughts about the environment."

"I don't hear a question, Mr Woodbury."

Rising to the bait wouldn't help. "Perhaps you can explain a little more about how your," I really wanted to use the word cult, but I knew it wouldn't help, "collective works?" Oh, how that cost me.

"Would you like to join us?" she asked.

I smiled. "Please just answer the question."

She spread her arms wide. "We are a small group of like-minded people who want to raise awareness that nature isn't just something we can use and abuse. Just as people who don't understand the sentience of animals, they don't understand that the Mother herself is sentient. We can hear her heartbeat. We can see her suffering. Father Sky gives us his tears even as we destroy our Mother."

Megan shifted restlessly. She didn't have my patience when it came to listening to overblown doctrine. It's something I'd noticed over the years: when I spoke to a vicar or cleric from an established branch of a traditional faith, then I'd have a down-to-earth conversation without the rhetoric of their faith getting in the way. With new branches of old religions, or cults, it always came down to digging through the preacher's doctrine before you found the truth of their beliefs. This blow hard nonsense was all taking time we didn't have, and if Luce was right, we could soon be looking at another murder.

"I'll be straight with you, Eloise, if I don't find the people responsible for this latest death, then I'll be forced to bring in other investigators who are far more likely to stomp all over your pretty speeches than I am. I'm the light approach, but don't think for a moment, I won't become the heavy approach if necessary. Cut the bullshit. Who are the people you recruit? What do you do? How do you survive? What brought you here?"

She blinked. "Your masculine dominance—"

"I've heard enough," Megan broke in. "I'm arresting you on a charge of obstruction of an officer of the law during their lawful investigation of a crime. You do not—" She moved in to take hold of Eloise.

The woman held up her hand to stop Megan's advance. "Fine. Once more the state wishes to control—"

"You just can't help yourself, can you?" Megan snapped. "Answer his questions here, or mine down at the station. Your choice."

Again, with that slow blink. "Last night we were all here. Together. We have nothing to hide. At dusk, we went into the woodland to the grove for Trystan to perform the rites that will sanctify the woodland once again. When this process is complete, and we have saved this place from the developers who wish to sanitise the countryside here, we will move on."

"Why not stay?" I asked, wondering if she was talking about the boy we'd seen.

"It is Trystan's mission in this world to call to the Mother through her sacred places. He is a gifted mystic and guides our duties. I am merely his guardian and priestess."

"You're talking about the teenage boy we've seen your people with?" Megan asked.

"Yes," Eloise said. "His name is Trystan, spelt in the Cornish manner."

"I take it you have paperwork to state you are his legal guardian?" Megan asked.

Eloise glared at Megan. "I assure you his presence here is perfectly legal."

Not quite the answer we wanted, but I didn't want Trystan to become the issue. Not yet. "We'll be checking that with Social Services," I stated. "You went into the woodland last night?"

"Yes, we perform a ceremony at dusk and dawn, and we will do so for as long as it takes for Trystan to connect fully with Mother."

I could practically hear Megan's teeth grinding. Silently, I willed her to keep her patience. I ploughed on. "You didn't see or hear anything unusual in the woodland at dusk? And how did you do your dawn celebration? We were here, and no one used the path. We didn't see you during the Beltane ceremony performed by the Cornish Sun group."

Eloise's mouth twisted as if my words put a foul taste on her tongue. "That group has little understanding. They're harmless, and useless. On that night we remained here, in silent meditation. It would've been pointless to perform our rites. We have a quiet way into the woods that doesn't require using the main footpath. We had no idea what had happened to the woman who has been sacrificed."

It was my turn to blink. "What makes you say sacrificed?"

Eloise shrugged. "I'd have thought it was clear. We've all heard about the stake, the ivy noose. Both women were killed the same way, with a stake through the heart."

And that's when I realised Eloise didn't know how they'd died. The small slice into the carotid artery near the collarbone.

"A difficult way to die," I said, watching her.

She nodded. "Sacrifices to the Mother and Father can often be brutal, but it is only humanity that is burdened with a conscience we have to learn to live with."

"What does this sacrifice mean to you? Spiritually speaking?" I trusted Luce's definition, but I needed more from this woman. I wanted to see behind her mask of doctrine.

Eloise smiled. "Isn't it obvious? They were chosen by the woodland itself. The spirits of the trees are trying to appease their god to stop the corruption of the developers and the council who allowed this horror to occur."

"And how do you know that?" I asked.

"Trystan hears them as he reaches out for the Mother. Their god is silent. He probably fled this place with the coming darkness of Christian domination and all the greed and horror that came in its wake."

I pushed that rhetoric aside. "You believe these deaths are being caused by spirits?"

"Why would a mortal want these women dead in this way, Mr Woodbury? Has it not occurred to you that these women died to give life to something so much more precious?"

Nothing in the world would give me greater pleasure than to demonstrate to this woman what was wrong with her theory. In doing so, I'd be able to knock her off her damned pedestal. However, what she'd said made perfect sense. We weren't looking for a human perpetrator, and I damned well knew it. Something else lurked in those woods, and I needed help to find it.

Megan didn't feel the same way. "You think the deaths of these women are justified?"

"I didn't say that, Sergeant. I am merely pointing out that the preservation of a sacred place should be a priority for all of us. Humanity is like an ants' nest. Just because a few ants die when they are out of the colony, it doesn't really affect the rest of the nest. The women are a natural cause and effect of those who wish harm to a unique woodland. We know Trystan can use this spiritually rich environment to speak directly to Mother, and he will guide us towards our destiny."

Megan's patience snapped, but she had the good sense to walk away for a moment and take a few deep breaths. Eloise watched her in the same way a child watches a wasp before swatting it.

"What do you think that destiny is?" I asked.

"Trystan, when he does connect to Mother Earth for a sustained period, will give us a clear mission. She will tell us how best to help her, and he will become her mouthpiece, so humanity can listen. Just as Jesus did centuries ago for people's souls, so he will for Mother's soul."

"That's a lot of weight for a boy to handle."

"That's why he has us to guide and support his efforts. My brother Will is one of our disciples who will become a warrior, and he will protect our Trystan when we begin our conversion."

"You're happy to be defined as a cult?" I asked.

"That's a derogatory term in modern parlance. Don't

forget your history, Mr Woodbury. All Romans thought of their polytheistic pantheon as cults, including Christianity. Cult is not a bad word."

"That depends on the nature of the people."

She smiled, and I saw the thin lines on her pale skin. She was older than I thought, maybe in her late fifties. "It does, but you've seen, we are peaceful."

"I certainly hope you are," I said.

# Chapter Seventeen

Megan's fury rolled around us like a thundercloud as we walked away from the cult. Sod it, I was using the word, even if they didn't.

"I want to take her in," she snarled.

"I know."

"All that peace and love bullshit. She just wants to be famous, and she's using a child to get there."

"I know."

"I want her stopped."

"I know and DoPI will step in if there are safeguarding issues—"

"Safeguarding? I fucking hate that phrase." She turned to yell at me. "Do you know how many children I've had to leave in terrible situations because they don't meet the safeguarding threshold? Because we don't have the fucking evidence needed?"

I had a sneaking suspicion I was about to find out.

"Dozens. Hundreds, probably over the years."

I doubted it would be that many, but even one was too many.

"I want Sid to do a number on her and her fucking band of freaks," she muttered darkly.

"You could—"

"I have to have justifiable cause, which, sadly, doesn't include being a fucking lunatic! Sid doesn't need the same permissions. You guys are going to burrow into her life and find something for me to use. Heartbeat of the fucking Mother… I ask you. She's just some used-up old hag who didn't have her own kids, or maybe they hate her, and now she's latched on to someone else. I'm going to have her."

Her fury amused me, but I had the good sense to keep my mouth shut. I remembered well the stomping, rage filled twelve-year-old girl who'd found a pony left in a field with no visible means of water and surrounded by dirt, not grass. The local animal rescue had stepped in when Aunt Iris called them, but not before Megan, with me in tow, had confronted the owner. Her blonde ponytail bounced every time she pointed her savage finger at him. Megan's sense of justice was a powerful force, and I had the feeling Eloise would fold under the pressure just like the rest of us did.

In an effort to distract her, I said, "It's time we spoke to the people who own the golf course—"

"I think they've done this," Megan snapped. Not listening about the golf course and firmly stuck on Anwen's Children.

"Maybe."

She rounded on me, forcing my feet to stop before I mowed her down. "Maybe? Did you hear her? She has utter contempt for humanity. She hates us. All of us."

"That doesn't make her, or any of them, killers."

"You think it's some mystic bloody force in the forest?" She threw her arms in the air and stomped about in a small circle. "Why am I not surprised? It can't possibly be some wack job who thinks it's a good idea to subject a child to occult worship. Where's she going with this? What will Trystan be forced to do next? Sacrifice a virgin on an altar?"

"They'd have a hard time finding one here," I muttered foolishly.

*Dammit, and you've been doing so well.*

"Excuse me?" Megan asked, her pitch rising.

I didn't snap back. It never ended well. "Megan, I know. Alright? I'm as worried about them as you are, but we have to take this one step at a time. You, of all people, understand that. DoPI will have a full report on Anwen's Children, and even if Social Services can't step in, we can and will if he's in danger. Any form of danger."

Megan's eyes filled with sudden tears. Always a consequence of her rage. "I don't want to lose anyone else to this monster."

"We won't. We'll lock down the site tonight. Your people can be posted in the lane and along the borders of the wood where it's near to the groups. Everyone will be protected until we catch this…"

She frowned hard while swiping at her face. "Say person."

"Okay, person."

"Thank you."

"Feel better now?"

"Marginally. Though, I think I've given myself a headache."

I chuckled, and Megan managed a wan smile.

"Thanks for putting up with me," she muttered.

"You know I love you," I said without thinking. The

heat inside the words rushed up my neck and face. "Cuz," I added far too late.

We stared at each other for a moment. Megan's eyes slid away from mine, and she sighed. In silence, we returned to the field's gate and found Sid and Luce eating lunch while leaning against the Mini.

Sid's awareness flickered between us, and when he met my gaze, his eyebrow rose. I gave a small shake of my head, begging him not to ask. Instead, he sighed with the air of a martyr looking at fools and pushed off the small car. I watched him rummage in his daysack, and two more sets of sandwiches appeared.

"Thanks," Megan said with all the joy of an Eeyore.

"Cheers," I said. "It was a difficult conversation. What did you find out in the woods?"

Luce, seemingly oblivious to whatever Sid picked up between Megan and me, said, "You were right. There are the remains of an ivy noose around the branch of the oak where you found Jennifer Mancore. I'd have bet forensics wouldn't have seen it."

"The ivy looked more like a necklace on Jennifer. I didn't see a knot as such. Are you sure it's the same?" I asked. The cheese sandwich was good.

"As sure as I can be," Luce said. "We have pictures. Though Sid wouldn't climb the tree, and as much as I'd like to know, I wasn't going to do that either."

"Fair enough. Anything else?" I asked.

Sid nodded. "Some serious EMF readings. Something in that wood is leaving a trail vivid enough for us to follow using the frequency readings, but it's not a ghost."

Megan grumbled something through her sandwich.

I ignored her. "Lower levels?" Which is DoPI speak for something that vibrated at a lower level than a spirit form.

We humans are the base; we vibrate at the lowest level, being heavy carbon-based life forms.

"Yes. It's far more corporeal than a ghost, but of a higher vibration than a human."

"What's that mean?" Megan asked, still sounding spiky.

"It means we have a *para* in that woodland."

"But we don't know what?" she asked.

"Not yet, but I don't think it'll be long before we know for certain. I can set up field cameras like I did at the gravesite, and we'll see what's recorded."

"That's a good idea," I said, just as my phone started. I fished it out of my pocket, trying to juggle the sandwich and my phone carrier on my belt. Megan rescued the sandwich. I swiped to answer the call, number unknown. "Hello?"

"Is that Griffin Woodbury?"

"Speaking."

"This is Steve Denzel."

"Hi, Steve, I was about to come and visit you."

"Ah, so it was you I saw this morning. Good. If you're in the area, can you come over now?" Steve asked. He sounded tense, and I heard other voices in the background.

"Sure, I can come over. Sergeant Ackley will be with me, is that okay?" I stared at Megan, and she nodded.

We finished the sandwiches, but I didn't bother unlocking the bike helmets from Quacker. It was barely a hundred metres down the lane to the entrance of the building site, then we'd be on a dirt track.

Megan sat on the back, keeping her body upright and away from me. Did that mean she was annoyed? Or was she preparing herself for whatever we'd be facing at the building site?

The moment the security officer saw us at the gate he lifted the barrier and waved us through. We both acknowledged him with thanks. The track, after the dozens of vehicles from the day before, had smoothed out, and Quacker had an easy ride. What wouldn't be easy was dealing with the crowd of men, and a couple of tough looking women, outside the farmhouse.

The foreman, Steve, stood a little apart, and his worried expression didn't bode well. I stopped the bike, Megan climbed off, and then I did the same.

Steve stepped forwards. "I'm representing my people, but they want to hear what you have to say when I explain the problem."

"We want the truth," said a big bald man with an anglicised Polish accent. "We are not going to continue working unless we get the truth."

"Okay, who are you?" I asked.

"Matty, people here call me Matty."

I glanced at Steve, who looked even more worried. Megan gave me a slight shrug. She knew I couldn't give them the whole truth. Partly because I didn't have it, and partly because Sanchez would flay me alive if I gave this many people the facts about DoPI.

Time to spin those lies like a good little operative. "What's happened to make you so worried? There are no more people in the protest camp who wish harm to any of you."

"I'm not talking about their bombs and guns. We heard about the dead woman. And we have seen with our own eyes. We are not stupid men." A cough nearby had him rolling his eyes. "People, we are not stupid people."

It was my turn to frown. "What's happened?" I directed this question at Steve.

"It's best I show you, but, Matty, can you please ask everyone to go back to work? We've had too much disruption already, and your bonuses are under threat. We deserve that money. *You* deserve that money. I've made sure you all have jobs away from the woodland, so let me deal with the police and I'll report back. I've never lied to you or steered you wrong. Let me handle this. Please."

"You tell him everything?" Matty wanted to know.

"Everything."

Matty grumbled, but finally the crowd of workers dispersed. I watched them and turned to Steve.

"What's going on?" I asked.

"I can't believe I'm saying this, but the men think there's something in the wood that's hunting them. They're scared, and I don't blame them. With that lot trying to blow us up—"

Megan stepped into the fray. "The saboteurs weren't trying to hurt you. They would've fired on the emergency services if we hadn't stopped them, but they weren't interested in killing your people. Though I understand why they're nervous."

"I wish that was all that bothered them," Steve said. "Come on, I need to show you."

Once more, we walked through the house and were handed yellow hard hats. Steve said to Megan, "You've gained some serious street cred with your handling of the digger the other night."

She grinned. "I learned to drive my first tractor at eleven."

I'd learned as well, but with me being absent during the term times, I never became useful on the farm.

"Well, it showed. You did a grand job. Thanks for not breaking anything."

Steve led us around the portacabins to a stack of wood held in frames that they'd use for some building project I didn't understand. I knew as much about DIY, and carpentry in particular, as I could write on the back of a very small stamp.

And my handwriting is large.

"Here is the most obvious problem," he said, pointing to the wood.

Every plank had large gouges taken out of it, as if it had been attacked by someone with an axe. Steve held out a chunk of stone to me. "I found this. It had fallen under the pallet. I'm no expert, obviously, but I've been to my share of museums and watched enough of the History Channel to know that I'm looking at a primitive axe. Like Stone Age." He paused and looked at us with genuine fear in his eyes. "How is any of this possible? What's happening?"

"Is there anything else?" I asked, avoiding a question I couldn't answer.

"In the cabin the men use for the breaks, we've found more of those berries and several ivy wreaths."

"Show me?" I suggested.

Here, Steve took his white hat off and scratched his scalp. "That's the thing. The men are getting jumpy. Some of them come from very rural parts of Europe, and despite being British citizens now, they don't forget their heritage. They've burned them. I came outside, and they'd put a bonfire together. The room has been destroyed by whatever lay those wreaths. All the furniture has been torn to shreds. If I didn't know better, I'd think a werewolf had been locked in there overnight."

He walked us over to a larger portacabin than the one he used as an office and opened the door. Megan stepped inside. I followed. He was right, the place was a mess. Mugs lay smashed on the floor. One of the windows was broken. Every cushion or spare piece of clothing had been ripped up. The posters hadn't stood a chance, and the fridge had vomited its contents all over the floor.

Megan went to the smashed window. She looked at me. "The glass is on the inside." Which meant they'd broken it from the outside. "Probably the place of entry."

I rang Sid. "You still here?"

"Only just, we were leaving."

"Do you have a dusting kit in the bag?"

"For fingerprints?"

"No, for spreading fairy dust."

Sid chuckled. "As it happens, yes."

"Come down to the farmhouse. We'll come find you. I want you to dust for prints."

"Or I could just sprinkle fairy dust everywhere?"

"You could do that, but I'll tell Sanchez."

He laughed. "Mate, there's no point in threatening me with that. You're almost as much in her bad books as I am."

I cut the call and turned to Megan. "I doubt we'll find anything usable, but it's best to check while we can."

Megan agreed and started taking photos.

Steve didn't enter the room, so I went back outside. "There's something else, isn't there?"

The foreman moved a rock around in the dust with his steel toe capped boot. "I've lost three workers this morning. Good men, but they won't stay here. Say the place is haunted. I'm a good Christian man, Griffin, ghosts are not high on my agenda. I'm also a rational man. This is… With the murders as well? Even I'm thinking of walking."

"The murders and this damage are linked, that much is true. What's doing it? I don't know. Yet. But I will."

"Shouldn't that be who?"

I managed a tight smile.

Steve continued, "We've been hearing noises as well.

Even during the day when we're working close to the woodland."

This made me pay attention. "What noises?"

"Chirrups. Not like birds, before you say anything about that. It's something else. The sounds are deeper, harder, and there is a definite back and forth going on. Then there was this odd whistling, but not like people make. It's an undulating sound that sends real fear running through us. These are not sounds I know, and I grew up in the countryside."

I nodded. "Okay, I understand."

"And the best news is, all this chaos is putting us behind schedule, so the owner of the site is coming down to check on progress."

"When?"

"Tomorrow. I don't know what to tell him. What do I tell him?" Steve's eyes were beseeching.

I thought about this for a moment. "I'll come back down and talk to him. We'll have more information by then. When's he arriving?"

"Midday. He'll come in a helicopter. Stomp about for an hour. Tell me that I'm not doing my job properly, threaten everyone, promise more money for working longer hours, and leave. He won't listen, and he won't be bargained with."

"Cash rich, empathy poor, kinda guy?"

Steve said it all with a look.

"I'll be here," I promised as we walked back to the farmhouse. I heard Sid's Mini chuntering along. "There are things you can do to help yourself and the men until we sort this problem out. You can lay salt at the doors and windows. Keep holy water on you. Maybe even use wood to protect yourselves. Rowan is a good one."

"Seriously?"

"Or prayer. Sometimes that works."

"You're making this sound more and more like something supernatural. That's not what I want to hear, Griffin."

I sympathised with the man. Who does want to hear what I was telling him? No rational person, that's for certain, but it didn't change the facts. "Just don't let any of your men into the wood, especially alone. Don't cut down any more trees. I think you'll be inviting more trouble."

The poor man rubbed his haggard face with both hands. "This makes no sense."

I gripped his shoulder. "I know. Please just keep your people safe. Keep the hysteria to a minimum, and I'll have answers for you soon."

"But those poor women." He looked glassy eyed.

"That won't be happening again," I promised.

We spent time trying to find fingerprints and failed. Sid and Megan managed to uncover more of those odd footprints, and we found hand and finger shapes, but not what a forensic fingerprint expert would think of as fingerprints. They were interesting though. Just like the footprints I'd seen several times, the handprints were not human shaped. The palms were wide, like an ape's, and the fingers spread out, long and thick. Ideal for heavy gripping. We found no lines or whorls. These creatures had smooth skin.

Before heading back to Redruth, Megan and I returned to the camp to speak with Leaze. We practically begged her to keep the young women locked up overnight. No one should walk outside the camp alone, and no one was to go into the woodland. Even in daylight. I didn't know if they'd listen, we were the authorities, they were the free spirits, the two things about as compatible as the oil they hated so much and the freshwater that plastic kept polluting.

When we returned to the bike, we were quiet, and on the trip back to Redruth, I felt a weight on me that left me deeply worried and almost itchy with the need to do something.

At the office, we did the necessary admin associated with the discoveries we'd made, but it yielded precious little information. Megan went down to her HQ and gave a full report to her inspector. That evening we returned to Turpin Cottage feeling uneasy.

# Chapter Eighteen

I paced around the kitchen, Sid and Megan watched, Luce had gone home.

"We can't just sit here," I said. "What if something happens at the camp?"

Megan sighed, her expression grim. "You want to go back down there and stake it out, don't you?"

"Don't you?" I asked her.

She nodded, despite her tiredness. "I don't want anyone else to die, that's for certain. Especially not like that. If the pattern holds true, someone will disappear tonight, and reappear tomorrow night, dead."

"We need to keep an eye on Anwen's Children. I don't trust them. There is something about that woman, Eloise, that's making me… itch."

Sid rose from the table and began pottering about the kitchen. "Well, if you're going out again, you both need feeding." He looked at Megan. "I assume he isn't going alone."

"Like he can keep himself out of trouble." She shot me a smile.

I'd happily take Megan on a stakeout, so didn't bother arguing. "What do we know about Anwen's Children, Sid?" Removing myself from the cooking area, I finally sat down at the kitchen table.

With his head in the cupboard where the frying pans lived, he said, "Eloise Windmaker, if you can believe it, changed her name after a nasty divorce from a man called Hubbard. Her given name was Danielle Elliot. Obviously not romantic enough. The divorce gave her a sizeable chunk of money, couple of million, so she's using it to create more wealth while living in a van building her eco-rhetoric. She has most of her money in hedge funds and invested in companies that are at least eco-friendly. From that point of view, she's legit. Despite these ethical investments bringing in less money, she's happy to keep her paper trail clean."

"What about her ethics regarding her budding faith?" Megan asked. "And the lad, Trystan?"

Sid appeared with a wok. "Well, that's where things get murky. There are reports of some very unhappy people in her wake. Anwen's Children was originally just a protest group. They've been around for years, moving from one battlefield to the next, like airport expansions, motorways, the HS2 railway, that kind of thing. About three years ago, Eloise got involved, and from what I've gleaned from old social media rants, she took over within months. She shifted them into more of a religious order, but not like a coven. It's far more than that. You have to truly believe in her vision of the whole Mother Earth vibe." He looked at us. "And it's not a democracy. They have a website, and I've tracked back some of the old members."

"Did you speak to them?" I asked.

Sid nodded. "Though, I think it could do with your touch, if you want more detail. I'm not an interrogator." He headed to the fridge.

"Mate, you don't have to cook—"

"I know that, Griffin, but I'm anxious and this helps. I can't go out there with you tonight. I'll be a hindrance if anything happens, but I can do this. Cook and worry. That's something I can do really well." He pulled out the chicken breasts and various vegetables. "Anyway, what these people said echoes the experiences that DoPI has recorded for decades. People give away their life savings—though they sign a covenant that states she invests their money in ethical products—and fully commit to her creed. She says that when they have enough money, they'll buy an island and live a fully eco-friendly lifestyle. It has to be somewhere with a strong connection to Mother."

"Lucky her," Megan muttered. "What about the kid?"

"That's tricky. Yes, she's his legal guardian, but his mother is currently in a private psychiatric facility in Switzerland, paid for by Anwen's Children. She was a member of the cult seven years ago, has terrible bipolar and is schizophrenic. She was deemed unfit, and Eloise was granted custody of Trystan. The lad is homeschooled. Their cult is focused on the boy. He's seen as a mystic and prophet of their faith. Or he's mentally ill like his mother. Or his mother is a sensitive like him, and Eloise betrayed her, locking her away. Who knows at this point? How much of all this is true varies depending on how angry the ex-members are with Eloise. If you choose to leave, you leave without your money."

Megan's eyes widened. "And that's legal?"

"Very murky grey area that people with no money can't afford to investigate. She closes them down with NDAs."

"Meaning they can't even talk about it afterwards?"

"They aren't supposed to, but the three I tracked down were more than happy to talk, but they can't go to the press or leave anything too terrible on the web."

I retrieved a beer for me and one for Megan. "That nails it. We're going down there tonight. I want to know more. What phase is the moon, Sid?"

He lifted his eyes to the ceiling in thought and said, "Full moon, due to rise at 23:30 or thereabouts."

We ate, and Megan borrowed a couple more layers off me to keep her warm overnight. We took two daysacks, food, water and weapons. Nothing fancy, but after the attack on the building site, I wasn't going back at night without at least one firearm. My Glock sat on my hip. We also had the asps, the iron dagger, some holy water, salt, two pairs of NVGs, so we'd see them from a distance, and I pressed a canister of Mace into Megan's hands.

"Keep it. There are few things made of flesh who can withstand that stuff," I told her. Oddly, the thought of Adrian came to me. As a police officer, she had to leave all the self-protection gear at the station each time she clocked off. At least I'd given her the means to stop a man in his tracks if he came at her, and I wasn't around.

We rode back down to Madron but stopped the bike a long way from the protest group. As dusk turned to night, we jogged through the small moorland that circumnavigated the camp's field at the summit of the hill and found our spot just as night settled over the fields but before the moon rose. We had cloud cover, but it wasn't thick or universal. I doubted it would rain.

The spot we'd chosen was a mound among the bracken behind the field, containing the camp. We lay shoulder to shoulder in the wind-burned fern and gorse. It had been oddly neglected by the surrounding sheep.

"You know this probably contains a dead king or something under here," I said, elbows in the soil, belly on the ground, NVG binoculars in my hands.

"Thanks for that, Griff," Megan said, doing her own watching.

"Just sayin'. If I really am attracted to the dead during the hours of darkness, maybe we'll see a ghost or two."

She removed her eyes from the binos long enough to give me one of her best glares. "Seriously? God, you're a twat sometimes."

I grinned. She'd been quiet, pensive and checking her phone too often. Tension radiated from her that had nothing to do with the case.

Without removing my binos, or changing position, I asked, "What's up, Meg? You've not been right these last few days. I know I keep getting it wrong, but you can talk to me."

She lowered her arms and rolled onto her back. "I know I can talk to you, I'm just not sure how much I can trust you."

*Don't overreact, she doesn't mean it.*

I bit back my flash of temper her statement caused. "I promise to listen."

"And not kill anyone? Or break heads?"

I removed my eyes from the binos. "Is he hitting you?" The question, outright like that, could go either way. It was certainly a risk, but I knew it was time to dig, and she wanted to talk to someone.

"No, Griffin. Nothing so simple. It might even be in my

head. I can't… There are indicators, but…" She sighed. "I thought he might be the one, and now… I don't know."

*That's as clear as swamp water.*

"Are you talking about coercive control?" I asked quietly, keeping my eyes fixed on the camp below us. People were moving about, but so far, I saw nothing to worry me.

"Yes. At least, I think so. It's…" She flipped back over onto her belly and resumed watching. "I was offered the deal for Bristol, right?"

"A promotion."

"A sideways move that would lead to promotion, yes. It turns out Adrian knows the man who made the decision to offer me the post."

"And that's a bad thing?"

"I think he manipulated them into offering me the post to get me away from my family, from DoPI and from you. When we were away in Scotland, I talked about you, about our friendship, a lot. He said I was too dependent on you, that we were too close. It wasn't healthy, and I'd not been able to form proper relationships because of it."

My belly turned cold against the mound. I feared that *Adrian* had a point, but I wasn't going to concede it.

"That's not true. He just wants to separate you from your base so you only have him to depend on."

"That's what worries me. He keeps niggling at me about my weight, my finances, which aren't great as I give what I can to keep the farm going, and even my hair."

"Your hair is great," I said, looking at her again.

She smiled. "Thanks. He showed me pictures of his mother and said he liked her hair."

I coughed to hide my desire to swear. "Red flag, Meg. If he thinks our friendship is a negative influence because we're cousins, then that is really wrong."

"I know. I tried to end it last week. If I go to Bristol, I'm going alone. But it's not that simple." She sighed long and hard while staring at the sky. "Who am I kidding, I'm not even sure I want the damned job."

*She's not going to Bristol. She's not going to Bristol.*

I tried to calm the jig going on in my head so I could think and not make the wrong move. "What do you mean by 'trying to end it'?" I asked.

"Just that. I went into the station, before all this kicked off at Beltane, and said we needed to talk. Could we have a break together at some point during the day? Which we did. I told him that I didn't think I could commit to a serious relationship with the career opportunity being offered to me in Bristol. He told me that I wasn't getting any younger, the clock was ticking, and I needed to think about my life, not just my career."

Even I knew that wasn't a good move to pull on Megan.

"He wants to get married," she added.

I put the binoculars down and turned to face her. "You said, no, right?"

Her eyes were too bright in the thin light given to us by the darkening night. "I tried. I don't know what happened. He just… He gets moody, says I don't understand him. Says I always think the worst of him. That I treat him badly, just like all the other women in his life. It's like a bloody soap opera, but the police can feel like that sometimes, and you get caught up in the drama of people's lives on long shifts. And then… There's you and Sid and Luce. The work we do together." She added quietly, "The time we spend together. It's always been so easy, being with you." She started watching the camp again.

*Warning, dickhead. Don't say it. Don't. Say. It.*

"Yeah, it's easy being with you as well." *Well done. Good*

*boy.* Was it wrong that I wanted to tell myself to fuck off, and stop being a condescending prick? Probably. Besides, this wasn't about me.

The time had come to ask her how much she remembered about the events in the cage we'd been locked in by the incubus. The things we'd hinted at and shared while under the influence of MDMA.

"Megan, I think—"

"Isn't that Eloise and Trystan?" she asked, fiddling with the magnification on her binos.

Exasperated, I dropped my head for just a moment, found my highly trained core, and focused on the job. Through the binos, I saw a tall woman and a shorter, slimmer lad. Their gaits were very different. I began to take note of the others I'd seen in their smaller camp. Body types, movements, clothing, hair, filing away their individual specifications and giving them identifying names. Including Eloise and the boy, I saw nine tangos.

A significant number in the occult. We watched the group walk in single file towards the woodland, with Eloise and Trystan at the head, the rest coming in behind. On the breeze, we heard low level chanting, but it didn't disturb anyone in the main camp. Their dwellings remained quiet and mostly dark.

"What do we do?" Megan asked.

"Follow, at a distance," I said, packing away the equipment. The two of us slid down the slope of the hillock and dashed through the crackling bracken to the wall separating the two fields. This would give us protection as we followed the group right to the edge of the woodland, where our moorland met the edge, then veered away to the east, whereas the camp's field wall contoured the woodland perfectly. They'd climb over the stones and be in their sacred forest.

"We'll need to follow them into the trees," I said, keeping my voice down.

"Are you sure that's wise?" Megan asked.

"No choice. I have to know what's happening in their ceremonies. For all I know, something they're dabbling in is causing these deaths. Nothing like amateur sorcery to cause a rip in the veil, allowing something to slip through."

"How is this your life?" she hissed.

I grinned at her. "Just lucky, I guess."

It took a while for the procession to reach the woodland's edge, climb over the wall, and vanish among the trees. They were using candles in lamps, they wore robes—which caused some difficulty as they clambered over the wall—and they had their chant. An endless loop of words I didn't understand.

"It's Cornish," Megan explained.

"They're all speaking Cornish? Why?"

"Seriously? You're asking me? How the hell do I know? You're the expert."

I shrugged as we climbed first one wall, dropped into the bigger field, then climbed over the next wall before dropping into the wood. The moment my boots hit the ground, I sensed the change in the atmosphere. A creeping fear started to nibble at the edges of me, making all my senses stand to attention and take notice.

Keeping my voice down, I explained, "It's not really known as an arcane language. Latin, Enochian, Greek, even Sumerian, but not Cornish."

She chuckled. "Don't worry, most of them aren't pronouncing it right. They'll end up summoning a mermaid in the middle of the wood at this rate."

"That's not at all reassuring. Mermaids are very rare."

She smacked my arm. "Stop winding me up."

"I'm not," I said in my defence.

Megan's eye rolling and head shaking made me grin, as she took point, following the faint lamplight ahead of us. In the dim light of the forest, the two of us easily tracked the group by switching to the night vision goggles instead of the binoculars. I did love DoPI's toys.

The path we followed ambled through the wind-stunted, but ancient trees. Spring leaves rustled in the rising wind that had a damp feel to it as sneaking fingers wriggled under our clothing. Despite it being May, the night was chilly, and I'd called it wrong earlier, rain would likely arrive before the dawn. We were careful during our stalking, but they weren't expecting to be hunted, and their prayerful murmurings hid the worst of our noise. It helped that the moon had finally put in an appearance, and her silvering dominance of the sky flickered and licked at the ground as it dodged the leaves.

The path wove downwards, towards the spring, and we followed until they crossed the small stream south-west of the cloutie tree.

Megan stopped. "Where are they going?"

"I don't know. I thought the druids' grove would be this side of the stream." We were heading towards the part of the woodland that backed onto the building site. We tried not to splash as we walked through the water.

Now they were going uphill, and within minutes we were forced to stop. The nine lamps were still, and the line now formed a circle. Megan and I hunkered down behind a tree trunk each and just watched. Trystan stood in the centre of the circle, and I tried to see Eloise. She wore robes like the others, but they were far more decorated, just as

Trystan's were. The light from the lamps flickered over the design, golden as opposed to the silver from the moon. I wanted to see what trees were around us, but to be honest, I couldn't tell in the dark. All the trees were so old and bent from the Atlantic winds, it was hard to tell the difference between them. Their trunks, though, held the mysterious shapes of fluffy mosses and lichen. It felt like I'd been thrown back almost two thousand years.

A prickling sensation surged up my spine as Eloise began to intone something in English. My heart ached, breath catching, and my throat closed as if I'd swallowed a football.

"Megan," I croaked, opening and closing my hand in her direction. "I can't..." Faint rustling as she crossed the distance between us, and her hand closed over mine.

"What's wrong?"

"I think..." My head hurt. Oh, damn, my head hurt so much my vision blurred. "Watch them." I managed to blurt out before something extraordinary happened.

*Old men in hooded robes filled the cleared glade. The trees were thick around them, but primary in the circle were the oaks. They rose tall and thick, with hazel, hawthorn and ash filling the gaps between the compass points. The glade was large and grassed, with a single stone rising in the centre above the height of any man. Among the trees, half-hidden in their shadows, were the people. Adults and children stood in silence as brown-robed men spoke and chanted in a language long since lost. Those who watched were mostly dressed in homespun woollen tunics with leggings and simple leather shoes or boots. Cloaks and hoods protected them from the wind. Behind the main man, who had a long silvered beard and staff of twisted willow, stood a couple. She with hair the colour of chestnuts, he with hair kissed by midnight. Their clothing was lined with fur, and gems caught the light, flashing as the day birthed new once more. Golden thread hemmed their sleeves and panels in their richly coloured tunics.*

*As the ceremony continued, the leader of the prayers, led the richly clothed couple towards the stone and for the first time the small hole in the ground came into view. The woman, weeping, lay a tiny bundle down in the earth. On her pale cheeks there were tears. Her hand reached out for the bundle, even as her husband and lord gently held her back. The grief in their eyes overwhelmed me…*

I sucked in a hard breath, unable to bear witness to what would happen next. The thought of it made my personal grief bubble to the surface and push away the terrible, brutal loss the royal couple had endured so many centuries ago.

Megan clutched my hand, but watched me, not the ceremony that was really taking place. She hissed, "What happened?"

I rubbed my chest with my free hand. "Later. Focus."

She whispered in my ear, making me shiver. "There's not much happening except a lot of chanting."

"The boy?" I asked, trying to force my mind to focus on the present.

"Still standing in the centre." She pointed, and I nodded. My heart pounded, and I barely heard the chanting. I needed to calm my racing heart. Deep breaths needed to be controlled, and I must force myself to return to my centre. My reality.

Trystan stood in the circle with his head bowed and unhooded. His straight golden hair hung around his shoulders and his hands were open at his sides. Even in the half-light, we could see his lips moving, and it didn't match the chant. Slowly, he lowered himself to the ground and placed his palms on the ground cover of plants. Mostly ivy and tufty grass. The atmosphere of the ritual notched up, the air becoming static as if a thunderstorm approached.

Megan gasped as the lad threw his head back and sound erupted from him. A deep sonorous howl rippled outwards from a body that was surely incapable of making such a noise. In DoPI's archives, I'd read of mediums being able to speak in pitch and accents far removed from their natural voices, but I'd never read of anything like this. The boy sat on the grass and vibrated with the depth of sound. It undulated like a whale's low frequency, or perhaps an elephant's rumble. His mouth stretched to release as much sound as possible.

The worshippers swayed and babbled, caught up in the religious ecstasy of the moment. They behaved like I'd seen Christian worshippers do when they spoke in tongues. Some of the people in the circle began pounding their chests with their fists and turning in jerky circles. Others raised their hands and jogged on the spot, as if dancing.

Eloise remained poised and focused on Trystan with a hunger I really didn't want to witness. Her shoulders rose and fell, demonstrating her heightened breathing pattern, and she leaned towards her obsession.

"Griffin," Megan whispered, "what's that?" She pointed towards the shadows at the back of the grove. A place far thicker with dense undergrowth than our area.

I caught the movement Megan had seen on the very edge of the light. Tall figures had gathered behind the worshippers. Fear rippled through me. Animal fear. Instincts honed by our ancient ancestors and carried through our DNA.

"What the fuck…?" I murmured, unable to help myself.

They were slim, with long, legs and arms, humanoid in shape at least. Even in the weak light of the lamps and the moon, they moved with sinuous grace and obvious strength. I couldn't see the detail of their faces, but they were nude, their skin colour—*was that green or brown, or both?*

The sound from Trystan began to rise in pitch, then drop, rise and drop. The shadow forms wove through the trees, forcing Megan to check our back. I sensed nothing behind us, but I was transfixed by the beauty of what we watched. This was nothing short of magical. That's saying something with my experiences. An invisible hand reached into my belly and stroked it with fingers wearing gloves made of terror.

The grove became something out of time, out of logic. I glimpsed the oily vision of the veil in the air above us, mixing with the tree canopy. These people were not play-acting at being a cult, these guys really had stumbled over something unique, and they were using it. Did they understand what they'd done? What they had summoned?

"I don't like this," Megan hissed. "It's not right. Something about this is not right."

I agreed. Whatever Trystan was, whatever he could do, this wasn't good. They'd unleashed a residual power here that they couldn't possibly understand, or control. Suddenly, I knew who, or rather what, was doing the killing. Those human-like shadows we could see, they had to be woodland spirits of some kind, and they weren't happy. My warrior instincts were on full alert, as if I were walking through an African town full of insurgents and their guns, just waiting for our patrol to reach their kill box.

"We need to leave," I whispered. "Keep low, quiet and slow. Match me where you can."

I was trained for this kind of exfil, though the Royal Marines expected me to be backing out of hostile territory in a foreign war zone, not trying to escape beings from myth and legend in Cornwall. Keeping my eyes forward, but allowing Megan to turn around, I used elbows and knees to back away from the scene. Trystan had begun to calm, his voice quietening, his body relaxing. Eloise stepped to his side and knelt, catching him as he fainted.

The shadow beings, whatever they were, retreated, as did the veil. It dispersed among the leaves. I hadn't realised it, in the moment, but the lamps had been far too bright for their small flames and now, the shadows raced into the grove. It would help our retreat.

I watched Trystan speak to Eloise, and she hugged him, but the gleam in her eyes twisted knots in my guts. As I moved backwards, I realised I'd made a terrible mistake. I thought we'd be witnessing just another druidic ceremony. Calls to the nature deities, a bit of an offering, maybe honey and milk, or wine. Praise for the moon. That kind of thing. Instead, we'd seen a major conjuring, and I'd been too dislocated to even consider taking a video of the scene. Sanchez was going to rip me a new one for that oversight. I'd warned her I wasn't fit for duty, and I'd just proved it.

Besides, what the hell had I seen? The vision that swept over me was a disaster for this mission. It reminded me of when I'd woken under the damned quoit weeks ago, before the events caused by the incubus. Was it the same time period? The same people? I had no idea. The previous event had been a vision I'd had while waking from one of my nightly episodes. I'd seen a tribe burying their leader with all the ceremony I'd expect from a Bronze Age people. This one had sadly shown me the burial of a child in this sacred place. It opened up a series of questions to which I had no answers, both as an archaeologist, anthropologist, and a DoPI operative.

"Bugger it," Megan muttered. "I've just crawled into the water."

I chuckled, unable to help myself. "I think it's safe to stand, but we need to get out of here. You might not be maiden, but I don't want to risk it. Let's use the footpath. They'll go back through the wood the other way."

Megan climbed to her feet, trying to brush bits of debris off her clothes. I did the same. I'd expected her to make some joke about my maiden comment, but she remained serious. Probably a more appropriate action, than mine.

Still keeping quiet where we could, the pair of us soon located the place we'd found Jennifer Mancore's body. From there, it was easy to leave. The energy in the wood felt very different tonight, and I began to sympathise with the workers from the golf course and hotel. It vibrated with a sense that predators roamed the darkness. A sense that something, long forgotten and vanished from our world, had returned in this tiny, ancient wood, and it wanted to feed. Or maybe it wanted revenge?

I thought about this. If Anwen's Children had used the thinning veil and Trystan's natural gifts to tap into the ancient sacredness of this location, then they'd pulled, or woken, an apex predator into our world and those beings were not happy... I tracked back to the beginning of my thought processes. Woodland spirits were manifesting, and their woodland was being destroyed. They wanted to prevent that, so they called on their god to help them. By sacrificing the best human women they could catch, performing the triple death ceremony, all in the hope of gaining their deity's favour. I needed to speak to Luce very badly. Too many ideas ping ponged around my brain for me to settle on one theory.

Megan and I splashed through the water and found the

footpath. From there it was quicker. I noticed she still didn't say much, I could only imagine what she thought. For a woman who, despite the evidence she'd seen with the incubus, still wanted to deny the existence of the supernatural, tonight was going to be difficult to incorporate into her world view. I'd give her some space to think. It was a hard adjustment for many of us in DoPI when our world view was shattered by the work we did. Time to adjust was the only thing to really help.

# Chapter Nineteen

When we reached the road, we both stopped. The feeling of being tracked and hunted backed off, and Megan leaned over to take some deep breaths.

"I never want to see that again," she said. "What the hell just happened? Why does that place feel so bloody scary all of a sudden?" Her eyes were wide, and she shook as she pushed stray hair out of her face.

I'd been feeling it since Beltane, but I didn't bother telling her that. "You're sensing danger on a primal level very few humans feel any longer. It's like being hunted by a bear or a lion—nothing like the danger you feel in enemy territory. This is deeply primal, pre-homo sapiens type fear."

"I don't like it," she pronounced, walking in a tight circle and shaking her hands out as if to rid herself of the massive overload of fight-or-flight hormones we'd both been left to deal with after our sortie into the unknown.

"Me neither. DoPI's really not going to like it, or the fact that I forgot to record what happened."

"Seriously?" Megan looked at me. "They expect you to think that logically under those circumstances? And what happened to you anyway? You wigged out for long minutes."

I decided to answer the DoPI question, with luck, she'd forget the other one. "I'm trained to expect the unexpected and react with strategic planning and forethought wherever possible. So yes, they would expect me to record an event like that. The fact that I forgot just goes to show I'm not the right man for this job. I'm too unreliable."

"You have a witness. I can testify to what you saw. Stop being so hard on yourself. It was…" She ran out of words for a moment. "Not normal."

I grinned, despite my fears. "Not normal sounds about right." I gripped her shoulder. "If you're okay to return to the bike, I think we need to leave the area."

"Aren't you worried about them taking another woman?"

I shook my head. "Not tonight. That manifestation at the grove will've cost everyone a lot of energy. Besides, we've warned those at the camp, and we can't be on point all the time. We need to sleep." I certainly did. The drive home would be a real test of endurance. Exhaustion snapped at my heels in a way it hadn't done for a long time. Megan looked pale and wobbled.

"I don't know why I feel like this," she mumbled, looking for water in her daysack.

I handed her mine. "For beings to manifest on our side of the veil takes a lot of energy, they'll suck it from anything in the area, including us."

She looked at me in alarm. "Did they know we were there?"

"I don't know. I don't think so, or we'd have been chased and probably caught. It's their territory, not ours. We wouldn't stand a chance."

"That's not alarming at all," she said. "I need food."

I found a high-energy bar for her. For a moment she looked as if she'd push it away, but her shoulders slumped, and she took it from me. "I'll run off the calories."

"You don't need to, Meg, and we could go running together."

"No, we couldn't."

I frowned at her. "What's that mean?"

"Now!" a voice yelled to my right.

Five figures came rushing out of the darkness. Two from in front, hidden by the thick shadows of the trees filling the hedgerow and stonewall. Two from behind, who could've been on the far side of the footpath entrance for all the attention I was paying at the time. One from the side.

Megan yelped and went down, her hand still clutching the food. She tried to roll, but someone stood over her and dropped onto her chest. I bellowed in rage and went for the Glock at my hip, only for a baseball bat to come at me from the dark and smack my left shoulder so hard my arm numbed instantly, and I dropped the weapon. I'd felt the bat move past my ear. These guys meant us serious harm. The pain in my shoulder and chest almost overwhelmed me, but training flicked that damned switch and I roared at my attackers.

The man with the baseball bat wore a plaid shirt and jeans like a builder might, and he certainly fit the profile. I charged him, knowing I needed a weapon. He raised the bat, but I came in faster than he thought possible, and low. Using my right shoulder, I barrelled into his belly and heard him grunt as air rushed out. Then the big muscles in my thighs took over. I rose and shoved his legs upwards with my right hand. The left didn't respond to my signals. The bloke tumbled over my back and hit the ground hard. I heard the bat skitter off onto the tarmac of the lane and went after it.

Despite being a lefty, I'd gone to a boarding school that believed in outdoor sport, regardless of the Scottish climate. Like many left-handed people, I'd learned to be as ambidextrous as possible. Moving effortlessly, tiredness long forgotten, I scooped up the bat. In the dark, I'd never find the Glock. I just had to hope no one else did.

"Right, you fuckers, come and get some," I yelled.

My first objective was stopping Megan's attacker. The punches raining down on her meant she'd curled into a ball and tried to protect her head. They were untrained haymakers, but still heavy enough to cause damage.

The bat rotated in my hand as I tested its weight. Expensive, wooden, good.

Three of the men came at me, two carrying bats, one a knife that caught the moonlight. It takes a long time to train well with both. Sometimes, just a swing and a chunk of luck isn't enough. The first person I smacked was the man over Megan's small body. I hit him hard enough in the side to hear something snap, and he howled, as she thrashed about with enough force to roll him off. She then scrambled out of my way.

A bat came in a wide swing at my head, someone else lunged with a knife.

Without my left arm operating properly, I'd struggle to have any kind of control over these jokers, so I needed to end this farce without any of my usual techniques. Rather than try to step back from the wild, one-handed swing of the bat, I stepped into the man's space. The most dangerous part of a baseball bat is the end. It moves fast and it is very hard. I'd avoided that, and I drove the rounded handle end of my weapon into the man's guts, just at the solar plexus. These guys smelt off. Their odour should be either of building sites or of aftershave and shower gel. This close, all I noticed was cigarette smoke and the smell of booze, and unwashed bodies. Like homeless, unwashed bodies. The man doubled over. I turned him towards the guy with the knife, putting a body between us, and fired down with my elbow into the centre of my enemy's back while also kicking him hard in the leg. I wanted to hit the knee joint, but I had the wrong angle. Still, he yelped and went down.

Megan moved in with her asp.

Next came knife boy. He was a boy as well, twenty at the most. Vicious looking bastard. Small and tough. He swung the knife like he'd seen too many martial arts films. I tried curling the fingers of my left hand. Still no action, but I did manage to lift it. That meant I probably hadn't snapped anything in my collarbone, but my God, it bitched like a banshee.

I didn't bother waiting for the knife to come to me. It didn't seem wise. Keeping the technique close and tight, as I would with eskrema sticks, I held the bat about halfway up its length. Taking a line from left hip to right shoulder, I whipped the bat up into his knife hand, forcing it to withdraw. At the apex of my attack, even as he moved backwards, eyes wide and surprised, I brought the bat down hard in the same direction. Under its own weight and the twist in my hips, the bat connected with the lad's head.

He dropped.

I turned to number three, who clearly wasn't impressed with the outcome.

Yelling a war cry, I lifted the bat and ran at him. The

poor bastard dropped his weapon and crouched into a ball, covering his head.

I pulled up and looked down. "That's new." I rolled my left shoulder and groaned. It really hurt.

"Help here," Megan ordered. She struggled with the man who'd been beating her as she tried to subdue him without causing additional damage.

I strode over and punched the man in the face. Hard. He went down. Again. At the edge of the road, I saw a familiar shape. My Glock. Picking it up, I felt the tension leave me. None of them carried firearms, which would make life safer for all of us.

"You okay?" I asked her.

She looked at me. Blood poured from a cut over her eye and her nose and lip.

"No," she croaked.

"Okay, go over there, sit down and wait." I didn't have long; she'd be going into shock. Experienced police officer or not, it's hard to take action after receiving a beating.

"Back up?" she asked.

"No point. They won't know anything useful unless you want to deal with the paperwork?" I asked her.

She shook her head, groaned and limped off, holding her side. I heard voices from the camp and saw Leaze running down the road towards us. Megan had help. That was good.

"Stay back," I ordered. "It's not safe here."

"Are they the ones who murdered my friend?" came Aggie's voice from the darkness.

"No," I said. "No, this is something different. Please stay away. Help Megan."

Turning my back on the people we'd met from the protest group, I squinted into the night. Just past the entrance to the footpath, I saw a dark van pressed into the hedge. These were not locals of Madron. The man who'd almost broken my shoulder rose to his feet. I lifted the Glock.

"I want answers. Nice and quick, please." I kept my voice low, not wanting an audience.

"Fuck off, you won't shoot me."

Covering the distance between us in three strides, I pushed the gun into his temple and glared into his eyes. "I'm guessing you want to go for round two. I suggest you think again. My friend over there might be police, but I am not." I pushed hard into his head with the barrel. "Give me a reason not to spray your life all over this road."

His eyes echoed the fear growing in his belly. "Alright, alright. What do you want to know?"

"Who hired you?"

"Some woman. She came into the city and found us near the train station. Offered us money and the van to come up here tonight and attack anyone we saw coming out of the pathway over there." His eyes moved to the footpath, his head couldn't.

So, Eloise wasn't beyond using hired grunts to do the dirty work her people couldn't in case violence went against their moral, eco-friendly, code of fucking honour. I was going to enjoy setting Sanchez on the damned woman. That would serve them both right.

"This woman, did she have a posh accent and long silver hair?"

"Dunno, about the hair, she wore a hat. The accent was posh though. She was tall. We just… We needed the money. The streets—"

"Not interested. When did she come to find you?"

"Yesterday. Said we needed to be here tonight, maybe

tomorrow, just in case someone turned up. I'm guessing that's you?" he muttered. "We was told to stop you going up this path, or get you coming out of the wood, depending."

"I want you to pick these guys up and put them in the van and fuck off. Never come back. Whatever she paid you isn't worth dying for, and if you think for a minute, I won't put a hole in any of you, then you're mistaken."

"Yeah, alright, tough guy, I get the message, you don't have to be a prick about it," he muttered, moving away from me.

I picked up Megan's dropped daysack, and the other bats, hurling them over the wall into the field.

"One more question," I said, as he lifted the knife wielding lad out of the road. "Did she supply the clothing?"

He looked at me and nodded. "Said we needed to look like builders. How'd you know we wasn't?"

"Wrong body odour," I told him. "Builders shower and use aftershave in my experience. You look too desperate, and you're all too thin to be anything but addicts."

"She said you'd be an easy mark. Never said nuffin' about no guns."

"She lies a lot. It's a bad habit. Don't let her find you. Go to a different city."

The man grunted, and I backed off, moving away while keeping my focus on the group struggling to reach their van. I berated myself. I should have checked our exit, but I never thought Eloise would do something so damned stupid. She wanted to perform the ceremony, knew I'd be here because of the deaths, and she'd set me up. When the van started, I watched them turn around, and I lifted the Glock one last time as they rumbled past me. It would help keep them honest and stop any bright ideas about running me down.

Once I'd seen the van leave the area, I jogged down the

lane to catch up with Megan. My shoulder moaned and bitched, but my fingers now danced as I tested them with guitar chord manoeuvres. It would be a while before it fully came back online, and I'd have some serious bruising in the morning, but for now, I felt lucky.

# Chapter Twenty

I found Megan sitting in the communal area of the camp, near the fire, with a mug in one hand and a cloth to her face in the other. Behind her, I saw TikTok girl. Christ, she was young and always there, watching, recording. Present, but never really part of events. The protesters moved out of my way in silence. Probably wise, I was in no mood to be playing tactful games of 'let's be friends'.

Megan looked up at me and winced as her eyeball hit the swelling. "You okay?"

I grunted. "Bastards didn't have a clue." My shoulder said something different, but I'm a Royal Marine Commando and the front of the manual ought to read 'No ouchies here'. It didn't stop me from flexing my left hand as feeling gradually returned in a rush of pins and needles. "The most important thing is, are you okay?"

She nodded, but her eyes were too bright, and she shivered. I moved closer and added my large bike jacket to the blanket covering her. My jacket was probably what saved my shoulder. Then I put a gentle arm around her shoulders.

Feeling her weight leaning into me made me feel able to hold her closer still. We snuggled.

"Where does it hurt?" I asked.

"He caught me on the side of my head. That's bad." She removed the cloth, and I saw her skin split over her brow ridge. A black eye and swelling down the side of her face made the anger surge again. I should've ground his face into the tarmac.

"Alright, we need to get you home. I don't think the bike is a good idea. I can phone Sid, or we can get in touch with one of your colleagues? Or Adrian?" I asked, hating the name in my mouth. Her fears about him still reverberated in my mind like little shards of glass stuck in my skin.

"Sid. I want to go home to your place," she mumbled.

I fished out my phone and made the call.

"What the hell?" he grumbled.

"We've been attacked. Megan's hurt. I can't bring her back on the bike."

"On my way," he said, without another word.

I hung up. He'd find us.

"Meg, do you want to go to the hospital? That swelling looks bad."

A man appeared in front of Megan. I recognised him but didn't know his name.

The next few minutes surprised me. It turned out he was a paramedic here on sabbatical. After poking Megan's face, he said there didn't appear to be any broken bones, but it would be wise to have an X-ray. She'd never lost consciousness, so a concussion was unlikely. Surface damage.

"I'm not spending hours in A&E to be told I've got some nasty bruising," was Megan's predictable response.

I asked him to check my shoulder, and after more

poking and wincing, he declared me fit. I watched him return to his tent, grumbling about idiots. He wasn't wrong; we both needed to be checked out properly, but we'd both taken a beating before in the line of duty.

"Why'd they always get my face?" Megan grumbled. "First week on the job, some sack of shit punched me on the nose and broke it." She poked the end of her nose. "You would think it wasn't big enough to break. I tell you, that bloody hurt more than this." She let Leaze put some arnica cream on it and agreed to some rescue remedy being dropped in her mouth. I've never been sure of the benefits of homeopathy, but it helped Megan's shaking.

"What happened?" Leaze asked once she realised I wasn't going to rip anyone's head off.

"Your great and noble priestess of Anwen's Children, hired a bunch of homeless guys from the city, bought them a van, and told them to wait for us. That's what happened," I snarled like a wolf guarding pups.

Megan glanced at me out of her left eye. "Really? She did that?"

I nodded. "You know how persuasive I can be when I want answers." She'd certainly witnessed it a few times since we started working together.

"You're a teddy bear," she murmured, snuggling even closer. She'd be in my lap any moment, not that I'd mind.

"More bear, less teddy, thank you very much."

"Are you going to report her?" Leaze asked.

"She'll be handled," I said ominously. "What do you know about her?"

Leaze shrugged. "Less than you, I expect. Her followers are very devout and seem honest. They sacrifice a lot for Eloise's vision of the future with Trystan."

"What do you know of him?" I asked. We'd have his legal details, but I needed hands-on impressions.

"He's a strange lad. Very quiet and self-contained. Speaks Cornish more than English, if he speaks at all. Knows the names of all the trees, animals, insects and birds, that kind of thing. He has schooling, but he's kept isolated from the other kids here, which I've never liked. It takes a community to raise a child, you know?"

I didn't, but I nodded.

"Some of us have been worried about him. It's not good to be the focus of so much esoteric law at that age. They go and have their rituals in the woods, or on the hill." She jerked her head towards the summit and its tiny patch of moorland. "But we aren't part of it. They aren't like the rest of us, and if we try to join, we're pushed out. Are you really saying she paid to have you beaten up?"

In the darkness of the now quiet night, I heard the Mini's familiar engine. Giving Leaze a tight smile, I said, "That's exactly what happened. There are things in that wood which are dangerous, Leaze. Things I don't yet understand, but you need to keep your people out of there and keep your young women safe. I know this place is important to you, but it might be wise to move away. I think Anwen's Children and the building site have disturbed something."

"Like what?" she asked.

How much to tell her? I didn't want to see any of them get hurt. "I don't know, Leaze, really. I can't tell you what it is, what *they* are, I just need you to be very careful. When I have more intel, I'll share it."

"Is this what Rural Security does? Deals with this kinda thing?" she asked, her voice smaller than ever.

"It's some of what I do. It's often a moving brief. For all I know right now, these could be people dressing up, hiding in shadows, sniffing glue, or coke, or something else I don't know about."

"You don't believe that, do you?" she asked.

Megan, who might've dozed off against me for a minute, said, "Just keep everyone out. If I could make my team in Redruth believe what I think I saw tonight, I'd have the place cordoned off forever. For now, let's make sure you guys are clear and the builders stay away."

Leaze considered this for a long moment. "I'll do all I can, and I'll make sure I don't mention the possibility of there being something in that wood which could give us a glimpse of another world." She was not a stupid woman. "That's what we're dealing with, right?"

Reluctant as I was, I nodded. My phone buzzed, and I texted Sid badly with my right thumb, to tell him where to meet us. After helping Megan to her feet, I said to Leaze, "Please, don't get curious. I will explain when we have more to share."

Leaze groaned as she stood, using her hands on her thighs to act as a lever. "I'll hold you to that, Griffin."

Sid's long legs were hurrying over the bare earth, looking like a dancing daddy-long-legs in the moonlight. It was good to see him. After hurried explanations, we bundled Megan into the Mini, and I climbed onto the bike. It wasn't easy to ride home, but using Sid as a guide, I managed to stick to the road.

The following morning, we all rose early. If the others were anything like me, anxiety kept us awake until the darkest hours, then nipped us into consciousness far too soon.

"Oh, Megan, that's terrible," I said the moment she appeared in the kitchen. She wore one of my t-shirts, and her legs were naked. I noticed this before the bruising on her face. I am a bad man.

"Thanks, love you too, cuz," she grumbled, heading for the kettle. Her face had swollen, and the bruising looked like a rainbow's evil twin. "It'll calm down after some more painkillers and another ice pack." She looked at me out of her left eye, the right almost closed. "You get any sleep?"

"Not much." I shooed her to sit down while I took over making her coffee and emptying the ice tray.

"Griff, what the hell were those things? What did I see out there?" She sounded more fragile than I'd ever heard before. It made my heart ache. I'd done this to her, shattered her world, and given it monsters.

"You don't have to go back, Megan. I can ask for another police liaison. Maybe Bristol would be best—"

"Fuck Bristol and don't be a twat. I took a knockdown, so what? Have you any idea how many times I've landed on my arse dealing with drunks and arseholes who think it's okay to hit a woman? Or even people who just see the uniform and wanna go to see how tough I am? I'm staying right where I am, Griffin Woodbury. Whatever is happening to Cornwall. Whatever weird shit DoPI's into. This is my county, and it's my job to protect it." She took a breath. "But you're cooking breakfast, and I want porridge because my jaw hurts."

I carried a large mug of coffee towards her with due reverence. "Welcome to the crazy train."

We were quiet for a while as I prepared the demanded sustenance. I heard Sid moving around upstairs and Luce's voice. Good, we'd need her help. None of us spoke about the previous night while we ate. For a moment, we just wanted to feel normal, to be normal. The spectre of the incubus and all the events surrounding the thing's banishment loomed large in the room.

Sid finally broke the taboo. "I need to collect the equipment down at St Day's Cemetery today. If you two have to deal with things at the woodland, then Luce has agreed to help me." He stared at me, waiting for a response.

My mother's grave. I'd not had an episode since we'd set it up, so would there even be readings to collect? Unless that weird vision I saw in the woods during the ceremony was an episode? I almost longed for the days when my mind threw up memories from my time in the Sahel; it would be easier to understand.

"We saw something last night," I finally said into our collective silence. The weight in the room increased.

"Isn't that part of the job?" Luce asked, looking at Sid, then me.

"You'd think, but this was something…" I rubbed my face, feeling stubble at least three days old. It'd be a beard in a minute. I'd never grown a beard.

*Yeah, because that's a helpful thought. Just tell 'em.*

I took a breath and started our weird tale. Between us, we described the ceremony, the graphic image of Trystan's communication—or was it just noise?—with the Mother, and the beings in the shadows. Then I explained to all of them the vision I'd seen take place millennia before, of people heartbroken by their loss.

Luce was intrigued. "You really think that was an actual event?"

I shrugged. "Who knows, but it felt real, just like the last one I saw down at the quoit."

"Could you draw the clothing? Maybe we could record your experience, so I can do some more research into the site? I need to look for evidence of the standing stone in the area. We know many of them were broken up and used for walls. If we find—"

Sid placed a hand on her arm to forestall the torrent of words. "I'm not sure if that's the bit we need to focus on right now, babe."

She frowned and removed her hand from his. "No, I don't suppose it is for you. I suppose you would like me to think about mythology, though you could just Google it."

"We need more abstract thought than AI can manage," I pointed out, trying to ease her sudden tension.

"There's not much more I can tell you than I did the other evening before all this began. There are various tree spirits in the world, but if the druids had specific names for their versions, then they've been lost to time. As the concept spans many cultures worldwide, it's safe to say the native religions here had the same ideas. That means we're looking at dryads. Though, it's an odd thing to say. In myth, they are traditionally women who are beautiful. Often causing problems for gods and men alike. Look at the story of Eurydice and Orpheus. He had to travel to the underwood to retrieve her when a snake bite caused her to die." She focused on me. "Do you really think they are the ones who caused the deaths?"

"It's hard not to."

She pondered this. "They are always peaceful unless you cut down their trees."

"That explains it," said Megan, who had another ice pack attached to her face. "I'd be pissed off if I were an ancient spirit and someone bulldozed my family home."

Luce tapped the tabletop, her frown deepening further. "But that's just it. We've been cutting down trees since forever, so why now? Why here? What woke the spirits and forced them to act? And if I'm right about the deaths, with the crone, matron and maiden, triple sacrifice, what are they calling out to for help?"

"I don't want to think about that one," I said. I'd spoken to Lorne Turner at length about what had happened at Clatworthy Reservoir and the local nature god they'd stumbled over. I didn't have a djinn to save me if I faced a god, even a small one. I'd be doing this alone. "As to how this happened… I think Anwen's Children have something to do with it. They've found a thin patch in the veil, and they've punched a hole big enough to let these beings live in our world again."

"Even if these are tree spirits of some kind, how do we stop them?" Megan asked. "They aren't going to give up unless the woodland is left alone. Right?" She looked at us in turn, seeking confirmation.

We all nodded.

I pushed back from the table. "I need to talk to the company that owns the site. Or I need Sanchez to start pulling strings."

Megan put down the ice. "It'll take time to do that, Griffin. The first thing we need to do is talk to Trystan without Eloise being around. If you want my advice as a police officer, the most important thing is to stop the murder of the maiden. That's our priority. We can start the process of speaking with the man who owns the building site, but I doubt we'll get anywhere. Trystan might give us a direct way in, and we might be able to head this off, or put these spirits back to sleep before anyone else dies. It's going to be impossible to control the number of people in that protest group. We'll never keep all the young women safe. Someone will make a mistake. Telling the protesters the truth will just cause more people to arrive. Hiding it from them makes them vulnerable. We need Anwen's Children on our side."

# Chapter Twenty-One

We gave ourselves the morning to rest up, do some more research, fill out reports, and just think things through. We'd take Megan's car down to Madron. She'd never get a bike helmet to be comfortable with the level of bruising on her face, and I wanted some serious security at hand if Eloise had any more surprises in store for us. Knowing at least some of this problem was human, helped. Going to the office, I trawled my shelf of toys and the weapons' cabinet for human-shaped issues: pepper spray, Glock 17 and three clips, asps, plasti-cuffs. Then the more unusual items: holy water for two of us, two sets of iron daggers, some tempered wooden stakes, an ointment our alchemists designed for protection made of several different berries, silver daggers because I had no idea how to kill a tree spirit beyond killing its tree. Not something anyone wanted to do.

I stood in the darkened, silent office, trying to figure out if there was anything I'd forgotten, or what else I could take to help. An offering? I Googled it. Anything from cornmeal and berries to shiny stones or crystals. Well, I had a lot of crystals here. Checking which were located in Cornwall, I took some quartz and the far rarer, Cornish turquoise. The quartz was rough, but the turquoise I held in my hand wasn't and I smoothed my thumb over the stone's surface. Without being really aware of it, I slipped the pendant Megan had given me, the witch's stone, out from under my shirt and rubbed that as well. Both felt warm to the touch, and despite my logical mind telling me I was a fool, I took it as a good omen.

Tree spirits. Who'd have thought? How many people had wandered that woodland over the centuries, leaving wishes at the cloutie tree or offerings at the spring, only to be watched by the spirits of trees? What an incredible concept. This entire mission was becoming so much darker, but at the same time, more captivating and beautiful than any other I'd experienced. I knew I should call Sanchez, give her an update and a full report, but sullying this with her cynical approach to the veil's hidden inhabitants didn't feel right. These were elemental creatures who had no desire to dominate or destroy humanity like the incubus, but we had woken them and were in the process of destroying them.

I did not want to kill tree spirits.

I did not want DoPI to kill tree spirits.

During the day, Megan called Leaze, no one had gone missing from the camp. I asked Luce about the timing of the crone, matron, maiden link we'd theorised, and she just shrugged. With Jennifer going missing, we'd had twenty-four hours before she'd been found dead. River forty-eight hours. These were a bit rough for timings, but it was the best we had. We also had just one day between Jennifer's body being discovered and River going missing. Another set of data to consider. We were already outside that time frame. We just didn't know if the time frame was important. If it was, we had our perfect crucible and a ticking clock. They'd be wanting a maiden and might not wait for one to wander into their home. They might just come and get her.

Considering what I'd seen during the ritual we'd witnessed and the state of the bodies, I'd say these creatures weren't going to be passive in their request for a maiden. The entire camp was under threat by something we didn't understand.

It also occurred to me, I wasn't telling Sanchez about this operation for one reason. Her remit was the preservation of human life and the current status quo with regard to the veil and its inhabitants. DoPI was there to research the hidden world and contain it. I knew without asking that if I couldn't settle this through peaceful means, DoPI would come in and flatten the wood, removing the threat. Doing such a thing would damage much more than just a few hundred trees. I had the feeling it would further weaken the veil.

Then, there was Trystan. I leaned against my desk and gave the lad a moment's reflection. That he was a natural mystic meant DoPI would want him and, to be honest, they'd be able to help him. We had experienced people who would offer the lad an education, enabling him to safely grow and develop whatever natural skills he possessed. The only problem was, what would DoPI want in return? They'd find out how to use him for their own reasons, and that made me nervous. Still, what was Eloise doing? Wasn't she using him right now? How safe was it for the boy to communicate with something—we didn't know it was 'Mother'—through the veil with people who had far less knowledge than the centuries of detailed information which DoPI could access?

Also, Trystan needed people his own age. He ought to go to school.

It sounded like I was trying to rehome a dog.

The quiet of the office, in the semidarkness lit only by Sid's computers and a few security lights, had given me a breather. Something I badly needed. It left me focused and centred.

In the last few days, I'd taken some serious physical, but mostly emotional shocks. The dead were in my life. Actively. I remembered one night, talking to Lorne, about how he'd felt haunted by the dead of his campaigns. Now we knew it was because he'd been a powerful psychic, only to have that enhanced by the djinn.

For me, something different had happened. I didn't see dead people. I didn't hear them. However, I had some kind of connection to the past that came through when I slept, or during those moments of high stress as a child, or if I'd been daydreaming too deeply. Was I psychic? Yes, that much I had to admit to, I worked for DoPI after all, but what kind?

Then, Megan loomed large in my thoughts. I had the feeling I'd be pulling Adrian's arms off fairly soon and hitting him with the wet ends. The image appealed and gave me the impetus to get moving.

Unable to put off what would be another long day, I left the office and climbed back on the bike. I'd be driving Megan's car, her right eye pretty much closed. When we reached the camp, we needed to come up with a plan to find Trystan on his own. I wanted him to open up to us without having to resort to arrests or any kind of violence. We needed trust, and we needed it fast.

*Take some damned dog treats with you.*

Helpful, Griffin, a really helpful thought.

By the time I returned to Turpin Cottage, Megan was dressed, and the swelling had calmed down a little, even if she now looked like a three-year-old had decided to use face paints on her, swirling all the colours together. Despite the obvious discomfort, she was… happy.

As I drove, I had to poke, as if her good humour was a sore tooth. "You seem happier than you have been."

She sat next to me, enjoying the view as we ambled back down to Madron through the Friday afternoon tourist traffic. "I am. I thought I wanted the city life. To be a city copper. Maybe look at moving into CID, but…" She gestured out the window. "Look at this. Why would I want to leave this?"

"Bristol's nice. Somerset is pretty," I said, knowing she'd hear the lie in my words.

She did. "Don't talk rubbish." Her Cornish accent kicked in. "I'm not leaving my home. I can't. I love Cornwall."

"What about Adrian?" Did I manage to keep the sneer out of my voice?

By the look she shot me, no, I did not. "I'll be dealing with him, Griffin. I don't need your help. I've two brothers who've never been much use in that department. It's something I've learned to handle."

"It's over between you two?" Be still, my thrashing heart.

Megan fell silent. Shit, I'd pushed too far.

"Griff, it's not that simple—" she began.

I rushed in. "Don't. It's none of my business. You're an adult. I'm here if you need me." In the slow-moving traffic, I realised my hands strangled the steering wheel. I forced them to relax.

Megan's head dipped in acknowledgement of my escape

attempt. "I spoke to Mum. When I asked her about you and me going for a visit to talk about Aunt Hazel, she seemed okay." She paused. "Well, no, that's not true."

I glanced at her and saw her attempted frown, despite the bruising. "She said, 'Well, I guess it's time he knew'."

"What's that mean?" I asked, senses pinging in alarm.

"I don't have a Scooby, mate. I tried to ask, but you know what she's like, she started rattling on about Dad and the cows and…"

"You gave up trying to keep her on point?"

"Hmm. Usually means she's hiding something. God only knows what, mind. It could be anything."

"When can we go down?" I asked suddenly impatient. Or desperate to know more.

"I think we need to sort this out first. Then you'll have headspace for it all."

I clenched my jaw.

"Don't do that, Griff. I know you want answers, and you'll at least be able to ask some questions, but we can't do anything about it now. We need a plan for talking to Trystan, maybe we should be doing that. After all, we can have Eloise on conspiracy to commit numerous crimes."

"Except you didn't arrest any of them, so we don't have details."

"She doesn't know that." Megan tried to wink and smile, but it hurt too much and she groaned. "I'm going to make the damned woman pay for this."

"How do you want to handle it, then?" I asked.

Megan considered her options. "I should've changed into my uniform. It's always a good place to start."

"Official badges and threats?"

"I think so. Let's scare them a bit."

"What if that causes Trystan to close ranks?"

"We need to separate him and get a different appropriate adult in to help. Someone outside Anwen's Children, but still a person he might trust."

"Leaze?" I suggested.

"I think so. We'll take her up the field, state that we have questions for him, but it isn't appropriate to have one of the cult with him, get him down the field and see where it goes. If this Eloise gets shitty, then we threaten Social Services, arrests, and we point out what we know about that attack last night."

It turned out we didn't need a strategy. When we arrived at the camp, things were quiet. I'd pulled the car into the field, dry now after several days without rain, and parked at the edge of the main area. Leaze and several others approached the moment we stepped out of the vehicle.

"Afternoon." We all exchanged greetings, things tense after the previous night's attack.

Megan smoothed things over. "Don't worry, we aren't here to cause a problem. I just need some help. Leaze, could we have a quiet word?"

The others, faces mostly marred by scowls, wandered away.

Leaze looked exhausted. The lines on her face had deepened, and her hair hung limp around her slumped shoulders. "What can I do for you?" She nodded towards the central meeting place. "They all want to know what's going on. Why we can't move around freely. What you're doing about these deaths? With the best will in the world, your actions are causing a lot of conspiracy theories to float about. It's hard to keep people cooperative when we're not getting the truth."

"The truth is dangerous," I said.

She huffed at me. "That's what all controlling authorities state. Around here, you're on quicksand with that answer."

A good point, but not one I could solve easily. If I told Leaze about the existence of DoPI it would be all over the internet by lunchtime, and I'd be hauled over the coals, maybe literally, by Sanchez come teatime. Our tech gurus would then spend weeks trying to chase down all references to our existence and removing them from the internet.

Megan approached the woman. "You're exhausted."

Tears filled Leaze's eyes. "I've lost two good friends in the last few days and seen more violence than I have in more than two decades of protests. Something is happening here we don't understand. I'm scared. We're all scared. And for some reason, I've found myself in charge of being your contact. I'm totally overwhelmed and out of my depth. Jennifer and River would've known what to do, and they..." She burst into tears.

Rather than push the poor woman any further, I walked away while Megan took over the comforter role. From my location, near the field's gate, I stared up at Anwen's Children's camp. I pondered my options. Subtle would be less disruptive, but after last night's attack, I felt some justification to just charge up there and bang heads together until they leaked some answers.

Then something happened. As I watched, a wave of hyperawareness hit me. The kind that usually swept over me the moment someone fired their weapon in my vicinity. My neck prickled, and a chill raced down my spine. A slim figure on the hillside stood apart from the decorated vans.

Trystan. I began to walk up the hill. He started to walk down. I became transfixed by his presence. The world turned hazy at the edges, but he remained incredibly clear. As if I were seeing him through the scope of a rifle. As he drew closer, a remarkable thing happened. Colour danced around his body. A tight armour, then these odd wisps of green and gold wiggled around his head and down his chest, as if they were reaching out to me. Was I seeing an aura? I'd never seen one before. DoPI knew they existed, but we hadn't learned to use them in any constructive way.

When we met in the centre, near a dizzyingly yellow clump of dandelions, Trystan stared up at me with his intense, grey-eyed gaze, and I stared at him. For the first time in my life, I had a sense of what a brother should feel like when he is close to you. That odd level of familiarity you only share with true family. It happened with Megan, but not with my immediate blood relatives.

"Hello," he said in his soft voice. Christ, he was young, but also ancient. This was very confusing.

"Hello. Do you remember who I am? My job?" I asked.

"I do. You are lying, but it isn't a bad lie. I know you can help me. I need help." His Cornish accent was thicker than a seal's blubber, but as soft as a fledgling's feather.

"I'm sorry about the lies. They are necessary for the moment. I will tell you the truth when it's safe to do so." The promise came easily, and I meant it. "What kind of help do you need?" I had an odd moment where I had to fight the urge to drop to one knee and offer some kind of homage to my liege lord. I knew I lived in Cornwall, but this wasn't King Arthur, and I wasn't Galahad.

He glanced behind me for a moment, and I knew Megan approached with Leaze. The lad said, "Maybe I should speak to you both? The lady—she's a police officer?"

"That's right. And Leaze wants to help make sure you stay safe. That we aren't infringing on your rights."

He nodded. "I'll come with you."

"What about your mother?"

"Eloise is asleep. She will stay like that for a while yet. We have some time." He didn't smile, and I saw a terrible sadness lurking in the background somewhere. If he'd been any younger, I'd have offered him my hand and led him down the hill.

Rather than doing that, we walked together, with Megan and Leaze behind us, back to the communal area of the camp. People stared as we passed them. I had the sense that Trystan rarely went anywhere without his people surrounding him. A quiet and odd kind of reverence hovered over the community.

When we reached the central fire pit, Leaze took over. "We'll go in my van. It'll be private."

I wondered if we'd all fit inside, but it turned out Leaze had a large horse truck, and the interior had more room than most touring caravans. We entered through the side door, and I tried not to fill up the space with my bulk. Not easy for me.

Trystan sat on a built-in sofa made for two and Leaze sat next to him. Megan took another built-in chair next to a small table, and I opted to lower myself to the clean rug on the floor.

We were all silent for a moment, the atmosphere one of peace, but also tension. As if secrets were about to be shared, and they weren't good ones.

Trystan spoke first. "You saw what happened in the woods, didn't you?" He said this to me.

"Yes." There wasn't anything to be gained by lying.

"Do you think I can speak to Mother?" he asked, his eyes soft and pleading. He wanted something from me, but I didn't know what.

The truth, it's all I had. "I think you communicated with something last night. I don't know if it was something we'd think of as Mother Earth. Do you understand what I mean when I talk about the veil?"

He nodded. "The barrier between us and the dreamlands?"

Well, it was close enough. "Yeah, we'll go with that." I certainly couldn't call it dreamlands. More like nightmares considering some of the crap that spilled out. "I saw you break through the veil, and that enabled something to talk through you. It's a very, very dangerous thing to do alone."

"I wasn't alone," he stated.

I glanced at Leaze, who frowned in concern. She said, "But it doesn't make it safe to be with others who don't understand the consequences of going too far with this stuff." The woman understood more than she was letting on about what Anwen's Children were up to in that wood.

Trystan's steady gaze went to Megan. "I think I need to be arrested."

She blinked in surprise. "Why would I do that?"

"I think I killed those women." His luminous eyes filled with tears, and they rolled silently down his soft cheeks. "I think this is all my fault, and I don't want to do it anymore. I'm really scared. It feels all wrong. When I saw you the other day, I knew, like I know other stuff, that we were the same." This, his longest speech yet, finished with his eyes on mine.

## Chapter Twenty-Two

We were the same? How? I tried not to let the panic rise. He certainly wasn't referring to me as a Marine or an investigator. Why would he? That meant he understood the hidden side of my life. The bit that confused me most. Did this kid know more than I did about my spooky night wanderings? I wasn't sure how I felt about that.

*You do know. You're uncomfortable.*

Megan, of course, went straight to the bloodied heart of the matter. "What do you mean you killed those women?" She sounded sceptical, and I didn't blame her. He couldn't weigh more than fifty-five kilos and hadn't yet grown into his arms and legs. There was more fat and muscle on a sparrow. He'd never be able to lift someone of Jennifer Mancore's size. Never mind capture and kill someone as powerful as River.

Leaze put a comforting hand on the boy's back. "It's okay, Trystan, just tell them the truth as you know it. Their job is to understand. We can get a solicitor if that's what you want?"

The boy sniffed and Leaze handed him a box of tissues. He surprised her when he leaned against her. "I don't need one of those people, I just need someone to listen."

Leaze hugged the boy close. "Okay, then you talk to these guys and they'll listen. I'm here if you need anything."

He looked at her. "Do you have any biscuits?"

Leaze laughed. "I've homemade flapjacks? How does that sound?"

"*Meur ras.*"

I glanced at Megan. She mouthed, 'Thank you'.

Once Trystan had devoured two flapjacks, and we all had one and a glass of juice, the lad started to explain what had happened.

"I know this won't make much sense, but it's all I have, and I want to do the right thing. The trees need me to be honest. I…" He studied the highly polished floorboards of the truck's interior. We all waited. When he started again, it was barely more than a feather's whisper. "I'm not sure I'm human. I don't know my birth parents. My mother left me with Eloise and ran away. She's now in a hospital. No one knew my father. Eloise says my mother never spoke of the night I was conceived. I was born on the road. Never even been to school." He said this as if it were the greatest failure of a parent's duty, depriving him of an education. "I've never had none of them immuni… Immun…"

Leaze said, "Immunisations?"

He nodded. "Yes, those. I've been taught other things. I know all the plants and animals. Their uses, and how to create healing potions. She taught me spells and stuff, but when we've been in the smaller villages and towns, I've asked about school, and she says I'm too special. That normal education will strip me of my gifts."

This was probably true. Routines and mundane learning

could dampen things down for the boy, but it would resurface soon enough. Though school hadn't calmed my nighttime sorties very much.

"Over the years, the rituals we perform have grown. We used to just do simple rites at river junctions, at ancient springs, under old trees and at crossroads in drovers' lanes. Places where the nature spirits like to play or live. We'd leave offerings and things. Then Eloise started wanting me to do more.

"I can see them. All of them. The spirits that live on the edges of our vision. I can talk to them. Not with words, but images in my head. Simple things. Like asking where the best berries grow, or the finest wild garlic in the spring. I can ask permission to take green wood from a tree. Water spirits will bring me fish. I am of the land."

Trystan had no doubt within him about the validity of his statements. The adults surrounding him didn't respond. I think we were all worried about his progress along this path at such a young age.

Megan leaned forward, elbows resting on her knees. "What makes you think you hurt those women?"

Trystan's eyes met hers and held them in a way most teenage boys couldn't manage with an attractive woman. He had the air of being two people at once—this grave young man, and a sad old one. He said, "I woke the trees up. I've given them a voice, a form. I've created this, and they are calling out to their god, but he's gone. Long gone. I can't find him. I can't help them, and I can't make them go back to sleep. This is all my fault." He started to cry again.

Megan and I shared a long, silent look. Luce had been right, and we had a mess to deal with before these tree spirits decided to kill a young woman.

When the lad calmed, I asked, "Is there something we

can do to quieten down these spirits you woke up? Or maybe we can strike a deal with them? Explain to them somehow?"

The lad's chin wobbled. "That's why I knew I had to talk to you. I knows you seen things, hear things. They might respond if you're with me."

"You want me to go into the veil and talk to tree spirits?" I asked him, knowing I sounded sceptical. "I don't think—"

"You've been in it before," the young-old man said.

I knew why people followed Eloise. It wasn't because of her charm, but Trystan's honest nature. He was compelling, intense, like every indie band lead singer rolled up into one and coated in the essence of a master politician. Except it wasn't an artful power with him, it just came naturally. People would flock to him, even if he sold double glazing, second-hand cars, and snake oil out of the same shop.

Megan tapped my leg. "Can we have a word?"

I rose from the floor and followed her into the outside world. It felt good to breathe in fresh air and to feel the sun on my face. That truck had become a cocoon of doom.

"You're not considering this, right?" she asked, her eyes flashing a warning for me to tread lightly, or she'd be giving me a slap.

I stepped back, so she'd struggle to reach to make contact without moving forwards first. "I don't think I have much choice."

Megan sucked in a deep breath and turned in her circle-of-frustration, trying to capture her temper before it escaped. "Griffin. This is madness. You don't know what you're walking into. You think it's this veil, but the boy might be some master hypnotist, and what we saw the other night was some kind of illusion. For all we know, they have some poison in the lamps that makes you see things when you inhale their smoke."

Her ability to remain in denial about some of the things we'd experienced together was beginning to bore me.

"You don't have to be there. In fact, it's probably best if Sid is around, just in case something goes wrong. At least he believes."

"Don't take that tone."

*That's not a tone, woman. That's me being annoyed with you.*

"I'm not taking a tone, Megan. This is my job."

"To indulge a spoilt child in his fantasies?"

I muttered something foul under my breath. "Look, I get it; you don't want this to be real, but it is, and I have a duty to help Trystan." I repeated, "That's my job. You don't have to be there. You don't—" I stopped as I caught sight of something we really didn't need right now.

Eloise and two of the men from Anwen's Children, walking towards us at a pace.

"Oh shit," Megan muttered. She pulled back her shoulders, as did I, and suddenly we were a single unit with one objective. Stopping Anwen's Children.

"Where is my son?" Eloise yelled the moment she was in range.

"He's perfectly safe," I stated.

The woman's eyes were wild, and I don't think I'd ever seen that much hate on someone's face. That included some Somali pirates we fought off during an attempted boarding raid in the Gulf of Aden. They hadn't been very happy either.

Her finger jabbed at the air in front of my face, and her usually pale skin was flushed an ugly red. "You have no business interfering in my family. I will make a formal complaint to the authorities—"

Megan cut her off. “You are welcome to put in a formal complaint to my inspector, but it won’t go far. Trystan came with us of his own accord, and he has an appropriate adult, chosen by him, to make sure his rights are respected. He may not be an adult yet, but in the eyes of the law, he is old enough for self-determination.”

I had no idea if this was true, or police bollocks speech. It sounded good, though.

Eloise’s nostrils flared. “How dare you?”

One of the men reached out to touch her arm, but she flicked him off. They both stepped back, eyeing me. Which was probably wise. I wasn’t in the mood for playing silly buggers after the previous night.

Megan stepped up to Eloise and, despite having to look up at the taller woman, she didn’t lose any of her power. Impressive. I have to admit to using my bulk on more than one occasion to force people to back down.

The police officer came out to play. “If you don’t turn and walk away right now, I will arrest you.”

“For what?” the older woman spat.

“For conspiracy to commit a serious offence? For multiple crimes under the Offences against the Person Act 1861. Including, but not limited to, assault occasioning actual bodily harm, or grievous bodily harm, with or without intent. That’ll be the Crown Prosecution Service’s decision when I report the attack that was made on myself and my colleague last night. We have the details of the men involved and who paid them.” Megan didn’t drop her gaze for a moment.

I kept my eye on the two useless guards Eloise had brought with her. I was surprised one of them wasn’t the young man from the other day. Maybe he was still on the naughty step.

Eloise stepped back, straightening. "I have no idea what you're talking about."

Megan stepped forwards. "I have recorded evidence."

"I am Trystan's mother."

"I'm sure Social Services will be overjoyed to hear that when I discuss with them the fact that his physical and mental well-being are at risk due to the nature of your lifestyle and living conditions. Don't play this game with me, lady. I can do this all day, and I have done for many years." Megan crossed her arms over her chest and gave Eloise a proper scary stare. She really meant it.

It was time I stepped in. "We need his help, Eloise. He came to us because the poor boy thinks his actions have caused the deaths of these women." I glanced at the men as they shifted uneasily. This was all news to them, and I guessed it was unwelcome. It's not always easy to lead a cult. Sometimes, when the curtain is torn away, it all falls to pieces. "Sadly, I believe he's right. Not his fault. Not even your fault. Your ignorance of the species of creature you've disturbed is monumental, but that's a problem for another day. Today, we have to close this down before someone else dies." I was going to set Sanchez on this woman.

"The death of a few humans—"

I stepped up behind Megan. "Will be on your head if you don't help stop this. We'll make sure of that, Eloise. Be very careful before you reject this offer of co-operation and clemency." I might have to offer the carrot of clemency to gain her co-operation, but I knew Sanchez didn't have to, and it warmed my cynical heart to think about it.

"I want to discuss this with my son." Eloise set her feet, crossed her arms and the colour returned to her cheeks as she clenched her jaw.

"That'll be up to him," Megan said. "I'll ask him. You will stay here. Woodbury, don't let them near the truck."

"Yes, ma'am." I'd follow Megan's orders all day if necessary.

Megan walked back to the truck, our personal issues long forgotten. At least for the moment. Eloise stared past my shoulder, ignoring me the way a young priest tries to ignore a heaving cleavage. I remained still but used the time to think.

We had to stop these woodland creatures, these warrior dryads, from harming people. How? What did I have to offer in exchange? Nothing. They wanted us to bugger off and leave them alone, but how the hell would we manage that? Trystan wanted me to travel with him into the veil, but every time I'd gone close it hadn't ended well.

The dream vision I'd had during the debacle on Bodmin Moor. All the events around the incubus. My absences at night that lead me to digging up my mother's grave. Let's face it, the veil scared the shit out of me. We were meant to stay on this side. Maybe a practiced psychic of some kind could get a glimpse through that oily rainbow, but most of us shouldn't even try.

When I'd first joined DoPI, I'd been a Royal Marine Commando who just couldn't handle the violence of the fight anymore. I'd had borderline PTSD from seeing the horrors offered by ISIS clones in sub-Sahara Africa and what we'd had to do to take down those groups. I had both feet planted in the misery of the real world, and I lived in denial of my dream self wandering off into loolaa land.

The Department of Paranormal Investigations, started to change that, rapidly. I saw the damage this unknown and unknowable, other world could do to normal people. The havoc it caused and the evil it contained. I'd come to understand that many artists, writers, musicians and others, touched this other world, and it leaked into their work. What Lorne Turner and the rest of his people had faced in Barle's Keep had been a perfect example of this. Grimm's fairytales are another example. They showed the darkness of the other realms. Mythologies from all over the world were full of warnings about what can happen to a mortal human, even a hero, if they touch this strange place just the other side of our reality.

The modern world has grown far from these stories. We glimpse it in our dreams, but we don't usually interact with it. That world has drifted from our noisy, smelly, greedy plane of existence. I often wonder if that's a good thing, or a bad one. We battered it with our religions, our controls over nature, and virus-like ability to spread. Now, however, it was pushing back. We'd made it retreat too far, and I suspected its very survival was on the line. If our world died, they would die as well. So, it was fighting back.

The skirmishes were chaotic, lacking any kind of cohesion, but they were becoming more powerful and far more frequent. What would the world do when it discovered dryads were real? That incubus existed? Or djinn? Just the thought of that level of instant insanity in the population made my heart race. The implications were enormous.

From where I stood, I could see the woodland that contained the druids' circle and the cloutie tree. The thought of going into it and trying to bargain with these creatures, terrified me. As it should. They'd already killed two people. It wasn't just that, though. I had to go into a world that wouldn't welcome me. Its inhabitants didn't like humanity, with good cause. We'd closed down as many of the places where our worlds touched as possible. The dark was scary, and we'd only been living with electric light for a little over a century. For millennia, these beings had filled us with reasons to be scared of the dark, scared of certain valleys, or mountains, wary of even our sacred places.

*Here be dragons, soldier boy.*

I had a very bad feeling about this. I should call London, get DoPI down here. Find an expert to transverse the veil with more skill than I'd manage. It always made me its victim. A lost mind spinning out of control, unable to save itself.

"Griffin," came Megan's voice from behind me. "Trystan wants to speak with you."

Eloise made to move past me, but I shifted my bulk. I'd pepper spray the damned woman if she pushed this, and I'd probably enjoy it.

"No," I said to her. "You'll have to wait. He wants his space."

"He's my child."

"He's not a child. He's able to make decisions. Respect that, and him. It'll go a long way towards this ending well for you."

The larger of the two men approached at last. He touched Eloise's shoulder. "I think we should leave. Let's be guided by Trystan. He is our mystic. We have always trusted his wisdom."

I almost laughed. They'd been trusting whatever Eloise decided was Trystan's mission.

"Well?" I asked. "Are you trusting your son to do the right thing?"

I saw it in her eyes. She really didn't want this. Something inside that woman hated humanity and whatever they'd conjured or released in that woodland, suited her purposes. If we hadn't arrived, what would she be doing right now? Using Trystan's natural gifts to raise more of these creatures? Or trying to control them?

That wouldn't end well.

With her lips pressed firmly together, her eyes a blaze of fury, she turned and stormed away. The two men scurried after her with anxious expressions thrown in my direction.

I turned towards the truck and sighed. Whatever happened, I just hoped I had the wits to stay alive with my sanity intact.

# Chapter Twenty-Three

I stepped back into the truck, and the weight of Trystan's world engulfed me. The poor lad felt like a leadened soul driven to the edge of human endurance. He should feel like light and energy. A fifteen-year-old lad ought to be out there on a mountain bike, or skateboard. He should be surfing, or boxing, or anything else but this terrible responsibility.

Looking down at him, I asked, "You ever heard of Joan of Arc?"

He shook his head, confused by the question.

I didn't bother explaining. What was the point? Another young mystic trying to stop a slaughter. She had wanted to save her people. He wanted to save the environment. I had to hope their fates weren't the same.

"Okay, kid, how do we do this, and where?" I asked.

"The circle, I suppose. It's where I feel them most." He sounded so sad. If he were a puppy, I'd be suffering the sad eyes and doubtless caving into whatever was necessary to make the puppy eyes happy again.

I didn't like the idea of going into that druids' circle of

trees, but what could I do? We risked these things escaping onto the building site or into the protesters' camp, and I doubted these creatures would stop at murdering only one more young woman. I had the feeling they were gathering momentum.

Leaze said, "Are you sure that's wise? It's where they'll have the most power."

"It's where the veil is thinnest," I said. "I need Sid down here, and Luce. We'll need a circle of people I can trust."

"What do you think will happen?" Megan asked.

"Hopefully, nothing. Worst case? My mind vanishes."

Megan's eyes widened. "You can't be serious."

"I'm really bloody serious, Meg. The veil is dangerous. I'm not trained for this."

"Who is? Can't you get someone from your office to come here and do this for you?" she asked, her concern for me clear.

"Maybe, but it'll take time, and I don't think we have it. The afternoon is already marching along, and another night here will not be safe for anyone. This is only going to get worse. Besides, Trystan is strong, and he'll be my guide. I'm there for backup. Right, kid?" I looked at the boy.

He nodded. "I hope that by the two of us travelling together, they will know that I am not alone, and it will make them listen. They need to understand that we are on their side. Their god cannot return. That we will protect their sacred place and their trees. We can offer them that, can't we?"

I'd move hell's high-water mark if I had to, so I said, "Yes. We can make this happen." With much more confidence than I felt.

My phone jangled in my pocket, and I fished it out. "Sid," I said.

"Where are you? I can't find anyone."

"You're here?" I asked with a frown.

"Well, if I wasn't, you'd only go getting yourself dosed by an incubus and lost in a mine, so yeah, I'm here."

I chuckled. "Good, I thought we'd have to wait for you. Hang on a second, we're coming out."

The moment I stepped out of the truck, I saw Sid's greying Afro bobbing about above everyone else's heads. I let out a piercing whistle, and he turned. So did every child and dog in the place.

As he came over with Luce, thank goodness, he looked grim. "We were kicking our heels back at base. I wanted to make sure you guys were okay. Even I have the spooks on this one."

"I'm glad you're here. We do need your help. We have the lad in the truck over there, and we're going to try to communicate with the spirits in the woodland. He wants me to walk the veil with him, to help him offer a message of peace."

Sid's eyes widened. "You're going into the veil? Isn't that like…" He fished about for words. "That's like Luke Skywalker going into the Death Star, mate. Seriously, it's fucked up. You shouldn't do it. We have experts—"

"All that will take time. It's daylight right now. We aren't near an equinox, fire festival, or solstice. The fluctuations in the veil will be minimal. We can't leave these people for another night. It's too dangerous. What if they manage to complete the ritual and do raise something? It might not be the god of this place. It could be…" I held up my hands, indicating anything from a demon to a worse demon.

Sid frowned hard, making his eyebrows meet over his nose. "We ought to inform Sanchez. I'm the last one to want the wicked witch down here, but this should be her call."

"No." In my heart, I knew bringing Sanchez into this would be the wrong choice. Whatever happened to me, I did not want to have the deaths of those tree spirits on my conscience.

Luce stepped in. "I think he's right, Sid. Whatever Griffin's abilities really are, he can surf this veil and return. Your DoPI won't help calm this situation. It'll just make things worse."

"I'm not convinced," he said. "I'm really not convinced. What's Megan say?"

I felt her coming up behind me.

"She said," said Megan, "that this is daft, but we don't want any more dead bodies on our hands. I just want to make sure Griffin remains in one piece. Can you help with that?" She looked between the two of them.

Sid puffed out a breath. "I guess we can make a circle of salt around him and the boy so—"

"It'll damage the ground. I don't think that's a good idea." Leaze had joined us. "Trystan says he can keep Griffin safe. I can come along; we can build a meditation circle. That'll help. If we collect some stones, form a circle with them, then use them to build a bubble around us with the stones as anchors…"

I'd heard of such things. "Good idea." Glancing at the sky, I realised we had a cloud bank coming in from the northwest. "Let's do this before the weather arrives. The sunlight will help keep things under control." I hoped. It would be at least two hours before dusk crept over the sky and wiggled his fingers between the trees. Rather than focus on what could go wrong with the operation, I focused on the tasks necessary to make it work.

Sid wanted to record the event, and I didn't blame him for that. When would DoPI ever get another chance to prove the existence of tree spirits? Trystan wasn't impressed. He said the electronic equipment would upset the energy of the place. He was outvoted. If his summoning didn't work, we'd try something else, but right now, we had to take advantage of the situation. If we could prove beyond doubt that these things were real, we'd have a chance to change humanity's view of the natural world. Or, DoPI would do what it normally did, and hide the evidence. Still, it couldn't hurt.

With Leaze, Denny and Aggie along, we all trooped along the lane towards the cloutie tree's footpath.

"You alright?" Megan asked softly. I watched Trystan, who walked with Leaze and Aggie.

"Define, alright," I said, trying for light-hearted, but the tension inside me leaked out.

"That's what I thought," Megan murmured. "You don't have to do this. Whatever we saw the other night—"

"It was real, Meg, please just go with it. I can't fight about the fact that you're a sceptic."

"That was unkind."

"True though." I glanced at her before returning my attention to Trystan's lean, narrow back. What was he thinking right now? What agenda did the boy have? The fact that he was willing to defy Eloise so easily made me uneasy.

Megan grunted in affirmation. "Fine. Okay, you're right. I've spent hours trying to rationalise what I saw last night. I want it to go away. To be some kind of mass hallucination, but…"

"You know it's not."

She hummed, a kind of agreement at least. "You didn't answer my question. Are you okay with this?"

What truth did I give her? The one where I admitted to being so scared that my knees felt the same as they did the first time I engaged real enemies in a firefight. It seemed an unnecessary burden to force on the poor woman.

I opted to lie, of course, because I'm a big, tough Royal Marine. "I'm fine. I just want this over with."

Our hands brushed on the narrow path, and I felt her little finger hook mine. It made my heart race and drew my full attention to my hand, rather than Trystan's back. In silence, with something fluttering in the breeze between us, we made our way up to the cloutie tree and beyond.

When Megan and I had to part because the path narrowed, my focus once more returned to the boy. He moved between the roots of trees and the stones as if we trod a path on a mowed lawn. When brambles threatened to snag him, he lifted them, spikes included, gently out of the way, and they didn't spring back. The birdsong seemed to grow louder, and little wings brushed through the air between the trees in a way they never did normally.

He turned to look at Megan. "*Tewal a dheffo.*"

We all looked at her. "Erm, I think he said, a storm is coming."

The lad was already moving deeper into the woodland. He moved from the shadows to the puddles of sunshine as if the dappled light was a cloak he wove with each step. We were all quiet now, the task ahead filling each of us with a different reaction to the possibility of witnessing something truly remarkable. I was scared, and that was making me anxious, which in turn made me scratchy and pissed off.

Sid was excited. Anyone could see it in his bounding steps. The others were just unsure but mostly hopeful.

Megan was obviously worried about me. Trystan, well, I had no idea what he thought. I'd be putting all my trust in this boy.

*Come on, doofus, think about what his agenda might be in all this.*

What could he achieve? He said he wanted a clean conscience. That he wanted the spirits to go back to sleep. That he wanted to explain their god was dead or gone beyond recall. He wanted to protect the woodland. However, if he took me into the veil and left me there, he'd be removing one of the major pieces on this chessboard. Without me, it would take time for DoPI to react. What would Anwen's Children do with that time? What could be their endgame in all this?

Eloise didn't like humanity very much. She didn't even seem to like her followers. Her only link to the real world was this slim boy. What could she be gaining from all this?

For the life of me, I couldn't think of anything, except the power of being worshipped as Trystan's priestess and controlling him. She had to know that world domination didn't come from a boy like this one. Or did she? Maybe that was the plan. Train him on the occult practices in the UK, then take him somewhere like the pyramids or the Nazca plains in Peru and really pull something incredible out of the veil. Something the world couldn't deny, and she would control. It had a whiff of dark magic about it, but wasn't completely out of the box most of us lived in. Especially if she wanted recognition for Trystan's gifts. Parents live through their offspring all the time. Even if she wasn't his biological mother, it had to be a strong driving motivation for someone who'd 'failed' at a normal life. I should've spent time with Sid going over her background more thoroughly.

We reached the grove. Trystan stopped walking. He

stood, and we gathered behind him. Putting his right hand over his heart, he spoke in Cornish with his soft voice and bowed low. Then he pulled a handful of sunflower seeds out of his pocket and scattered them over the low-lying foliage.

Luce whispered in my ear, "He's asking permission for us to enter with an offering of food."

Megan added, "I understand enough. He's asking for protection and guidance as well."

When he'd finished, he stepped into the glade. The light bent around him, and once more I saw those strange colours surround his body. A young blond god.

"Let us find stones for us to anchor our shield," he said.

We decided we needed four large stones for the compass points, or the elements, depending on your perspective. Then smaller ones at the half points between them.

Trying to squash the panicking voice in the back of my head wasn't easy. What was I doing? I'd be facing down, on their territory, murderous spirits with only a child for backup.

*I can't believe I'm saying this: You should've called Sanchez.*

Great, now I was being nagged by my internal critic. That really helped the nerves, which were behaving like squirrels making nests in my guts.

Trystan asked me to sit in the centre of the clearing. The others would be on the inside of the circle but spread around the edges. When I sat, I realised I took up the same space the standing stone had been in the vision. The one where the child was buried. I shifted sideways and wondered if the stones we'd placed in the circle were the remains of that silent sentinel.

Overhead, I saw a buzzard circling a thermal. Crows rose from the trees around us and flew upwards, aiming to chase it off. Watching their battle for the skies would be my preferred pastime right now.

Using slow breaths to calm my nerves, I tried to use some of my firearms' training to bring my heart rate under control. When I looked down, my eyes met Megan's. She smiled but couldn't hide her worry. This scared her badly. Turning, I saw Sid behind me. If anything, he looked even more worried.

"Come on, people," I said. "I'm not about to die. Have a little faith."

"Don't mention dying, Griffin. We've seen two bodies already," Sid said.

"No one will die," Trystan told us in a voice that held a surprising amount of authority for such a young man. His eyes met mine. "You need to leave your gun behind and any other weapons."

Silence. "No," I stated.

He shook his head. "You cannot go into their world armed. It would be seen as a declaration of violence, maybe even war. That we don't really mean it when we ask for peace."

"Trystan," how to explain this to a boy like him, "if I don't take my sidearm with me, then both our lives could end really fast."

"Or they end quickly because you do take it with you," he countered. "If you don't leave it, we won't be going, and I'll return to Eloise."

I looked at my team. Luce said, "He has a point. You have other ways to fight, right?"

True enough, but I'd rather shoot someone than offer an arm wrestle if it came to me or Trystan dying.

Sid added, "We need to know more about them, soldier boy. It's all part of the deal. If we want peace, we have to lay down our guns. After all, human destruction of their woodland started this." He was right as well. We had to know our enemy, and sometimes you had to lay down your arms to start the vital conversation that brought about peace.

Megan's turn. "Are you fucking crazy, Marine?"

*You gotta love her.*

I smiled at her furious expression. "Can you keep the gun for me?"

Her eyes rolled, she stomped in one of those tight circles of hers and grumbled, but when I handed over the Glock, she accepted it. I removed everything else as well, even the holy water.

Trystan then walked around the circle, touching each stone, and muttering a prayer over it. He also placed his hand on everyone's heads, giving a quick benediction. Then he came to the centre and sat next to me.

"Take my hand," the boy said, offering me his slightly grubby palm. I took hold, the smallness surprising me. He looked at me. Those pale eyes were wide, magnetic in their intensity, and worryingly calm.

"What's going to happen?" I asked.

Trystan shrugged. "I never really know until it starts, and I've never done this without Eloise, or taken someone else. I'll start with a prayer. Just make sure you all keep seeing a bubble of blue light surrounding us. Make it really clear. A strong dome that goes far into the ground." He looked at Leaze in particular. "You understand?"

She nodded. "I understand."

"You are the anchor," he said. "You are the one I will trust to bring us home."

Her eyes were soft as she gave him a gentle smile. It looked like the kind of expression an indulgent cook would give an urchin as he licked a spoon clean of cake mix. "I will follow your prayer and bring you home." She looked around the small group. "All of you follow me, if you can. Our chant will act as a beacon in the other world."

Megan and I shared another long glance. She mouthed: *You don't have to do this.* In return, I just offered a smile and a small shrug. Trying to convey: *If not me, then who?*

Trystan placed his free hand on the scruffy grass, and I did the same. He pushed his fingers into the dirt, and I mirrored. Then he began to speak.

I understood not a single word. It could've been Cornish or Elvish for all I knew. Closing my eyes, I felt the world begin to shift.

In all the years I'd been experiencing my visions, the PTSD from conflict, the night wanders, I'd never known anything like this.

## Chapter Twenty-Four

The world turned black. I sucked in a breath, and it was ice-cold, burning my lungs cold. My breathing shifted, and my left hand twitched, desperate for my sidearm. Disconcertingly, a wave of peace came from my right hand, and light came with it.

A thought arrived, and it wasn't mine. *We are inside the veil. Be calm.*

Inside? I had assumed there would be an oily, twisting rainbow. Isn't that what I usually saw? What I'd witnessed on Exmoor that time? Why was this just a black space? We stood in a void. Our feet were planted on nothing visible, but it was solid. Wasn't it?

A moment of vertigo hit me and I swayed. I think, if Trystan hadn't held me, I'd have tumbled forwards, perhaps forever.

That's when the rainbow showed up, giving me the perspective my brain needed. Our feet were on a wild, shifting surface of colours. They drifted, lapped against my sturdy boots, and sent chills through my body. It was like looking into a fathomless, endlessly wide puddle that contained clean car oil in thick drifts. This rainbow didn't float on the surface; it wove through the black. A constant dance of colour. I sniffed the 'air', nothing. I smelt nothing. Not even myself. Somehow, this disturbed me more than anything else. Even with stuffy sinuses, humans could smell their world. This one held no scent.

*Come, we need to ride the rainbow.*

Well, if ever there was an album name waiting to be snagged, that was it.

Trystan remained passive beside me.

I said, "Aren't you scared?" The words came out flat. No echo, or sense of vibration.

Trystan looked up at me. *Why? No harm will befall us.*

I seriously doubted that, but what choice did I have? We needed to calm these tree spirits.

"Take us where we need to go," I said. The deadness of my voice unnerved me.

*Don't show fear. Generations of shamans have walked these rivers.* Trystan bowed his head and stepped onto the greenest of the rainbow's colours. He whispered something the moment I followed him, and the nothingness world misted away. It was the only way I could describe it. We began in the black void, and then a light came for us. The rainbow arrived under our feet, then that reality dissolved like tendrils of cloud might, to reveal something else.

A woodland, I realised. Just like the one we'd left, but not the same. No, this was far more like the forest I'd seen in my vision of the grieving parents. The trees were thick and tall, but the ground was cared for, and in the centre, that large standing stone. It had swirled carvings etched in bas-relief on the surface and animals like wolves, bears, eagles and boars. All of them new and painted, not weatherworn and barely visible as they would be in my world. The air now smelt, but it was different. More liquid, richer, cleaner, I guessed. Overhead, I saw the blue of the sky, oddly familiar and a comfort. The trees here were actively alive. I felt them, like I would if I were standing in a roomful of strangers, all of whom knew each other, but not me. Like walking into a local's pub, and everyone turns to watch you as the foxes bark on the moorland outside, and you've brought in the cold.

*Don't stray off the path.* I really needed to stop watching horror movies.

We were standing in the silent crowd until the wind set off a whisper that shimmered through the leaves and twitched branches. I ached to have a weapon in my hands. This place did not want me here.

"Stay calm," Trystan instructed. "We are safe in this circle."

"I don't feel safe."

"There's not much I can do about your feelings, so I suggest you control them. These are elemental beings, and they'll sense your fear." There's nothing quite like being told off by a teenager.

I rolled my shoulders in an effort to relax. It didn't work for long. Figures began to move behind the trees.

Unlike the previous night, I could see these beings in the daylight of this place. They were captivating. Not human, but ethereal and beautiful. Each movement, as they stepped out of the woodland and onto the edge of the glade, was precise and delicate. Like a ballerina stepping over gravel. Their limbs were long and slim but corded with muscle. Their skins brown and green in swirling patterns that gave the illusion of a tight bodysuit. Hair covered their heads, but it was made of living leaves. Ropes of it tumbled down their backs. Each part of them was formed to blend with their forest environment. Soundless, and eerie as hell.

Every one of them carried a weapon. Mostly types of spear: hewn wood fire blackened to a point, others with flint points tied with well-made rope. A few held axes, their wedge-shape familiar to me from my university days. I saw no bows, or arrows. All the figures were male.

"Don't look at their eyes," Trystan whispered.

"You might've mentioned that before," I growled, dropping my gaze. I'd looked into one face only. The strong cheekbones and wide jaw weren't human. What had Luce called them? Dru. His nose was wide and flat, almost human, but thicker, with narrow nostrils. The eyes came straight out of the world of elves, upswept and vivid green, but not large. Their otherness scared me, but somewhere deep inside, I recognised these creatures. With that recognition came a terrible sense of fear. As if the core of my being had known humanity once suffered from being hunted in the great forests of the world by beings just like these. That big Dru, he held a stone spear. A very sharp-looking stone spear.

Trystan released my hand and stepped forward. The grace I'd seen in his movements through the woodland was nothing compared to these creatures. He bowed low to the male I'd noticed.

A soft murmur of sound issued from Trystan. Rather than speech being his primary communicator, a tide of emotion gushed from the boy. How I sensed it, I didn't know, but it overwhelmed me. My vision swam for a moment before adjusting itself. Again, I saw the energy rippling around him. The soft browns and greens of the forest we stood in, with long tendrils licking outwards. Now, though, I also saw other colours, and the tendrils formed shapes.

The big Dru watched these for long moments. So, did I. With his mind, Trystan formed images of the dead woman, River, hanging from the tree, and the colours used were sad, muted reds and purples, yellows and greens, like old bruises. He then created something I didn't understand. It was a complex shape of swirling colours that were brighter and swifter than I could follow.

Sound shimmered around us, and the emotions in the glade shifted from wary but mostly benign to outright hostile within a heartbeat. It was like feeling a dog trigger at the scent of an enemy combatant. One second peace, the next, threatened violence. Nothing in between.

I'd been in some scary arsed negotiations in some shitty places, but this gave no room for compromise.

"What the fuck did you just do?" I breathed, trying to keep my eyes down while watching for the coming storm.

Trystan looked back at me, and I saw fear in those big eyes of his. "I tried to explain about their god not returning."

"Well, that didn't go down well. Why am I here, Trystan? What can I do to help?" Keeping my eyes down, I stepped up beside him.

His hand slipped back into mine, only this time, he sought comfort. "Can you give them an image of the building site stopping its work on the woodland?"

I took a breath, and inside my head I formed a clear image of the farmhouse, and the surrounding land free of big machinery. I then populated it with more trees planted by people. The colours I chose were made up of dusky light, and I picked a guitar riff that sounded very much like *Black Magic Woman* from *Santana*. I'd spent months learning that back in the day. Though I'd never really do it justice. The notes drifted through the scene, meant as a quiet offering. I also removed the crystals I'd brought from the office, and I placed them on the ground before us.

Trystan grunted quietly, "Clever."

"I have my moments."

The big Dru came closer. He'd entered the circle I knew the others held in our reality. That shouldn't have been possible. I saw his feet in the short grass. Those long toes and high arches looked perfect for climbing, but also for holding something down. Hard. His ankles and calves were thick and corded with muscles I'd never have. This creature was all power.

"I thought the circle with the others would keep them out?" I whispered, trying not to panic.

"So did I," Trystan confessed, and his hand grew clammy in mine.

When the violence came, I had no chance of preventing it. Two of the large Dru lunged for Trystan and ripped him from my grip before I had a chance to tighten my hold. Four came at me. I stepped back, preparing to fight, but I was hauled upwards by an immense strength and hurled through the air.

When I landed, I hit hard. I hit blackness very hard.

The nothingness of the veil surrounded me, and one enormous Dru stood over me. Unable to help myself, I stared into his eyes. They were not human. Nothing in there was human. It was like looking into the eyes of a stingray I'd swum with once. Cat-like but horizontal. A predator's eyes, not one that belonged to prey.

I held up my hands in a gesture of peace. "I can help you," I said, unable to form images to communicate and falling back on human speech in my fear. "I will help you. Please."

The Dru held the quartz crystal in his hand. I watched him close his fist, and the stone turned into chunks and dust.

*Well, I guess peace is off the table.*

"Where's the boy?" I asked, pushing myself away from the creature. I'd never felt like this before. So fucking insignificant in the face of a being that reeked of forces elemental and powerful. My mind could barely comprehend it. I was beyond fear.

The Dru took a step forward. His long legs wrapped in corded muscle, the patterns on his skin shifting. They were sharper, angrier and darker. I had no doubt rage fuelled this creature. The feet, the prints I'd been tracking, might be long and narrow, designed for climbing and running through tangled woodland, but they were also savage weapons.

While scrambling backwards, I managed to gain my feet, but where to run? I existed in a black void with only the oily rainbow lapping at my boots. I wanted to return to my world. To step out of this veil and never, ever return. Thoughts of my mother drifted into my panicking mind. Would she return to me and help, like she had in the long barrow?

How close to death did I need to be before she appeared?

When the Dru came at me, I'd steadied myself enough to take a fighting stance. The creature didn't bother. He just rushed me. I dropped my weight, expecting a rugby tackle, or a judo takedown, but this was worse. Far worse. He hit me, with no care for himself, and knocked me clean off my feet. His knees came down on my chest, and I felt my ribs bend. If I'd been any smaller, he'd have crushed me.

Those long fingers went around my throat and closed. Then the Dru screamed at me. His teeth were like a chimp's. Designed to rip meat and chew vegetable matter. They were long, savage and far too close to my face.

I writhed under him. Never before had I been so small and insignificant. Fingers made from the strength of centuries old oak, closed around my throat. I scrabbled at the thick wrists, desperate to break his hold. Terror filled my mind. I had a dozen ways of breaking from this attack if my opponent was anything close to human. With this thing? I stood no chance.

My breathing was closing down. The weight on my chest, the hands around my throat. Was I dying in this void? Where would my soul go? Could it escape this place?

Mum! Help me now! Please…

Nothing came back. Nothing. She's abandoned me. Again.

Then, I thought of the only other person that meant anything to me. Megan. Rather than hold the impossible wrist. I grasped the witch's stone she'd given me days before. I held it. Thoughts of her drifted through me, even as I began to die. I wanted to scream, but I had no more air. I held the river smooth stone, its coolness a balm among the hot rage of the Dru. For one moment, it aligned with my fading vision long enough for me to look through the small hole.

The black void surrounding us wasn't there, inside the hole. In that space I saw my Megan, kneeling in the circle, over me. Over my shaking body. Tears of panic in her eyes as she held me down. Her voice a dim echo as she yelled for water.

Megan. My Megan. The love of my life. I didn't have to own her; I just wanted to be beside her. Always. Even if we could only ever be friends.

The hole in the stone moved just a little and the Dru's face swam into view even as my brain started to go as black as the void. How it happened I couldn't know, but sparks of blue light shot out of the stone and into the creature's skin, like needles. But his face. His beautiful, terrible, fierce face was dying. The skin rotted, eyes dulled, the hair gone. The Dru's eyes widened. Those pupils dilated hugely, and he screamed into me.

The hands released my throat, the world shuddered and the fall I'd sensed as Trystan pulled me into the veil, occurred again.

## Chapter Twenty-Five

"Griffin! God, please, wake up. Please don't leave…"

The pain in my throat and chest forced me to roll, heave in air and gag. Sound rushed in and back, an overwhelming tide of muddled voices and vision. My eyes weren't focused. Was that… what was that?

I shook my head and tried to groan. It hurt too much. Hands everywhere. I struggled for space until… "Griff, relax. It's okay. You're safe. I'm here." My arms folded, and I collapsed against a soft, warm body. "Shhh, it's alright. You're safe."

"Trystan's woken up," came another woman's voice.

My hands closed on the forearms wrapped around me, and I clung to them. I clung to them as if they were a piece of driftwood shorn from the bloody Titanic. I did not want to slip away into that void. The darkness, the terrible vision of the Dru trying to kill me. Being so fucking alone. I shivered and felt panic begin to spread again.

What if it came for me in the night? What if I slipped through the veil again during one of my episodes? Could the Dru come find me in Redruth? I'd die. He would drag me back into the black, and I'd die. Lost. In the void.

"I need some help here," Megan called out over my head. "Griffin, it's alright. You're back, and we're safe. You are safe."

"What's wrong?" Luce's voice.

I kept my eyes shut. I wanted to block my ears, but if I did that, I'd have to let go of Megan, and I didn't think I'd survive. It hurt to breathe, and my heart—

"He's having a panic attack."

"What?"

Hands began to rub my back, and another body pushed against me.

"Just hold him. If we keep him contained, he'll start to feel safe. Keep talking. He needs to block out the noise in his head. I've had these since I was a child. Trust me." Luce sounded so confident.

Oh yes, that noise. A roar of sound that came from nowhere and everywhere.

"Griffin, breathe with me. You are safe. Breathe in." I heard and felt Megan take a deep breath. I tried to match her but didn't manage it. Again and again, she went through it. Someone stroked my hair and my back.

Slowly, very slowly, the noise in my head eased back. My spine unwound a little. I risked a glimpse at the world. I didn't see much. My nose was buried in Megan's chest. Shame I was too freaked out to enjoy the novelty. When I managed to look at something other than Megan's shirt, I saw the glade and Leaze bent over Trystan.

That gave my brain something else to do rather than just hamster-wheel in blind terror. The lad needed help. We both needed food and hot tea. Also, I never wanted to come back into this damned wood again. Right now, I was tempted to call Sanchez and order a strafing run from the nearest military airbase. Followed by ordnance being dropped on the site. Bollocks to the damned trees.

I pulled away from Megan, and Luce detached herself from my back. Sid was with the boy. We were okay.

Denny hurried over with a flask. "Bit of brandy. Nothing special, but it'll help. I've had my share of panic attacks."

I found my hands didn't work, and I'd left huge red marks on Megan's arm.

"I'm sorry," I mumbled.

"Just drink, you big lug. Bruises heal. I'll be fine." She stroked my hair back, and it felt so good I wanted to cry. Holding the flask to my lips, she poured some into me, and it burned with a wonderful intensity that only a cheap liquor can manage.

"He'll be alright," Luce said. "Can you tell us what happened?"

"Can we get out of here first?" I begged them. Staying here, and talking about what I'd seen, might well invoke it to appear. I saw my Glock poking out of Megan's waistband and snagged it back. No way did I want to go anywhere unarmed ever again.

The journey back to the road happened in a blur of motion for me. With unsteady legs, I felt jostled by the trees and tricked by the stones. The mud conspired against me, and I'd never experienced such a lack of confidence in my body. When you are fit, strong, and you've been trained to be an elite Royal Marine, you don't understand what it is to know frailty. That Dru made me feel wickedly vulnerable.

Reaching the tarmac at last, I almost dropped to my knees to kiss the damned stuff. My spine unravelled a little more, and the coiled, paranoid spring in my chest relaxed.

"I'm never going in there again," I muttered.

Sid stood close. "You scared the crap outta me. What the hell happened?"

I eyed the remaining trees bordering the path. "We're still too close."

He frowned. "Griffin, they can't get you the other side of the veil."

"You sure about that? I think Jennifer and River wouldn't agree. Come on. I'm not going to be happy until I'm surrounded by concrete." Forcing the others to keep up, and choosing not to look at Trystan, I began to double-time it up the lane. Megan kept pace and remained silent, just offering her support.

When I saw the car, I started to relax. Escape was now truly possible. I leaned over the roof of the old Vectra and took in a few deep breaths.

"What the hell happened, Griffin?" Megan asked.

My throat hurt when I swallowed. "I almost died. It was… It was like trying to reason with a shark and just as deadly. I lost Trystan. It, he, the Dru, threw me back into the veil, then tried to kill me." I reached up for the stone still hanging around my throat and managed to meet her eyes for the first time. The blue had a greyness to it that reminded me of a stormy sea. "You saved me."

"What? How? Is this more of your metaphysical, waffly weirdness?"

"Pretty much. I was dying. He was choking the life out of me. I grabbed the stone." I felt it now. "The veil… It's nothing but blackness and that weird rainbow I've described." I swallowed again around the swelling in my throat. "Trystan rode the rainbow to find the Dru. That's what they were—male-looking dryads. They are so powerful, Megan. And fast. Like nothing I've ever seen. They want us gone forever. I saw you through the hole in the stone. The witch's stone. Then I saw that thing, and it… He screamed and let me go." I wasn't making much sense.

"That's when you woke up?" she asked.

I nodded. "What I saw through that hole was not what we saw last night. The hole revealed a dying thing." The more I thought about that brief glimpse, the more terrible it became. "It was like…" I stared off over the fields, trying to fish for the words I needed. "It was like the poor bastard had a kind of leprosy. He was mutated and ugly. As if he'd been poisoned by something."

Luce had caught up with us, along with the others, as they trailed behind her. She'd heard the last part. "It could be the ruin of their home. They can project one version of themselves, but the witch's stone, inside the veil, shows their true nature. Even to themselves. They are a dying race because of us."

"Really?" Megan asked.

Our resident academic shrugged. "It's not like I have proof to show you, but fairytales would back up that possibility. A mirror reflecting your true nature, for instance. For some, they'd glimpse beauty even if on the outside they were seen as ugly. For the beautiful, the reverse. This stone showed the Dru how much damage had been done to it." She looked worried. "Which might make them even angrier."

"Oh, good."

Trystan, with Leaze helping to keep him steady, arrived. "I'm sorry," he said to me. "I've never seen them like that. It's never been so violent. They often scare me, but that's just testing. Nature tests us all the time, we no longer understand that, but they've never…" His eyes were wells of sadness. "They are very angry. I don't think they'll welcome me again." The poor kid looked beaten. "I should've listened to Eloise."

Leaze rubbed his shoulder. "Don't be daft, lad. You did the right thing. That's what's important." She looked at me. "We still need to keep an eye on our potential maidens?"

"I think so. Trystan tried to show them that their god wasn't coming back, and that's when everything went wrong. Even more wrong than it already was." I ran my dirty hands through my hair. "I can't see a way to stop them. They don't listen. We can't talk, and with all due respect to Trystan's obvious gifts, his way of communicating is too blunt."

The boy frowned at me. "It's not like they talk the way we do. It's not that kind of place. It's far more subtle. You just picked up the basics. They understood. The male tree spirits are more warrior-like, and the female ones didn't want to speak with us. I did the best I could. You're asking them to give up their god. I woke them up in this world, gave them the ability to transverse the veil, but they're alone. With no guidance. That's not how it should be. The damage we are doing to their world is just..." He looked lost himself. "It's so vast. They are all connected."

Sid asked, "What do you mean by that? How are they connected?"

"The mycelium. That's their... well, I guess you could call it their internet. Though it's a lot slower obviously." He looked at Sid, willing him to understand.

My friend nodded, fully grasping the boy's meaning. I had no idea what he was talking about, but to be fair, I didn't want to be close to the wood when night dropped over Madron. Right now, I needed human normal. A fish supper, some downtime and, hopefully, a restful night. My thoughts needed ordering. Part of me still wanted to bomb the damned wood and then send in the bulldozers before salting the earth and covering it in tarmac, with a sodding great shopping centre put on it.

The more rational part of me heard the crows boisterously owning the sky. The distant storm still threatened to advance onto the land. Then the spring gift of evening birdsong. A beauty that just never sounded the same in a built-up area. I loved Cornwall.

"We need to come up with a new plan," I said. "If you, Leaze, can keep the camp safe, then we need to go back to Redruth and do some serious conferring with our experts."

Leaze's eyebrows rose. "Rural Security deals with mythical beings a lot, does it?"

I tried not to smirk at her sarcasm. "We have our moments."

She huffed at me and started to corral her people back to the camp. "I'll do what I can, but I have you on speed dial, so be warned."

Watching her go, I looked at Sid. "We should get a team down here to keep an eye on the protesters."

"What if Sanchez wants to destroy the Dru?" Sid asked, looking worried.

"Right now, I'm tempted to let her," I told him. "Let's just go home for the moment. I need some space from this."

He nodded, and we parted to take our separate vehicles. I headed for the driver's side when Megan stopped me.

"I've only a black eye, Griffin. You're still recovering from a panic attack and whatever else just happened to you. I'm driving." She held out her hand.

Feeling like a damned fool, I handed her the keys.

Being locked inside the metal cage of the car, with a seatbelt and the foam of the cushions giving way to my weight, made the real world just that bit firmer than it had been for a while. We were silent while Megan wove through the narrow lanes, following Sid's Mini.

"I'm sorry for being such a flake," I muttered. An episode of PTSD flashbacks felt less humiliating than this.

Megan glanced at me. "I've had a panic attack or two over the years. One night while I was on duty about five years ago, some fucker in a squat tried to stab me. If I hadn't been in my full tactical gear, I'd have died. When the knife didn't work, he threw himself at me, knocked me down and started banging my head against the floor. He was completely out of it. Barely aware of what was happening. I saw nothing human in his eyes as he tried to kill me. Fortunately, my partner on the call, Big Steve, makes you look like a Hobbit. It took a long time before I was confident on call again. I even moved back to the farm for a while. You've nothing to be ashamed of, Griffin. I don't think your tactical training includes facing a giant tree spirit bent on your destruction."

I tried for a chuckle, but it didn't work. A huge part of me just wanted to hide under a duvet and never come out. "I don't know how to solve this problem." The confession burned.

Megan reached out and gripped my knee for a moment. "That's why we have a team. I'm just a lug, like you, but with less training and knowledge. Sid and Luce, they'll figure this out. Or you'll have one of your blinding insights, and it'll all fall into place. Have faith, cuz."

I gazed out of the window, watching the Cornish countryside slide past. Suddenly, tears pricked my eyes as I remembered the beauty of the Dru's grove in those few fragile minutes I'd spent in their world. "I don't want to see that woodland destroyed."

"Okay, that's a good place to start. How do we stop that from happening?"

I drew a shaky breath. "Talking to the landowner."

"Get the landowner to leave the wood alone, and the problem should just go away?" She pulled out into the traffic on the main road. It was busy heading towards Land's End. At least we were heading east, which would make life quicker.

"That's the first thing to do," I agreed. Just saying it made me feel, not better, but more confident in my ability to remain alive while keeping the trees safe. "I'm wondering if we can use Anwen's Children to make the woodland go back to sleep."

"What on earth did they do to wake it up? I mean, why there?" she asked.

"I think it's the cloutie tree, the spring and the druids' circle all being in the same place. The cloutie tree has kept the site a place of living nature worship. The spring water was used by the early Christians and for pagan worship, probably until the modern historical period. What I saw through the veil was a far larger and grander place long ago. It's a husk of what it once was. Then, Anwen's Children arrived, and Eloise took Trystan into that place. Whatever he is, he's a natural. His gifts flow through him like water. With the three things—a thin place in the veil, the continued worship at the site right up to modern day, and Trystan's mysticism—the place just…"

"Woke up."

"Basically."

"Only to discover their reality was being torn down and making them sick."

"Yeah."

We were both quiet for a few miles, contemplating the damage caused to the place.

"What happens in the veil when we destroy something like Madron's woodland?" she asked.

I sighed. "It's difficult to know. We have a few mystics in DoPI, but none like Trystan as far as I'm aware. We have impressions of the place, but I think Trystan took me further inside it than any of our people have managed to get. His ability to communicate, the way he communicated, it was incredible. The boy's the real deal."

"That's going to be bad for him, isn't it?" Megan accelerated past a caravan.

"It'll make living in a city very difficult. Having a normal life is almost impossible. In the past, mystics like him have had a nasty habit of being burned at the stake, stoned to death, or just dying from starvation because they get lost in the other worlds they can touch. Or they go mad. He needs help. Real help, not exploitation."

"Can DoPI help him?"

"Yes, but they'll also exploit him."

"Everything in life is a transaction, Griffin. Will they use him to set up a cult and create followers who give the chief crazy lady loads of money?"

I chuckled. "No. That won't happen. They'll train him and use him like they use me, I guess."

"Exactly. He'll have a home, an education and a job. Those aren't bad things. If Eloise keeps going with him, she's going to create something terrible that even DoPI can't control."

"You mean if the Dru do wake up this god of theirs."

Megan shook her head. "How am I having this conversation?" She glanced at me, and I chuckled, making her roll her eyes. "Basically, yes."

"If they wake up a god, then all bets are off. That's just the kind of thing DoPI can't afford to happen. The risk would be enormous to humanity. Not just the destabilising of all traditional faiths, but the ramifications of what else is possible for people. Proving a god, or the God, exists…" I made a puff sound to indicate the grand scale of the possible cock-up it would cause.

"I can see why it would be bad," Megan said.

"I just need to lower the temperature of what's happening. That's the goal, I think."

"Then we have a plan. We just have to fill in the details." She smiled, and despite the bruising, she looked amazing.

# Chapter Twenty-Six

That evening, the four of us sat around the table in Turpin Cottage, eating Chinese takeaway, and sharing our experiences of what had happened during the afternoon. I did most of the talking.

While I explained what I'd seen inside the veil, and then those brief moments Trystan and I had tried to communicate with the Dru inside their version of our world, I found it hard to hold anyone's gaze.

Luce was, of course, fascinated and muttered frequently about how she wanted to do what I'd done. She'd studied the myths, legends and fairytales of many cultures, and to have a chance to glimpse them, to experience their otherness, was turning out to be catnip for her.

Sid stuck his phone on the table to record what I said. The more hours between me and the meeting of the Dru, the more the memories were fading. The bruises were still there, my shoulder was killing me, and swallowing hurt, but the clarity felt like trying to grasp coloured smoke. Apparently, this matched other experiences people had throughout history when they crossed over. Only people like Trystan, mystics, could retain the detail.

This made me feel cold inside. Not only had they bested me with ease, I'd been as lost in fear as I was with my night-time episodes in this world. It meant more confusion and nameless horrors to live with. Just what I needed. The more I spoke, the more withdrawn and sadder I felt. Megan and I might've spoken about some kind of plan, but to be honest, I didn't hold out much hope. How could I? Negotiating with beings so bent on our deaths was never going to work. Their language alone was so alien, I didn't stand a chance of becoming competent. The skills necessary weren't there inside me. The thought of failure meant I'd have one option: destroying the woodland.

This brought me nothing but bleak horror. I didn't want to kill this grove. How much damage would that do? Trystan had possibly spoken with the Earth's heartbeat, for goodness sake. He was the most extraordinary young man I'd ever met, but even he failed to reach through the Dru's rage. How much more damage could the Earth take before something as amazing as that scientifically proven beat, deep inside the planet, died?

Life would end, and I wasn't strong enough to stop it from happening. This bleak view of the world—a grey world—was at least an honest one. For the first time, I knew I was being honest with myself. This was something at least. Acknowledging your weaknesses and failures was important. Right?

"I need to call it a night," I said, unable to finish my beer or food. It all tasted like sawdust, anyway. I hurt everywhere. A shower, painkillers and some rest might help. I probably needed to make reassuring noises to everyone, but to be honest, I didn't have it in me.

Pushing away from the table, I just left them to it. Someone else could clear up. What did it matter anyway? We were all fucked. The planet was going to burn, and humanity would face mass extinction. Saving one bloody grove of trees and their strange inhabitants wouldn't change anything, and if they killed another woman and did manage to summon their god, well, that'd just be icing on the cake of doom we all faced. Another indication of my failure as a protector.

During my explanation, I'd heard from the others how things had played out for them. Inside the circle we'd supposedly created to protect us, they had seen Trystan and me slump as if sleeping. Then, a few moments later, my body lunged backwards, and I started to shake all over as if fitting. The glade of trees had darkened around everyone, and Trystan collapsed forward onto his face. They'd felt a terrible chill in the air, the wind shrieked for a minute or two, then fell silent as I came around in Megan's arms. They hadn't seen the Dru, fortunately for them.

I lay under the duvet, in my t-shirt and boxers as usual, and tried to find something positive in all this, but it was more ephemeral than the damned memories. My usual mental coping strategies weren't holding me up this time. Even in my darkest moments as a child or a Marine, I'd tried to find a spark of something to hold on to that would keep me going. Even if it was just the knowledge that everything changed eventually, and change brought hope in its wake. Right now, the thought of change felt like too much weight to carry.

Alone and very sad, I curled up and, for the first time in a very long time, I let myself sob quietly.

Ever since returning from the other side of the veil, this sense of losing something, like captured moonlight in a jar made of sunlight, became a weight on my heart. That weight was growing heavier with each breath.

Minutes turned to hours, and eventually, even the despair could no longer keep me awake.

My phone jolted me to consciousness. I pulled it closer to my ear while swiping to answer, "Woodbury."

"Griffin? It's Steve Denzel from the golf course. I have some news that might help."

I blinked, trying to breathe through the heaviness in my chest. Trying to suck in enough air to speak. "Help would… help…" I felt like my brain was full of razor blades. They slashed through my thoughts. *Swish, swish, slice, dice. We'll turn your brain to mince.*

"Are you okay?" asked the voice.

"Yeah, tell me," I said, sitting up and trying to rub some sense into my head by rubbing my temples.

"Mr Alanson is definitely coming. He's arriving tomorrow morning at the site. Hopefully, we can make him listen to us if we want to save the woodland. He'll be here by ten. Can you make it?" Steve sounded hopeful. The damned fool.

"I'll be there." Though what the point would be was anyone's guess.

"Good, thank you. I'll see you then." Steve ended the call.

I sat in my bed and stared at the phone for a long time. Light leaked through the gaps in the curtains, and I wondered if I should go for a run. Rolling my shoulder, I also wondered why I should bother.

Reaching up to my neck, I held the witch's stone and stroked its smooth surface. Somehow a natural hole had formed in this small pebble, and Megan had seen it on a stream's bed as she walked the mountains of Scotland. It was the only thing that had saved my life, I knew that, but I didn't remember what I'd seen through the hole. I just knew it made me terribly sad.

A soft knock on the door dragged my attention into the day. "Griff, it's Megan. I have tea?"

"Come in," I growled through my still swollen throat.

She opened the door. "Hey. I stayed in the spare room last night. I hope that's okay?" The tea was offered to me like a talisman to a questing knight.

"Fine. You know that. Thanks for the tea. How are you this morning?" I touched the side of my face where she had the bruise. It looked like the painting of a memory of ending grief.

She managed a brief smile. "Oh, it's okay. Sore, but so long as my big brute of a cousin doesn't try to poke it, I should be fine." Her eyes were soft, and the swelling had reduced considerably today.

"I won't poke it."

"Good." She sat on the edge of the bed. "Griffin, it's past eight. Are you okay? Sid said you never sleep in. We're worried. You didn't seem right last night, and I'm in the room next door. I heard you…"

Heat rushed up my face. "Heard what?"

"Nightmares."

Oh. At least the lessons I'd endured as a boarding school brat still held true. I knew how to weep without making a sound. That was something at least.

"I'm fine."

She studied me. "No, you're not. Something is wrong. I can feel it." Her smaller hand reached for my inert one on the surface of the duvet. "You can talk to me."

I didn't want to talk. Pulling my hand away from hers hurt, but it was a pain I deserved. "I've just had a call from

Denzel at the golf course. The owner, Sir Pierce Alanson of Whist Industries, is going to be arriving this morning. We need to talk to him."

Though how I'd convince him to change his plans was anyone's guess. The weight of the blackness over me was suffocating.

Megan rose. "Drink your tea. Have a shower. Meet me downstairs." She was frowning as she left and closed my bedroom door.

I didn't want to do any of those things. The effort it took to shower, brush my teeth, and dress drained me completely. Each footfall down the stairs emptied me further. When I made it to the kitchen, I found the others, all eating and chatting about the day. I sat slumped in the chair and wondered if I could choke down a slice of toast.

*What the hell is going on! This isn't you, it isn't us, come on…* The small inner voice we all have babbled at me incessantly. I tried to ignore it. I wanted to, but my god it could nag.

Sid's face hove into view. "Griffin? Look at me."

I lifted my eyes but struggled to meet his gaze. "What?"

"Shit," he muttered. "We have a problem. I think he's brought something back from the veil."

"I'm fine," I said, pushing back from the table. "If we're meant to meet this bloke who has the golf course, we need to leave."

"Griffin, you need to read the file on the man—"

"Send it to my phone. I'll take a look on the way down. We're bound to hit traffic." I slumped out of the kitchen, not meeting anyone's gaze, and picked up my bike jacket. "Megan, you're driving." I had no wish to take the bike. It'd be too much effort.

Silence behind me.

I turned to look. All three of my companions remained in the kitchen.

Sid handed Megan a set of keys. "Go around the front, lock the door from the outside. Leave the keys in there. Come back in the back door and then lock that. He's not leaving in this state."

The tall man marched towards me. "Living room. Now. No arguing. I know you can knock me over like I'm a matchstick man—"

"You look like one," I muttered.

"Thanks, mate. Just go in there and wait." He pushed me onto the sofa and made me sit. I wanted to put my head on a cushion and go back to sleep. I didn't want to eat, or drink, I just wanted to sleep.

The cushion felt nice as I collapsed sideways.

"Oh, no you don't," Luce said, pulling the nice squishy thing away, making my head thump hard against the armrest. "You aren't sleeping. That would be bad. Remember what happened to Snow White? Or Sleeping Beauty? You've been fairy spelled."

I frowned. "What the fuck are you talking about?"

She crouched before me, watching my face with those big dark eyes. "We can see it in your eyes. They're heavily dilated and your skin tone is grey. Something is sucking you dry, making you want to sleep. It's a familiar trope in many a story of travellers who return from the fairy lands. They might sleep until they die. Or time warps for them. Perhaps they return with an appetite for raw meat, or rotten vegetables, and poison themselves. Maybe, they return mad. You," she tapped my kneecap, "can't leave this house until we've smudged you."

"What?"

I heard Sid call from upstairs. "I've found it." His feet

pounded downwards. "I've found the kit. Just as well I didn't leave this in the office with the other stuff. Have you showered?" he asked me, appearing suddenly in front of me.

"Course," I managed.

He grunted and muttered, "Huh, that should've helped." He opened a small wooden box. The grain of the wood shone a soft amber. The inside of it had a deep purple felt lining. "We might need a blessing from a vicar or priest," he muttered, "but let's see how we get on." He looked at the women. "Either of you christened?"

"Farmer's daughter," Megan said. Then, because of Sid's confusion, she added, "Yes. Farming is dicey enough without annoying the Almighty, according to my dad."

"Daughter of a vicar," Luce said, holding her hand up. "I've done the lot."

Sid nodded. "Good. Then you can lead the prayers. We need the Lord's Prayer and this one." He handed Luce a piece of paper. "Saint Patrick's Breastplate. That'll help. I'll do the smudging with the sage, and we need to get some of this blessed wafer and water into him."

"Is that some kind of spiritual first aid kit?" Megan asked.

"That's exactly what it is." He looked up at Megan. "When I give the order, unlock the back door, then the front one, as quickly as possible."

"It's cold and raining today."

"Good. The rain will help wash the thing away from the house and the host." Sid lit the sage. I coughed. "Get praying, you two."

"I'm an atheist," Megan protested.

"Not now, you aren't. Not if you want soldier boy back in one piece." Sid rose and began circling the sage over my head.

I felt so tired and dazed, I didn't have the energy to protest as the strange smell enveloped me. I coughed and my stomach lunged. The two women began to repeat the Lord's Prayer, then the next, and during the second round, Sid joined in, adding his deep baritone to the mix. By round three, I started to feel really sick and dizzy. Sid had forced a thin slice of wafer onto my tongue and made me wash it down with some water. The smell of the sage attacked my senses; it burned in my nose and throat. Made my eyes smart, and my skin itch.

"Stop it," I said, sounding loud and shrill against their hypnotic litany. "I don't like it." I moved to stand and leave. Sid shoved me back down and ordered Megan to hold me in place. Her small, but strong hands, gripped my shoulders. Somewhere inside me, I knew I could move her easily, but the lethargy left me weak and unresponsive.

Round four began and my stomach plunged. My mouth started to water, and I knew I was going to puke. Sid noticed something in my face change.

"Megan. Doors." He reached for the metal waste-paper basket he'd bought because he liked the dancing pigs circling it, and I grabbed the thing just in time.

My stomach heaved.

"Keep going," he ordered Luce, who'd let her voice peter out.

Round five. I was sick until I'd begun to dry heave. The cold air rushed around the house, moving the sage out of the living room and wafting it everywhere else.

The final, *amen*, came on round six. I sat back on the sofa. "What the hell just happened?" I asked, blinking. Turned out, the world wasn't made of grey shades after all. Colour rushed into my brain, overwhelming me for long seconds until my mind readjusted. My mouth tasted foul.

"Go shower again." Sid wasn't done with his orders. "Then you need to eat."

"Sid—"

"No arguing. I should've done this last night. I knew something was wrong. Go," he ordered, and pointed to the door.

Megan stood there, puzzlement making her look years younger. "Why do you look different?"

I walked past her and winked. Not only did the world contain colour again, it held possibilities that filled me with hope. "Sid's a wizard."

She grinned. "Of Oz?"

"Naw, Peckham."

She laughed. "Almost as strange."

By the time I returned to the kitchen, I felt… No, I *was* completely different. Light filled the room, and I knew what I had to do today. I needed to convince a powerful, wealthy man that he had to move his damned golf course to another part of the country. Or not build the damned thing at all.

I glanced at the clock on the wall. "Shit, we only have forty minutes to get down there."

Megan held out the bike helmets.

Sid stepped between us. "I don't think that's a good idea. You aren't going to be on your game, and we need to talk about what happened."

I grabbed some soggy toast and stuffed it in my mouth, then slurped at the cold tea. "Later, Sid. Promise." I stole more toast. "How bad is the rain?" I asked, peering out the window.

"Mizzle." Megan pulled on a set of waterproofs.

"Don't either of you want to know what just happened?" Luce asked.

"No," we said together. Then we grinned.

Sid pulled Luce away. "They are the pointy end of the spear. They aren't very interested in the healing process. Let them go. We'll sort it out later. I need to write up what he was saying yesterday."

The ride down to Madron was full of excitement. The roads were wet, the wind strong and the traffic busy. I didn't think about anything other than keeping Quacker on the tarmac and Megan safe as she held on behind me. It was fun.

We made it to the building site before ten, and the security guard waved us through the barrier. I gunned it going down the track and may have made more of a show of stopping than strictly necessary.

Megan laughed as she climbed off the back and removed her helmet. "That was a bit saucy. I'm very glad I know where all the speed cameras are."

I grinned. "I feel great. Why do I feel great?"

Megan waved a hand over me. "All Sid's magical smudging and my oh, so helpful prayers." She pressed her palms together and tried to look like an angel.

"Daft tart."

"Stupid boy."

Steve Denzel walked out of the farmhouse wearing his white hard hat. "You're just in time. He's due any…"

We all turned at the sound of a heli coming in from the east.

# Chapter Twenty-Seven

I've dealt with some obnoxious people in my life, but Sir Pierce Alanson had to be top of the list. A man dressed like an overpaid caddy, with the weight of a bloated monarch behind him, and before him. The face of a flappy fish suffering from sea lice. His hair was a shade of brown I'd never seen in nature, and however much he paid for the plugs, it wasn't enough.

As he came off the sleek helicopter, he wore a hat to protect the quiff, but he behaved as if he'd just landed in a war zone. Which, to be fair, if I failed in our current mission, we might end up living in, but he didn't know that, and it irritated me. He also had two suited, booted and armed security guards with him. Their concealed weapons were all too obvious to me.

The air stank of aviation fluid. I muttered, "This isn't going to go well."

Steve said, "We can but try."

Megan just scowled.

Rather than pull out my Rural Security ID, I removed

my Royal Marine credentials. Being only a corporal probably wouldn't help me, but he might not notice the lack of rank. I should've worn my uniform. Hanging about with the protesters had made me lazy with my appearance. I squared my shoulders and took on a parade-ground stance.

The foreman stepped forward. "Sir Alanson, welcome. It's a pleasure to see you."

"Is it, Steve? You sure about that?" He had a hard Northern accent. A pair of deep-set, hooded eyes turned to me. "Who are you?"

At the last moment, I changed my mind. Being a corporal in this arena wouldn't help. His security probably outranked me; they'd certainly been in the military. I withdrew my ID and said, "Griffin Woodbury, Sir Alanson. I'm from the Department of Rural Security."

The man frowned. "Never heard of you."

"That's the idea, sir." I didn't elaborate. He could interrogate his contacts in Whitehall to suss us out. "This is Sergeant Megan Ackley, my police colleague. We would like to speak to you about a sensitive matter."

"I'm not here for subtlety, Mr Woodbury. I'm here to find out why this project is off target, over budget and late for delivery." He glared at Steve. "You are my project manager. I suggest we go to your office." He turned his annoyed gaze to me. "If you'd like to make an appointment with my office—"

"This is a police matter, sir," Megan said, stepping forward as the heli's blades began to slow and the noise died.

"And they sent a sergeant to speak with me? Contact my lawyers. I don't speak to the police."

Respect from the wealthy and powerful goes a long way when the upper echelons of our society deal with the plebs.

That was us. After all, there are a great many more of us than them. Megan's jaw bounced a little as she bit back her immediate response.

"You aren't under any kind of suspicion of wrongdoing, sir. We simply need to talk with you, explain a few things, and ask for your help and co-operation." She managed a smile that, if you didn't know her, you'd think was bright and shiny. I did know her and saw the crocodile in her eyes ready to snap her jaw shut, do a death roll and stash his body underwater so she could feed on it for several days.

The man took a deep breath, and I watched as he laid a veneer of bonhomie over the truculence of his true nature. "Well, I guess I should do all I can for the local constabulary. As I understand it, you've done all you can to contain the damned fools over the road. Anyone would think that bringing jobs to the area made me the criminal." He smiled, walked past us, and began striding towards the portacabins. Over his shoulder, he said, "Steve, catch me up on progress."

Steve scrambled to catch up. "Sir Alanson, we've made good progress in certain locations, but I've requested that Sergeant Ackley and Mr Woodbury be here this morning because we do have problems. Perhaps you've read about the deaths in the area?"

"Hippy women, right?" Alanson asked.

"Well yes, sir, they came from the protesters—"

"Then I fail to see what they have to do with me and my golf course. The deaths weren't on my land, as I understand it, and unless the police know differently, I didn't kill them. If one of the men *your* company hired did, then that's not my problem." He flung open the door to Steve's office and strode in, stamping mud off his glossy wellington boots as he went.

Unable to help myself, I knocked mine on the breeze blocks set up outside for just this task, so we didn't tramp the mud into the foreman's office.

"Let's face it, Steve. We're two weeks behind schedule. You still haven't cleared the section of woodland we need shifting, and I've landscapers waiting to go, while the damned farmhouse is an eyesore. Hitting the targets is part of your contract, Steve, and you aren't hitting them."

"Sir—"

I couldn't watch this man humiliate Steve Denzel any longer. The poor bugger was under immense pressure and wanted to do the right thing by everyone. An impossible task. I said, "Sir Alanson, I think we need to walk the site with you and try to explain how you can help us make this project work more smoothly."

Though, trying to tell this man to leave a bunch of trees alone wouldn't be easy. Now I'd met him and listened to his voice, I recognised him. Not all multi-millionaires were in the headlines on a daily basis. Many of them ran their organisations with a quiet hand, unknown to the public. They might show up on a red carpet, but they wouldn't be recognised by anyone but the business press, and unless their children or spouses hit the headlines for something nefarious, no one cared about their lives. This particular rich bloke had interests in the worldwide mining of rare minerals, off the back of his father's legacy in the oil industry.

"I don't have time—"

Megan tried, "I think you'd want to help in a murder inquiry, sir. The publicity of the protesters at this location is already damaging your brand. It might be wise to co-operate with the police and our Rural Security colleagues.

Of course, I could go through official channels, make some noise about the lack of—"

Sir Alanson waved a hand and chuckled. "Alright, Sergeant, alright, you've made your point. At least it's stopped raining. Show me whatever you need to so I can get this over with. I've a lunch appointment in Paris."

Well, that was a start. The man's mood seemed to have shifted, and we'd be able to communicate our concerns more easily. I hoped.

The security team was outside the cabin. Sir Alanson said, "Wait here. We don't need any more mud in the chopper than is necessary. I don't think those hippies are likely to start taking potshots at me."

I wasn't so sure after the other night. He must've received a report about the shooting and potential bombing of the site.

That's when he looked at me properly. "You're the ones who stopped those damned freaks from blowing up my golf course, aren't you?"

"We're part of the team," I said. It wouldn't do to escalate our role. I wanted to keep this meeting focused.

Sir Alanson stood and wagged his finger at me. "No, no, don't do that. My people told me a commando and a police officer saved my site."

I glanced at Megan. She gave a quiet nod. I said, "We were just doing our jobs, sir. Rural Security is a small force of highly trained individuals that can act with the military precision the police can't with current legislation. We are used in very specific instances where we believe there might be specialist problems."

"And you think we have those problems here?" he asked.

"I know we do. The deaths of Jennifer Mancore and River are proof of those difficulties." While I spoke, I managed to get the man moving again towards the trees. "All we did the other night was to prevent more deaths, either among the protesters or your employees."

"You did a fine job, Mr Woodbury. Though, I'm guessing that you hold a rank in the Royal Marines?" He smiled at me, and I suddenly found myself almost willing to like this man. His initial brashness and irritation with Steve, his foreman, had set me on edge, but I realised Pierce Alanson just didn't believe in mincing his words, tempering his attitude or backing down from his goals. How he'd retained his Northern credentials despite growing up in wealth, I had no idea, but he had that earthy quality that made it possible to talk to him. Really talk.

"How do you know that, sir?" I asked, a nibble of paranoia making me terse.

"I see it in you, son. My grandfather was a Marine. You have a way about you."

We did? That was something to change. "I'm only a corporal, sir. My work with Rural Security keeps me outside the usual mechanics of the Armed Forces."

"You're a commando, though, right?"

"Yes, sir."

"You saw action?"

Ah, now I knew why his attitude had mellowed; he was a fan. "Yes, sir. Africa and the Gulf. Mostly protecting shipping lanes, dealing with pirates, then moving inland to tackle religious groups destabilising places like Mali and Niger."

"I have business interests out there, Corporal. I appreciate your work. It's been difficult with the rise of these death cults."

"Religious—"

He waved a hand to cut me off. "No, Corporal. These

people aren't religious anything. They are death cults. I work with Muslims all over the world, and I have a lot of respect for their beliefs. Those heathens aren't part of Islam. Still, we aren't here to debate that, are we?"

"No, sir. Though it is related." I felt the nerves that always accompanied this part of my job. Trying to explain the unexplainable, without revealing the truth of DoPI's work and the existence of beings from other planes of reality. A man this powerful and wealthy would give even Sanchez pause for thought. I should've phoned her and requested her presence here to take this meeting. If I fucked up, she'd skin me. Alive!

We were now standing in front of the woodland. It made my heart ache, and I watched Megan's fingers trail over the remains of an ash tree stacked on the ground among so many others. The earth here after the rain was thick with mud, puddles and torn out roots, stumps and fallen limbs. It looked like a war zone where one side had ballistic missiles and the other, stones and spears.

"Sir, we need to discuss this woodland."

The man's brow furrowed, or it tried to at least. "I fail to see why. I have all the permits I need. The council wants to see good jobs and housing brought into the area. The woodland was up for sale, as was the land. So long as we don't touch the water source, and the ancient monuments, we'll be fine."

I wondered if appealing to him through the medium of history might work. "That's just it, Sir Alanson. You are touching an ancient monument. In that woodland, we have the remains of an ancient druidic circle, pre-Roman. Isn't that worth preserving? There could be an archaeological team here—"

He held up his hands. "Whoa there, slow down, Marine.

You start bringing in archaeologists, and the price of building goes up tenfold."

"Important historical—"

"You can throw a rock in any direction in Britain and hit an ancient something. I can't stop business investment because of ancient or modern hippies doing their thing."

My eyes flickered to Megan for some backup, but her focus was on the trees. I glanced at Steve, who stood on Sir Alanson's other side. He was frowning and leaning forward, as if trying to hear something.

Knowing what I'd faced the day before, dread swept up and over me so fast, my knees turned to pudding. I breathed out slowly to bring my racing heart back under control.

Pierce Alanson kept on about the importance of his portfolio and the work he'd be providing the locals in Cornwall all year round, and how focusing on long-term commitment to rural locations would improve education, prospects, and health. All of which I agreed with, but there were better ways to do it than digging out trees that could fight back.

I turned at the sound of rustling. The wind didn't cause that. It moved around us with sullen inefficiency, full of water, making it limp. The shadows among the trees were thick. The hair on my neck and arms rose.

"Megan." She didn't take her eyes off the woodland but gave a brief nod. "We need to leave."

"Are you listening to me, Corporal?" Alanson snapped.

"No, sir. Not right now. I want *you* to listen to me. Steve, you too." I glanced at the foreman. His eyes were wide, face pale.

"What the hell is this?" demanded Alanson.

"Sir, I want you to step back from the trees. You and Mr Denzel need to move quickly, but with great care, back to the portacabins. Lock the door. Do not run." The surrounding air thickened.

Steve dared to touch his boss's sleeve. "We need to listen to them, Sir Alanson, please. Let's leave. We can talk more about this later."

"No, I want to know what the hell's going on." Again, a demand.

I ignored him. "Megan, step back towards me. If something comes out of those woods…"

"We need to slow it down?" I heard the fear in her voice. She didn't know exactly what we'd face, but she had seen the state of me when I'd woken up in her arms. Anything big enough to knock me on my arse was going to do untold damage to her.

"No, I want you to run. Get to the security team. We'll need their guns. I'm not carrying."

"Griff…"

"I can handle it, Meg. Follow orders." I'd put my hand out, taken hold of the sleeve belonging to a knight of the realm, and started to shove him in the direction of possible safety.

The rustling became stronger. An earthy smell hit me. One of rotting leaves and animal flesh. Overhead, the clouds grew thicker impossibly fast, the sludgy white turning dark grey. Rather than a thin mizzle in the air, rain began to fall. Big fat drops. Thunder rumbled. I thought of Eloise's Father Sky and wondered which side he was on. I guessed it wouldn't be ours.

The petulant light caught something shining at the edge of the woodland. A reflection. Two flashes of silver, further off the ground than any mortal man. Two more appeared and then vanished back into the shadows. Crows burst from the crowns of trees, their cries to Father Sky more like screams than caws.

"What was that?" asked Alanson. "I saw something in the trees. Is that an animal?" He managed an attempt at a laugh, but I felt his fear. It leaked between us, staining the air with his heavy musk. "Has the Beast of Bodmin moved down here?"

"No, sir. Something far worse. Move. Now!" I ordered, and I really shoved him back, putting my body between him and the trees. *Would I die for this man?* The thought flashed through my head. I knew I'd make it to the portacabins alone. So would Megan, I'd make damned sure of it, but Steve wouldn't, and neither would Sir Pierce Alanson.

In my periphery, I saw Steve's workers. Their instincts were already honed to the site's odd atmosphere, and they were on edge. Several languages burst over me as men yelled and began running. The two suited guards who'd arrived with Alanson took notice and appeared from the side of the cabin. They were moving quickly towards us.

"Run!" I bellowed, pushing Alanson in the shoulders, then grabbing his arm, pulling him with me. "Just bloody run!"

Confused, both men stopped moving. Alanson slipped from my grasp, and I started to backpedal in an attempt to make him move. I saw their eyes widen, their jaws drop, and I knew what was coming from behind me. I felt it. Every fibre in my body yammered and gibbered in terror. Three shapes, tall, impossibly elegant, their smooth mottled skin vivid in the raining light of the day, rushed past me. In that glimpse, I saw they carried stone spears and knives on thick vines around their slim waists.

Before either security guard had a chance to pull their weapons, the Dru attacked. One of the creatures grabbed at the suited man, and before he could release a round, the warrior gripped his head and twisted. I'd seen it done in films, but breaking someone's neck is not easy. This wasn't just a break; the Dru twisted it so far, the guard's surprised eyes were turned away from us. The warrior dropped him into the mud. Then, he turned his attention toward us. Steve screamed and stopped moving altogether.

I glanced behind me and saw three more Dru stalking forward out of the woods. If anything, these were even larger. Their shoulders dwarfed mine. Thick and solid as an oak, ash or yew. Tall as an elm or sycamore. As fluid as willow. We didn't stand a fucking chance.

They rushed us. I threw myself at Alanson, but a hand made of roots strong enough to force stone to move, closed over my damaged shoulder and I found my feet leaving the ground. I didn't even have time to yelp in agony. Flying backwards, I hit the log pile, and my head cracked against the wood, air bursting from my lungs.

Megan.

Despite my dazed brain, I struggled upright and watched the bloodbath. The Dru took no prisoners. Sir Pierce Alanson and his men were torn limb from limb. I watched, unable to move despite trying, as a pair of the Dru grabbed Alanson's arms and just ripped them from their sockets. Blood fountained into the mud. Alanson's screams clawed at the glowering sky. Thunder rolled through those clouds. Frantic, I searched the battleground. I saw Megan trying to drag Steve away from a Dru who'd locked his savage teeth into the foreman's ribcage. Those terribly strong hands were scrambling to reach her.

Training kicked in. Fear fell backwards into the mud and floundered there, drowning. I ran towards Megan and Steve Denzel. Leaping over the remains of a security guard,

I landed and used the momentum to smash into the far larger figure of the Dru. His energy rippled over me as we tumbled in the mud. Megan bellowed my name, but I had no time. That energy felt like poison ivy, stinging nettles, and blackthorn spikes. It, and the smell, made it hard for me to breathe. I'd caught the Dru by such surprise that I found my feet planted in his belly. Even as his teeth gnashed at my face, Steve's blood falling hotly on my skin, those alien eyes savage with their hate, I pushed upwards with all the strength in my thighs. The Dru weighed less than the leg presses I'd been doing at the gym. I shoved him off me.

"Griffin! Taser!" Megan screamed from behind me.

I twisted, still in the mud, and she threw something at me, even as she dragged Steve away. The other Dru were still pulling at the corpses of the men they'd downed and... My God, they were eating them. My hand went up and caught the black weapon, even as my eyes saw a man's ribcage opened and organs pulled free.

In one almost fluid motion, I twisted back to the Dru I'd stopped, and I fired into his body with the Taser. The needles hit.

A scream, high, pitched to hurt human ears, filled the war zone. The other Dru stopped their dark feast and screamed in unison. The sound rebounded from the low clouds and made me want to cower in terror. All the creatures arched their backs. The one I'd hit dropped to his knees and clawed at the pins in his chest. He should've gone down. Nobody could stay conscious with that many volts in their body. He didn't. Those lethal hands pulled the wires away. Two of his battle brothers ran to his aid. They lifted him and, without a backward glance, they ran back into the woodland.

The battle was over. For now.

## Chapter Twenty-Eight

Silence, except for Steve's sobs and groans. Not a bird tweeted. No sign of a crow or buzzard. Megan, tear-stained and muddy, wobbled for a moment, then collapsed into the filth. I scrambled towards her on all fours. The rain was cold on my back. My limbs were weak and disorganised.

"Meg, talk to me," I begged.

Her eyes were wide and shocked. "I… I…"

"I need you. Steve needs you. Do you understand, Sergeant?" I asked her, trying to get her eyes to focus on my face. They were drifting about in her skull, her attention far away from the moment. "Megan." I shook her very gently, but it was enough to snap her back.

"Ambulance."

I breathed. "Yes. Lots of them, and we need DoPI." Sanchez. Oh, the fallout from this would be bad. We weren't just covering up the death of some internet manosphere influencer this time. We'd be covering up the death of a peer of the realm.

"Griffin…"

“Not now. I promise later. But not now. Now, I need you to be a police officer. Can you do that for me? We need a cordon. Get people to stay back. We can’t have them marching around.” While I gave her instructions, I pulled off my bike jacket, then the jumper and shirt and finally my t-shirt. Wadding it up, I put it on the bleeding wounds covering Steve’s side. Then I put his hands over it and ordered him to press down. I redressed.

Megan nodded as I barked more orders. She moved far too slowly for me to hold much confidence in her. I saw people rushing towards us. Workers from the site, people from the protest camp who must’ve heard the screams, and the site’s security guards. Too little, far too late. I had to keep the area clear of civilians.

I pulled out my phone, but couldn’t make it work until I realised, I’d smeared blood all over the screen. After wiping it clean on my shirt, I called Sanchez.

“What is it, Corporal? I’m in a meeting.”

“Ma’am, we need a cleanup team down here at the cloutie tree site, stat. It’s a war zone. The trees attacked us.” My voice shook.

A long pause. “Did you just say the trees attacked you?”

“Yes. We can’t contain this one. I don’t think… I, um, I’ve fucked up, ma’am. I’ve really fucked up.”

I heard a sharp intake of breath. “Stop whining, Corporal. We’ll have a team dispatched immediately. Use locals for now. Think of a damned good cover story. We’ll back you. Then I want a full report. I can’t come down there myself. You’ll have Markin on site.”

Talking to that ice-cold woman’s voice shored up my trembling spine. “Yes, ma’am.” I had a command structure; I wasn’t alone.

She killed the call.

I took one long, smooth breath and moved into action. Looking at the site and the people about to arrive, I made a series of decisions.

"Megan." She turned to look at me, still wobbly and glazed. "Help Steve. I'll deal with the cordon." I ran off towards the group of workers on legs that didn't really feel like mine, but they worked, mostly.

A group of the men headed in my direction. "I need you to help keep people out of the area. It isn't safe. I want a simple fence, just like you've seen on the TV crime shows. Can you provide me with that?"

"What happened?" one of the men asked me in an Eastern European accent.

My brain scrambled for a moment. Whatever I said now would be the line DoPI took. It had to be good. "The storm," I said. "The thunder, there was ball lightning, and I guess, marsh gas. It looks like everyone near the wood has been breathing marsh gas. Or that radon gas Cornwall has problems with. The lot just… It's bad. You don't want to see it." I was almost babbling.

"Steve?" asked the same man.

"Alive. We've called an ambulance. Please get people organised and away from the site. If there is another pocket of that stuff, we could all go up." It was bollocks, but the human mind is a funny thing. When someone sounds like they know what they're talking about and speaks with enough authority, most people will believe them. I see it all the time out there in the world beyond Cornwall.

I turned and had the maddest thought. If I wanted the lightning idea to really stick. If I wanted to keep people away from the bodies, I had one ace in the hole. Running through the pieces of the dead men, I found one of the weapons. A Glock. Good. I also found something I really didn't expect. A suppressor. What the fuck was this dude doing with a firearm *and* a suppressor? Even on security duty for the Royals, we didn't carry that kind of equipment. What was Sir Pierce Alanson so worried about? Whatever it was, it didn't matter now.

Shaking the thought away, I headed towards the heli, waving my arms like a puppet suffering from apoplexy. The pilot opened his door.

"What's going on?" he shouted.

"Move!" I screamed. "There's lightning and marsh gas from the building work."

The pilot took a few seconds to understand the strange words. To be fair, anyone in his position would've. He couldn't have seen the Dru from his angle, but he'd obviously heard the screaming.

The man slipped from the helicopter and started to run. He sat on gallons of aviation fluid. The moment he was clear of the area, and hidden from my view, I screwed the suppressor onto the Glock's barrel. Checking my surroundings, seeing everyone clustered the other side of the old farmhouse, or the portacabins in Megan and Steve's case, I considered my idea one more time.

Happy I'd made the right call, I opened fire on the heli's fuel tank. *Phat, phat, phat…* The dead sound of the gun's discharge wouldn't travel far in the wet air.

I planned on emptying the clip, it only took five rounds. The boom, the flash, the percussive force of raw energy knocked me over. Heat ripped the air into pieces. Metal and fiery foam cascaded outwards. I huddled in the mud. Deaf to everything but the screaming in my ears.

When I dared to look up, I saw a scene that should've been in a war film.

"Oops," I murmured, or shouted. I wasn't sure.

The sight shocked me. To be honest, I hadn't really expected quite so much drama. Still, it would help explain the bits of body everywhere. The crime scene would now be so confused that DoPI could make up any narrative it wanted about Alanson's death. I hid the Glock and suppressor in my jacket.

During that long morning, I took on the mantle of 'the man in charge' and I did my job well. The emergency services, when they arrived, were directed through the site by the workers. The protesters were kept back with building site warning tape rather than police issue and stakes in the ground. When the protesters grew restless and demanding, I had them provide food and tea for all, using the site's facilities. I asked more of them to go back to the road to help direct traffic, and still more to provide blankets to anyone who needed them. They were all agog at the heli's explosion. Exactly what I planned.

At one point, Leaze caught hold of me. "You're talking bollocks, Griffin."

Gently, I peeled her hand off my arm. "Please don't interfere. My people won't like it. Your priority has to be keeping your friends safe. Get them off the site, Leaze. Leave. This is going to get worse."

She frowned and studied me for a long moment. "What's happened?" Her voice was soft, gentle, and far too much like the mother figure I'd missed all these damned years.

I was desperate to tell her the truth. To have someone take this weight off my shoulders. Instead, I patted her shoulder. "We'll tell you, but not right now. Right now, I need to be what I am." I stared around. "Leaze, where's TikTok girl?"

She blinked. "Who?"

"The girl with the phone? She's been all over the place. Far too young to be out on her own. I keep seeing her because she looks like she should be glamping, not camping."

"Oh," she said. "You mean Isabelle. I'm not sure. I haven't seen her in a while."

"Leaze, you need to find her. Lock her up and don't let her near the fucking wood. Now." The damned girl should be here recording this, and if she wasn't, what the hell was she recording? DoPI would be monitoring all social media coming from this location, doctoring and removing where necessary. I'd give them a call and warn them about Little Miss TikTok, get her accounts closed down.

For a long moment I wondered if Leaze would argue with me, then she started to understand. "Oh, oh, goddess, yes. You're right." She turned and yelled, "Denny, I need you," before hurrying off.

When, almost three hours later, I heard the familiar *thump, thump, thump,* of DoPI's Puma heli, I almost dropped to my knees in thanks. It landed near the wreckage of Alanson's machine. The remains looked like a melted Lego toy in comparison to the military bearing of the Puma. The ambulance crew had taken Steve, checked over Megan and me, then left when I'd said Rural Security would be dealing with the remains. I just kept repeating the story, marsh gas, or radon, and lightning. Helicopter exploded. The rain had yet to let up, but it added to the chaos, and sometimes that's a liar's best friend.

The team from DoPI, in their black fatigues and carrying assault rifles, looked like the response in the war film I'd created. Markin had twelve experienced operatives with him and a press officer. Suddenly, I was redundant. They took over talking to the police, the remaining medical teams, and pushing people back further than I'd managed. It felt good, and I retrieved Megan, moving us towards the farmhouse and out of the rain. She shivered and didn't say much. Steve's blood covered her hands, face and clothes. In the farmhouse, we used the old sink to wash up as best we could. I used a clean rag to wipe her face. We still didn't speak. Her eyes were very distant.

When Markin finally deigned to talk to me, I heard Sanchez's dulcet tones in every word. I listened; he was a sergeant after all, and didn't respond. He made all the valid points I'd made to myself. I'd ignored the chain of command. I hadn't reported in. Furthermore, I'd underestimated the enemy because I didn't do a proper risk assessment of my operation… and more.

He finished with, "Frankly, Woodbury, you'll be lucky if the boss doesn't throw you in the brig."

"Yeah, well, that's her decision, not yours. Now that you've finished yelling at me, there are some people who need my help."

He hawked and spat at my feet. Disgusting habit. "You aren't going anywhere but back to London."

"Actually," Megan said, coming in from my left, "he's coming with me. I have a police warrant for his arrest. You can check it with my inspector. I think you'll need to argue over who has authority over him, and in the meantime, I have to take him in." She grabbed my arm and snapped a handcuff over my wrist.

I offered my other arm and smiled at Markin. "Sorry. She's the civil authority on site."

Megan led me away by the elbow, ignoring Markin's shouted orders completely. "How deep is the shit pile you're in?"

"So deep I'll be lucky to see the light of day if I don't solve this problem ASAP," I muttered.

"I don't think I like Sergeant Markin."

"I used to be Sergeant Markin."

She looked at me. "You could never be him, Griff."

I wished I believed her. Since touching the veil for the first time on that beach, I'd been different. I knew it. Or maybe the changes began at Barle's Keep? It's hard for me to understand if it's an awakening to a different way of life, or something closer to a smashing of the old one. Maybe it's both?

For a long time, I'd been less and less a Marine, and more of a civilian who does a weird job with weird people, and happen to handle a gun really well. Let's not forget the running and fighting, I'm usually pretty good at that bit too. It's just Markin had a point. I'd disregarded all protocols and people had died.

We reached the bike, and Megan released the handcuffs. "I know both of us are a bit…" She breathed out, turned in one of her tight circles, tugged her hair for a few seconds and forced herself to look me in the eye. "I know I'm not handling what happened. I'm probably going to need therapy forever, but Leaze and the others need to know how much danger they're in. My conscience won't let me walk away, and your lies aren't going to help."

I gripped her shoulder. "I know."

Her eyes suddenly started to shine too much, and her breath hitched. "Griff…" Blood stained her clothing and despite washing her face, neck and hands, I still saw patches we'd missed.

"We saved Steve, Megan. You did that. We did that. The others—" I shook my head. "Megan, we didn't stand a chance of stopping the Dru. I wasn't armed, and that's on me. Markin was right. I didn't do my job, and people died. None of that falls on your shoulders."

This time, her hand gripped my arm. "We were here to talk to a businessman about his project. We weren't here to fight tree spirits. They've never come out in daylight like this. We had no reason to think we were in danger. His security detail failed to save him. This isn't on you either. I'll be writing that in my report."

I appreciated the solidarity but knew the hard truth of the situation. As a Royal Marine, I am supposed to be prepared, but I liked my softer civilian life too much, and that meant I didn't run around the Cornish countryside with a sidearm unless necessary. Then, a horrible realisation struck me. Opening fire on the Dru would've broken a piece of my heart I'd never have healed.

They were elemental beings fighting for survival. They weren't anything like the damned incubus, looking for domination and power. These creatures just wanted to be left alone and to have their home returned to them. Just like tigers or polar bears.

My phone burped to life. When I looked at the screen, I saw Sanchez written across it. "I have to take this," I said to Megan, turning away and accepting the call. The dread in my belly this time was knowing I faced a metaphorical firing squad. At least I hoped she wouldn't put me against a wall.

"Ma'am," I said.

"Corporal. Markin has informed me that the situation is containable." She sounded as if she were double-checking our homework.

I began to pace up and down the lane to burn off my anxiety. "He has the site locked down. Requested I leave the area. I need to speak with the protesters. They are still in danger."

"The explosion motif was a wise move. We can use it to help hide what happened to Alanson. However—"

"I know, ma'am. I've let you down. My protocols have slipped. I'll understand—"

"My God, Woodbury, will you stop with the self-flagellation? Yes, your protocols have slipped considerably, and we will be doing a full review; however, you are our first remote office. You have operational control, a fact that I've just reminded Markin of—you're welcome, by the way. I chose you for this assignment because I needed someone who could act independently. If I didn't want you to make your own decisions, I wouldn't have let you go down there. It's tough, making the hard calls, and when it goes wrong, it's even tougher."

To say I was shocked by her words was an understatement, and my brain scrambled to keep up. "I understand, ma'am."

"I doubt it, but you might, given time. It's a shame you never saw action as a commanding officer. It would've helped with a slightly more pragmatic view to making operational mistakes, but still, you'll learn. What I need from you now is a plan."

She didn't mean come up with one in a week, or even a day, she wanted one now.

I surprised myself with what came next. "I do have a plan, ma'am. I think it's something that DoPI might want to use as a blueprint for the future. This isn't going to be our first encounter with something like these tree spirits."

"I believe you're calling them Dru?"

"Yes, ma'am. They are male dryads. It's not a term

usually used in traditional mythologies, but Doctor Carmichael feels it's appropriate. They are fearsome warriors. Immensely strong and interested only in defending their home. If I can communicate with them, using a natural mystic we have access to down here, then I think I can negotiate a peaceful resolution, but I'll need your backing on the practicalities." I held my breath in the hope she'd agree to hear more.

"Go on."

I breathed out and continued, "We need a preservation order on the woodland. No one is to go in there to cut down the trees. A proper management team should be brought in, and we must expand the woods. If we can show these creatures that we have peaceful intentions, then we have a blueprint for future encounters worldwide. With the ruptures in the veil—"

"Yes, Corporal, I understand the implications, and it's not as if we can move the damned trees."

"No, ma'am." I remained silent, knowing she was thinking through more implications of my plan than I'd considered.

She said, "It's like we're encroaching on their land, isn't it?" Was this turning into a proper conversation again?

"Yes. Just now I was thinking it's like polar bears, or tigers, even wolves, I guess. Where human activity has unbalanced the natural world so much, the animals are coming out and pushing back."

"Alright, Woodbury, I'll allow you to keep the lead on this. Don't let me down. We can't contain these things the way we have in the past. We need a new dynamic for elemental contact of previously peaceful species."

After centuries, DoPI was changing its protocols? This

was huge, but I didn't have time to think about it. Relief shot through me instead. "Yes, ma'am. Thank you."

"Don't let anyone else die."

"No, ma'am." The call ended.

Megan strode over to me. "Well?"

"I'm not fired, and I'm not going to the brig." To say I was astonished was an understatement. I kept pushing the boundaries of my remit, and Sanchez kept backing my play. To what end? What was she going to get out of this?

"This is a good thing, right?" The shaking had stopped, and she'd started to eat one of her energy bars.

"It's certainly surprising. Not the usual DoPI behaviour, which is making me suspicious, but time will tell on that score. Come on, let's talk to Leaze and Trystan. Did you hear the plan?"

She chuckled. "That was a plan? Don't they usually involve something saner than talking to trees?"

We both mounted Quacker, not bothering with crash helmets, and I rode up the dirt track to the gate. "You can't remain a sceptic forever, Meg."

"No, you're right. As much as it pains me to admit it, there are creatures out there that shouldn't be real, but they are. However, can I remain a sceptic about an all-knowing deity having created the universe?"

I laughed. "Yeah, sure, you can totally own that one."

Her forehead hit my back. "Good, then the rest I can learn to deal with." We flashed our IDs at DoPI's people, who maintained security at the building site and headed for the protesters' camp just down the lane.

A number of colourful vehicles were pulling out of the field. Obviously, this much scrutiny from scary men in black uniforms with a Puma helicopter for their transport was too much for the paranoid. I couldn't blame them, and the fewer people, the less potential for violence or victims.

When we reached the gate, I rode Quacker onto the grass verge and Megan climbed off the back. "What are we telling them?" she asked.

"If my plan's going to work, I'll need their full co-operation."

"So, the truth?"

I waggled my hand from side to side. "Mostly." We shared a grin. "Come on. I'll explain what I have in mind when we speak to the others. Assuming Leaze is still here."

"Oh, I don't think she's going anywhere. The woman's lovin' the drama."

"What's not to love? Psychotic, pissed off tree spirits murdering your friends."

Megan smacked me on the arse as she walked past. "Let's not forget the hulking great Royal Marine with the big puppy-dog eyes."

I followed, confused. "What's that mean?"

Megan shook her head. "You really have no idea, do you? All-male boarding schools have a lot to answer for in this country. Come on, soldier boy, let's get that charm to do its thing again."

Slightly mystified, I tried to focus on the plan I'd been thinking about while waiting for the DoPI team to show up. Having thought I'd be immediately returned to base and facing charges of insubordination, my ever working brain had developed a handover strategy and a way to move forwards with this problem, without anything else dying. I guessed this might be one of the reasons Sanchez hadn't dropped me off the roof of her office building in London. She actually trusted me.

That was a revelation.

*Don't get your hopes up, Superman. Things'll change fast if she decides you've cocked up another mission. Getting comfy is a bad idea.*

Reality checks never hurt.

Yeah, because giving myself a reality check during a mission that involved murderous trees was just the thing to motivate me. Sometimes, I baffled myself the most.

# Chapter Twenty-Nine

We found Leaze sitting at the community fire pit. The poor woman looked so forlorn, and she'd obviously been crying. The huge wad of tissues in her hand looked like it badly needed replacing. The few people moving around avoided her and us.

Megan sat next to her and placed an arm around the woman's shoulders. Predictably, it opened the floodgates.

Like most blokes, I'm not great with other people's tears. I'm not great with my own, but I've come to accept that there are times when even a Royal Marine just needs to break down and let go. I remembered my mother crying a great deal when my father came back on leave, and I'd seen Megan cry during our shared childhood misadventures. Then the girlfriends I'd lost over the years—some of them cried a lot when they were ending things. Which always mystified me. The tears of boys at school, of course, but we all tried to hide those. A woman like Leaze? In this situation? I was lost to that one completely.

I said, "I'll go and speak to Anwen's Children." Climbing the hill would be easier at this point.

Wishing I'd had the opportunity to speak to Leaze and Megan, I went through my plan again, hoping it would be enough to convince Eloise to help us save her damned grove.

The moment I was spotted by one of the Children, a shout went up to rouse the others. By the time I was within speaking distance, I faced several men and two women, all of whom carried makeshift weapons.

"And there's me thinking you were all about the peace and love," I muttered, coming to a halt. In case of potential violence, I rolled my shoulders. My left screamed in protest. That bruise was going to be a problem for a while.

Eloise appeared in robes, and Trystan stood next to her, his head lowered like a grovelling dog.

"Why are you here?" Her crisp Home Counties accent rang out like a preacher in a pulpit.

"Why do you think?" I countered. "I'm hoping we can prevent more deaths. If that's okay with you?"

Trystan looked up, and our gazes locked. I saw the grief in them and the confusion. The kid was heartbroken. He tried to step towards me, but Eloise put a hand on his shoulder and he stilled.

"You can't expect us to help," Eloise said, "after what you did to Trystan. Forcing him to commune without my guidance. I believe it almost cost your life, not to mention the damage it did to my son."

Humble pie straight in the face. Fair enough. She had a point, and she was going to keep scoring with it. "I know, but you kept blocking me, Eloise, and ultimately, it's you who woke that woodland up."

"You don't know that," she snapped.

Trystan stirred next to her and ducked his shoulder to avoid her grip. "Yes, he does. He can prove it was my fault."

I frowned. "No, kid, that's not what I meant. Don't take that onboard. This isn't your fault. We're the adults here."

He backed off from Eloise and came towards me. He asked, "What do you need?"

"Trystan!" she barked.

"No, Eloise. No. Griffin is a good man. I can see it in him."

"He's a murderer."

"He's a soldier. That doesn't make him bad. He carries The Watchers mark on him, no one should have to endure that, and now he needs my help."

I carried what now?

*Focus, doofus.*

"Look," I said, trying not to think about Trystan's pronouncement too much. "I need your help, Eloise. I can't do what I'm planning alone. You can make it possible. Or at least, it'll be safer with you helping us. Please come down to the camp and listen to my ideas. Bring your friends. You really need to hear the truth."

She turned her back. "You people have no interest in the truth."

"You don't know who my people are, so don't go making up conspiracies where none exist." Except they did. After all, I was at the heart of a secret government organisation.

Her gaze went over my head and into the distance. For the first time since I'd met her, those shoulders relaxed. Not by much, but I'd take it as a peace offering of sorts. She flicked her head towards the building site. "What happened?"

I couldn't help myself; I looked over my shoulder. From

up here, I saw into the chaos. The Puma sat on what might once have become the eighteenth hole. Black-clad people moved around, some of them carrying large, heavy-duty black bags between them. The grey clouds overhead gave the site a muted iron tone.

"The Dru attacked us. I didn't have time to move everyone out of the area. Three men died, one is seriously injured. They are fearsome warriors, Eloise. However, we're far worse, and we're disinclined to allow them a chance to hurt us again. I need your help to stop those men down there from setting fire to that woodland and destroying everything in it."

"The spirits didn't hurt you?" Trystan asked with obvious concern.

"They tried, but their focus wasn't on me or Megan. They aren't tactical fighters like humans. We weren't the threat. We were just collateral damage." At least, I thought that's how the fight had gone down. It was hard to know for certain.

All eyes turned to Eloise. She asked, "Do you really think they'll kill again?"

"I know they will. It could even be one of your people. I have to find a way to communicate with them, or I'm going to be left with no choice. The team down there will fry the woodland, and it'll be one more holy site destroyed. Please, I don't want that to happen."

It was true. I really didn't want it to happen. We had to find a way to strike a balance. Not all *paras* should be destroyed. It wouldn't help our species to lose that connection. The war DoPI had been fighting for centuries needed to end.

She bowed her head for a moment, and I watched her people watching her. The level of control she had over them disturbed me greatly, and we might be playing nice right now, but I'd have DoPI keeping an eye on her. We didn't like cults that messed with the veil.

When she lifted her head, I saw resolution in her eyes. It reminded me way too much of some Bible thumper agreeing to talk to the 'savages'. "I will consent to listening to your plan." She looked at the oldest of the women in the group, preventing my infiltration of their inner sanctum. "I'd like you all to prepare for a questing ceremony."

They bowed and, without a single murmur of curiosity or dissent, they dispersed.

Frowning in disapproval and trying to keep my tone neutral, I said, "We'll need Trystan."

"Of course." She nodded in a way that made it obvious he'd remain with her. I very much doubted she'd let me anywhere near him again.

In silence, I led the way down the hill. She didn't seem the type to indulge in chitter-chatter, so I kept myself quiet and let my thoughts race through my plan. I poked holes in places, ripped at other ideas, and rebuilt where necessary. By the time I reached Leaze and Megan, I thought I had it presentable.

When we arrived, Leaze had a mug of steaming tea, and Megan held another. She smiled as I looked at it longingly. "Yours is by the fire."

"Awesome," I murmured, retrieving it and taking a scalding gulp. There are few things a cuppa won't sort out for you.

"Let's all take a seat, and I'll explain what I know, and what I'd like us to do." I sat on the nearest straw bale. "Hey, guys," I yelled over the heads of Eloise and Trystan, "get over here, I need you in on this as well."

Denny came over with a few other people I recognised.

TikTok girl was among them, and I breathed out in relief. We hadn't lost a maiden among the chaos of the day.

Quietly, I asked Leaze, "Is she the only teenage girl on site?"

"She is now," Leaze said. "Don't worry. I've made her move her tent next to my van, and I'm hoping she'll sleep in with me tonight. Or even use River's. I tried to get her to leave, but she won't."

Shaking my head, I said, "Alright, we'll figure it out later."

TikTok girl's hands went to her slim hips. "I have over two-million followers, all of whom want to know about how we can save our planet. I'm not a child."

"You're not an adult, either," I told her, with a scowl.

"Griffin," Megan warned, "don't do that. It won't help. Let's just talk about your ideas. Isabelle, sit down and listen." The police officer pointed to the bale next to her, and the girl sat. I swear, Megan's the only person I know who might stand a chance at herding cats.

I had everyone start with a simple team-building exercise. We shared our names and one significant thing about ourselves. The girl had all the confidence of a socialite and about as much sense. She said her name was Isabelle, and she'd arrived to document the protest for her worldwide following. Her hair was still clean and styled, her fingernails even cleaner. She didn't have that outdoor smell to her that comes with camping—that's camping, not glamping—but she now looked tired and strained around her large blue eyes. Trystan watched her with the shy intensity of every fifteen-year-old boy who doesn't mix often with young women.

I looked at the motley crew I had before me. Peace loving do-gooders on the whole who'd never stand a chance in a real world combat situation. If my plan didn't work, I'd be getting some of them, if not all of them, killed. That thought, and the pressure accompanying it, added a weight to my shoulders I didn't need.

"Alright, here's the plan so far. We've come together to powwow it, and it's an important phase in any potential engagement with the enemy." I was trying to keep my language civilian, but it wasn't easy. "I'll need you all to think of potential problems and solutions."

Megan hid her smile. The damned woman knew exactly why I was struggling. In a situation like this, I'd normally speak commando, a hybrid language that bonded us as a unit, but excluded everyone else. Not what was needed here.

"For those of you who don't know, I work for Rural Security, and it's part of my job to keep things safe for people like you who want to go about their lawful business in the countryside. However, we now face a threat that none of us really understands, and it's certainly nothing we've faced before. The two deaths that have occurred in the woods, Jennifer and River," I didn't want to lose my audience by minimising their friends' lives, "died because Sir Alanson and his building project threatened the woodland. He is also dead."

A murmur went through the crowd.

"I don't know what will happen to the site, so don't ask. He died at the hands of something that lives in those woods. I know I'm speaking to many people here who believe in all kinds of things. That doesn't stop what I'm about to say from being… well, being odd, I guess."

"Just get on with it," Eloise said.

I almost flipped her the one fingered salute. Instead, I

ignored her, a far worse fate for such a person. "During various ceremonies and without any ill intent, Trystan here woke the trees up."

A murmur swept through the crowd of twenty or so people.

"It's not the kid's fault. No one could possibly have known that their ceremonies disturbed several warrior, very male spirits, who are bent on two objectives. One, that they stop the destruction of their home. The second, that they summon their god."

Someone asked, "What's wrong with that?"

Leaze spoke up. "What's wrong with summoning a god? Oh, I don't know, maybe we can all take a moment to think about worst case scenarios."

I held up my hand, trying to forestall an argument. "It's not possible, and it's not really the point. The point is we need to settle things down. I've spoken to my team in London, and they will be putting together a rescue plan for the wood, but we need to do our thing as well."

"The trees are saved?" a woman's voice came at me, but I couldn't make out who spoke.

"Yes, hopefully, so long as we convince them to go back to sleep." I wasn't going into the complexities of the veil and that we'd actually be asking the Dru to return to their version of our world for good. The crowd seemed pleased so far, which was a start.

Denny asked, "What's the plan?"

"With as many of you as possible, I want Eloise and Trystan to summon the Dru so we can speak with them and create a dialogue that will ensure no one else dies. Including them. We'll be doing it tomorrow at midday, ensuring we have maximum daylight to help act as a control."

Megan muttered darkly, "Yeah, because daylight helped this morning."

"That was the Dru's choice, not ours," I said to her. "This will be different."

"Do we really need this many civilians in the way?" she asked. "It doesn't seem wise."

Trystan stirred at last. "It's sensible. Inside the druids' circle, the more people we have, the lower the energy resonance. The Dru aren't so different from us. They just exist at a high frequency, which is why we don't see them when they choose to move through our plane of reality. We might catch a glimpse if we're vibrating in a dream state while awake, but generally we don't notice them or other beings of energy. The god they want to summon isn't that different from our old religions, but he's dead. Gone the way of many others in these lands. Their attempt to call him will go unanswered, but what that'll do to them…" He shook his head, deeply saddened by the idea. "I can summon the Dru, but I need people around me to keep them and me grounded."

I had to hope everyone else understood what he was talking about because I wasn't sure I did. Though several people nodded sagely, I wasn't convinced.

"I'll do it," said Isabelle.

So she could plaster it all over TikTok? "No, you're the last person we need in the ceremony," I told her.

Megan held up a hand to stop the argument. "I'll explain, Isabelle, but now isn't the time."

"The point is," I said, "I need each of you to think hard about whether you want to remain here and take part in this ceremony. It could be dangerous. It will be unpredictable. I'd ask the men in the black over there," I pointed towards the building site, "to help, but I think we all know that would end badly." Christ, I used to be one of those men in black. "We need peace and love, folks, but it comes with risks. So far, five people have died, and they weren't easy deaths. I've been attacked twice." Three times if you counted the spirit I took home with me. That had been unpleasant. "This is dangerous," I repeated for the hard of understanding.

"But the trees are safe, with or without our help?" someone asked.

Megan's eyes shot to mine, and a warning look flashed bright and hard.

I lied. "Yes."

She looked down and breathed out slowly. Leaze's colour rose as if she was about to spill the can of worms all over the beans, but Megan squeezed her hand and the woman remained silent. It couldn't have been easy for her. She knew that if I failed, we'd be flattening the place, one way or another.

It took a couple of hours to settle everyone down. Megan and Leaze convinced Isabelle that she needed to remain in the camp, locked inside Leaze's van. The young woman had only brought a small tent, and I had the feeling her appearance here was more of a protest against her parents, and a desire to be the world's next big eco-influencer than any real affiliation to the cause. There were a few other younger women, but she was by far the youngest and most vibrant, just like Jennifer and River. We did what we could to once more impress on all of them the importance of staying safe.

I returned to the building site long enough to ensure Markin had set up the correct perimeter for the night. He scowled and growled a fair amount, but we had the civilians contained. At least for the moment.

By the time Megan and I climbed back on the bike to head home, we were both wrung out.

"I hurt everywhere," Megan said, leaning against my back. "Even my hair hurts."

I rubbed her leg. "I'll have to take it steady going home, but we'll be there soon enough. You want me to drop you at your place?"

"No. If something kicks off in the night, I need to be with the team."

I smiled. "Roger that."

Through another thin mizzle, I rode home, focusing only on my job. Keeping me and the bike upright.

## Chapter Thirty

*"I can't wake him up, Sid. What the hell do we do?"*

*"It's possible that we just have to let this play out."*

*"He'll be heartbroken when he knows we've seen this."*

A long pause in the sounds. They come to me through cotton wool, and I don't fully grasp their meaning. I have my mission. It's important I reach *her*. She will give me the answers I need, so I understand my truth in this world. Everything I have experienced so far has brought me to this place and this time. It means I must continue my mission.

*"Megan, just give him the tools. He's going to rip his hands to pieces if we don't—"*

A ringing sound reaches me. It's very odd.

*"Shit, it's Leaze from the camp. Hello? What's wrong? Calm down, Leaze, I don't understand… Right… Yes… Yes… We'll be there as soon as possible. Take a breath. Take another. We have a plan, let's just initiate it sooner rather than later… Yes, that's right, gather them together."*

*"We've gotta wake him up."*

*"This isn't going to go well."*

Pain radiated up my arm, and I came to, yelping in shock. The electric feeling released instantly, and the pain stopped except for an orangy afterglow.

"Oh, Griffin, I'm so sorry."

"What the hell?" I blinked against the torchlight in my face and realised I was soaking wet. Megan knelt in front of me, a raincoat covering her. Sid stood nearby with an umbrella. We owned one of those?

I was also sitting in the graveyard, and once again Cornish mud covered me. "Fuck."

Megan's eyes were full of pity. I couldn't bear it.

"We need to get home," she said, talking gently. She made no reference to the fact that I stood in my mother's grave again. "That damned girl, Isabelle, has gone missing. Leaze can't find her anywhere, and the DoPI team isn't helping to look. They won't listen to her."

Sickness rose in my gut, but I didn't have time to indulge. "Do you have the car?" I asked Sid. I avoided Megan's hand, offering to help me out of the pit I'd dug in the grave. Every bone hurt.

"Yeah, sure, of course," he said, watching me. "But, Griffin, I don't think you're in a good place to—"

"I need to change, and we need to get down there. Can Luce come? We might need her help. I don't trust Eloise—" I strode through the graveyard, forcing Megan and Sid to double time it to keep up. I had to swallow down the nausea and dizziness threatening to sweep me away.

"Yes, you said all this last night. She's at home. I hope. Megan heard you leaving, so we followed you."

I'd lay money on Megan feeling as battered as I did right now. "Obviously."

I saw Megan's Vectra, thank goodness, rather than Sid's Mini. Trying to get all three of us in that wouldn't be a joke.

Besides, covering the Vectra's interior with mud was one thing, daring to dirty the Mini would mean I'd have to spend my next clear day—assuming I survived until then—cleaning and polishing the damned antique inside and out.

Thinking about cleaning Sid's car was preferable to just about anything else right now. Option one was thinking about the Dru and the upcoming confrontation with them. Option two was having a conversation with Megan about my latest nighttime adventure. Neither filled me with joy, and the second scared me more than the first. What the hell must she think of me? Every time I thought I'd become the type of man she could be proud of, I did something stupid. This obsession my subconscious mind had with my mother made me look like a freak. What was I becoming? Norman Bates? Was I going to stab…

*Don't go there, buddy. Just don't go there.*

I sat in the back of the car as we returned to Turpin Cottage in silence. Once there, I walked swiftly past Luce, who tried to speak to me, and hurried up the stairs. When I had the door to my room closed, I slumped against it.

"Oh, God," I murmured. I'd left the house in nothing more than my jogging pants and a t-shirt. My feet were sore, my hands bleeding. I had soil all over my legs, arms and belly. I stared hard at my ceiling, trying to fight the urge to just collapse and weep in shame and frustration.

*You don't have time for this, Marine. A girl is out there alone, possibly with the Dru already preparing her for death.*

Now, I just wanted to scream.

I pushed off the door, headed for my shower and cleaned up, leaving my soiled clothes in the washing basket. Then I dressed and forced my swollen feet into my boots. I needed to spend some serious time with a tub of Savlon, never mind a tube.

Through the wall, I heard Megan. Whoever this Adrian bloke was, whatever kind of control freak, she had a better future with him than with someone like me. Rather than talking her out of going to Bristol, I should be packing her stuff and driving her up there myself.

"Get your damned head in the game," I muttered, yanking on my body armour.

When we'd returned to the cottage earlier that day, I'd left Megan and Sid to deal with the food while I took her car over to the office. I'd needed to load up with some defensive gear, including the ballistic vests we'd used before, my Glock, and an assault rifle with three magazines. Next came two communication units that I'd share with Megan. Then the usual array of knives. I also took a flask I'd only needed a few times in the field since working with DoPI; it contained quicksilver. Mercury couldn't be turned into anything useful, unless you wanted fragile bullets in your firearm, or you were into using arrows, which I wasn't, but as a backup it might prove useful this time. Regardless, some instinct told me to take it, and I wasn't going to ignore my instincts.

After dressing for war, I headed downstairs to the kitchen. Megan was suited and booted, ready to face whatever was necessary during our return to the woodland. Her eyes were clear of fear, and she knew better than to talk to me about my grave digging before the coming operation.

She took a long, hard look at the L119A2, which is a C8 carbine used by the UK Special Forces. It wasn't the usual weapon for a Royal Marine, but I'd always preferred it, and DoPI let me pick my toys.

"It's better to go in heavy than wish we had it but didn't," I said.

"I know. Especially after what happened yesterday. It's

just difficult to get my head around," she said, chewing on a protein bar.

I grabbed three. I'd need the calories. We also took several bottles of water and a med kit. Sid and Luce appeared.

"You two are purely for backup. I do not want you involved in the ceremony. Luce, remember, I just need you to keep track of what Eloise is talking about. The damn woman confuses the crap out of me with her mystical bollocks, but you stand a chance of understanding her. Also, you'll know more about Trystan's needs than I do. Understood?"

She nodded, though I read the apprehension on her face. I didn't blame her after what happened with the incubus.

I reached out and gripped her shoulder. "Nothing is going to happen to you. Sid's staying out of the ceremony as well. I need you both to remain firmly in the real world."

"I know. I'll be fine." She managed a smile.

"Sid?"

"I have everything I need. You don't have to worry about us. Luce can help with the recording equipment. The more we understand about what you're doing, the more scientific our report to DoPI."

I went over my plan once more, outlining how I was going to attempt to communicate with the Dru again. This time, hopefully we could come to some kind of truce with them. Sid insisted we needed to keep track of any data we produced. If this was going to be a blueprint for future *para* events, then we needed all bases covered, the esoteric and the scientific. After all, it was his job.

We took both cars down to the Madron site, and at three in the morning, the roads were quiet. Megan and I didn't talk much, and when we did, it was about the mission.

When we reached the protesters' site, things were in uproar. I strapped the C8 to my chest and jogged through the drizzle to reach the epicentre. In the confusion of torchlight and the thin rain, it wasn't easy to see what was happening, but it looked like Leaze was trying to batter Markin. They had a crowd of protesters around the DoPI operatives, and the men with the big guns were uneasy, hands on their weapons, barely visible in the darkness.

"Hey, what's going on?" I called out, pushing through the crowd.

Leaze turned at the sound of my voice. "This prick won't help us."

"Alright, back down, Leaze, I'll handle this."

"No," she said, adding a stamp of her booted foot in the mud. It made an unhappy squelch. "She should never have been allowed to stay. She's seventeen and had the road sense of a hedgehog."

By this, I guessed she meant, 'living on the road' sense. "And I told you; I don't have that kind of authority. She's seventeen, I can't control a young adult."

Leaze tossed her hands up in the air and stomped away from us and Markin. Megan went after her, hopefully to gather more intel.

"What happened?" I asked him, forcing him away from the others.

"We've been patrolling both sites. For all we know, the damned girl got fed up with the rain and went home."

"She was on foot," I growled. Was I ever this cold towards the vulnerable? I didn't think so.

"Look, they should've all been moved off-site. I told

Sanchez that, but she said it was your call. This is your cluster fuck, not mine." He turned his back on me.

Every instinct inside me yelled for action. I wanted to take his bloody head off his shoulders. This was not what DoPI operatives were about. We operated on domestic soil, and due to that rather large inconvenience, we had to show more damned respect than this prick obviously did in overseas operations.

"Get your people to the outer cordon," I called after him. "I don't want them interfering." His people. They used to be my people. In fact, several of them responded to my presence with a nod of welcome and a look of relief.

I returned to Megan. Leaze had stormed back to her van. Sid and Luce were arriving, carrying the large holdall I used for DoPI's portable equipment.

Megan stood gazing after Leaze's retreating back. "She's not happy. I didn't know what to say. Can we go into the woodland and look for Isabelle? Markin's men stopped Leaze and the others from going. There were threats made."

"I can imagine."

"Did you used to behave like that?" she asked.

"I'd like to think not." No, I'd never been like Markin. He reminded me of my brother in particular. I was the Marine they sent in when a job needed a soft voice and calm attitude.

"What's the play?" she asked.

We walked over to join Sid and Luce, both of whom eyed the weapons held by the DoPI team.

"I don't think it'll be safe to go in there at night, right?" I asked Luce.

"Probably not, but Isabelle is little better than a child. We only have an idea of how long they'll keep her alive."

She was right. We were back to that damned ticking clock. I felt it in my bones, and it made me twitchy. At best, we had twenty-four hours before Isabelle died. I detected movement behind me and instinct had me turning and lifting my rifle before I'd visually checked my six. Trystan stood in the crosshairs of my scope. His eyes widened, and his hands went up.

I lowered the weapon. "Sorry, kid. Next time, call out."

"We have to go in and get her," he said, keeping a 'safe' distance from me. "I can do it. I can help." The boy's courage was admirable, but I had the feeling it might have something to do with Isabelle's long blonde hair and pretty smile.

"Let's talk to Eloise," I said to the group.

We found the wicked witch of cults, with Leaze of all people. Anwen's Children had come down from their hilltop eyrie.

When the two women saw me, I felt like I'd become a moth pinned to a board. Whatever they wanted from me, I had the feeling I'd probably be following orders rather than giving them.

*Man up, Marine.*

"All very well for you to say," I muttered. Megan looked at me and frowned, but I shook my head. She didn't need to know the inner workings of my cynical mind. "Ladies," I said, not hiding my apprehension.

"We are doing this, right?" Eloise asked without explaining.

I took a deep breath. This wasn't going to be easy. "Night is their preferred hunting time. It's when the veil is thinnest, especially this close to dawn. We've still over an hour before we see the sunrise. Also, it's their territory. We'd be at another disadvantage. None of us, not even Trystan, can know that place well enough for safe navigation under pressure. If we need a swift exfil because we're under attack, we'll really be in trouble. I cannot protect a large group of people."

"What about them?" Leaze asked, waving a hand at the shadows in the dark.

I glanced over my shoulder, thinking through her question. I was tired and sore. Despite my desperate attempts to rely on my training and the compartmentalisation of what happened at the cemetery, I knew I was in trouble. My focus was split, and that's never a good thing for an operator.

"We could use them," I admitted. "I have operational oversight, but they might just make things worse. Besides, they're designed to kill things, and I don't think any of us want to kill the Dru unless we have to?"

"We sacrifice Isabelle?" The potential for tears in Leaze's voice didn't help.

"No. But we need to modify the plan and know that if it fails, we have the potential of facing a nasty death."

Trystan came up beside me. "That won't happen, Griffin."

"Kid, they've already tried to kill me twice." I didn't want to explain about the spooky banishing we'd performed at the house. I still didn't understand that one. "They're playing for keeps."

"But I know more now," he said.

I wiped rain off of my face. How much could a fifteen-year-old really know or understand? Though, he'd spent longer training in his world, than I did before I faced my first deployment. He understood the lore better and spoke a language the Dru might recognise.

"This is going to be something I regret," I muttered to my boots. I faced the group. "Fine. We go in, but only those people who really understand what this is about. Eloise, that's your group and Leaze, hand pick those who are truly aware of what we might be facing. Not those that just want to," and here I used air quotes, "have an amazing experience with the universe, man." I always felt air quotes pack more punch when you're wearing tactical gloves and have an assault rifle strapped to your chest.

I turned to Sid and Luce. "I want you there, but not part of the ceremony. If things go south, get the civilians out ASAP. Understood?" Both of them nodded. Though, I had a sneaking feeling Sid might need an extra nudge. "Sid, you leave the toys behind if we have to run. All the toys. Got it?"

He rolled his eyes at me. "Yeah, alright, soldier boy. Leave the damned toys."

"I want to state, here and now, that saving Isabelle is our priority." I held up a finger to keep their attention on me. "However, we cannot do that by sacrificing ourselves." I doubted any of them had seen *Black Hawk Down*, but that's what came to mind as I spoke, and it didn't make me feel any better. "We have multiple tangos—"

"Griffin." Megan warned me and I stopped. Military speak might make me comfortable in this situation, but it wouldn't help the team building I had to conjure from a standing start of barely concealed hostility between the groups of people.

"The Dru are bloody dangerous. We are highly vulnerable. All of us, including me, have to trust Trystan," I put a hand on his shoulder, "and Eloise. They are our guides. We need to be a unit with one objective. What is our objective?"

Several weak arsed comments came back.

"Not good enough people. Our only objective is to save the girl. We are doing this for Jennifer, for River and for

Isabelle. So, what's our objective people?" I asked in my best—we're about to go into a skirmish completely under-prepared—voice.

"To save Isabelle!" came back.

We did it twice more with added heft on each effort. It's a quick way to bond a crowd.

"Those of you who remain behind. Be ready for us to come back. If you have med kits, find them. We hope they won't be necessary, but we don't know for certain. Have hot water available, blankets and dry clothes, places to rest." My mind raced, wondering what I'd forgotten. "When I say follow Eloise's instructions, I really mean it. If she asks you to visualise a unicorn farting rainbows while galloping through the field of stars, you do just that. Understood?"

A few yes came back.

"Am I understood?" I bellowed, feeling like I was suddenly a pantomime dame.

"Understood," said most of the crowd. A few of them had sloped off into the darkness, which suited me. I turned to Eloise. "How many people do we need other than yours to make this as safe as we can? I want the minimal number. I don't want people there who aren't necessary."

"Well, the best number is 999, but that's not practical." She frowned, suddenly uncertain with the weight of responsibility I'd just dropped on her shoulders. Well, she wanted to be in charge, welcome to the world of making the really hard decisions.

Trystan said, "I want two circles. Each person will represent the trees that once stood in the grove, forming the wood henge. Our people will be on the inside, Eloise and eight others. Then the rest of our people will take the compass points on the outer ring and everyone else will fill in the gaps. That should be…" He paused, and his gaze drifted inwards. I wondered what he saw. "That will be eighteen in total. Nine is a derivative. Two layers of nine." He grinned at me. "It might be bending the rules, but who really knows?"

I lifted an eyebrow. "You're supposed to know, kid." His maths made no sense to me.

The ballsy little bugger just winked at me. Since when did he grow a backbone and a personality?

Unable to offer any guidance as to who went and who remained, I strode over to DoPI's team.

"What frequency are you using?" I asked Markin.

"Channel five."

I put my earpiece in and switched my radio so I could pick up their chatter. Coms were quiet for the moment.

"Listen," I said to Markin, "I know you don't approve. But I need you, and your team, to cover our six. Can you deploy up the footpath so if we run into trouble, we can fall back, and you'll protect the civilians?"

Markin's jaw bounced, obvious even in the dim light cast by our torches that pointed to the ground, so we didn't ruin our night vision completely. "Yes, I'll do that. Do you want NVGs? I noticed you and Black Widow over there aren't wearing them." Was he referring to Megan? She'd like that, Black Widow, I'd have to tell her.

"No point. We'll need to use torches to get through the woodland and get out. I don't want anyone blinding me by accident because they shine a light in my face while I'm using the goggles."

"Fair enough." Markin shifted his feet. "Listen, Woodbury, I don't understand why you're doing this when we could just concrete over the entire site, but I have to respect the chain of command. I just want you to know that if me, or my people, see a viable threat, we're taking action. I can't afford to let whatever is in that wood escape."

"I wouldn't expect anything less."

"So long as we're clear?"

"We're clear."

He held up his fist. "Then good luck with the hippies, brother."

I chuckled and gave him a fist bump in return. "Thanks. I'm going to need it."

"Roger that."

After our 'bro' moment, I felt better as I walked away from the operatives. Part of me longed to be with them, rather than the mad hatters, but that wasn't my job anymore. I had to deal with the fluffy bunnies, the sky dreamers, the Pooh Bears, and the dope smoking caterpillars. We stood about as much chance of getting Isabelle back alive as we did finding hen's teeth in that wood.

# Chapter Thirty-One

Our motley band entered the woodland, and night swallowed us whole. With the constant drizzle, the ground beneath our feet was thick Cornish mud. No moon or starlight came to help, and we couldn't move silently. People muttered and cursed. The air began to smell of disturbed earth and leaf litter, rather than just rain. Clothing caught on branches and brambles that I'd swear weren't there on the other days I'd walked this damned track. The stream had risen as well, and in several places, we sloshed through water up to our ankles. The other thing that made me wince repeatedly was the torches.

I asked everyone to keep them down, facing the ground to minimise exposure to our eyes and the—enemy?—hostiles. I'd call them hostiles. That felt okay. Of course, it was impossible to keep the light contained. This many untrained people couldn't follow a series of simple instructions if I ran up behind them and battered them with the handbook. Which is pretty much what happens when you're a recruit.

Roving back and forth, one hand on the assault rifle, while the other pushed down the torches, I tried to contain my growing anxiety. It rippled through me as I thought of all the ways this adventure could go horribly wrong. It wasn't even my lack of understanding of the events we were about to instigate that caused the mental shuddering. Rather, it was the unknown element of the hostiles. We had no idea, and no way to predict multiple facets of this demand to parlay for the girl.

How many Dru would Trystan and I face? What would happen if they stormed through the veil as a horde? How many civilians would they kill if we failed to contain them?

There were more nagging 'what ifs', but those came with the territory of working with paras.

When I reached the front of the column for the third time, Megan caught my arm as I headed back down. "Slow down, Griff," she said quietly. "You're going to make them nervous."

"They should be," I growled, knowing I frowned.

"They are, but you shouldn't be. They know what dangers they face."

I huffed out a breath. "No, they don't. They couldn't possibly, or they wouldn't be here."

Her hand slipped from my arm and curled around the fingers gripping the optic on my rifle. She squeezed. "You're worried about who will get hurt, aren't you?"

"Aren't you?" I asked after a long sigh.

"Of course, and I don't even fully understand what's likely to happen. Not like you and Trystan will."

I shook my head as we walked. "There are just so many variables, Meg."

"I know, but the only other option is to destroy this place, and neither of us wants that to happen. You'll do it.

You'll save her." She pulled my hand away from the weapon and laced her fingers through mine. "I know you'll save her."

Megan's faith in me came as a shock. A part of me swelled at the thought of being the man she turned to in times of crisis, and I could give her answers, solve her problems. Then a huge part of me just wanted to curl up and die at the thought. Didn't she realise that just a few hours ago, she'd found me digging up my mother's grave? For heaven's sake, I was an unqualified nutcase. The thought of failing her almost crushed my resolve to go on with this mad plan. I should just turn everyone around and order Markin to flatten the woodland.

Thoughts of leaving the Marines and DoPI flitted through my head. Moth-like thoughts that flamed in the rising and falling fires of panic inside me. Never before had I wanted to run so badly as I did right now. Run from all my responsibilities. I wanted to stop making hard choices. That's why I'd left the Marines as only a corporal. I wasn't built for command. Whatever Sanchez saw in me was just a set of big shoulders that managed to fake confidence, but I didn't have what it took, not really. I'd only made it through my training because I'd been doing it for years under my father's bullying gaze.

"We're here," Trystan said. He'd led the procession with quiet dignity. I wished I could maintain his level of calm.

The grove of trees didn't feel welcoming. As we filed in from the barely there footpath, silence held the group. Despite the dim light, I saw people's eyes were wide, they licked their lips and shuffled their feet. A few of Anwen's Children were more self-contained, they prayed quietly. Eloise maintained her poise, and Trystan looked almost relaxed.

I approached him. "What do you think? Is this still a viable option?"

"I think we must do our best to save Isabelle and this holy site," he said.

"I don't need a politician's answer," I snarled.

He had the good grace to look away from me. "There is hostility here that I've never felt before, but also…" I saw him close his eyes. "I sense something else. Something trying to reach out."

I glanced at the sky, just visible through the canopy of tangled tree limbs. "I've no wish to put another wound into the world, but this is going to be difficult."

"It's possible you're too burdened by your imagination, Griffin."

Rubbing at the bruises that still made it painful to talk and turn my head I said, "Experience, kid. It breeds paranoia for a reason."

"It also deadens the potential to reach for something so beautiful we can hardly comprehend it. Try to find the light, not the dark. You have an affinity for this, a gift. The dead you feel, they are the ones strong enough to show you the way. They are the ones you hang on to, the only ones you listen to, but you don't listen very well."

I frowned harder. "I don't understand."

"I know, but you will." The damned child then patted my shoulder, his young-old eyes full of compassion. "Come, it's time. Dawn isn't far away, and these clouds are dispersing."

They were? I glanced up, and the night still held all the playing cards, clouds and rain being just two of them.

The stones we'd used in our previous attempt to talk to the Dru remained in place. Eloise took over and began instructing the crowd. She picked who stood where and explained what everyone should visualise. I'd always struggled with the concept of visualisation, despite Lorne Turner using it to his advantage more than once, but for some reason science couldn't really explain, it often worked. I just had to go with it.

Sid approached. "You okay?"

I stared at my boots and wiggled my sore toes. "Not really. What are you going to do?"

"Don't worry about us. We'll just keep clear. I don't want to be a part of what this is." He drew circles in the air with his hand. "I'd just like you to come back in one piece without bringing anything through with you."

"It's time," Trystan said. "Now is the time. I can feel it."

Sid and I shared a final nod, and I felt his hand grip my forearm. I returned the gesture. "Stay safe, brother," he murmured. I gave a single nod.

Megan didn't say anything. We shared a long look that probably said far more than it should, before she retreated to her given position on the outside of the people henge Eloise had built.

I returned to the centre of the circle with Trystan. We stood over the spot where I'd seen the standing stone and the burial of that poor child centuries ago.

Trystan took my hands and held them tight. "You need to leave the guns."

"Forget it. I won't be fooled again."

He recognised the resolution on my face and bowed to my demand. Still holding my hands, he lowered us to the ground. My knees just about made it, but I wasn't as limber as a teenage boy. That's when I realised the rain had stopped, the air cleared of the damp, and a faint silvering of light filled the grove.

The lad grinned. "Told you."

"Alright, smarty-pants. Let's do this without anyone dying, and I'll be a happy little camper."

"Just like before. Close your eyes, breathe with me, and follow me through the veil."

*Great, just great. That feeling of your spidey sense tingling and pinging? That's me warning you that this is one of your stupider ideas. When it goes wrong, don't go blaming me.*

I sucked in a breath, closed my eyes and tried to ignore the nagging whisper in the back of my head. Who am I kidding? It wasn't a whisper; my instincts were practically screaming at me to run the hell away from this place and keep running. I'm a Royal Marine Commando, so I can run a long way.

I mirrored Trystan's breathing and felt his hands relax in mine. Opening one eye, I saw the veil. Eloise and the others surrounded us, and I heard their prayers. The group of people on the outside repeated the mantras of those on the inside. It all sounded very Catholic to me, but I was hardly an expert. Between them and us rose the veil. It came from the ground. A thin curtain of that oily shine rippled through the air. It rose in a dome over Trystan and me, the light within our bubble somehow brighter than that on the other side. My eye strayed to Megan, and I found her hard to see, harder to focus on with each muttered word Trystan said in his Cornish language. The veil was taking me.

I closed my eyes and relaxed my shoulders. Trystan's fingers twitched in mine as if giving me approval. The smell inside the bubble became more intense. The incense from his clothing. A drift of his personal body odour, the waft of mine. The very maleness of it.

"That's right," he murmured in English. "That's the

problem. Try to find a different aspect of yourself to present to them. A softer version."

His words instantly made me think of Megan. The version of me that moved around her with a tenderness I rarely displayed for other people, except the Turners' children. They brought out that side of me as well. A more patient man, a better man. The one I wanted to be for a potential family. Someone who listened, rather than just forcing through his solutions to a problem.

The veil took us.

That never ending blackness swept in, and I felt as if I'd dunked into a freezing lake. I struggled to take in air, but whether this was from the cold or my fear, I didn't know. My hands tensed over the smaller ones.

"Breathe," came the command. "Don't fear this place. It's nothing more than a cosmic bus stop."

That made me laugh, and I opened my eyes. Trystan and I stood, as before, on the rainbow that lapped at my boots in the endless nothingness. "You should give that personality more airtime, kid. Eloise keeps you locked up too much."

He gave me an indulgent smile, as if telling me I understood nothing about his existence, then pulled me into the rainbow under our feet. The terrible vertigo hit me, threatening to dislodge what little I'd managed to eat. My bowels and bladder clenched like they did before battle, and I grunted hard as something solid rushed up to meet me, caught hold, and held still. The ground?

Panic swept over me. With my eyes now firmly open, I released Trystan and put my hands on the weapon's stock. We were standing in the grove of trees once more, ancient and foreboding. All my senses were on their red setting.

"Where are they?" I growled. Despite my fear, I registered how differently everything smelt in this place. The air was like liquid gold as it slipped through me, filling me with a vigour I never remembered feeling before.

Trystan eyed my weapon. "That won't help."

"It helps me." I stalked forward, the butt of the rifle in my shoulder.

Movement to my left. Without thinking, my body moved into fully engaged mode. I looked through the weapon's scope. Several figures seemed to drift through the trees. I placed a finger on the trigger and depressed to the halfway point, while also flicking off the safety. Oddly, my breathing and heart rate calmed.

Gradually the figures came out of the green gloom of the far thicker forest. When they breached the sunlight flooding the grove, I moved back towards Trystan in confusion.

"What are they?" I murmured.

He whispered, "You'll know them as dryads."

I glanced at him and frowned. His expression was one of awe.

"Have you met these creatures before?" I asked.

He shook his head. "No, not like this. Not so clearly." Despite his obvious desire to keep his eyes on the coming creatures, he managed to glance at me. "I've never spoken to them directly."

This worried me. We had no relationship with these beings, no precedent. I licked my lips.

Think, Marine, think. If these were villagers rather than local combatants, what would you do?

I dropped my weapon and relaxed my stance. Holding my hands up in the universal gesture of peace, I placed my body between them and Trystan. From this position I could be firing in seconds, so I wasn't concerned I'd hindered our defences too badly.

For the first time, I allowed myself to take in their appearance. These tree spirits were definitely female. They weren't as tall as the Dru and had no martial attributes. Only three came into the sunlight, but there were more shadows in the background. Their skin held the same mottled colours as the Dru, but I saw flashes of red among the green and brown. They were slim, not like humans can be. These beings were too finely made to be the same as a skinny person. Lithe, that was a better definition. They had breasts, but only as small mounds on their narrow chests, and they were naked, just as the Dru had been.

Trapped forest sunlight seemed to colour their hair, and it resembled the finest tendrils of moss. Their faces were enthralling. I understood the myths I remembered, the longing a god or mortal might feel when gazing at these creatures. Their very alienness just added to the mystique. With rounded ears, but almond eyes, they had an oriental cast to their features that reminded me of the young women I'd seen in Thailand, or Vietnam. Those eyes though, they weren't dark, they were formed from the silver of the moon and stars.

The dryad in the centre of the three was clearly older. Her skin had far darker tones to it and a roughness where we might have wrinkles. I wondered if the bark of her tree would be deeply fissured, like an old willow's trunk. It was impossible to tell what kind of tree they came from. There were no oak or holly leaves for identification.

She stepped towards me, eyes sweeping over me and resting on the rifle. Her head tilted.

Trystan, who now held the webbing at my waist,

murmured in my ear, "She wants to know why we've brought death to her home."

"You can hear her? She's speaking to you?" I asked over my shoulder.

"It's more like images and emotions, but they are nearer to speech than the Dru."

"Can you explain about self-defence, and I wish them no harm?"

A moment passed.

He whispered, "You just did. I think they have a firmer grasp on humanity than their male counterparts."

It made sense, I supposed. There weren't any complete surviving myths about the Dru, just a few mentions here and there, but dryads? Well, we all knew of the female nymphs and their tricky ways.

"She requests our counsel must be held in peace, or her warriors will come." He looked at me nervously. "That won't be good, Griffin."

Understatement, kid.

It made my insides jiggle about in protest, but I unclipped the carbine from my webbing and placed it on the ground. Next came the Glock from my left thigh. I'd gone from fully dressed to naked in seconds. Rarely had I felt this vulnerable.

All three dryads bowed their heads in acknowledgement of my good intentions.

"Say aloud what you want to happen," Trystan said.

I took a deep breath. Placing a hand on my heart, I offered the beings a deep bow. "I am here to seek a resolution to the conflict in our world. It is important that you understand our intent towards you. That there may be peace and safety for all."

Trystan said, "You have an agreement. State your purpose."

"If we can have the girl returned to us, then I can vow to you that I have the power to protect your homes and your people."

A soft rustling of leaves filled the grove, and there were a few clacks, like branches being knocked together. It sounded angry. My hands itched for the smooth polymer of my weapon's stock in my shoulder.

Trystan shifted behind me and grunted. "It's a bit overwhelming, but I think some of them want that, but others don't believe you and want the Dru to summon their god. To complete the ritual." The kid sounded like he was trying to talk through a migraine. I maintained my focus on the dryads. Back in the shadows, something stirred. I tensed, watching, listening, even smelling the air, trying to second-guess the potential for this parley to go FUBAR.

"I understand your mistrust. All I can offer is my word. My vow. I will protect this sacred place. We humans need you. Your connection to the world is so much stronger than ours, and if people like Trystan," I yanked the lad around my shoulder and presented him to them like a puppy hanging from my hand, "can hear you, we will all learn. Eventually. I do have the power to stop this destruction."

Many more rustling and banging of wood against wood. It was eerie, to say the least. The three dryads before me bowed their heads for a moment, and I realised they were communicating with the masses. This must be the mycelium, the plant equivalent of the digital highway.

"They don't know how to trust you." The lad sounded panicky.

"Any ideas on how I make that happen?" I asked him,

keeping my eyes on those shifted shadows and the dryads before us.

"They want to keep the girl as a hostage."

I wondered if I dared to look through the witch's stone, what I'd see among the dryads. Were they as damaged by humanity's cruel hand on their home? Or maybe, I didn't want to know, they were just too damned beautiful.

"No. I can't do that." I directed my next words to the dryads. "I'm sorry. I can't leave her. She is a child, and her family want her home. If you keep her, or hurt her, I will lose control of my people, and they will tear down the woodland, the cloutie tree, the grove, everything, and we will lose our connection to the veil at this site. To you, who can teach us to live in harmony, by giving us your peace when we come to visit. By returning the human girl, I can offer the expansion of your woodland. We can repair the sacred site."

This elicited great rustling, and the pitch of the knocks changed upwards. I guessed that was a good thing, though my eyes flickered to the rifle at my feet. I'd need three, maybe five seconds. If there were Dru in those shadows, especially at my back, I'd be screwed.

Trystan said, "They want to know more about repairing the sacred site."

To be honest, I hadn't given it a moment's thought. The idea had just tumbled out. I floundered, then saw the way forwards clearly, as if I'd just been given inspirations by the gods themselves. Yeah, I could convince Sanchez this mad plan would work.

"With your guidance, through this emissary," I placed a hand on Trystan's shoulder, "we will return the woodland to its greatest glory. We will raise a stone in the centre of the grove once more. In our world, we call it rewilding when we return a place to its previous condition, and I can promise this will happen. It is time we built trust between our people. If you return the girl, we will return your woodland."

A softer rustling, more akin to soft autumn winds cradling leaves as they tumble to the ground. No twig banging accompanied the softness of sound. The shadows kept too far back in the woodland for me to see clear shapes, but I felt them. Something was coming.

"Did I do the right thing?" I asked the boy without looking at him.

"I'm not sure. They've cut me out," Trystan said with a frown.

*That doesn't sound good. Get ready for action, soldier boy.* Really? Even my internal dialogue was being disrespectful. *And you're surprised by this?* I forced it into silence.

On the edge of the grove, a figure stepped from the shadows into the sunlight. I tensed. It was the massive Dru who'd attacked me. I saw a scar on his right cheek where I'd looked at him through the witch's stone. My mind wove frantic plans together, and I pulled the stone out from under my protective gear. Oh, my hands ached for my weapons.

In the paler shadows of the treeline, I saw more Dru and between them, they dragged the inert form of Isabelle. Was she even alive? Did they bring their victims through the veil to kill them before returning them to our reality? What had that been like for Jennifer and River?

Trystan began to speak at the same time as the increased rustling began. I had the feeling it was the Dru speaking to him, not the dryad. "Our people hear our Mother's heart beating in pain, and we cannot help her. In summoning our god, we will be able to give her back her strength. You have never understood this. You cannot hear her without your…" Trystan frowned for a moment, obviously struggling with whatever concept they wanted to share. "Machines. We can't hear the planet without machines."

"They aren't wrong," I mumbled, thinking of Sid's gizmos.

The lad ignored me. "You might think our god is dead, but you know nothing of his power." Trystan glanced at me. "That's coming from the Dru."

"I guessed."

"The dryads are saying they want peace. They want to give you time to be trusted. The Dru aren't listening. There's a conflict here we don't understand. It's moving too fast. I'm losing the connection." He touched his head as if in pain.

"Let it go, kid. Don't waste your energy." I wanted to back us up, but that would put too much space between me and our only means of escape if this went south.

Trystan peered into the trees, gasped, and slipped from my grasp. It was like trying to hold a cat before you wormed it. "Isabelle," he cried out in desperation.

Shit.

If I moved forwards, would it be taken as a form of attack? I really didn't want to put my guns at my back to go after the lad. One glance at the Dru and I held my ground. If I moved, he'd come at me. Seeing what they'd done to Alanson and his men, meant I stayed, keeping the truce.

Trust. This whole thing would come down to trust. I had to trust them with Trystan, with Isabelle, with other people who would wander into their wood.

I watched, helpless, as Trystan dodged past the dryads and the massive Dru, who also made to catch him with about as much success as I did. The boy made it into the treeline and grabbed Isabelle. Much to my surprise, the Dru holding her up released her.

The young human couple looked like something from a fairytale as Trystan tried to carry Isabelle into the grove. Bless him, he wasn't yet man enough to take even her slight weight, and I watched him go to his knees, cradling her head and shoulders like some romantic hero.

He was calling her name, sobbing it, when she didn't wake to his princely touch.

It's like watching a bloody Disney film.

"Or reading the Iliad," I muttered aloud. It had been required reading at my school.

The dryad shifted in unease. The Dru's eyes narrowed. The other males shifted. I counted ten in my eye line and death just behind them. I tensed, ready to drop, roll and fire if anyone so much as twitched near the pair of youngsters playing Romeo and Juliet.

It seemed the dryads were visibly moved, and more of them came out of the shadows in the treeline. Some of them formed a circle around the pair until the elder, who'd been 'speaking' with me, pushed them back, clearly indicating I needed to see them. I registered the gesture as a kindness.

"Please," Trystan begged. "Please let me take her home, and I promise I will make them protect you. I will listen to you, and I will be guided by you. Please, you know me. You know I can hear Mother Earth and Father Sky. You don't need to bring back your old gods. I will help you. Your gods… What they ask of you, it's not fair. I know how it hurts you to kill even our kind. I know you don't want war with us." He said all this on his knees in the dirt, staring up at these powerful beings and just offering his heart. It was all very Arthurian. He finished with, "If you go to war with them," he threw his arm out towards me, "they will win. You know it. They have been winning since forever. It is your place to endure, from earthquakes to fire, but what if you had allies in our world? Powerful allies? Like him." This time, Trystan pointed at me.

The rustling grew around me. It seemed to come in waves as they passed ideas back and forth among themselves. Like a tree version of a Mexican wave.

The Dru snarled at me and stomped around the older dryad. I heard their voices for the first time. A high verbal sound, not painful, more like a nightingale than a painful whistle. It warbled beautifully and became a cascade of language. They were certainly going at each other. I wondered if I needed to step in to defend the dryad. Not that I'd stand any chance against the hulking Dru. If death waited for me in this grove of otherworldly trees, would my spirit find the way home?

The argument ended when the dryad put her hands on almost non-existent hips and proceeded to turn into an Italian grandmother telling off some random child for dropping litter in the street.

"Oh, you're in trouble now, big man," I muttered. The other Dru began to move back into the thicker shadows. I did not back down from *DEFCON 1*.

She cut the conversation with the Dru dead with a slice of her hand through the air, before turning her back. The two younger dryads stepped towards Trystan and Isabelle, helping him to his feet and lifting the girl with no discernible effort. It made me realise I wouldn't want to fight either gender in a weapons-free arena.

Trystan and the girl were brought to me. The three dryads were now very close. They laid the girl down on the soft grass, and she appeared unharmed except for a few contusions.

The boy said, “You have a moon’s month to prove you can be trusted. In that time, we must see evidence of your good intent. Returning the woodland to its former glory will take a long time, we understand this, but we have to see progress quickly. If you fail, you will return with a maiden for our sacrifice, or one shall be taken, and war will be declared. You will not just face our kind if such a thing happens. Do not betray us. We are not foolish to your lies and wiles.”

I gave a single grave nod. “I understand. I vow we will commit to our plan.”

“Then we have a bond.” Trystan looked up at me. “She wants you to touch your palm to hers. It means they’ll have a sense of you for all time. A sense they’ll share with each other.”

“Is it dangerous?” I asked, knowing it didn’t matter, I’d do it anyway.

“I honestly don’t know.”

The older dryad held out her hand as if to shake mine, however, when I reached to do that, Trystan grabbed my hand. “No, smooth your palm along her forearm and palm.”

I swallowed and looked into those silvery eyes. She stared back. We were trying to read each other, but I think she had more success than I did. As my fingertips brushed the inside of her elbow, a tingle raced up my arm. I was touching an elemental being. This was…

Magic.

It whispered over my skin, and she smiled, revealing teeth a bit too pointy for me to feel completely safe. I glanced at the big Dru. His top lip rippled in anger. I felt the sweat trickle down my spine. We were so close to getting out of this alive. I just had to hold it together a little longer.

Trystan spoke again, "She says you are special. Born special. There is much you don't know, but you will."

"Thank you, gracious lady, for your help. For interceding on our behalf. We will not betray your trust."

That strange but beautiful sound came to me again, and I realised she was trying to actually speak to me. Trystan said, "She knows you can be trusted, but people have short lives. Make them remember this for all time."

I nodded my understanding and bowed as our palms slipped away from each other. In the process, I realised I might just have fallen a little in love with the strange and beautiful creature.

Trystan rose, and I lifted Isabelle. As this was all her own fault, I slung her over my right shoulder. Ruining the muscles in my arms and back by carrying her across my chest wasn't going to happen.

"Trystan, get the guns."

"But."

"Do it." The order would not be disobeyed. "You don't want them to have that kind of hardware here."

He scrambled to pick them up.

## Chapter Thirty-Two

When my eyes fluttered open, I heard a cry and, seconds later, a body knocked me over. Megan. I wrapped my arms around her, even as another body pinned my legs down.

"Are you hurt?" she asked, checking me over none too gently.

I laughed. "No, I'm fine. It was scary, but it all worked out. More or less. We did it, Meg. Trystan did it."

The young man cradled Isabelle while Eloise tried to maintain discipline among the crowd. Her words were drowned out by questions and calls for water, blankets and food. Sid and Luce rushed over to join Megan, and they helped me up off the ground. I was lightheaded and my limbs a little disorganised, but other than that, I felt great. Better than great. I felt like I'd really achieved something significant for the first time in my life.

"What happened?" asked Luce. "We saw something amazing."

"You saw the grove and the dryads?" I asked.

They all frowned. "No, just the oily rainbow thing you've been talking about," Luce said.

"That's the bus stop. Right, kid?" I asked Trystan.

He grinned at me as Anwen's Children and the protesters helped him and a now awake Isabelle up off the ground. I realised it was daylight. Dawn had come and spread her wide fingers over the land, reaching between the trees to steal the night's shadows and hide them for another day.

Oh, it did feel good to have that light on my face.

"Are we safe?" Megan asked.

I turned to face her again. Oof, the world was so vivid. Fast. Everything was loud and bright and sparkly. The birds. They were perfect and melodious. I wanted to reach for my guitar.

"Griffin," Megan said, grabbing my face and forcing me to look at her. "Are we safe?"

I started to nod, then thought my head would fall off. I stopped. "So long as I convince Sanchez to protect this woodland and make significant headway into healing this place within twenty-eight nights, then we'll be fine. I've so much to tell you guys. Make sure you're recording it all, Sid. I don't want to forget anything, and I've a feeling I'm not going to be able to hold on to all the images. I spoke to dryads, Meg. Actual dryads. How cool is that..."

I realised I was as high as a kite whose string had snapped, and it was caught in a hurricane. Regardless, I just kept babbling at Sid, who held his digital recorder under my nose. I tried to describe everything I'd seen, all I'd experienced. I wanted to capture the smell of the air, the feel of the grass, and the sounds. Things that in the stress of the moment I didn't register, but I remembered them now and they mattered. It all mattered. I'd touched another world, walked in it and made a deal with the fair folk.

Just a few hours ago, I'd woken in my mother's grave, desolate and ashamed. Now, I'd been touched by a dryad. Her skin had brushed mine. When I got to this point in my story, I pulled up the sleeve of my old army jersey. There on my arm was a ribbon of pale green and red intertwining, like a faint tattoo. "Wow," I said.

"We'll need a skin sample." Sid poked it with interest, then tried rubbing it off, until I slapped his paws away.

Slowly, because my feet were not to be trusted right now, Megan led me and the others out of the grove. I kept looking over my shoulder, not sure why, but I feared I'd never again feel the magic of the place, and I didn't want to lose it. Something had happened to me, and it was…

Miraculous felt like the wrong word. Too religious. Fantastical? Yes, it was certainly that, but also so much more.

"I haven't asked?" I managed to say between babbling monologues. "What happened on this side of the veil?"

Sid, who walked next to me, said, "Brother, I've a recording. I'll show you, but man, it was wild. Nothing as wild as your story, but still, it was like nothing we've seen before. The moment Eloise began her chants and everyone joined in, the air and light in the grove changed. As if we had the moon right overhead, but it wasn't. Then hovering around you and the boy, this oily, sinuous rainbow appeared, and it seemed to smother you."

Megan added, "I panicked and threatened to break the circle, but Eloise kept me steady. She said it was important that we not move. We'd become anchors. If I broke the spell, we'd lose you both."

Luce, who walked behind us, said, "You were gone for

ages. I think even Eloise started to get worried. The chanting faded, and we just waited. It took forever. We watched this astonishing storm of colour surrounding you like it was a…" She looked at Sid. "A funnel?"

He nodded. "Yeah, that's it. The veil was like a funnel into the pre-dawn sky."

"Father Sky," I said.

Megan laughed. "Yeah, okay, Father Sky. Mind your foot, big man, you're about to trip." She guided me around a large stone.

"Anyway," Luce continued. "The funnel wobbled a few times."

"Yeah, that's probably when the big Dru threatened to rip my head off."

"Seriously?" Megan asked.

"He wasn't pleased, but he didn't really get violent with me. Not this time."

We walked onto the proper footpath, almost back at the lane now, and Luce said, "Then the sun came up properly and the funnel just started to fray. Eloise made everyone begin chanting again. We all got louder, and it felt like we were calling you home."

"There was a flash of light." Sid took over. "I think we all blinked, and then you'd fallen over, but Isabelle was in your lap."

"The rest you know." Despite being on firmer ground, Megan laced her fingers with mine. I didn't argue.

My stomach made itself known, and it was not happy. "I need food." Then I yawned wide enough to crack my jaw. "And sleep."

We didn't make it back to the protesters' camp. By the time I reached Megan's car, I was on my knees with exhaustion. We'd gathered the DoPI team up as well, and Sid gave

Markin a verbal report. We watched the DoPI operative walk away grumbling and cursing.

Sid looked at me. "If you aren't here, it's going to be up to men like Markin to solve these problems, and I don't think he'll give a damn about sacrificing virgins to tree gods. Or bulldozing sacred sites."

"Yeah, I know. Maybe it's time to leave the Royal Marines behind, though. Would Sanchez go for that?"

Sid gripped my shoulder. "Mate, she just loves the fact that she has a commando at her command. No, I don't think she's going to let you leave the Marines."

I puffed out air, making the curling hair now covering my forehead lift. "Well, that's a bit bollocks."

Megan laughed. "Come on. We need to get you home."

"No," I said. "I want to go see your mum."

She frowned and stepped back. "Mate, I don't think—"

"No, we go. We go, and I need to speak to her. Now, Meg." An itch under my skin had set up, and I wanted an honest conversation with the one person in my life who might just know something.

She looked at Sid, who shrugged. "I don't do family drama." Luce had already climbed into the Mini.

"Fine, we'll go see Mum. At least you'll get breakfast."

It would take us nearly an hour to reach the farm near Baldhu. The moment my head hit the backrest of my seat, my eyes closed, and I zipped away into dreamland.

A vague mutter of, "Bloody Marines sleep anywhere," drifted to me before I left the area completely.

Megan shook my leg to bring me back. "We're here, soldier boy."

"Not a soldier," I grumbled, peeling open an eye.

"Yeah, but it got you to wake up." She left the car, and I followed suit, though it took considerably longer. As I stretched, my spine cracked, and it made Megan wince. "You're going to have terrible back problems when you get old."

I grinned. "Yeah, but I have to get old first."

Predictably, she punched me on the arm. I looked around the farmyard. The first time I'd come to visit after moving to Cornwall, I'd been shocked at the decline in the farm. It wasn't that the place looked any different; it was still tidy, as clean as a farm can ever get, and organised, but everything looked old and tired. The paint on the tractors had faded, the roofs on the barns were patched, and various other pieces of machinery had make-do-and-mend fixes with odd pieces of mismatched metal welded over rusting holes. I'd noticed a place where machinery that could no longer be used had its own section in a nearby field, and they'd cannibalised pieces. The Ackley family farm was struggling.

The farmhouse itself was large, with white paint covering old stone and cob walls, in places two or three feet thick. In many patches, the rendering had fallen off, and the white was greyer, but it still felt like a home to me. With three windows upstairs at the front, and two down, I couldn't help but notice the slowly rotting wood. The front garden was neat, with the spring flowers in full riot. The roses rambling up their trellises were heavily pregnant with buds. The roof sagged in places it shouldn't, and I knew they had a problem in their centuries-old beams. Time would stop being kind to the house soon, and the small problems would become big ones.

In the distance, I saw the movement of cows. "Your dad's out."

"Dad's always out. He seems to think that if he keeps working hard enough, something might change."

She sounded so sad and bleak, I put my arm around her shoulders, landing a kiss on her head. "I'm sorry, Megan. Conor is a good man. He deserves better."

"I just wish Peter or Daniel could put the time into doing the research for new farming methods, new initiatives, but they aren't academic enough. I do what I can, but it's just not enough. We can't afford the experts we need to pull us into the new decade and teach us how to handle climate change."

We walked up the path to the faded green front door, and Megan lifted the ancient latch. The warmth of the spring morning fled, and the cool chill of a stone house wrapped around us. A threadbare but clean carpet covered the entrance hall's flagstones. Inside the wattle and daub walls were drab in their white paint and the ubiquitous cobwebs, but pictures of generations of Ackleys having fun, from the grandchildren, back to Iris's parents and my mother took the edge of any despair. It smelt slightly damp, but also of a fried breakfast.

I bent to take off my boots, wiggling my toes in my Mutley socks, and inhaled. "Oh my God…" I let my nose lead me to the back of the house.

Megan laughed. "I rang Mum to warn her."

"Griffin, my favourite boy." Iris turned from the huge Aga and smiled just like Megan.

"Oi," said Peter from the table. He was dark where Megan was fair, taking after his father. "Hey, cuz," he said to me with an edge to his voice.

Iris waved a spatula at him. "He's my favourite because he remembers his manners. Pete, get your elbows off the table. A fork is not a shovel. Seriously, I don't know how Delia puts up with you, and if you teach—"

"Yeah, okay, Mum. I didn't drop in for a lecture. I need

to get out to the south field, fencing needs seeing to. Delia's up at the school, inset day or something before she goes back to work tomorrow."

"What does she teach?" I asked, trying to be polite. At almost forty, Peter didn't have my discipline for fitness, and it showed. His hair was thinning, and his features were meaner than I remembered. He had a bitter streak a mile wide and didn't like me. We'd never been close as kids, and once more I was the cuckoo who threatened to make him look like the fool I'd always considered him.

"Modern languages," he growled without meeting my eyes.

The oldest of the collie dogs, Bandit, came over for a cuddle, and I obliged. He was blind now, walking was difficult, but his tail kept wagging, and he loved his humans. They had two younger dogs, but they'd be working with Conor.

"A difficult subject to teach but rewarding, I should imagine."

He sniffed. "You'd have to ask her that." He pushed away from the table, making the wood of the chair leg screech over the floor tiles. Mopping up the last of the baked bean juice with a thick slice of homemade bread, he said, "Right, I'm off to do some real work." I watched him cram the food in his mouth, and it turned my stomach.

A huge part of me wanted to explain that his sister and I had just saved the damned world—well, okay, a woodland, but it counted—but of course, I couldn't. Instead, I just smiled benignly, which seemed to irritate him more.

Iris sighed. "Some things never change."

I declined to comment.

On plates I remembered from my childhood, heavy earthenware glazed green and blue, Iris served me a fried breakfast able to break the belly of any operative in the world. I grinned.

Megan sat with a black tea and tried not to look at my plate.

"Seriously? After the night we just had?" I asked.

Her eyes narrowed.

Iris murmured softly, "I have plenty left, Meggie."

Megan's gaze shot warning darts at her mother's heart.

I pushed my plate away. "Fine. If you won't eat, I won't eat." My belly howled in protest, but I was a commando; I could take the pain.

*No, you bloody can't. Get the scran down your damned throat!*

I stared at Megan, who glared back. Finally, she huffed like a preteen and said, "Fine, I'll eat a week's worth of calories in one sitting."

It took half a second for me to pull my plate back and start eating. I managed more decorum than Peter, but only just.

Iris sat eating toast and homemade jam, watching us with an indulgent expression. "Is one of you going to explain why you've dropped by at this early hour?"

I wondered if my mother would've looked like this as she'd aged. The blonde hair turning silver in places, the features blurring gently. Then again, my mum had been finer boned, naturally slimmer than Iris and considerably taller.

"We had work down in Madron," I said. "Thought we'd swing by on the way back."

Iris's darker eyebrow rose, just like Megan's did. "No one comes to Baldhu because they're swinging by, Griffin."

Her thick Cornish accent turned me back into that anxious and grief-harried child that arrived on her doorstep at the beginning of the school holiday. "Can I ask you some questions about Mum?"

She blinked. Then, inexplicably, colour rose in her cheeks. "Of course you can. Ask me anything."

Well, that was a lie. I was a trained interrogator and investigator; I knew when to call bullshit. Megan frowned, obviously detecting the same tells Iris broadcast. Then Megan's phone started to ring. "Shit." She pulled it out, her face clouding, shoulders tensing. "I'll just be a second."

*That'll be Adrian. Fat-face git-bag.*

What is it about going to your childhood home that instantly turns you into an idiot? We watched Megan step outside.

Iris returned her focus to me. "I'm not sure about this new fella."

"Me neither," I growled, watching Megan pace outside the kitchen window. She was using the path separating the house from the veg patch and lawn. "Iris, do you have any papers that might've been Mum's?"

"Papers? Like what?" She licked her lips, and an index finger started to curl strands of her blonde hair.

"Like anything. Photos, school reports, anything."

"Why now?"

"I've the time and distance to go through it now I'm living down here. It's been more than twenty years, I think I need to know more about her life before me." I watched her, but she couldn't meet my gaze. "Iris?"

Rather than reply, she rose from the table. "Give me a few minutes. I have to find the box."

I watched her leave the kitchen. Unable to remain still, I started to clean up the breakfast dishes, putting them into the old dishwasher, called a Belfast sink, and starting to run the hot water. I heard Iris moving around upstairs and

Megan talking rapidly on the phone outside. She didn't sound happy, and somehow, she looked smaller, as if her life was being sucked out even as I watched.

*You could pull his arms and legs off. You saw how the Dru did it to Alanson.*

I frowned and tried to concentrate on the washing up. Iris returned carrying a large cardboard box. "I've a chest upstairs that contains some of her old clothes, a quilt she made for you and other bits. I've kept them for when you settled down, had a home, maybe a wife."

My eyes chose that moment to flicker to Megan.

Iris smiled. "I think I should've done this a long time ago, but… Oh, Griffin. I'm sorry. This is going to be difficult in some ways but in others…" She looked at her daughter through the window. Megan had stopped talking and no longer held her phone. She'd walked to the back wall of the lawn and stood staring out over the fields and hedgerows.

With a pat on the nearest kitchen chair, Iris continued, "Leave that, it isn't important. We need to talk properly. I know you haven't been back very long, but Megan says you seem to be staying, so maybe now is the time. I didn't want to explain all this when you were a boy—"

"Iris, you're freaking me out."

She gripped my hand and stared into my eyes. "Just know that this changes not one thing about how much I love you, Griffin. You are my third son, and I will always, always be here. So will Conor. He feels just as I do. It's never mattered to us, it never mattered to my parents, or your mother. We are family."

"Okay," I said. A hollow feeling beginning to open in my chest. Breakfast shifted about uneasily.

Iris took a deep breath. "When Meggie rang this morning, I knew it was time. I've been dreaming of your mum a lot recently, probably because you're home."

*Yeah, you aren't the only one. Get to the point.*

I kept my silence, waiting for whatever sword Damocles decided to drop on me this time.

Iris let go of my hand and opened the box. She stood up to rummage for a moment before handing over an age-tarnished envelope. It was thick, good quality and official-looking. It just had my mother's name, Hazel Tudor, her maiden name, written on the front.

"I don't understand."

"You will. It's best for you to see it, rather than me explaining."

I opened the unsealed envelope and withdrew the single, neatly folded, heavy piece of paper within. Flicking it open, with my heart racing and mouth dry, I read the words. Then I read them again.

"This is a notification of adoption," I said.

"Yes."

"My mother was adopted?"

"Yes."

"But you look alike."

"Do we?" Iris asked. "We were both blonde and blue-eyed, but other than that…"

I glanced out of the window. Megan remained with her back to the house, but it looked as if she was crying. I wanted to go to her.

*And? Come on, get with the programme, idiot.*

"She's not my cousin," I whispered.

Iris's hand closed over mine. "Technically, no, but we're still your family."

My eyes returned to the piece of paper in my hand. "Then who is my mother? Where? How? I don't—"

Iris patted the box and said, "Everything is in there. It's not much, but our parents kept all they had, and I did the same after your mother…" She swallowed hard and tears shone in her eyes. "After she passed."

"Why didn't you tell me sooner?"

"I think you can work that one out yourself, Griffin. How much more miserable would you have been if you had thought we weren't blood? Even your father didn't know."

I looked at Megan's back again. Yes, she was crying. This was too much. Wasn't it?

"Meg needs me," I said, pushing away from the table. "I'll take the box. We need to talk more." Wearing just my socks, I padded out onto the lawn and headed for Megan.

She tried to wave me away when she heard me coming, but her face was puffy and pink. I wrapped her in my arms and just whispered, "It's all going to be okay. I promise."

As she sobbed against my chest, I stared over her head, out at the rolling hills. A buzzard screamed, launching crows from the nearby wood. Sheep dotted the fields, and I heard the cows. The air smelt of spring and the future. My future.

I had no idea what this meant, but I knew something: I wasn't going to lose Megan again.

## Chapter Thirty-Three

When we left the farm, I asked Iris not to tell the family what she'd shared with me. While Megan cleaned up a little, Iris explained some family history I didn't know. Ultimately, I wanted to process the information in the box, and she owed me that much. This needed to be handled with care. As I cradled the contents in my arms, Megan drove us back to Redruth, and my thoughts spiralled down a rabbit hole and bounced off the sides on the way to a bottom I couldn't see. If I were honest with myself, I was scared.

My entire worldview had tilted off to one side, and I didn't know what it meant. I had no idea who my mother really was, or, and this was important, where she came from. Iris had always thought of Hazel as her sister, and until their parents had died, she hadn't known Hazel was adopted. By that point, it was too late to speak to her sister. She also didn't want to invade her family history; her grief was too overwhelming. Then there was little me: a boy with no love in his life. She'd barely glanced at the paperwork involved and had done her best to forget it. The mother in her just wanted to protect me.

I hardly remembered my grandparents. They'd moved to Southern France the moment Iris and Conor had taken over the farm. Apparently, the large family they wanted wasn't going to happen after Iris's birth, so they adopted Hazel, who was three years old when she arrived. Iris was five. Children's memories being fairly elastic, it wasn't long before Iris forgot that Hazel had never been a baby. She just assumed all sisters arrived in a car driven by a woman in a uniform.

On the way home to Redruth, Megan kept glancing at me, but she had troubles of her own and didn't want to share. It kept us silent and oddly distant from each other. The bubbling, and let's face it manic, high I'd been on since leaving the grove had vanished. It was time to order my thoughts, collect my resources and do some very personal investigations.

When we pulled up outside Turpin Cottage, Megan said, "I'll leave you to it. Is that okay? I want to get my head straight, and I need to go see my inspector. He's going to want to know that Madron's safe for the moment."

I nodded, needing space. "Yeah, sure, but maybe we can pop down there in a day or two? Check on Leaze and the others? I'm concerned about Trystan's future."

She smiled. "That would be good." Reaching out, she patted the box. It made me pull it away from her, and I watched her eyebrow flick upwards. "Whatever is in there, I'm here to help. You know that. Right?"

"Yeah, I know." I wanted to reach out, to touch the healing bruise on her face, to… I faltered in mid-action. It suddenly occurred to me that I had no idea if she felt the same way I did.

Something in my expression must've changed. She frowned. "Are you sure you're okay?"

A small chuckle left me.

*Keep your damned shit together, Marine. She's going to need time as well. Patience.*

"Sorry, it's been the weirdest day of my life, and that's saying something."

"What the hell did my mother tell you?"

I reached for her hand and held it, rubbing my thumb over her knuckles. "Give me a day to think about it all, and I'll let you know. I promise."

Megan's fingers twisted in mine as her eyes searched for something. Then I watched tears gather, and her hand closed over my wrist. She managed to whisper around a lump in her throat, "Griffin, I need your help."

"I know. I'm here."

She gave me a watery smile, then looked down at my boots. "I ended it with Adrian, and he hasn't taken it well. The guys at work are going to think I'm the crazy one. I want to report him, but it's going to ruin me down here."

This vast bubbling of something rose up inside me. For years, I'd been sitting on the lid of an oil gusher, and suddenly it had enough pressure built up behind it to explode. I couldn't have stopped it even if I'd tried.

"Meg, we aren't cousins. Not by blood. My mother was adopted. Iris just told me. I have the paperwork here." I patted the box. "We aren't related, Megan."

The tears in her eyes spilled over and rolled down her pale cheeks. I reached over with my big, rough and still grimy paw, and wiped the tears away. The roiling, boiling tension between us flared so hot I almost gasped.

She closed her eyes and whispered, "I'm dreaming right now."

Which made me laugh, and the tension snapped. Her eyes opened, and they were the colour of a summer midday Cornish sky. "Today. We take today to rest and think," I said. "Tomorrow, we'll talk. Yeah?"

She nodded. "Dinner? Maybe on the coast?"

"We'll take the bike. It'll be easier to park."

"A date?" she asked.

My grin might've become wolfish. "Oh yes, very much a date."

She leaned over the old Ford's gear stick, and the wolf inside me became a rabbit. My heart thrashed. Feeling her lips against mine, the pressure soft and tentative. It made the entire universe—

*Really? The world not enough for you?*

Damn straight it wasn't enough. The entire universe flipped around us. That's all she did, just that one all too brief kiss, but it was enough. When she leaned back in her seat, she grinned. "Well, that answered that question."

I could barely breathe. "What question?" Did I always squeak like a mouse?

"Whether we had the spark."

"You doubted it?"

She blushed and turned coy on me. Not something I'd seen often, and it was cute. Yep, that was one I'd be keeping to myself, she'd kill me for certain.

"A girl never knows until that first kiss."

"Glad you approve."

She shoved me. "Get out of the car, lug. I need to go home, shower and get some more sleep before going into the station later."

"Sorry, you lost me at shower." I opened the car door and managed to make my boots move. "Any problems with anything, I'm there."

Her smile softened. "I know, Griffin. We'll talk later and go out tomorrow."

Somehow, I managed to close the car door, but I watched her drive away. That's when I realised, I still had my assault rifle in her boot. Well, it would give me a good excuse to go check on her this evening.

*You get possessive over her, and she'll pop through your fingers like a bar of wet soap.*

Fair enough. I'd message her and warn her it was in there. Maybe she'd invite me down to the flat, not that I'd visited it yet, she liked Turpin Cottage too much, or she'd come up?

My stomach did a jibbery-wibble at the thought. What a bloody strange day I was having.

By the time I rocked up to the house's back door and began stripping off my boots, Sid had appeared. With the Land Rover not parked outside, I guessed Luce had gone home, which was a shame, I wanted to talk to her about some of the things I'd seen, though, just like before, the memories were fading.

"You have new belongings?" Sid asked in surprise, looking at the box I'd placed on the floor. "I thought your entire life fitted into a single bag for life."

"Ha, ha. That's from my Aunt Iris. It's about my mum." Except she wasn't my aunt, and Megan wasn't my cousin. *Tee* bloody *hee*.

I could see his fingers twitching to get in there. I'd discovered Sid had no personal boundaries when it came to boxes of stuff. He just wanted to get in and poke around. This time, I really wanted to keep the private stuff to myself for the moment. All the private stuff.

Distracting him seemed wise. "Has Sanchez spoken with you yet?"

He nodded. "She wanted you to call when you came back. Markin's given his verbal report."

I put my boots to one side, knowing I'd need to clean them later. "Bet that was fun."

"Apparently, we come out of it, if not smelling of roses, at least we don't smell of dead sheep." We'd found one of those in a field a few weeks before and the scent still haunted him.

I laughed. "I'll make us a cuppa and call in."

With tea in hand, I retreated to my room and phoned the boss lady. I gave her the full report.

After a long silence, she said, "I have to get a bunch of tree growers down there, and we're going to be building a forest?"

"It was that or war with the Dru and a lot of dead dryads," I said. "We can't move them, ma'am, but we can study the environment there. The grove, the holy spring, the cloutie tree. We can build them a new henge for their worship. Imagine what we might learn from them? I want Trystan to teach our other mystics how to reach them. He's powerful and shouldn't be left with Eloise. Not without guidance. You'll have to help him, ma'am." I wanted to add, 'She's a match for you in the wicked witch department', but I valued my new life too much.

"It seems you've struck quite the deal."

"If the veil is thinning and dangers are coming through we don't understand, it's important we start to build allies. These Dru are powerful warriors. I'm not saying I want us to stick an M16 in their hands, but they know how to fight and die for their people."

Sanchez made a humming sound. "I suppose I can get a heritage order slapped on the area. We can then talk to the Duchy of Cornwall about using it as one of the Prince of

Wales' re-wilding projects down there. Having royalty involved will maintain the project for generations."

I fist bumped the air and did a silent jig around my room. "Thank you, ma'am."

"And they need to see changes within a moon month?" she asked.

"Yes, ma'am. Or they're going to sacrifice a virgin."

"That's not the kind of behaviour we need to encourage, Corporal."

"No, ma'am, that's my thinking exactly." Did she just make a joke?

"Then I think, once Sid's sent up his evidence and I have your full report on my desk, we can make this happen. The prince is very interested in our work. This will be the kind of project I need to keep him distracted."

I wanted to ask why he had to be distracted—oh did I want to ask!—but I knew her too well. If I pushed, I'd never learn anything. Instead, I said, "If anyone needs a guide down here, I'm happy to help." I quite fancied meeting a royal for a chat about trees; it sounded like a fun day out.

"Well, good work, Griffin. I hope this successful outcome puts your personal problems into perspective, and we'll have no more nonsense about you leaving DoPI or the Marines."

Warning shot, meet bow.

"Understood, ma'am."

"Good, my job is not about mothering anyone."

I almost laughed. After almost five years of knowing her, I wouldn't call the two conversations we'd had about my meltdowns, mothering, but I guessed it came in all shapes and forms. My eyes flickered to the box on the bed. Yep, mothers could always surprise you.

Sanchez ended the call with her usual abruptness after

offering me a week's leave. I snapped at it, knowing I could get some surfing in and general larking about with Megan if she could wangle a few days off as well. Besides, I had that box to investigate and a hole to fill in the graveyard down the road.

That brought me back with a bit of a bump.

"Well, Mum, I guess I have to start somewhere with all this. What are you trying to tell me?" I whispered as I flicked open the box's lid.

## Next in the Griffin Woodbury Supernatural Detective Series

vinci-books.com/CathedralOfDemons

**She's not summoning salvation—she's setting a trap for Heaven.**

A ritual killing draws operative Griffin Woodbury to Truro, where a woman plans to summon demons—and trap angels—in revenge against the Church. With one child left, stopping her may already be too late.

Turn the page for a free preview…

# A Cathedral of Demons: Prologue

*Thirty-four years ago*

The skin around her belly felt like it would split under the pressure from the shifting lump of human who'd taken up residence. Her back and hips ached all day, and nerve pains were tormenting her legs at night. Everything had swollen, especially her boobs. They were huge and kept leaking this horrid white stuff onto her clothes. She refused to call it milk. It made her sound like a cow. Her mother tutted and muttered under her breath constantly, and her father couldn't bring himself to look at her.

Elena wanted to cry, and each time she felt all that sadness well up, she turned it to anger. The only part of her life she had any control over. Rather than seek comfort in her confirmation gift of a golden cross hanging from a fine chain, Elena now wore a quartz crystal around her neck. She'd removed the simple wooden cross she'd prayed to every night since she was a small child. In its place hung a picture of a full moon over the sea. Bollocks to the damned Church.

Over nine months, her rage had built to catastrophic levels. She wanted to tear down buildings, rip out trees and hurl them at her parents, the teachers, her missing friends. Cowards. The moment they'd found out she was pregnant, they'd fled from her side. Like it was catching, or something. Yet another betrayal.

She sat on her narrow bed in a room decorated with posters of Take That. Her favourite was bad boy Robbie Williams. That crooked smile and blue eyes just melted her heart. Maybe that's why she'd ended up in this state.

*He'd* had twinkly blue eyes and a cheeky smile. His congregation loved him for it. She'd loved him for it. Those damned tears threatened again.

She yanked open the drawer on her bedside table and removed her diary. The pink, sequined surface looked offensive to her now, like it was for a little girl, not a fifteen-year-old woman of the world. She threw it back in the drawer and pulled open another.

A 'so called' friend had given it as a birthday present. It was a witch's diary and spell book. Elena, heavily into the Church at the time, had shoved it away.

Maybe this magic stuff was something that would never betray her, never force her to make impossible choices? Did she need to follow a new path? Anxiety made her stomach twist again, and the nausea rushed back. She opened it and the first thing she read was: *Your Mother loves you. She is always there for you.*

Below this was the image of a beautiful woman dressed in robes made of butterflies, ears of wheat, birds, squirrels and more. It was beautiful. So different to the misery of Christ's suffering on the cross. So different to her suffering.

Elena wanted to be loved by someone like this. No one in her congregation loved her, that was for damned certain.

She rubbed the huge, round belly. "You're screwed, you know that?" No tenderness echoed in her words. She hated this lump. By the time she realised she was pregnant, she'd already crossed the threshold for a legal termination. So, she'd drunk a bottle of vodie, having stolen the money for it from her mum's purse, and thrown herself down the stairs.

It hadn't worked. In the process, the nurses, then her parents, discovered she'd ruined her life forever. The screaming and blaming had started at the hospital and hadn't seemed to stop for the next five months. She'd basically been a prisoner here, in her bedroom, for all that time. Her mother had refused to buy maternity clothes, just pulling out the old ones from the loft. They dated from the bloody seventies, it was old hippy shit. Elena spent her days in her dressing gown, which just about covered the obscene bump.

When she'd finally confessed to her furious father which bloke had knocked her up, he'd gone deathly quiet. The look of confusion on his face was comical, not that she'd dared to laugh. It took him several attempts to speak, and when he'd managed it, he'd said: "You'll go to hell for lying. You know that?" Despite being Protestant, he was still from Northern Ireland. Hell was a big, and very real place, and the Church mattered. Its reputation was as important to him as his own. It was her fault. She'd been the temptress. Her skirts were too short. Her tops too tight. No girl of fifteen should be in heels or makeup.

That's when he started in on her mother.

Elena knew that just to keep the peace and to stop the fists, her mother would side with her father and she'd have no one to defend her. No protector. In the stupid books she read, there was always a man out there who'd save the heroine. Alas, her fate wouldn't be like that; she was destined to be the bad girl.

Elena snarled. She yanked open the first drawer, removed her old, pink diary, and methodically began tearing out pages. If she was so unlovable, then she'd just have to learn to live with it.

Tears dripped onto the ripped, shredded soft pink paper. Her fingers ached with the effort of tearing each page into tiny pieces. Every time her eyes stopped blurring enough to see the writing, she'd catch sight of her secret name for *him* or a little love heart over a letter. Pages of her signature with her new name. *His* name. That's what he'd promised. Now, he'd gone. The Church spirited him away somewhere else. She'd never see him again. He didn't even fight for her, just did as he was told and left.

Her grief, her shame, her loathing overwhelmed her so much that when the first wave of pain hit, she thought it was just another emotional overload for her body to cope with. Right up until fluid poured out from between her legs to soak her bed and the rug on the floor.

---

*Twenty-two hours later*

She lay back sweating, and breathing like she'd just run the school's cross-country at record speed. A joy she'd never felt before filled her exhausted limbs, her fuddled mind, and most of all, her heart.

"Let me hold her," Elena called out to the nurses in the corner of the room. She tried to reach out, hearing the weak wail, and her entire body reacted to the sound. Was this motherhood? This odd sense of connection to another being? A desperation to provide and protect?

The midwife turned back to her with a smile on her face, but Elena realised it didn't reach the woman's eyes. "Just a bit more work to do on her first, dear."

Elena frowned. This wasn't how it worked on the telly, unless there was something wrong with the baby.

Her heart plunged into the agony between her legs. The vodka. The trip down the stairs. The months of hate and shame she'd poured into the lump, wanting it gone. What had she done? Tears filled her eyes again. "Please let me see her. I promise to be a good mum. It doesn't matter if she's not right—" Her shaky voice was ignored.

Elena struggled to sit further up in the bed, ignoring the cooling bodily fluids covering the mattress. If she could move, she might be able to stand.

The weak cry became stronger, and Elena's entire body screamed to provide. "Please," Elena said, making her voice more forceful. "You can't keep her away from me."

The door to the room opened. Elena had hoped it would be her mother. That maybe both her parents would now forgive her, and they could all be a family together.

Instead, an old man walked in. He wore a black woollen coat, black trousers and shiny black shoes. His thin hair was another shade of black never seen in nature, and he'd used some kind of oil to stick it down to his white scalp. Elena hated him on sight.

"Who are you?" she called out, trying to cover herself.

He glanced at her with such disgust, Elena felt like she'd been punched in the face. "You have it?" he asked. This was addressed to the midwife.

She glanced at Elena. "Is this really necessary? We have

the ability to support young mothers. This seems cruel and archaic."

"It's what the parents want. She is underage." He held his arms out.

Elena, who'd never been stupid, foolish perhaps, but never stupid, suddenly understood. She'd glimpsed the man's throat, seen the dog collar.

"No!" she yelled. "You can't!" Curses poured out of her.

The child started to scream. The baby started to scream. The midwife tried not to weep.

---

*Five years later*

Elena strode out of the university grounds clutching her degree to her chest with a wild grin on her face and in her eyes. This was the first step on a long journey to make sure no other young woman had to suffer the way she had. With this degree, she could join any medical school in the country, even without her pathetic parents.

First though, she had to go home. Her flatmate had sent a message to her pager, telling her that a recorded delivery letter had arrived. Elena was almost as excited about the letter as she was about the qualification.

Hurrying down Bristol's busy streets, then catching a bus to the St Paul's district, she navigated the area like a native. Despite being white, most of the locals treated her like one of their own, and they'd offered her kindness over the years. She'd always felt safe here.

Breathless by the time she'd run up the three flights of stairs to her flat's front door, she let herself in. Her flatmate would be at work by now, but the letter was on the small kitchen table they used for their essays when not in the library.

Elena grabbed the envelope and ripped it open, hardly daring to breathe. She'd finally uncover the history of her baby girl. When not studying, or learning about her new spiritual path, she'd spent hours, weeks, months, figuring out how to track down what had happened in that hospital maternity ward. Who the man was that took her daughter and where she'd been taken. This letter should tell her who'd adopted her baby without her permission.

She scanned the letter, her entire body fizzing and popping with excitement.

The words didn't make sense.

She read them again. The fizzing turned into nausea. The popping excitement turned into dread.

"No," she said aloud. "No, this can't be right. This can't be true. They must be lying. They're doing it to me again."

The words: *We regret to inform you of your baby's death,* lifted off the page and floated about her head. *Eighteen months old. Sepsis after a short illness. So sorry for your loss. Our deepest condolences. Her burial was held at…*

Elena screamed.

She clutched the quartz crystal pendant around her neck and vowed vengeance on them all. Every fibre in her body would be turned into a weapon. They would all pay. She'd bring down the entire fucking Church of England. And when she had burned it, she would dance on its ashes.

## A Cathedral of Demons: Chapter One

Riding my retro-style Kawasaki Café 800 from home to work used to be an easy pleasure. This being Cornwall and not central London during rush hour. Now, the short ride between Turpin Cottage and the Department of Paranormal Investigations satellite office—or Rural Security, depending on who asked—proved to be a juggling act between the four wheeled traffic and his desire to reach work in one piece. Perhaps that should be a high-wire act while juggling, in a high wind.

I threw my bike lid at the sofa, which caught it. Then I swiped a hand over my sweating face and grumbled, "I swear, even without the school run I'm going to end up a smear on that piece of road."

Sid looked up at me. He drove a Mark III red classic Mini, which was barely more visible on the high wire we navigated every day than my bike. "Tourists," he muttered before turning back to his screens.

This made me chuckle as I headed for the coffee

machine in our small kitchen. "We're worse, we're incomers. Besides, if you want to call tourists anything, it's *emmets*."

My friend, colleague and housemate, grunted. "I drove through a ford in my Mini. I am now a local," he declared in his Peckham accent.

"You might want to discuss that with Megan."

"If she ever shows her face again, I will."

The coffee machine snarled and growled while I stripped off my bike gear. Despite being a Royal Marine Commando and DoPI's spear point in Cornwall against the *paras*, I was not tough enough to be riding my bike without my protective equipment, regardless of the heat. I switched on the fan in the kitchen area and fluffed out the front of my t-shirt, trying to dry it. High summer had brought high temperatures and sudden, sometimes catastrophic, storms. Climate change was giving the UK a nasty slap around the chops, and we were going down, hitting the deck hard. Only time would tell if we got back up and found a way to fight back.

I pondered what Sid had said about Megan's prolonged absences since May. He had it right; we'd hardly seen her. More importantly, I'd hardly seen her, and we were supposed to be in a new, and romantic, relationship. Or at least heading that way. I'd encouraged her to take up the opportunity for firearms training with DoPI. She didn't want to train through the usual channels as a police officer; it would force her into becoming an Authorised Firearms Officer or AFO, and that wasn't part of her career plan. Besides, it would take her away from DoPI, and despite her atheism regarding organised religion, she would now admit to worrying about what might lurk under the bed or in the back of a wardrobe. She was also battling her day job.

I worked full time for DoPI, as did Sid, but Megan was

my police liaison, which meant when she wasn't needed for DoPI work, she had to do 'normal' police work. The summers kept the Devon and Cornwall Police Service very busy. It felt like the rest of the UK descended on the county in such numbers that the narrow peninsula might snap off from the mainland under the extra weight, and drift into the Atlantic. Her role as beat sergeant meant her shifts were long, and she'd taken on overtime to help her parent's farm financial situation. I'd offered to help as well, but despite being family, sort of as it turned out, Conor Ackley didn't want my money. I didn't press the issue. There would be other ways to help, and my sort of uncle would just have to put up with it.

Sid leaned back in his chair, making it groan in protest. "Any news about the ex-boyfriend?"

I grunted. Unused to navigating ex-boyfriends who didn't know when to give up, I'd turned to Sid for advice. He'd told me to leave it to Megan.

"No, she's still being elusive about Adrian *bloody* Hess. All I've managed to glean out of her, is that most of her colleagues think she did the dirty on him with me."

Sid frowned. "You didn't though, right?"

"No. I mean, it was pretty tight between her breaking up with him and us discovering we aren't biological first cousins, but it wasn't like they were living together, engaged or even that serious."

"In Megan's eyes."

I sighed and carried over a mug of coffee for Sid. "Yeah, that's the problem. He doesn't seem to think she's able to make her own decisions. A 'real' man needs to tell her what to do."

Sid laughed. "He never said that to her."

"I doubt it, he's too clever for that, but it's the impression she gave me. Their colleagues are certainly making the most out of the drama."

Police stations were way too much like schoolyards for my liking. We'd never done the dirty, but that didn't stop the fuel being ladled on the fire by good old Adrian.

I leaned one thigh against Sid's desk. "Are you sure I can't just hunt him down?" The desire to do just that burned through me constantly.

Sid eyed me. "I really hope that's a joke, mate."

"It is, I guess. If I do anything like that, I'm going to be no better than him." Even to my own ears, I sounded like a stroppy teenager.

Sid tried to suppress a smirk. "Trying to be the better man?"

I grumbled, "Right now, I'm not sure I want to be. Throwing her over my shoulder and forcing her to stay in my cave while I kill any trespassers feels like a better option."

Sid laughed. "It's tough being a twenty-first century man."

"Don't I bloody know it."

After finding out Megan and I weren't blood relatives everything in my life had changed. It felt like the ties weighing me down had been cut, but equally, being adrift was disorientating. My inappropriate desire for Megan had oddly kept me locked down and welded into a state of self-pity I now thought of as comfortable. I was currently adrift in uncharted seas.

It had also unmoored me from the only real family I'd felt good about. No one knew where my mother had come from, and the little evidence I had left, didn't reveal that secret. Sadly, it seemed Mum had never discovered her origins either.

I finally plonked Sid's coffee down on his desk and received a grunt in response, before heading for my less technically enhanced office area. The box full of my mother's paperwork sat on the floor beside my chair. It whispered its half-disclosed secrets almost constantly, but that's all they were, half of the secrets she'd contained. I knew she'd been adopted by the Tudor family, but no one knew from where, and that nagged at heart and head. My mother was not a normal woman, and whatever genes she'd passed down to me had brought more with them than half my DNA.

Sid had done a deep dive, but all her details were pre-digital, so only the basics were found online. I'd even considered contacting my father, but that would be the very last of last resorts. For heaven's sake, I was a trained investigator; there had to be something I could do to figure out her origins.

Most of my work over the summer, so far, had been down at Madron. Some of the protesters remained, including Leaze and Denny, and we had the unremitting irritation of Anwen's Children, who refused to leave Trystan in DoPI's hands, but plans were moving forward rapidly. Trystan, a very young and gifted natural mystic, had really started to come out of his shell. The woodland and its Druidic circle were gradually taking shape under his guidance.

The Duchy of Cornwall had agreed to the project, as land management wasn't really in DoPI's remit. You can always trust the Royal Family to keep a state secret, and so far, they had been doing a great job at blurring the lines. The press hadn't caught a whiff of the secrets we were hiding down there. Though, it had taken all my diplomacy skills to coax Denny into signing a non-disclosure agreement and the Official Secrets Act.

Rather than think about tree spirits, I pondered where next to take my investigation of the real Hazel Woodbury. Sid had suggested past life regression under hypnotism, though I failed to see how this would help; it was her life I wanted to understand, not mine. Besides, even for an operative of DoPI, this stretched the bounds of credibility. Then he decided LSD might be the answer. This one I closed down fast. After my one and only experience with MDMA, I wasn't going to be using drugs again. I had to be missing something in that damned box.

Just as I bent to pick it up for the hundredth time since May, the phone rang. Sanchez.

"Ma'am," I stated. She'd thawed recently, but not so much that we had pleasantries to share over the phone.

The moment I heard her voice, my office vanished, and I stood in front of her desk, doing my best to ignore her choice in mind-melting artwork. "Corporal Woodbury, I need you and your police liaison to go up to Truro to speak with Bishop James Chadwick. They have a problem that's come to our attention, and we need to keep on top of it." Her inner android was in full control today.

"Of course, ma'am. Are they expecting us?"

"Yes. Today would be best. Details will be arriving now."

I suppressed a sigh. The woman didn't seem to understand that Megan had an actual job and wasn't always at my beck and call, unfortunately. It also meant dealing with August traffic. "Very good, ma'am." Not like I could refuse a direct order.

"Report back once the issue has been dealt with." She paused for a moment. Then: "And Woodbury, try not to make this into another shitshow we have to hide."

"I'll do my best, ma'am."

"Thank you." The call died.

I checked my secure email and found the briefing. "Sid."

"Got it."

We both read the file for a few minutes while drinking coffee. Sid finished first. "Seems simple enough."

"Why do they need us?" I asked, still going through the details. "It's a bloke with a problem, surely they need the police if it's stalking?"

We didn't have many details, which meant I was probably missing something important. The basics were there, though. A man in his forties seemed to be stalking members of the cathedral's staff, both women and men. Several people had complained he'd followed them home and watched their houses and families for a few days, before he moved on to someone else. He'd also been found in the private areas of the cathedral and its grounds. When challenged, after he'd been discovered making chalk marks on the door to the sacristy, he declared he was a demon hunter and wanted to keep the holy items and vestments of the church untainted. That's when the bishop had called the Archbishop of Canterbury, and his office had called DoPI.

The bishop would know me as Rural Security, but the archbishop, the Security Service and the Monarchy know they'd be sending a DoPI operative. At least that's how close we tried to keep the circle of trust. It was proving harder now that the veil between us and the *paras* was thinning so much that the monsters just kept leaking through no matter what we did to stop them. Social media didn't help either.

"I've got a photo of the man," Sid said. "Do you want me to do a background check on him?"

"Sure, dig up what you can. I'll call Megan." At which

point my stomach flipped on its arse. An uncomfortable feeling.

Sid chuckled. "You should see your face right now, soldier boy."

I flipped him the one-finger salute as I speed-dialled Megan.

"Hey, Griffin," she said after three rings. Three. That was a long time. Did she contemplate switching me off, like I'd seen her do to Adrian?

*Really? The poor woman is probably out on patrol somewhere wearing more clobber than you did as a Marine, and she'd have to fish the phone out of some Velcroed pouch on her Batman belt.*

Good point well-made.

We hadn't reached the endearments stage, so I stuck with our normal routine. "Hey, Meg. I have a DoPI job if you're up for it."

"Really?" She sounded excited. "Oh my God, that would be amazing. I'm due to provide security for a politician doing the rounds while on their summer holiday down here, so I'd love to come with you. Also, the pile of paperwork on my desk is beginning to resemble the Leaning Tower of Pisa."

"Do you want to come up here, or shall I pick you up at the station?" I asked.

"Now?"

"Roger that," I confirmed.

"Erm, bike or car?"

"Traffic to Truro?" I asked.

"Bike."

"My thoughts exactly. So…?"

"Pick me up outside my flat in twenty minutes. I need to change into something practical," she said. I heard a soft shush of fabric moving against a stab vest. Her voice came over more quietly. "It'll be good to see you. I've missed you."

My heart raced like a greyhound on amphetamines. "You too." Though it was sad she had to whisper for fear of being overheard. Megan killed the call.

The grin on my face made Sid roll his eyes at me. I gave him the one fingered salute.

Grab your copy...

**vinci-books.com/CathedralOfDemons**

# About the Author

Joe Talon tolerates reality by escaping on a regular basis into strange worlds and spaces that appear from a muse who likes to take the darker path. Be it murder in Glastonbury, or monsters on the wilds of Exmoor and Cornwall, Joe feels the tug of words and enjoys the company of many invisible friends. Mostly, Joe really likes seeing the bad guys suffer.

While living a small life in rural Spain with far too many rescue dogs, Joe battles demons, slays dragons, and imagines what the apocalypse will really be like when it comes and are there enough lentils in storage to make it through.

With an addiction to stories, collecting dogs, and trying to grow vegetables (mostly unsuccessfully), Joe really hopes that the darker paths those stories take aren't real. Though, in the quiet of the night, when the moon is bright, the air is still and a fox barks as an owl screeches, Joe's fairly sure they offer adventures that cannot be resisted forever.

Joe has a degree in medieval stuff, grew up on the edge of Exmoor, managed to survive gaining martial arts black belts in three disciplines and loves to walk. Which is just as well with all the dogs.

## Acknowledgments

I hope you enjoyed this story. It was a joy to write. Combining real life with the supernatural can be a challenge. How far should I take it? This is one story that I wish could be real. Seeking out the magical places in woodlands where the dryads might dance with their male counterparts, is definitely one adventure I'd love to have. Saying that, cloutie trees are a real phenomenon in Cornwall, and this particular one I visited while enjoying one of my many holidays down there. I didn't leave a wish or a prayer among its boughs, but I always wondered what story I would write for the tree. I can't imagine for a moment anyone would want to build a golf course down there, but if they do, they have been warned.

Many of you know by now, I pick a strange location and weave the story around some obscure, little-known fact. There are references to Dru in Greek myth, but very, very few, and it might even be one of those AI driven ghost-in-the-machine type things. I'd never heard of them until researching for this book. They aren't in any of my mythology books. Still, it's a great thought, to have warrior tree spirits ready to defend their homes.

As always, I owe a huge debt to my editor, David Luddington, who pulled in some great additional plot lines and made me beef up the sense of dread. Griffin wasn't too happy about that, I can tell you! And to Jeff Jones, who corrals my commas like a pro. I'd also like to thank the team at Vinci Books, with a special thanks to Nicole, for being the support structure a neurotic writer needs.

Finally, my Taloneers. Guys, you're amazing. I've been through it the last couple of years and you have offered me the kind of virtual support that I never expected, thank you. I love sharing my newsletter with you, and my endless free stories. I especially like it when you find the weird ones funny. Your patience has been very kind. You guys are going to love *The Cathedral of Demons*, it'll be with you soon.

www.ingramcontent.com/pod-product-compliance
Lightning Source LLC
La Vergne TN
LVHW030915080826
845145LV00013B/2900

* 9 7 8 1 0 3 6 7 1 6 4 3 1 *